Christobel Kent was born in London and educated at Cambridge. She has lived variously in Essex, London and Italy. Her childhood included several years spent on a Thames sailing barge in Maldon, Essex with her father, stepmother, three siblings and four step-siblings. She now lives in both Cambridge and Florence with her husband and five children.

WHAT WE DID

Christobel Kent

sphere

SPHERE

First published in Great Britain in 2018 by Sphere

1 3 5 7 9 10 8 6 4 2

A CIP catalogue record for this book is available from the British Library.

Hardback ISBN 978-0-7515-6878-3
Trade Paperback ISBN 978-0-7515-6879-0

Typeset in Bembo by Palimpsest Book Production Ltd, Falkirk, Stirlingshire
Printed and bound in Great Britain by Clays Ltd, St Ives plc

Papers used by Sphere are from well-managed forests
and other responsible sources.

MIX
Paper from
responsible sources
FSC® C104740

Sphere
An imprint of
Little, Brown Book Group
Carmelite House
50 Victoria Embankment
London
EC4Y 0DZ

An Hachette UK Company
www.hachette.co.uk

www.littlebrown.co.uk

For all the women who have supported and tolerated and argued and encouraged and listened and warned and loved, without whom life would be impossible.
They know who they are.

Acknowledgements

I'd like to thank my steadfast and sharp-eyed agent, Victoria Hobbs, for her tenacity, her warm heart and her cool head, my editor Maddie West at Sphere for her insight and patience, and the inimitable Sarah Crichton at Sarah Crichton Books in the US for her fierce commitment and brilliance.

The Sphere team: Kirsteen Astor and Emma Williams deserve many medals for their publicity and marketing genius and the eternally forbearing and kind Thalia Proctor a halo for services to proof-tidying and much much more.

To Richard Beswick of Little, Brown/Abacus, without whom I would never have dared write anything, I owe a debt of thanks and love for close on thirty years of good humour and friendship, and most of all I need to thank my husband Donald, for lying awake worrying about the bills, fixing bicycles, looking after children, making coffee and for generally being the best and kindest there is.

My Life had stood – a Loaded Gun –
In Corners – till a Day
The Owner passed – identified –
And carried Me away

EMILY DICKINSON

Chapter One

The university sat tall and dark above the town: three towers looking across the roofs and out over a grey estuary. Perhaps Rose Hill had been wild once and covered with a pink-petalled tangle of briar roses but now it was groomed to smoothness, cropped lawn and concrete in the shadow of the towers.

It could have been a woman's name – and there had been an incident, far back, decades ago, not long after the towers went up and regrettable, when a young woman from the town gained entrance to the towers, took the lift to the fourteenth floor and smashed her way through the security glass. Apparently an impossibility but there are circumstances – the psychotropic drugs popular then, or the more common or garden misery, or rage, or madness – under which the unfeasible can be accomplished. Her name wasn't Rose and besides, the hill had been named long before but her death was now wound into the story, part of the name that was too soft and pretty for the way it looked.

The only relic of a former landscape was an older building that sat at the foot of the hill behind dense hedging, grey brick and something like the Victorian gatehouse to a grander structure long vanished. Perhaps it had once had a rose garden, but there was no longer any sign of that, either.

Bridget stood at the shop window and looked out, down the cobbled curve, watching the light leave the narrow sloping street.

November wasn't always a quiet month, but this one had been, for whatever reason — the papers said it was uncertainty, by which they meant everyone worrying about money, and the world turned upside down. The short days and the light dimming to grey so early gave the lane a melancholy look too, in spite of the strings of lights, their mirrored gleam on the cobbles and the tinny sound of Christmas music — but Bridget liked Christmas. She'd learned to love Christmas: kids did that for you, just one kid did that for you. Even if he was sixteen now, and a foot taller than her.

Finn, Finn, Finn. Matt, bringing tea this morning, had lowered his voice and said he had a few ideas about what to get him, before sliding back in beside her for those nice five minutes before work. It would involve something for his bike and a lot of stuff for his computer. Bridget would get him clothes: gone were the days when she could work him out, but he didn't seem to hold it against her. Still planted a kiss, absent-minded, on her cheek shuffling down to breakfast with his hair sticking up and his eyebrow grown thick and dark as caterpillars overnight. Clothes she could do: she knew what logos he liked, nothing bright, warm stuff, practical stuff. Socks. Her mind wandered, down the little cobbled hill, into town.

There was a music shop on the corner, further down and out of sight but if it had been there when she was considering the premises, she would have looked elsewhere. The sight of the instrument, the curve of varnished maple, the inlays, the snail curl of the scroll and something happened in her head, a buzz, white noise. Notes on a page, an orchestra tuning up, did the same thing.

She was on her own in the shop. Her shop.

Four thirty on a November Tuesday. So quiet she'd sent Laura out to the post office. One of Bridget's regulars from across the county had phoned for a specific dress and — though Bridget hadn't really got into selling online because she was wary and stood resolute in the face of Laura's hints and pleas — they'd boxed it up between them as a favour and off Laura had gone, sailing down the darkening street bearing the box high. Close on a grand's worth of dress: Bridget didn't want that kind of stock out for two weeks to someone she didn't know only to come back again, never mind getting lost in the post.

That was the wariness she expressed to Laura, anyway. Just like when she got up at two a.m. and did her stretches in the living room because she couldn't sleep: she told Matt she was fretting over the VAT. Who didn't wake in the middle of the night, these days? If it wasn't recession it was people out rioting. Matt would reach out a hand to her when she climbed back in, resting it on her until

3

eventually she would get back to sleep. It wasn't the VAT, though, it wasn't fretting about stock getting lost in the post. She couldn't say to Laura, after all, I don't *want* people to find me on the internet. She couldn't say, I don't want people looking at pictures of me. It's not worrying, either. It's terror. Laura would think there was something wrong with her.

It was a relief, sometimes, to have Laura out of the shop. Ten years younger, so certain of everything, so pink and white, so blonde and pretty. So pregnant it set Bridget's nerves jangling, though Laura had told her, babies were always late in her family and she wanted to work. Needed the money: didn't we all. Perhaps they could close up early: perhaps Bridget could send Laura straight home when she got back from the post. She would take her time anyway, she'd dawdle and look in baby shops and buy herself a chocolate flapjack and pat her belly, anxious and satisfied at once. Bridget remembered that feeling: she'd like to jump to a month ahead and Laura sitting up in hospital with the baby safely in her arms and Nick the sainted husband at her shoulder. She turned her back to the window and surveyed the shop.

Home early, why not? Last night had been a late one, after all. Monday the shop was closed but she'd been in anyway, on her hands and knees repainting the old wooden floor, another layer of cream eggshell and all the stock swathed in dustsheets, along with the velvet chair, the sofa for husbands, the mirrored cube for the newspaper to sit on perfectly centred. Laura had once called her OCD in an unguarded moment, for her straightening of rails and scrupulous repainting of the floor once every six months, if it needed it or not. *How many layers must there be, by now?* Bridget had laughed. She didn't really know what OCD was, but she was fairly sure it didn't cover what she had.

Last night Matt had picked her up without being asked, taken her hands in his, sore and cracked from the white spirit, put her bike in the back. The party dresses had all been hanging straight again and the dustsheets folded and back under the rails in the stockroom. She'd hung up her coat and made the tea, though, because he'd been at work too and it was only fair. She didn't want their little world falling down round their ears for lack of sausage and mash. Besides, pretty much the only time she saw Finn these days was when he heard the table being laid.

It was normal, everyone said so, although what would she know was normal? Bridget's teenage years were a blur. Her quiet, shy, kind husband and her big, soft son wouldn't have known her, if you showed them a picture of fifteen-year-old Bridget O'Neill standing with her huge eyes staring out, gawky and angular, all knobs and bones. Whereas she'd seen Matt, an old yellowed photograph of him standing by his bike in glasses at that age, frowning with shyness and had known it was him straight away.

Something moved under the velvet chair in the back and immediately Bridget was over there on her hands and knees. Moth. In November? She must be keeping it too warm in here. It fluttered, velvety: Bridget didn't like moths and catching them was like trying to catch a bird, but it had to be done. Kill it? She didn't want to kill it. She had it between cupped hands when the bell pinged over the door and she looked up, expecting to see Laura.

A man and his daughter, more likely granddaughter: the

5

man half turned away from her under the downlighters but she could see bushy eyebrows, the sheen of scalp under thinning hair. He was holding the door for the girl and she walked in, bright, upright and excited, face upturned. Fourteen, maybe fifteen but looking young, with her hair pulled in bunches either side of the head, though Bridget knew that was the look. She didn't have the skinny jeans on though, that would have completed the look but a knee-length school skirt and her coat was tweed, like something from fifty years ago. Scuffed school shoes. Pretty.

And then abruptly Bridget felt a flutter of panic, sudden and extreme and in that moment she couldn't tell if it came from inside her own chest or was the caged moth, its wings beating furry between her hands. She stood hurriedly and moved past them, apologising, to put it out into the dark before the door swung shut again. When she came back the man was standing at the rails, turned away from her and frowning down at things like he knew what he was looking for, and the girl standing in the middle of the room, all eagerness.

Then the man spoke.

'Tell the lady what you want, Isabel,' he said, and from nowhere, nowhere except the sound of his voice, a prickling heat rose through Bridget's body. She couldn't stop it, she couldn't name it: she reached blindly for a rail to hold on to.

'We're looking for a party dress,' the girl piped up. The man raised his head then, quarter profile towards her. Unsteady suddenly, Bridget caught the edge of a smile before turning to focus on the girl. Isabel. His hand was on the girl's shoulder, slowing her down.

'What kind of party?' she said, as he moved along the rails behind her. The girl was too young for almost everything in the shop: the thought nagged at her, troubling. Bridget's stock was geared towards women of her own age and older, thirty-five to seventy, women who liked to dress up for weddings and the races or a weekend away in a country house hotel.

'Oh, it's a recital,' said the girl, shuffling and shy suddenly. 'And then there's a reception thing afterwards.' She started for a rail and pulled something out, bright silk and short: Bridget smiled at her. 'Why don't you choose what you like first?' she said, wary. The man had moved off, was leaning down to pick up the newspaper beside the sofa, sitting down.

A recital. The word set up a pounding inside her and Bridget swallowed, her mouth suddenly dry: in her head she saw a row of black-clad girls, gazing over their instruments. *Think of something else.* But she could still feel it as she stepped closer, had to stop herself putting her hand to her mouth as the girl held something against herself in the mirror. Maybe fifteen going on sixteen after all: but jumpy as though it was all an act, being grown-up. Isabel. Behind her the man turned a page of the newspaper.

Focus on the girl. Isabel was moving from rail to rail, bright among the muted tones, the cream and grey, but growing in confidence, pulling things out. None of it looked suitable to Bridget, something like panic pattering at her, *ridiculous, stop it* and she didn't know if the words in her head were for her or Isabel. She couldn't say anything, not yet, she didn't want to crush the girl.

'Ready?' she said, and Isabel nodded, excited.

The fitting room was in an alcove at the back, with the velvet chair beside it. As Bridget pulled the curtain around the girl and stepped away, the man got up from the sofa behind her abruptly, saying nothing, and crossed to the velvet chair beside the curtain. He moved the chair so that his back was to Bridget and the window, and sat down, crossing his legs. A bit of skinny ankle emerged from brown trousers.

Father or grandfather? You couldn't ask. The girl hadn't called him anything. But there was no accident in his sitting down right there, between her and the girl: he was paying, and he was going to have his say. The ticking of anxiety that had set up with her first sight of them, that she might have expected to settle down, wouldn't go away. Bridget had a sudden sharp irrational desire out of nowhere for them to leave. She'd seen it before, husbands, fathers, criticising. And it was late, she was tired. If Laura would come back—

The curtain rings clicked softly and the girl came out: she'd pulled out her bunches and was blushing as if she knew. The dress was a mistake: black, low cut and too long, a bit of beading on the shoulder. Bridget saw the man shift, his profile to her for a second, saw him half smile, superior, she saw him nod and in the tilt of his chin – older now, sagging, dusted with grey stubble – she could suddenly see him as sharply as if she had a telescope on him. She felt her mouth open and they turned, they were smiling at her, and suddenly her insides were liquid.

Something happened, she didn't know what, something spun, the world turning, back, back, too fast. She would be sick. Bridget put out a hand to steady herself against the wall.

He beckoned the girl over and she obeyed, hesitant: he sat there unmoving so she had to bend, in the low-cut gown and seeing the shadow between what were not yet breasts, seeing her expose herself unknowing Bridget felt her throat close; her hand was at her mouth. She saw him whisper something in the girl's ear, she saw the child's chopped hair swing forward to hide their faces so close together.

'I don't—' Bridget had begun to speak but she didn't know what came next, she had only wanted to stop what was happening: she saw him turn at the words – again superior, amused, and knowing and she felt it, tight and knotted and terrible under her ribs. And something that crept, something that brushed the hairs on the back of her neck. He looked at her. She saw the tip of his tongue flicker at his upper lip.

And then the door behind her pinged and she could hear Laura come in, breezy, mid-complaint about something, the post office queue, the cold, her aching feet, the everyday world beyond the door that was so remote, in this moment, that she might have walked back in from China.

Turning around she saw Laura falter for a second at her expression then, looking back again at the cubicle, saw the tableau all quiet, the curtain closed, the man with his back turned in the chair, hands resting on the padded velvet arms, very still. Blindly Bridget retreated behind the till.

After a moment's hesitation Laura was set back in motion, fishing in her pocket for the receipts from the post office, putting the kettle on. Bridget knelt behind the cash desk, pretending to be looking for her pins, hearing Laura begin to make conversation with them. Standing up again she saw that something had changed: Isabel was bright again, chattering, and he had smoothly become gentler, more grandfatherly. She saw him move his chair, though, an inch or two, to get further away from the great curve of Laura's belly as she leaned to confide advice.

They decided on a different dress, between them. Simple, short, a black shift with a white lace collar that Bridget couldn't remember even having ordered in, it was too schoolgirlish. And expensive. She waited behind the desk as Laura led them back over with a quick inquiring look: it was usually Laura dozy at the till or in a chair while Bridget gave encouragement and advice. But Bridget was numb, she couldn't even deflect Laura's glance, only returned it with a glazed smile.

Her fingers were rubber as she took the credit card, pushed it into the machine, processed the transaction: she had to enter the price three times. Laura was plumped down now on the sofa, oblivious, with her cup of tea on the mirrored cube, flicking through a magazine. His hands across the desk from her, the backs furred with sandy hair, as they reached for the card. Bridget felt as though she could hardly breathe, then she began to feel something else, something she couldn't control, it wound its way up inside her, a tapeworm; a viper; a dragon. He was putting his credit card away when abruptly he looked her in the eye, and she had to hold his gaze.

Older, hair thinner, turkey neck. Sandy eyebrows. He smiled. He smiled at her.

He had been married, when she knew him, but they had no children. The girl standing beside him, peering eagerly at the carrier bag as Bridget slid it over the desk towards her, she wasn't his daughter, nor granddaughter. She bent her neck to look inside, her shirt collar shifted and Bridget saw something else: there was the old familiar mark, the callous rough and reddening on the soft skin of her shoulder. The concert: of course. Isabel was a student of the violin. Not father, not grandfather, but teacher. Teacher.

What did the word say, to most people? Authority with kindness, that's what it was supposed to be. The teacher is stern and wise. The teacher leans over the student and places her hands on the bow, on the stem of the instrument, his mouth is close to her ear. The teacher knows better.

'All right if I take one of these?' He spoke in his soft, deep voice: how had she not known it straight away? She realised that she had, that from the moment he came in there had been a hum in the air, of electricity, that had stopped her hearing anything properly.

He was asking if he could take one of the shop's cards. She pulled herself together, and some hazy idea formed, some plan that had something to do with behaving normally. She was making conversation.

'You're not just visiting, then?' Her voice sounded like it belonged to someone else. Could he hear the fear in it? She knew he was listening: he was probing, circling.

'I'm at the university. A visiting Fellow, in the Music department – well—' and he was taking the card, he was putting it carefully in his wallet, casual. 'It might be more than visiting.' He smiled. 'They seem to rather like me.' Isabel had drifted towards the door. 'Do you have a mailing list? Would you like my details, perhaps?'

Laura was looking up from her magazine at the sound

of Bridget's hesitation, so she leaned down, extracted a form and pushed it over to him. 'Just the email address is fine,' she said, but he was writing it all, address, telephone, laborious. That handwriting: copperplate, Mum had called it, approvingly. Classy, old school.

Anthony Carmichael.

The girl was waiting obedient beside him, swinging the bag.

Bridget watched, very still, as he signed with a flourish, handed the form back to her and for a moment his fingers rested on her forearm. He held the door for Isabel as she walked out in front of him.

Anthony Carmichael. *Call me Tony.*

Laura said, 'Nice guy, right?'

Chapter Two

From the turning into the close Bridget saw the lights on downstairs and up: that meant they were both home. As she wheeled her bike up to the back door in the wet dark, anticipating Matt, the past came abruptly up to meet her.

Bridget couldn't remember her own father, not really. A closed door and music behind it, frowning over his glasses at the dinner table.

In the dark, she paused. That wasn't true. She could remember his hand stroking her hair when she was very small and had a temperature, and the smell of his ironed shirts. She could remember his face, lost and bewildered, at the door to his private room in the hospital, when he was dying. It was just that, after that, with Mum run ragged looking after her and Carrie, twelve and seven, while working shifts at the surgery as a receptionist, it seemed wisest not to remember him too often.

A light was on in the kitchen, and another one upstairs

in the little back bedroom. Finn was up there – it was where he did most of his living, these days. You could hear him laughing loudly, earphones on, or whooping over his computer, talking to whoever it was he gamed with in Arizona or Penang or Stockholm. Matt told her, it was fine. They had the usual filters in place, all the kids were doing it – and Matt should know. It was his job, computer officer, at the university. 'It's just a new kind of socialising.'

There was a girlfriend, too, now, at least. Shyly Finn had mentioned her: Phoebe, six months older. When he was online with her there was more laughing, but softer. A lot of clicking on the keyboard and sometimes they would hear him pad over to his door and close it.

Matt had worked at the university for fourteen years; the computer office had grown to four times its size and he was in charge, now. Monitoring usage, sorting out glitches, updating the systems, reprimanding students, when he had to, for exceeding the limits set on traffic, for streaming movies illegally when they should be working. It wasn't a glamorous place, it wasn't the sandstone and turrets of the university city in whose shadow Bridget had grown up and from whose shadow they had fled, eventually, she and Carrie and Mum. In search of cheaper accommodation, and a change of air.

It was a practical place, a hardworking place, built on idealism, was how Matt defended it even if the bricks and mortar, or rather concrete and glass, had failed it somewhat; sick building syndrome had been talked about, and in high winds it swayed. You could see the towers from everywhere: at night the red lights gleamed, they'd followed Bridget on her cycle ride home. At the back door she wiped her face, took off her helmet and turned off her lights.

The university suited Matt down to the ground, but why would someone come here from one of the old places, where dons have rooms and gardens? Matt might have passed him in the corridors. Anthony Carmichael. 'They seem to like me,' he had said, across the till to her. Matt might have been summoned to set up his internet connection.

She could see Matt moving behind the glass of the kitchen door, a slight, dark shape: she heard the tap running.

They'd bought this house – a new build, small and neat – when she got pregnant, barely in their twenties and choosing a kitchen on a plan. Four years left on the mortgage and they would be safe: God knows they wouldn't be able to afford anything if they were starting now; standing on this doorstep always sparked that thought, of how lucky they were. The trees that had been saplings had grown tall, red maples alternating with cherries, bare and dripping now in the yellow streetlight on the gently sloping street, and you could see the estuary from their bedroom window.

The violin had been a lifesaver: she'd heard Mum use those words often enough, anyway. *Keeps her out of mischief,* and the proximity of the ancient university meant there was a concert hall, *seems like she's got quite a talent for it.* There were lessons for underprivileged students. *Her dad would be so proud.* Dad, sitting in the car all on his own listening to the stereo, waiting in the drive till it had finished, a silhouette with a finger raised to conduct. Bridget remembered that too, out of the blue, as she stood lost in the blur of the past at her own back door. Where had that

15

memory been? The door opened and there was Matt's anxious face: she'd been standing there too long in the rain.

With a sound – half exasperation, half tenderness – that she knew very well, he reached past her and took the bike, leaning down to trace a squeak to its source. 'You're soaked,' he said and she stepped inside. He would wheel the bike to the garage, wipe it down, check the squeaking pedal, lock the garage up again after him.

He was cooking *puttanesca*, everyone's favourite and Matt's signature dish, he always said. Meaning what he'd cook if it looked like she was going to be too late or too tired, information he seemed to absorb out of the air before she knew it herself. She stared at the rich red sauce, smelled the tuna and oil and saltiness and felt sick. In that moment it was as if she had felt sick her whole life: she'd told herself memory was boxes, with lids, neatly stacked, but all the time it was like a sea, it was like seething space, a forest at night. It was all around her and it moved, in the dark.

Then Matt was back in the kitchen beside her and planting a kiss on her cheek, a whiff of bike oil and the wet outside on him. Matt who had wooed her with stammering persistence when she was nineteen and starting college, two stone underweight, jumpy and frightened and clinging on, for dear life, to normal. Matt gangly and awkward and obsessed with bikes, pushing his glasses up his nose. Matt who seemed to have seen everything about her at first glance: he had seen it all and never mentioned any of it.

'All right?' He peered down into the sauce, not looking at her.

16

And then Finn was on the stairs, jumping, humming under his breath, 'Mum?' he called, happy.

'I could do with a cup of tea,' she said to Matt, making her sigh sound just weary, and taking the kettle to the sink.

In the shop Laura hadn't seen Carmichael's hand, sliding down the girl's back as they walked out, and the girl jumpy as a foal under his touch, sidestepping. Laura hadn't seen him turn his head a fraction to catch Bridget's eye, his face all planes and shadows under the downlighting. 'Bless,' Laura had said, patting her belly. 'Buying the kid a party dress.'

And now even as Bridget turned on the tap she was wondering, could they move? How would she put it to Matt? To Finn, with his first girlfriend? Finn horrified by his mother, his soft mother whom he stopped to kiss on the cheek every time he passed her.

Something came to her, the batsqueak of a memory. A man's fingers on her arm and Bridget made a sound. Leaning over the sauce, Matt didn't respond, but he heard. She knew he heard.

Finn was already at the table, knife and fork upright in each hand, impatient, when they came in with the food. His knee under the table was tapping, cheerful but also itching to run, to be back upstairs. He ate like a wolf, forking the pasta in, oblivious.

Bridget ate, because if she didn't Matt would know, one alarm bell was one thing, more than one – well, she didn't know what would happen then. How many had to go off before he asked questions? The thought was horrible: Matt had never asked. It was why they were happy. Never asked why there were things she couldn't do, or listen to, or eat: he treated her like she was normal and in turn she did the

17

same for him. Mr and Mrs Normal: she knew it was why plenty of her customers came in, they could be sure there'd be no hysterics, no loud music, no clothes with bits flapping or unexpected holes. There'd be the magazine perfectly centred on the mirrored cube and the bright, soft colours. Tomorrow she'd have orders to place, boxes to unpack. She could set it to rights.

Matt poured her a glass of water. He didn't ask her if she wanted any more to eat though the bowl was still half full. He sighed. 'Long day,' she said, automatically. 'Sorry to be late. There was – we had a couple of customers come in, just as we were shutting up shop.'

'Laura must be nearly due, isn't she?' Pushing his glasses up his nose as he inspected the pasta on his plate. Matt was shy around women, unless there was something that suggested they needed practical help of some kind. Laura needed all sorts: chairs pulling out for her, doors opening. He liked Laura.

'Nearly,' said Bridget. 'A fortnight, she says,' and she saw his focus shift. Bridget remembered Finn being born, the shock of that, and Matt stepping up to help, not needing to ask. A small boy pressed against her, on her knee, arms tight around her. He couldn't know: could never know. Nor could Matt. The way they would think of her.

There was a sudden scrape and Finn was up and out of there, throwing a *thanks, Dad* over his shoulder, pounding on the stairs, and they were alone together. Before anything could be said she got up too and went to Matt, arms around him as he still sat there in the chair, breathing in his hair, his skin, his healthy smell. 'Let's go up too,' she said.

They had their routines, never made explicit, mysterious.

Quiet, intent, kind sex. Early in the mornings, late at night when Finn's door was closed, Saturdays in the days when he used to go off to football at eight. The first time she had panicked: she had thought somehow he would know she wasn't like other girls. But he knew nothing: they had been a pair of virgins, after all. They had lain there quiet afterwards in the student bed and for a moment, nothing had been wrong. Nothing at all.

It was like a piece of precious old glass, though. You had to keep it safe, you had to hide it, you had to wrap it up the same way every time, as careful as you could be, or it would break.

Four in the morning was the bad time. In the silence she could hear a hum from somewhere. Finn's computer, the big one he'd built with Matt, updating some mega-game or other in the dark across the landing. He could sleep through it: it occurred to her briefly that he might not be able to sleep without it, eventually.

It had begun normally, with Matt turning off the light and touching her. Matt wasn't a talker, not emotional or demonstrative, this was how he made sure everything was all right. He always put his mouth on her breasts first, one and then the other, certain that she liked it, because she did. But then he had shifted in a quick movement and knelt over her and suddenly there was something else there. With the lights out Bridget was only aware of the breadth of his shoulders over her in the dark, then of how practised he was, and she felt the panic bubbling up, she had to control herself. Her breathing was too fast: she was frightened. But then something slipped back into place and she came, too quickly, too suddenly.

19

Nothing could be different, not even this kind of different. This violent feeling. Matt had responded to her, reliable, instantaneous, and then fallen asleep in the moment after. She must have done too but an hour later, perhaps two, she had started awake in a surge of fear, sweating.

Why was Anthony Carmichael there? *Call me Tony.*

How could she get away?

They would move. She would say Carrie was ill, Bridget had to be near her. But schools? Jobs? Close the shop? She tried to talk herself down in the dark. It wasn't that he wanted contact with her, he hadn't come after her. She could have sworn he had no idea, when he walked into the shop. Why would he? She must have fallen asleep again, and woken again, in the same lather of violent fear.

And then it was four o'clock and she was wide awake. A man had come to the shop with a child. He could be her father or grandfather but he wasn't. Isabel, Isabel: in the deep dark she remembered the girl's innocence, her admiration, her glee at being special, it blazed. Bridget had been special once, as she frowned down at her instrument, the instrument burnished and warm from her touch, trying, trying, trying, her heart in her mouth. Him watching her, impatient.

He hasn't come back for you. He isn't interested. He will leave.

Do nothing. She lay still and waited for dawn.

Chapter Three

It took almost a week of uneventful days for the panic to subside. Going through the motions, eating, drinking, working: they went out to the reservoir on the Sunday, just her and Matt, because there was a dinghy he wanted to look at. He'd always wanted to sail.

That had been a bleak, cold day, the cloud lying in grey layers with lemon-coloured sky in between, and the dinghies all under tarpaulins. The owner of the one Matt wanted to look at came out of the little clubhouse, a clapboard shanty, with a pint in his hand, and with the other lifted a tarpaulin for them, revealing a pretty small boat, varnished wood. She could just see Matt out here sanding it happily for hours on end.

'You'd come too?' he said suddenly, as if he knew what she was thinking.

'Yes,' she said, and a smile came unbidden. It felt like months since she'd smiled and she didn't quite want to say anything else, shoving her hands in her pockets. It was freezing. As Matt and the owner chatted she looked out over the still water, the reeds at the edge black against the silvered surface, some bare trees standing on a steep bank on the opposite side. It was a flooded quarry, Matt had told her, very deep and very cold.

'I'll let you know,' Matt had said to the man with his pint, their breath making clouds in the air, but he'd been in a good mood, driving home. Humming, tapping his hands on the steering wheel. 'We'd bring it over to the estuary of course,' to himself. Making plans.

Eating, drinking, working: sleeping, even, eventually. Talking to Matt about the summer holiday. They'd go walking somewhere. Corsica, or Elba, some island.

'Fancy that, Finn?' Matt had asked him and he'd raised his shaggy head from his phone as they sat side by side on the sofa and gazed, mildly uncomprehending, his mind somewhere else. 'Walking in the Med?'

Their holidays followed the same pattern – didn't every-one's? Canoeing or walking, camping or modest hotels, usually somewhere they could drive to. Cornwall or France or Spain at a pinch, nothing flash. Just the three of them, with their happy routines of making tea on a camping stove and staying at the beach till it was dark.

'Uh, well, I, sure – but some of the lads. Phoebe.' Looking back down at his phone and frowning.

It wasn't even a sentence but they exchanged glances, both knowing where it was going.

'Come on, Finn,' Matt said, smiling. 'You're only just sixteen. Come with us for one last year.'

'Auntie Carrie said she went on holiday on her own

when she was fifteen,' looking back up mildly. 'Just saying.'

Bridget sighed. 'That's Auntie Carrie, though,' she said. Matt gave her a look and she grimaced at him.

After a couple of weeks Carrie had stopped talking about their father completely, but perhaps it was just a matter of not having the words, at barely seven and always more about energy than contemplation, because she kept the teddy he got her for that last Christmas under her pillow until she was a teenager. He might still be there for all Bridget knew, worn smooth, hauled from bedsit to squat to communal living experiment. Carrie wasn't one to give much of a toss what people thought, of that or much else either.

They were back on terms, her and Carrie, since Mum died, though it had taken a while and the terms were more theoretical than practical. Living in London with her girl-friend and not much time for Mrs Vanilla with her nuclear family, everything neat and proper and conventional, when there were drugs to experiment with and clubbing and sex. Finn talked to her more than Bridget did, via Facebook. He'd been to visit her once or twice, kipping on the floor in her shared house, going along to one of her DJ sets and coming back home grubby and tired.

Carrie was still angry when they did talk, and Bridget could see why: Carrie's childhood had ended up lonely. When Carrie had been going on holiday alone at fifteen Bridget had been long gone, at college and living with Matt.

'Auntie Carrie's different,' she said.

'You can always go camping with the lads too,' said Matt, folding his laptop closed and looking at Finn.

'Yeah,' said Finn ruminatively, then. 'I s'pose.'

Good old Finn, easygoing Finn. 'Sure, sure. Corsica sounds nice.'

It had sparked panic, though, nothing major but a pattering that ran through her, that she had to damp down quickly.

Things would change, Bridget wasn't stupid, she knew that. Kids grew up. Went on holidays with their girlfriend instead of their mum.

But she had had none of this when she was a teenager, no boyfriends, no family suppers. Winging it, then, but it could still work, she knew that. As long as you kept trying. In that moment, on the sofa next to Finn not for the first time Bridget wished her mother was alive so she could ask her: how much did you really know? Where did you think it all came from, the starving, the hair coming out, the cutting?

'When are we going to meet Phoebe, then?' she said. Finn smiling, ducking his head, shoving his phone down between the cushions then retrieving it.

'Bridge—' Matt was going to warn her off. But Finn stayed where he was, trying to control that shy smile. She'll be besotted, thought Bridget. This Phoebe. My lovely boy.

'Next week sometime?' she said bravely.

'Bridget—'

But Finn's head was bobbing, up and down. 'I'll ask her,' he said, and then he was scrambling up to his feet. He'd been in the sitting room with them a whole half hour, after all. 'Maybe – maybe Tuesday? I'll ask her.'

She and Matt looked at each other as the door closed behind him. 'All right,' she said defensively.

24

'No,' said Matt, edging up next to her, his arm going around to her. 'That was good. Good.'

In the mirrored interior of a lift, with London's Christmas traffic somehow audible even through concrete and steel and wood, someone had strung green and red lights. You could try and avoid the season of goodwill, thought Gillian Lawson, trapped among the bodies and going down, but it came after you. You could run, but you couldn't hide.

Gillian – Gill to everyone but her sister Chloe, who insisted on Gilly, still, *here's Auntie Gilly* – caught a glimpse of herself over a wool-clad shoulder. The light was fairly unforgiving at the best of times, but then journalists didn't need to look like supermodels, did they? Gill could picture a row of grinning blokes at their hot desks telling her otherwise, and mentally consigned them, one by one, to Siberia. In their jockey shorts.

Her roots needed doing, Gill could see that much. The lift was slow: she willed it on, down. Steve was somewhere in the building, and she didn't want to bump into him. He might be on the way home himself, to his wife and kids, he might have taken the stairs because he was trying to keep the beergut in check and he was daft enough to think walking down was as good as walking up. They stopped on the eighth floor and a gang from the newspaper's ad sales department crowded in, padded in their coats and scarves, and Gill was squeezed to the back out of sight of her reflection, which was just as well. She didn't need reminding that her suit was four years old or that she could do with getting a white wash on before she left.

The ad sales lot were chattering away to each other.

Camaraderie. She remembered what that was like, long ago and far away, when she'd started out on a regional paper.

Chloe's theory was that all her problems were down to the job: her theory as to why her big sister was single, lonely, friendless, poor – *thanks*, Gill would interrupt, *I've got the picture and besides there are – I've got friends* – but then she'd have to stop because Chloe would just look smugly triumphant and say, *Well, there you are then.* When Gill had to admit what she had by way of a social life was Steve (who happened to be her editor) a couple of still-single schoolfriends who got increasingly huffy when she called them up for a drink after months of silence, and a bit of casual sex.

And then of course there was him: Anthony Carmichael. Her life's work, her magnum opus, the bloody millstone round her neck.

Gill pressed herself against the back of the lift. An elderly woman she didn't know was next to her, holding a plant in a pot with a ribbon round it. Single – yes. But lonely? Gill resisted that. She liked being on her own. She needed it, too, because how did you think straight, when you had to be looking after other people? But sometimes. Maybe, yes, sometimes, maybe when the kids pelted out of Chloe's front door, Rose and Janie, Gill's two stocky little dark-haired nieces bellowing her name, maybe then she got a glimpse. Not of loneliness exactly but of its opposite, what-ever the word for that was.

Fourth floor: legal department. The doors opened, then closed again because no one got in. No room – and just as well. The legal department weren't too fond of Gill, though they probably wouldn't know her to look at. Next to Gill the elderly woman shuffled, darted a glance. She'd retired, or *been* retired, was that it? A month before Christmas, with a pot plant for her trouble. Gill grimaced back, apologetic, and they both looked away.

Poor – well, yes, that too, or at least not rich. Tiny flat, no car. Newspaper journalism was on the way out, and Gill was on six-month contracts that so far had been renewed on the dot (because she worked like a dog, and because she could write) but the pool of hungry freelances grew bigger and more shark-infested by the week. What she needed was a big story, was what Steve no longer said.

The job. Her sister Chloe thought of newspaper journalism as something for blokes with no homes to go to, men with nicotine-stained fingers and greasy hair who'd do anything for a story, men who lied and spun. Gill's hair might need doing but she'd never lied. She might have spun, where necessary, though she tried to avoid it. When she got her big story – the one Steve wouldn't talk about – she wouldn't need to lie. When she nailed him finally, she wouldn't need to spin.

Third floor, and the woman with her pot plant began to struggle to get out – maybe she was going to crown someone with it – then there was a tussle between two blokes, one carrying a big wrapped present, over who got to take her place.

Gill would be going to Chloe's, of course, for what the paper called the festive season. She didn't need to think about that yet. Presents – yes. She could always manage presents, who didn't know that Christmas was about presents? It was a while since Gill had been a kid but she could remember that much.

When did you stop being a kid? That depended. Fifteen? Eighteen? First kiss? First time you worked out adults weren't all they were cracked up to be, maybe then.

Gill and Chloe had had a good childhood. Uneventful. Parents in love with each other till the day they died, the one always reaching out for the other, and Mum sang around the house. Dead within two weeks of each other, Mum of lung cancer and Dad's heart gave out just like that. It was from other families Gill had learned not all adults took that kind of care of each other, or their kids. Stacey Jarvis's stepdad trying to feel her up when she sat next to him at the cinema, Stacey's thirteenth birthday treat. Routine behaviour. Gill had just sat there like a stone, when she should have stood up and shouted *pervert*.

The doors closed, then opened, there was a final crush and they stayed shut, sheepish apologetic grins among those squeezed too tight against each other. Gill concentrated on breathing, in and out. She wasn't great in crowded places, parties, none of that. But she didn't want to see Steve because she needed him to take the night thinking it over. It was why she'd emailed him her proposal rather than walking into his office and asking him. Kneejerk reaction was not what she wanted. She'd put it so carefully. I'd be up there three, four days at the most. Sandringham, the Royal Christmas, I could put together a nice little feature.

Steve wanted it both ways. He wanted a big story, of course he did – but he didn't want her within twenty miles of the bloke, not since he'd set the lawyers on the paper last time. Four years back, when she'd doorstepped Anthony Carmichael outside his Oxford college, in full view of the porters. It hadn't come to court, even though she begged Steve to take it there: the paper had paid Carmichael off, and given him written promises that 'Ms Lawson's harassment would cease'.

Not even two months on from the settlement though, they'd been in the pub, a quick one on Steve's way home that turned into a quick three. 'Of course I want you to nail him,' he'd said, before emptying his third glass. Wiping his mouth. Meeting her eye for the first time in what felt like years. 'It's what this job's about. I want the fucking story. But I want it nailed down, watertight, I want it on the record.' Standing up. 'Until then, if I find out you've gone near him——' and he was gone.

Gill had gone to college, a degree in English for all the good that did, then ten years on local papers. That was where she'd seen Anthony Carmichael first. How old would he have been? The age she was now, forty-something. Standing between two girls in front of their school on the edge of an estate somewhere, a hand on each of their shoulders, the girls ramrod straight with violins held out in front of them. Thirteen-year-old girls, stiff and scared. Gill had interviewed him, making notes, him droning on about young talent, all so dull and boring, but the hairs had been up on the back of her neck the whole time.

When one of the girls went missing and was found hanging in the wood behind the estate, she knew. Gill knew. Enough of a slacker to still be on the same paper and she hadn't forgotten him, in all that time. She had alerts on her phone.

And then last week, ping. Dr Anthony Carmichael,

inaugural lecture, Wednesday 22 November. The university of the arse end of nowhere: that had piqued her interest. Been sent to the badlands, has he, or what? The university's address was Rose Hill. Pretty name, Gill had thought: she'd looked up trains. How close it was to Sandringham. Not very close, was the answer to that.

Ground floor. The doors opened and with a collective sigh the lift emptied. Catching sight of herself again in the glass Gill smiled, experimentally. She looked all right. She looked almost human, Christ. Maybe smiling was the answer.

And then she turned to look out at the marble foyer, and there was Steve, and she must have not yet managed to wipe that stupid smile off her face because he looked startled.

'There you are,' he said. 'A quick word?' Trying out a smile of his own. 'Before you go?'

Chapter Four

There was something on the television, the late news.

It had been another quiet week at work. Laura moved slower and slower, sat down more and more, and Bridget found herself encouraging it, bringing her glasses of water and leaving her there when a customer did come in. A flurry of Chinese girls – university students – chattering incomprehensibly and then buying a job lot of handbags. The regulars, coming in less and less, women she'd known ten years or more and had seen marry and divorce, have babies, get cancer, survive. Business was shifting; the high street was not what it was. They came in and looked at the stuff, the younger ones, the twenty, thirty-somethings, then bought online. Even Matt had started to suggest she should think about it. She agreed, and did nothing.

There was no sign of Anthony Carmichael or the girl he'd come in with, not even walking past the shop. Isabel. Tuesday, Wednesday. She felt herself subside, slowly. He would stay away. Just visiting. He would go back where he came from.

On Thursday, getting ready for the weekend and December on the horizon, they dismantled the autumn window: red and yellow leaves scattered under a sheet of Perspex and a big piece of mossy log she and Matt had brought home from a walk. It weighed a ton, but he'd carried it uncomplaining. He was used to her window ideas, and he liked helping.

Bridget hauled it out again with difficulty, getting firm with Laura when she tried to help. It sat on the floor, making a mess of the cream rug, Laura's nose wrinkling at the flaking bits of bark and moss. 'Chuck it?' she said eagerly.

It was a prize, though, in Bridget's eyes: the moss was deep green and velvety, the smooth wood showing under ridged bark, and it smelled of the woods.

'I'll – I'll just—'And before Laura could have another go at her – nest-building, she told herself, even knowing it was irrational to hang on to a bit of wood – Bridget was in the stockroom and hauling out the stepladder from under the garment rails, so she could stash the log out of the way.

She heard the door ping while she was in there, and for a moment she froze on her hands and knees, but looking round the door she saw Laura was talking to the postman.

The postman helped her shift it in the end, looking from one woman heavily pregnant to the other dishevelled and flushed. 'Go on then,' he said glumly – with Laura shaking her head disapprovingly from the sidelines as they found a space for it in the kitchen. Not so much a kitchen as a cubby hole at the back of the shop and off to the side, so customers couldn't peer in while they ate their lunch standing. Not much room for more than a sink and a kettle but even in here, running out of room for stock, she'd had

32

to put shelves up high and it was up here, between two cardboard boxes of T-shirts, that they found a space for it.

On the stepladder Bridget took it from his hands, lifting it over her head as he grimaced. She got a piece of twine and wound it round to secure the thing high up in the tiny space, smelling of the outside. She was pleased with herself for her ingenuity: seeing it made Bridget oddly happy, she couldn't explain it, though she knew Matt would have frowned at her improvisation. And then as they started on the Christmas window together — a job lot of tinkly chandeliers and spray snow — she was triumphant, exhilarated, although still out of breath with the effort. She felt strong, in her prime. Silly, really.

And now here they sat side by side on the sofa, she and Matt with the late news on, Bridget with a mug of tea set carefully on the table at her elbow. She had found herself being particularly circumspect these last weeks, as if readying herself. As if there had been warnings of an earthquake or high winds or disaster, as if the door might burst open and something rush in. The images on the screen changed. A radio personality she remembered from her childhood had been arrested.

She'd made herself take certain things in her stride, long since, certain images or sounds, or words. *Recital*. Matt had learned to flick channels if the Proms came on, any of that stuff and probably would have said, if asked why, *she doesn't like classical music*, but: this was different, of course. This was new. Old men with their faces sagging with fear, being led through crowds. Historic cases resurrected, as if suddenly the times had changed, a switch had flipped and what had been normal, what had been acceptable, suddenly wasn't. A light coming on. There was a discussion on the statute of limitations that Matt had been listening to so she couldn't turn it over casually. How long was too long to wait, before you accused someone of something?

'Whisky?' she said, smoothly, getting to her feet. 'I'm having one.'

'Mmm,' said Matt, not really hearing her, she thought as she walked out of the room, not fast but steady.

A music school had come under investigation, twelve, fifteen years ago, not one Bridget had attended and no names had been mentioned, at least not on the news. But it had been a violin teacher they'd referred to and sometimes she thought that had started it all, a rock pushed off a hill. *Tell someone.* It had got into the television news and she hadn't been able to escape it, to walk out of the room quickly enough. She had gone to the local police station pushing Finn in the buggy, fast asleep, and she had stood outside. Pushing him back and forward, rhythmically, so he wouldn't wake. But what would she have said? With the building in front of her, the men moving to and fro behind the windows, her mind had been a blank, wiped by terror, wiped by shame. She hadn't gone in.

She poured carefully, two small glasses, and then stood a moment to wait for the trembling to pass, leaning back against the counter. Looking around the little kitchen, the row of jars, the bread on the side like she didn't recognise what it was; food didn't look like food any more, nothing looked the same. It's good, she told herself. This investigating, exposing people, it's good. He wouldn't dare, would he? Not now.

When she came back in with the tea Matt was watching *Die Hard* and he looked up at her smiling, innocent of it all.

34

Chapter Five

It was the Saturday when Carrie phoned. Almost two weeks had gone and Bridget had almost stopped expecting to see him again.

It was busy at last, with a chaotic Saturday mix: a privately educated girl gang, all with long expensive hair, occupying the sofa while the one shopping flicked contemptuously through the rails; a young, pale woman trying to persuade her mute boyfriend to pass an opinion on a succession of party dresses, and a mother of the groom, disapproving of everything.

The wedding wasn't till May, months away, and they didn't have much to offer her, in November. When Bridget and Matt had got married Mum had already been ill, swaying at the registry office — it was why they'd done it quickly. Matt in his only jacket and Bridget in a cheap chain-store dress. Pretty, though: she still had it somewhere. His parents had come, nervous and modest, just like him, his mother – still alive now, though his father had died ten years earlier, bequeathing Matt his tools and his kindness – had worn a purple hat and beamed all the way through the ceremony and the quick two rounds of drinks at the pub after. This woman, the customer – menopausal and angry – wasn't going to be beaming, Bridget could tell; she kept rounding on Bridget, her hands on some innocent piece of clothing, to explain another affront perpetrated by her future daughter-in-law. Bridget had just managed to persuade her into the cubicle with two sensible dresses and a duck egg blue lace suit when the phone rang.

Of course, it would be busy, because Carrie had a sixth sense like that. Once upon a time the phone would go when she was changing a nappy, now it would be when she was setting the alarm on the shop. She was oblivious, too caught up in her own stuff, but Bridget wouldn't have wanted it any other way.

Laura had taken the call on the shop phone and shrugged when Bridget mouthed, *who?* She took the receiver.

'Hey, Bridge.' A sniff. 'Bridge?'

'Hey, Carrie.' She reversed into the doorway into the tiny kitchen. She could smell the woods in here, and glanced up to see the log.

'You all right?' she asked warily.

There was silence, then a sigh. 'Sure.' Airy – for about a millisecond, before Carrie launched into a litany of complaints about work – the web design company – finishing up triumphantly with, 'The guy's an arsehole.' Bridget had long since stopped advising her little sister to be less confrontational: she always walked into another job, something completely different half the time. There was a

36

pause, and she knew there was more, because pausing wasn't Carrie's style any more than backing down was.

'What else?' she said.

A deep breath. Then, sulkily, 'Ella's – well. Things are a bit tricky with Ella and me.'

Sweet-natured, feminine Ella, all eyelashes and lipstick; prone to singing and yelling. They'd been together three years. Ella seemed to love Carrie's energy, her dash, her wiry schoolboy looks, melting adoringly against her in the Facebook pictures Finn showed Bridget. And Carrie looking almost bashful.

'What have you done now?' said Bridget. 'Carrie?'

'Why do you always think it's me?' Blustering.

'It wasn't?'

A longer sigh. Then, 'Listen, I thought I might come and visit.'

'Really?' Her nerves jangled: Carrie meant chaos, she brought it with her, into their little house. Finn loved her for it, shaking things up, but he'd been twelve or something the last time she came to them. She'd managed to break one of Matt's bikes on that occasion – for which he had forgiven her sooner than Bridget had.

'What?' said Carrie and Bridget could just see her, pale-faced and defiant, the little pointed chin up, on the alert for insult and rejection and going at it head on. 'You don't want me to come?'

It was always there between them.

She'd been nine when Bridget started the violin. Fierce little Carrie watching Bridget from the sidelines, watching her come back from a recital flushed and hyped. Carrie watching her stop eating, watching her hair fall out. Always bright, always inquisitive, tomboy Carrie. Bridget had told her she wasn't good enough to play an instrument, that had been the beginning of it.

Then it had been Carrie angry with her big sister over the dinner table, when Bridget pushed the food around, when she hid it in her pockets. Angry when Bridget was hospitalised weighing five stone, and when Bridget threw the family into chaos. She'd raged against it, aged twelve and having to leave her school, her mates. 'But I don't see *why*.' Bridget started to get better, the tide ebbed, but it left a changed landscape. It was how families worked: that was what Matt said, Matt who had no siblings but still knew, he watched. You think they're fixed, but they shift.

These days the pattern it followed was Carrie pushing Bridget to scold her, and Bridget getting more and more conciliatory and Carrie raising the stakes, angrier and angrier. Over nothing, on the surface.

'Of course I want you to come.' And she did. Whatever else Carrie was, she was a distraction. And it would make Finn happy. 'What, now? Today?'

'I dunno,' said Carrie, airy again, now she'd got the reaction she wanted. 'Next week some time. Maybe.'

So Ella hadn't actually chucked her out: that was something. 'Well, just give me a ring to say—'

'Got to go,' said Carrie, and hung up.

The mother of the groom flung back the curtain of the changing cubicle and stood there in the pale lace suit, glaring. It was as if a rhino had got tangled up in someone's curtains.

Bridget set the phone down. 'So,' she said carefully. 'What do you think?'

38

But what with the bashful couple and the rhino and the teenagers and someone trying to sell her a range of scarves, she didn't get time to think about Carrie or anything else herself until the late afternoon, and things slowed.

She'd been aware of Laura watching her, waiting for her chance to be nosy, and had headed her off a couple of times already. But then there was a lull, just after lunchtime and she found herself cornered in the kitchen. It was a confined space at the best of times, and with Laura in the doorway Bridget was trapped.

'Cup of tea?' said Bridget, warily.

'Trouble, is it?' said Laura, her head tilted sympathetically. 'With your sister, I mean?' She'd met Carrie once, two or three years before and even then, in her early twenties, had been disapproving.

Then, 'No, no tea, thanks.' Patting her stomach, complacent. As if tea might bring on labour, or acrobatics.

'I hope not,' said Bridget. Sometimes Laura made her want to scream. 'She's coming to visit, that's all.'

But Carrie had known Anthony Carmichael. In passing, at least: peering curiously into the car when he brought Bridget home from the lessons. Her stomach knotted at the thought. If Carrie bumped into him, here. *That man.* What would she say? What would she remember? *Call me Tony.*

'Family's family, though, isn't it?' said Laura dreamily. 'Nick's always saying—'

'Listen, Laura,' Bridget interrupted. Because if she had to listen one more time to the wisdom of the sainted Nick, whom Laura had after all found online, not at a ball with a glass slipper in his hand, Nick who was just some smooth salesman not a Nobel prize-winner – and now Laura was gazing at her, puppy-like.

Bridget ploughed on. 'Don't you think – maybe, now that – now the baby's going to be here any minute—' Laura's eyebrows drew together, a tiny wounded crease appearing above her perfect nose. 'Maybe you might want to move to doing half days?' Bridget concluded lamely.

Laura stepped back, uncertain, ready to be offended – but she was out of the doorway, at least.

'That window,' said Bridget briskly, stepping past her. 'While it's quiet, I'd like to get it finished off.' And before Laura could offer to help, 'You've been on your feet all day, why don't you have a sit down?'

When Bridget, fastening the last tinkling miniature chandelier to the last piece of fishing line, stood up, triumphant in the window, Laura was still behind her humming tunelessly on the sofa examining her nails, her back to the street. With her blouse untucked from her skirt and her hair coming down, Bridget had knelt to extract herself from the display when he was there, walking past.

She didn't even need to look up to know, for the sweat to break under her arms. Behind her Laura sighed but it might have been in another room, another world. Bridget couldn't move. She looked up.

In a sheepskin coat, head high. Walking on, not looking, not breaking step.

Just walking past.

And then she moved, reversing ungainly in her haste, and feeling the flush burn her neck, her face. Once out she stood up, pulling her skirt down, and turned her back on the street, unable to move further. Stood there in silence a whole minute, another, until even Laura registered some-thing, putting the magazine down, turning, looking up at her. 'What—'

Then, heedless, Bridget ran jerkily to the door and tugged it open, hearing the bell ping, loudly, to see him still just visible at the end of the street, jaunty, upright. He slowed – did the bell have to be so loud? – and she ducked back inside.

Laura stared up at her in astonishment. 'Nothing,' said Bridget, ragged, 'I thought I – nothing.' And walked jerkily, blindly away, into the stockroom where she closed the door behind her.

That night she couldn't eat, not at all. Finn, blithe, inno-cent – happy – asked if she was all right and she said she thought she had a bug. He told her Phoebe was looking forward to coming on Tuesday. 'Is it still all right?'

'Of course,' she said, stiff and bright. Matt pushed his glasses up his nose and reached to clear the plates. 'There's been something going round at work,' he said. 'I'll sort this.'

She lay in bed with the light off, listening to the murmur of Finn and Matt in the kitchen. She saw clearly that everything could just slip, out of her control. She had to be very careful. Methodical: she went over the options again. Do nothing. Leave.

Go to the police.

Maybe he will just die.

She dreamed.

Chapter Six

Sunday

When Bridget woke up, later than usual and Matt already gone from the bed, she couldn't remember the dream. Eyes closed, she felt the ghost of it still, moving in the dark spaces of her head – then Matt called up the stairs and she opened her eyes to thin sunshine and swung her legs, winter-pale, out of the bed.

They had their Sunday routines; maybe one day Finn would stop going along with it all but so far he'd always been happy. More than happy: it had always been his favourite day, revelling in staying in his pyjamas till midday. There would be a roast lunch which Bridget bought things for over the week: a joint of lamb, roast potatoes, Yorkshire puddings, mash. Garlic and rosemary and apples for crumble and carrots. They'd go for a walk while the meat cooked.

Finn loped round the kitchen with a bowl of cereal in his hand as Bridget sat at the table, peeling potatoes. He leaned down to give her a kiss, the milk slopping just to the brim. The bug had gone quietly unmentioned: *I'm feeling better*, she rehearsed, but no one asked. There was a pan with carrots already done and the tablecloth was out of the drawer, the glasses polished. The sun had strengthened, flooding through the big window and gleaming off the glasses.

Matt came in from the garage, cheerful and dirty with chain grease, and started to wash his hands. 'Ready, then?'

They walked up the river towards Rose Hill in the wintry sunshine. The fields were soggy with rain but Finn ran ahead like a kid, laughing when his boots sent up a wet squelch. Bridget found herself setting their path at a careful angle to the university campus: the towers were visible everywhere, from their own back door on a bright day, and deliberately she now made them just a tall shadow on the edge of her vision, looking beyond them to the estuary.

The country park was dotted with Sunday walkers. She could see the outline of a man with a baby in a backpack, an elderly couple, a family with a floppy-eared dog going into the clump of bare trees at the foot of the slope.

Finn zigzagged slowly down ahead of them.

'How's work?' she asked and Matt turned to look at her, quizzical. It wasn't a question she asked. Could he hear anything in her voice? She was asking now because of Carmichael, Carmichael with an office up here, Carmichael her husband's colleague: Matt couldn't know that. Matt couldn't know that since Carmichael had walked into the shop he'd been there, at the back of her every thought, while she was chopping carrots or opening garment boxes or talking to Laura about caesareans.

With Matt's eyes on her the dream came back to Bridget. She had been lying in bed and she knew without looking that the man in bed next to her, the covers pulled up and covering his face, wasn't Matt, it was Anthony Carmichael. Turning her head she could see the backs of his hands, the sandy hair on his knuckles. And Finn, not Finn now but the small Finn, three or four, had run in and begun to tug at the covers. *Wake up, Daddy.*

Don't, don't, don't.

Now she smiled a stiff smile and Matt turned away and then they were looking up at the towers after all. They'd been there all along, only bigger, taller, dwarfing them all. He turned back to her and nodded gravely. 'Work's fine.' Giving her a gentle squeeze. 'Same old, same old.' Happily.

She shifted, getting the towers back on to the periphery of her vision. Finn was jogging now, elbows up, straight down towards the copse.

'He's got energy to spare,' said Matt cheerfully. 'Nice, isn't it?' Not looking at her but smiling. 'Him being like this.'

'Do you think it's the girlfriend?' she said cautiously. Finn had never been difficult, but he'd been moody on and off for a year or more, frowning under the newly thick eyebrows as he came out of the bathroom, or monosyllabic under questioning. Now it was as if the sun had come out. She pushed her hands down into her pockets. 'Phoebe?'

Trying out the name: this girl might become almost part of the family, calling for Finn, coming to tea. Phoebe.

'Probably,' said Matt, drawing his shoulders up. 'It's been known.' He waved: Finn was spinning round and waved back. 'At that age.' She looked at him and he was smiling, awkward.

'Were you like that?' Bridget asked tentatively. She remembered Matt's quiet determination, nearly twenty years

44

ago now, waiting for her to answer when he had finally asked her if she'd like to go to the pub with him. 'Just for a drink,' clarifying, pointlessly. When she'd said *yes* he had just nodded, bobbing his head up and down quickly two, three times. He hadn't done any skipping – but she might not have gone for a drink with him if he had.

'Well, I was twenty,' he said seriously. 'When it happened to me. Not sixteen.'

She began to smile but up ahead Finn had finally run out of steam, breathless, and Matt was running down the hill after him. He had a characteristic running style, a steady economical jog.

It came to her that when she wanted to feel good, calm, *happy*, she thought of Matt in the garage on his knees in front of a bicycle, a box of tools and bike parts beside him and oil on his fingers. When he was fucking her he had the same focus, steady and careful. *I love you, Matt.* They never said it: if she said it now he'd know something was wrong.

They were at the trees when Bridget caught up with them, on the edge of a thick clump of silver birches where only the odd stray golden leaf clung to the black branches now, almost December, but before she could say anything Finn plunged in between the trunks to where a stream trickled across the foot of the copse. He'd always liked to splash there when he was small, in shiny red Wellington boots. It seemed a long time ago.

Then the floppy-eared dog was jumping up at Finn and the owners had come up to call it and they were all laughing, a father and mother about the same age as her and Matt, only rangier than them. A boy of about six or seven was trying to grab the dog's collar and then his older sister, flossy hair under a beanie, long-limbed, gawky, was intervening. It was Isabel: she was Isabel and for one second she saw Bridget: the girl held her gaze.

In instant fear Bridget took a step back, wanting to hide somewhere, behind one of the silver tree-trunks too slender to hide anything, wanting to turn around, to bend and pretend to tie her shoelace, to run away. But then Matt was in front of her engaging with them, Finn was saying something to Isabel and before Bridget could do anything at all suddenly it was over. It was done and she could see their backs as they were walking away. And it was too late.

She should have taken hold of the parents, the tall, unmade-up mother with hair flying round her face, the lanky father in his cagoule, and said, *Do you know what's going on? Your daughter's at risk.* She'd been too frightened—

Of Matt's face, if she did, turning, bewildered, to look at her, to see something, someone he didn't recognise. Finn stopping and all the light and movement and happiness draining away. And Isabel: Bridget hadn't needed to say anything to know what would happen to Isabel's face because there'd been a look, before they stepped away from each other, that had contained it all. *Don't.*

Something hit the side of Bridget's leg, wet and heavy. She turned to see that Finn was laughing and at her feet was a soggy old football; he must have found it and kicked it at her. 'Sorry, Mum,' he made a face then, registering something about her, a momentary uncertainty flickered.

Bridget made herself smile. 'Oi,' she said, and she made herself begin to tell him off, joking, pushing at him so he had to turn and couldn't see her.

All these tiny moments, their life. All these depend on nothing changing. Pretend he never came here, she doesn't know him. It never happened.

Except now there's Isabel.

'Home,' she said.

Back at the house she went through the motions, waiting till they'd eaten, the whole ritual observed minutely. The table laid, plates, cutlery, glasses, the right napkins, the timing. Yorkshire puddings and gravy and the warm kitchen smelling of roast lamb. Nothing must burn, nothing must go wrong. Nothing went wrong.

Matt was in the other room on the sofa searching for a movie to watch. Finn always helped her load the dishwasher.

'Did you know that girl?' she said, when his back was to her, leaning over the machine. Casually. 'The one we saw this morning on the walk, the one with the dog?'

His answer was muffled: she made herself wait, smiling as he straightened and handing him a bowl. 'No?' she said.

'Mum—' he frowned.

She held up her hands palms out: 'Sorry, nosy—' she said, apologetically.

He went on looking at her, only puzzled. A second passed. He shrugged. 'Not really,' he said. 'I've seen her around, at school. She's not in my year. We did the maths challenge together last year. She's good at maths.'

Good at maths: the information went in and out again, she couldn't retain it. Hastily Bridget said, not even knowing where it came from, if it was a smokescreen or what it was. 'She isn't Phoebe?'

Had that thought been there all along? She knew the

47

girl's name wasn't Phoebe. She needed a way in, to finding out.

'No—' Still bewildered. 'Phoebe's—' and Finn tipped his head, trying to work out what was going on: something was going on. 'If it had been Phoebe I'd have said.' Indignantly.

Quick. Quick.

'Sorry, stupid, yes, of course you would,' and then Bridget was laughing it off, she was turning to steer him into the sitting room so that he wouldn't remember how her face had looked, back there among the silver birches where he had used to splash in the stream in his red shiny boots.

Because it was a look all children knew: the look that says, caught out; guilty; frightened. Terrified. And the first time a child saw that in an adult's face, in a parent's face, suddenly everything was different.

Chapter Seven

Monday

Bridget was on her knees in front of the fridge in old jeans, mopping water: she was defrosting the freezer. It had taken her a year or two of running the shop to understand that almost no one went shopping for clothes on a Monday. Who knew why: too gloomy at being back at work after the weekend, too domestic after a family Sunday. Whatever: Mondays she kept it closed and did everything that needed doing at home.

Matt often came home for lunch on Monday and on the table in the kitchen was nice bread with a dark crust he liked and some cheese and pickles from the deli. It was half a mile away in the older streets where the town began, a little place on a Victorian corner with an old bacon slicer and shelves full of bright jars like jewels. November tomatoes: she'd spent a good five minutes surreptitiously picking out the good ones, the ones that had a distant smell of summer on them. We could go on holiday, she had thought, holding the tomato, a spark of hope, now, tomorrow, next week. Somewhere, anywhere, disappear to a bothy on a Scottish beach or a cheap hotel in

Tunisia. Anything. She'd even got as far as taking out her phone, to tell Matt.

But it was term time: another month for Finn, another fortnight for Matt. And Matt's mother invited for Christmas. Christmas seemed as far off as summer: the holiday conversation seemed almost as impossible to have safely as the emigration conversation.

Her knees were wet, her hair coming undone where she'd tied it back. Over the jeans she wore an old soft green sweatshirt, faded almost to grey. Her customers wouldn't recognise her but this was Matt's favourite Bridget. He would put his hands up under the wide sleeves of the sweatshirt to hold her forearms, as if he just wanted to feel her skin. As if the clothes didn't matter but her body underneath them, as if she was something lovely. She stood up and reached for the big blunt knife she used to chip at the ice.

Plenty of men had presided from the shop's sofa with the newspaper on their knee giving their demands – frowning at their wives, shaking their heads. Tighter, brighter, shorter, they mostly wanted, though others were more precise about it. It had to be a certain length, a certain height of neckline, or heel. Or, *isn't that a bit young for you?* And the woman's face falling. She dug the knife in harder, sawing at the ice, working up a sweat. Trying not to think of a man wanting to doll a woman up. A child.

But mostly men stayed away, and Bridget was much more at her ease that way. She could focus on the women, because even bad-tempered ones, dissatisfied ones, could be coaxed round usually. She had perceived a difference: the happy ones were more beautiful, whatever their actual attributes. Make them happy and they will look good.

Was she happy? She paused, with the knife in her hand and her fingers numbing. Before this. Yes. Yes.

Then there was the inverse. The girl wanting to please him. Inverting the formula: make them insecure, make them think they look bad and they'll be unhappy. They'll try harder, looking for the happiness. The unhappy ones spent and spent and spent and it didn't work: they stared at themselves in the mirror trying to see something, someone else.

Isabel's parents had looked kind. How could you tell? You could. But were they clever enough to know what was happening? A big chunk of ice came loose and Bridget dropped it into the bucket at her feet: nearly there.

There must be a way of getting her away from him. She reached for a tea towel and mopped at her face, then picked the knife up again.

There was a sound at the front door.

'Matt?' She stood there, the knife in her hand. An indistinct sound came in return: had he lost his keys? She padded down the corridor, cheerful, but as she reached to pull the door open, something shifted. The shape of a head through the wavy glass, or the quality of the light outside: she didn't know what did it but in that moment the world – her world – seemed to divide itself. There was inside and outside, there was home and there were strangers, and the door was there to protect her.

The bell rang, loud, and with the sound time subdivided, there was one fraction of a second left in which she could hide, stay inside. Never leave. She opened the door.

It was the postman, a man she knew with a bulbous nose and a cheerful smile, holding out a small parcel addressed to Finn. 'Another computer game, is it?' he said, and that was what it looked like. Bridget had to sign for it on his electronic pad, squinting to see in the brightening light and then, raising her head as she handed it back, she saw him. She froze. There, over the postman's retreating back, standing on the far corner of the close beside a flashy little black car with his hands in his pockets and looking around.

It was Anthony Carmichael. He stepped away from the car and turned, slowly.

She swayed, blinked, then stepped back into her hall so fast she stumbled, held on to the doorframe, then flattened herself against the wall. The door sat open: step into the light, it said. Show yourself. She fumbled with an outstretched hand trying to get a purchase on the door's panels without being seen and then it moved, she could reach the latch and pull it towards her. Her fingers on the latch were like someone else's, nerveless and uncooperative. The door clicked to, quietly.

Call me Tony, he'd said, after the first lesson in his big living room, with the mirror over the mantelpiece and brocade sofas and oil paintings – and with his wife, always out somewhere when he gave lessons. Drawing his finger down her cheek while she stood, mesmerised by the newness of it, a man she didn't know touching her face. Shocked and fascinated: what would happen next? She had had no idea.

Now she stood in the hall with her heart racing so fast she thought it could kill her. That would be all right, she thought for a horrible empty moment, drop dead here, natural causes, *all right*. She squeezed her eyes shut but his

52

image was imprinted on them, details: the way his head moved, how his neck looked, emerging from his collar, the thin hair. He had been wearing a leather jacket. The kind of leather jacket a man buys when he has no idea what it makes him look like. She even knew what it would smell like, like a leather settee, leather too new, too cheap, an animal smell, and she felt suddenly so sick she opened her eyes.

Her hand hurt: she looked down. She had dropped the parcel the postman had brought but was still holding the knife she'd been using on the ice. The handle broken, the tip snapped off, useless, but the blade had dug into her palm. She unclenched her hand but kept hold of the knife and walked, two steps, three, across the hall and into the sitting-room doorway.

The room was flooded with light from the big bay window that looked out into the close but Bridget stepped back, feeling her heart pound in her throat, a pulse so strong she thought it must be visible through her skin. In that moment she became acutely aware that she had no bra on under the sweatshirt, she felt the thin worn fabric against her breasts. She felt naked, as exposed as if she was standing in the wind on the street corner naked and all the neighbours at their windows. She blinked, swallowed. Go away. She made herself advance, a millimetre, a centimetre.

From where Bridget stood she could see only the mound of privet that bordered their little piece of front garden, two palings of their picket fence, a foot of pavement. The close was suddenly so quiet that she could hear the high drone of an aircraft turning to fly out across the estuary towards Europe. She edged around the door, behind the sofa, hands behind her feeling for the wall, until she was at the corner of the bay where the curtain hung. There was a shadow on the pavement, two pillars of shade that might have been legs, a man standing lordly outside her house, then the cloud moved, the light uncertain, and there wasn't. She heard footsteps then the clump of a car door and then she darted forward, then it was too late to run out and shout at him, *Leave her alone. Leave her alone, you fucker.*

The close was empty, bleached pale in winter afternoon light. Then a flicker as a bicycle turned the corner, a head down over handlebars. Matt. Matt. Home for lunch.

Running clumsily back into the house Bridget threw herself on to her knees in front of the fridge. She was still there in her rubber gloves, bathed in sweat, when Matt walked in five minutes later.

'What was this doing in the hall?' he said, half laughing, half frowning. He had the old breadknife in his hand. She stood, shaky. 'Are you all right?' he asked, putting his hand up as if to touch her cheek and she flinched. 'Is it that bug?'

'No – it – the postman – I was holding it and I had to answer the door,' she said, although she had no idea when or how it had got there. Matt had put the knife down on the table and was taking off his backpack, peering down at the lunch. He said nothing about seeing anyone leaving the house. About a little black car passing him on the road and a man in an ugly leather jacket turning to examine him, her husband on his bike.

Matt only ever stayed an hour, for their Monday lunches.

He was uneasy with pushing rules, and they needed him, up there on Rose Hill. The busiest man in the university, as they all came to him to sort their connections or salvage their hard drive and patiently he would comply: happily.

Carrie had said once, wonderingly, 'I did think he was boring, to start. Your Matt. Mr nerdy.' She didn't say what had changed her mind. The thought of Carrie set something off that Bridget had to push out of her head.

When he pulled his waterproof jacket back on she said without turning from the sink, 'I thought I might cycle back up with you. For the exercise.'

Because she couldn't stay here, cowering behind the front door, too scared to make a noise in case the neighbours heard. Never mind that Rose Hill and the university might be where *he* was, Carmichael: never mind that. Let him see her walk up to *his* front door.

'You sure?' he stopped with his backpack halfway hoisted on to his shoulder.

She shrugged. 'I just fancy some fresh air,' she said.

They cycled side by side, Matt upright with one hand keeping his handlebars straight. Daring a glance sideways Bridget wondered: perhaps she could tell him what happened. She could point to Carmichael, and say, *That man—*

The last stretch uphill to the university was a slog, heads down: as it levelled out and they sailed past the car park she scanned it, but saw no jaunty little black car. It was cold in the deep shade as Matt locked the bikes, and there didn't seem to be anyone venturing outside except the odd figure hurrying between the buildings. Bridget didn't come up here often, occasionally to meet Matt after work.

For all he sung its praises, it wasn't hospitable. A constant stiff, cold breeze blew, eddying around the foot of the towers, lifting and scattering the water in the concrete fountain. The campus had a concert hall, a theatre, a bar: she could see the student café from where she stood, orange plastic chairs and some posters lifting at the corners in the wind. The views from the towers over the river were supposed to be breathtaking but Matt's office was on the ground floor, a place of constant traffic.

'Stop for a cup of tea?' he said shyly, handing her the key to her lock. They set out across the deserted piazza to his room.

They'd heard about the suicide when they arrived, it had happened years before, even then: a PhD student who'd thrown herself out of a high window, and it turned out she had been having an affair with her tutor. She didn't even live in the towers but in digs in the town: she'd come up for the purpose, and they never worked out how she got through the glass. According to the caretaker, now long dead, who'd liked to tell the story that the sound of her battering against it had gone on for twenty, thirty minutes before she made it through, but no one had thought to trace the noise to its source.

She hadn't fallen between the buildings, said the old man telling the story in his subterranean office all that time ago, but on the far side, facing out to sea. She'd have looked out across the famous view, as she'd hammered against the glass: the estuary that looked brown or green or silver, according to the time of day and the state of the tide, its muddy banks appearing delicate as lace from high up in the tower.

56

For once there was no one waiting outside Matt's office, and he busied himself with the kettle, pleased to have her there. She stood talking to his back, looking out of the window towards the ugly fountain instead of at him.

'One of your colleagues came into the shop, the other week,' she said. 'From the Faculty of Music, he told us he'd just arrived.' She stopped then, she didn't dare say anything more because Matt would know, just from the tone of her voice, that something was up.

He turned, holding out the mugs, pleased with himself. He'd hardly heard what she said. The idea that she could tell him, she saw clearly now, had been a fantasy: it would all become public, unstoppable. Matt would go to the police.

'What?' he said standing beside her and for a moment she thought she'd have to repeat it. 'Oh, yes. Faculty of Music.' He looked across the piazza at the far tower, where the concert hall was. Bridget had never been inside: Matt had stopped mentioning what was on there years back but she didn't think he was that bothered. He'd never been into classical music. 'Did he say what his name was?'

She shook her head. 'Not far off retirement?'

'Dr Carmichael,' said Matt without hesitation. 'Yes, we were lucky to get him, apparently; some connection with the place, I suppose. Everyone's falling over themselves to keep him happy. Very eminent, he's taken up a two-year appointment.'

Two years. Her heart sank. Matt was speaking levelly, looking out across the windswept space, not giving anything away. 'It's good people like him want to come and work here, isn't it?' Perhaps Matt just wasn't interested. That would be good.

Why, though? That was what Bridget needed to know. Why had he come? To make him leave, you had to know why he was there.

Had it really been him, standing on the corner of the close? The car had been real. A little black car, how could she have imagined that? But now she didn't know. The man in the ugly leather jacket, could it have been any middle-aged man?

As if he could hear her thoughts Matt was musing on it. 'By all accounts he's just a nice guy,' he said, echoing what Laura had said, but not convinced, frowning. She knew Matt's face as well as she knew her own. She wondered if he'd actually talked to Carmichael. 'He's involved in some community music scheme, the other music fellow's idea. Talks in schools, that kind of stuff.' He turned to her, his head elsewhere. 'I did wonder if we should have got Finn into it. Music.'

At the thought of Finn Bridget felt panic surge, uncontrollable. 'Oh, Finn,' she said, at random, 'that reminds me. I've got to – got to—' Matt was looking at her. 'He asked me to get him a new jumper,' she said, and it was even true. 'I'd better – before the shops close. Get going.'

It was downhill into town and Bridget rode it at speed, reckless. The sun was low and she had no lights: she went straight to a men's shop that was a bit grown up for Finn but cool, and they knew her in there. Their shops had opened around the same time and she and the manager, a nice guy with a beard, saw each other at the dreary meetings for independent retailers, winking across the stuffy room in the town hall. Everyone knew everyone else, didn't they? It was what Carmichael had said. The manager chatted with her as she paid, about how time flew, how grown up Finn was getting.

'He's got a girlfriend now, can you believe it?' she said, feeling herself calm, among friends. Finn would grow up, get married, to Phoebe or to someone else, she and Matt would retire.

Buoyed up just enough she went to the supermarket to get something for dinner: browsing the shelves, she sent Finn a text asking what food Phoebe liked.

He answered straight away, obediently. *just anything mum, she's very cool. not fussy. but i'll ask her, i'm seeing her after school not sure when I'll be home.* She gazed at the little screen, the words conveying worship. Bridget wondered what she looked like.

Loading the bags into her bike basket – the sweater, a chicken for roasting, pasta and salad and Finn's favourite ice cream – she had a glimpse of the future: Finn would leave home, he would have another life.

Knowing about Carmichael would blight that, would blight everything, would send him running. She wanted him to always want to come home again, bringing his girlfriend with him.

She's very cool. What was she going to make of their small, odd family? For some reason she had identified Phoebe with Isabel: her family looked happy, orderly, loving, normal. That was the kind of girl Finn would want, he was like his dad.

The light was almost gone and a soft, light rain had begun to fall as Bridget cycled out of town again for home, and she hurried, anxious: cars hissed past. Lights were coming on in the suburban houses, their curtains were being drawn.

59

She had begun to believe their family – hers and Matt's – was completely ordinary, she had worked hard to make it that way. There was Carrie – but even Carrie, eccentric and wild, turning up wearing jodhpurs or lederhosen, bringing burlesque girlfriends, was a family tradition; didn't all families have one of those, a black sheep?

Finn had met his grandmother – their mother – they had their Christmas routines. Now Matt's kind, anxious parents doting on him, their only grandchild, Matt their only child. This was what families were like.

As she turned into the close in the dark she hoped Matt wasn't back yet because he hated her riding without lights. Not Carrie the black sheep, but her. Careful quiet Bridget, all alone, riding without lights, headlong into darkness. For another void, dangerous second she thought of riding off the road, or into the path of a truck, then it passed. Couldn't afford too many of those.

But Matt wasn't home yet: he got back just as she put the pasta on, and only nodded, weary, when she told him Finn was out with Phoebe. After dinner they sat side by side and watched TV, a programme about repairing cars, and she felt him relax, the day falling away from him. Matt had always been good at it, dropping into sleep like a stone, leaving the world on the doorstep.

When he caught her looking at her phone later, as they climbed into bed, he shook his head. 'Leave him,' he said, placing a soft kiss carefully on her lips, before turning on his side. 'He'll be fine,' he said over his shoulder. 'He's out there being young.' Bridget laid the phone down beside her, and turned out the light.

They worked hard, she and Matt, for what they had.

60

For these relationships with colleagues and friends and family. A small circle but safe. Not any more, however she might have fooled herself, chatting as she paid for Finn's jumper. Lying there still and listening to Matt's steady breathing Bridget felt her heart rate rise, stay high. It pattered in the dark, round and round like an animal on a wheel.

Watching the light that filtered through the curtains, listening to the distant traffic grow quiet, it came to her that the memory was still there, intact: she remembered what it was like. Long, long ago, when the only way she could get to sleep was by resolving to kill herself.

When Finn came in it was almost one in the morning, but Bridget was still awake. She listened to him pad softly upstairs and then, at last, the light went out in her head, and she slept.

Chapter Eight

Tuesday

When Laura came through the door, groaning under her own weight, it seemed to Bridget that she'd doubled in size over the weekend. She paused halfway through the door to lean against the jamb, exhausted already. Then she was inside.

'Laura,' said Bridget in alarm, hurrying to reach her. 'You – are you sure you should – look.' Catching her own breath. 'Just sit down.'

Laura smiled, tremulous, letting Bridget take her arm. 'Nick says—' and she paused, lowering herself gingerly to the sofa and letting her bag drop. Bridget made herself smile, patient: they heard a lot about what Nick said. Laura looked up at her, big swimming eyes.

'What?' said Bridget, helpless.

'He said it was the same with his first wife,' said Laura, sniffing. 'The minute she stopped work she turned into an elephant.'

'Nice,' said Bridget. 'Why did they get divorced, again?'

Laura blinked, wounded. 'So it's still all right if I move to mornings only?' she said, with conscious dignity.

'I – did we—' Serve me right, thought Bridget, for

getting impatient: she'd forgotten she'd said it. The thought of long afternoons on her own set up a little tic of anxiety. Get someone else. Some school leaver. Laura was smoothing the big round of her belly anxiously. 'Yes. I mean, of course, it's up to you, Laura.'

'Nick says—' and Laura paused, as if finally, dimly aware of how often he began her sentences, and changed direction. 'Can we see how it goes? I've arranged to meet him this afternoon but—'

'Sure,' said Bridget hastily. 'Sure. Play it by ear. Is he taking you out somewhere?'

'Baby shopping,' said Laura happily. Bridget and Matt had gone to just one baby shop, all that time ago, and he had stared, aghast, at all the bright plastic stuff, the mats and baby baths and nightlights and mobiles. They'd bought a cot and that had been it. Sometimes she wished that they'd gone the whole mad route of buying everything and anything. But the thought of Nick doing it with Laura, second time around, happy families – it made her uneasy.

'Washing up,' she said to escape and retreated to the kitchen.

Tuesdays could go either way in the shop: dead or busy. It looked like this one was going to be busy. A big, untidy woman in red lipstick breezed in at noon, on her lunch break, looking for a party dress, talking as she came in through the door. Pleading.

Some customers were like this, they needed you to know the whole backstory – her husband, her grown daughter, how great they were – and this woman was a talker. The daughter was getting married, there'd be dancing in the evening. 'I need to be able to move in it,' and the woman stretched her arms up and turned, in the middle of the shop. One of those who'd try anything on she was given and just shrug cheerfully when it didn't fit, and keep going.

For twenty minutes, half an hour, looking for sizes and colours and in and out of the stockroom, Bridget stopped thinking: she even relaxed. Laura joined in, moving slowly to and from the rails and there was banter, about birth and children. The woman had a loud, infectious laugh. She kept them busy, but busy was good.

In the end she brought a green silk dress to the till, sighing over not being able to buy everything, but they had all admired the dress, or her in it, swaying and posing in front of the mirror, delighted. It was expensive but without comment Bridget had given her a discount, on impulse, for being a good, happy, willing customer, just when she needed one. And in return, holding the door open for her and saying goodbye, Bridget had been rewarded by a hug, quick and warm and highly perfumed, that seemed to have more in it than just gratitude for money off.

It'll be all right. I can handle this.

But when the door closed on the big, happy woman the shop felt abruptly empty: she had seemed to fill the space up all on her own. At one thirty Bridget sent Laura home.

Lunch hour over, the lane was deserted and quiet except for the relentless jingle of the gallery's Christmas soundtrack, just down the hill and out of sight. Bridget mopped the floor, did some paperwork, moving to and fro. She was conscious of not wanting to stop, and think, to keep moving so as not to be seen, not to turn and look out of the wide window, where someone might look back.

64

In the stockroom a delivery was waiting to be unpacked, and finally Bridget gave in and retreated there. Last-minute party dresses, drifts of red chiffon: she stripped them of their plastic, hung them up, steamed them, priced them, thinking, soon it would be December and the shop would be busy. Then they were all done, pristine and bright and Bridget stood there in the debris, hot suddenly. Hungry, suddenly.

A cup of tea and a sandwich: that was what she needed. Seizing on her appetite she waded through the litter of emptied boxes and garment bags and headed into the kitchen. Bridget took tomatoes and bread from the little fridge, filled the kettle and it began to hiss, she washed her hands and the big water heater on the wall gurgled. As she tried to extract a knife from the draining board a cup fell into the sink with a clatter and she was suddenly, acutely aware of the craziness of the tiny space, the shoe boxes stacked up the walls; a piece of twine trailed and following it she saw that it had come loose from the log she and Laura had stashed up there, what seemed like weeks ago.

For a second she was tempted just to walk out and leave it. All of it: no more painting the floor, no more labelling boxes or filling out VAT returns. She could see Matt's face aghast. No. So she fished the cup out of the sink, emptied the bowl, got the stepladder, rested it against the shelving. The kettle boiled, so tea was next because – who'd told her? Mum, it would have to have been, and years ago, how long ago? – the water had to be freshly boiled or the tea tasted of iron, and the stepladder could wait, the log could wait. So when the doorbell jangled, Bridget was standing in the kitchen doorway, with the kettle in her hand.

And when he came inside there she still stood like some kind of idiot skivvy with her hair limp with steam and her face red with working, her skirt creased from kneeling among boxes.

'Well, look at you,' said Carmichael, easily. He wasn't wearing the leather jacket, she registered automatically, today it was a greenish wool coat to his knees, Germanic looking, horrible. For a second she wanted to rush at him with the boiling water in her hand.

'What,' she said, but it could have been anything, she didn't know what she was saying. The door swung to behind him and there was the gentler ping as it closed, admitting no one else. Beyond the window the street was empty again. Where was everyone? Where was the world looking in, when she needed it?

He stood there. 'I didn't recognise you at first,' he said, merry. Eyeing her. 'None of us is getting any younger.' Looking her up and down: the insult glanced off her, tiny, but she heard it. 'Your own shop, too, quite the little businesswoman.' Condescending.

'If it's about your purchase,' she said for the benefit of the world outside, the quiet lane.

He laughed – but something had happened, the spell interrupted: he moved. Slowly, towards her, so close she could smell his sour breath. 'Don't think,' he began, 'don't think you can—'

What would anyone see, if they did look in? A middle-aged man in a green coat, his sandy hair thinning, respectable, harmless. A woman with smudged mascara, brandishing a kettle.

'Why did you come here?'

He smiled. 'I was invited,' he said. 'By an old friend.' Then, amused, feigning surprise: 'Oh, no, no – you thought I came for *you*?' Shaking his head. 'I'm sorry,' and his eyes were cold, cold as flint. Carefully, carefully, holding her breath, feeling it rise like vomit in her throat, Bridget set the kettle down on the draining board just inside the door but turning back and seeing him still there she felt a great wave break over her, of panic, and fear – and rage.

'I'm going to the police,' she said rapidly, just to stop him taking another step, and before she could shut herself up. His face, his eyes were on her. 'If you don't leave me alone I will go to the police and I don't care what happens.' The words falling over themselves: this was it. She had to stop him. She had no choice.

But it didn't stop him: he advanced towards her, across the painted floor, on to the pale rug, quite calm. He began to talk in a way she remembered, with horror. And although she tried to blot the words out the tone was so familiar, the memory bringing sickness up inside her, up from her gut: he was very reasoned, smiling all the time, although his eyes were different. She remembered that, too: his eyes dead and flat and cold while his voice was smooth and warm.

'Don't be silly,' he said now, anyone listening would think him so reasonable, still walking across the floor. He had crossed the rug now, reaching to unbutton his long coat as he came – that too, Bridget knew that gesture too. 'We're old friends. There's no reason why we can't continue to be friends.' Talking, talking, another button undone. And then he stopped, a foot from her standing in the kitchen doorway. 'We have such a lot of history together.' Persuasive, tender even.

Bridget felt so abruptly sick she put a hand to the doorframe to steady herself. She remembered him talking this way while doing things to her body. Images flashed into her head, blinding her. The shock, the horror of it, the first time it happened: the violence of a hand pushing her down, wool choking her. She backed away from him, into the kitchen, the room so small the stepladder clattered as she bumped into it.

He touched her. 'We were lovers,' he said.

'Never,' she managed to say. 'Never,' but she heard the weakness in her voice. 'I'm going to the police.' The words were indistinct behind the roaring in her ears: could he even hear her? His eyes were pale, he was so close she could see the sparse gingery stubble on his chin.

They were both in the kitchen now, the space was so small. There was the boiling kettle behind her, the knife she'd got out to cut tomatoes. He took another step, and now he was stroking her cheek, his hand on her hip, she could feel the heat of the kettle on her back. They were hidden here, concealed from the world outside. He could do anything.

She could.

'You were a rather poor musician,' he said gently, kindly. 'But your little cunt.' His face so close to hers. 'You liked it, don't you remember that?' His head was tipping towards her, prying, looking, a hand on hers, holding it down. 'You were heartbroken, don't you remember that? Don't you remember why? You begged me. You cried. You begged me to keep going. Not to leave you.'

Frozen under his hand, her whole body was consumed with shame, loathing – and something else. Liked it? *Liked it?* Had she liked it? She could smell his breath. He never had good breath, he was careless with hygiene. The smell made her want to vomit, it transported her back so vividly. Blindly she groped behind her on the work surface until the knife was in her hand. Only a small knife. He reached past her and removed it from her hand, looking at it, smiling.

Bridget did remember. She remembered pleading with him, her blouse undone on his green plush sofa, silver-framed photographs on his piano. The way he had made her feel, when he had turned cold, standing up from her, pushing her hand away – and she wanted so badly to please him. What had she said? *Don't. I'll try.* She would have said anything.

'She's coming back,' said Bridget, making herself say it calmly. She didn't want to use Laura's name, didn't want him knowing the name of any girl or woman – but he just shook his head slowly, sorrowfully.

'I waited until she went,' he said, resting his shoulder in the ugly green-brown wool coat against the doorframe, leisurely, examining Bridget. 'She looked like she was going home. At that stage of pregnancy she shouldn't really be working, should she?' A little wrinkle of distaste. 'Couldn't you get anyone else?'

Bridget remembered him shifting to move away from Laura's belly when he'd come in with Isabel.

'I'll tell Isabel's parents,' she said, brave suddenly. His eyes were stony and she pushed on, reckless. 'I'll tell your wife,' she said, and he smiled with sudden pleasure.

'She's dead,' he said, melodious. 'Five years ago. A stroke.' He put on a mock mournful expression. Bridget remembered a flush at the woman's neck, his wife's neck, the

69

dislike she emanated as she reached for her coat to go out, while *Anthony* taught in the drawing room with the silver picture frames. *Call me Tony.*

'I will go to the police.' Bridget was stiff with holding herself away from him, she was rigid. Could he tell the idea terrified her? He smiled again, merry, teasing.

'I don't think so,' he said, and for a second leaned back, away from her, checking the room and who could see them. Then he was back. 'Don't you remember those little photo sessions we had?'

Bridget's hands rose in front of her, palms out: she didn't feel as if she had control over them, she felt as if her body wasn't hers, the hair that rose on her scalp symptom of something primitive, not her. His head tilted, examining her.

There had been a door beyond his kitchen that she had seen his wife glancing at once, in fear mixed with dislike. And then one day, drawing the curtains in the big room with the fireplace, in the music room, he had got out a camera. The photographs he took couldn't have been sent away for developing: the door beyond the kitchen had led to his dark room. Telling her how to pose: Bridget uncomfortable, smiling at his camera, fixed. She never saw the photographs.

There had been another man's face in the dark behind her eyes, of course. The doorbell had rung and he'd said, *Oh, yes. Someone I'd like you to meet,* and left her there waiting, then led him in. How could she have forgotten. Something opened up inside her, bottomless.

'All sorts of things I could do with those photographs,' said Dr Anthony Carmichael, respectable in his Loden coat in her shop for anyone to see, but he was a monster, with rank teeth and hair, this close she saw his waxy ears, his nostrils. 'People ask me all the time if I have anything to show them.'

People? Bridget didn't know what he meant, she was stupid as mud. 'There are places you can look, on the internet,' he said easily, looking down to brush something invisible from his lapel and then the word hit her. The internet. How had she thought she could escape? It would always be on her, his touch, his fingers, always. Her hand at her mouth, to stop it coming out. 'I always kept those pictures for myself,' he said, 'but it would be easy to share them.' Fixing her with his cold bird's eye. 'I wouldn't have to be the one to do it. I have to be careful. Of course I would never do it. Not unless I had to.' He put his hand on her then, on her cheek, stroking and she felt it rise and break in her like a wave, unstoppable.

'*No*,' she said and clawed him off her, pushing back with violence and caught off balance, he fell heavily against the stepladder that knocked into the cupboard. Something shuddered, teetered. And in that small moment everything shifted, the crockery on the draining board clattering, the kettle tipping: the tiny room seemed to turn, spinning around them. She saw his face change and loosen, uncertain at last, looking up. And looking up too she saw it. She saw it move.

Suddenly so much bigger, in the small space, it tipped in a flash of green, she felt a flake of bark brush her cheek in the split second she had to think. How much had it weighed? The wood's grain dense with wet and age. It had taken two of them to lift it up there.

The log came down.

It hit them both, a glancing, hard, painful blow to her shoulder and upper arm but the heaviest part, the big trunk, had come down on his head. There was blood, she saw a bright rush of it filling his eye: he staggered and fell to his knees, a hand to his face.

The log had broken in two: Carmichael was on his knees half in half out of the kitchen door, and as she stared down at the blood, he lurched against her. His green woollen arms were around her legs. He made a sound, mumbling, and his grip tightened, dragging on her. His bald spot, thin hair caked with blood. She found herself with a piece of the branch in her hand and she brought it down on him, to get him off.

He fell back.

Dropping the wood and kneeling, the buzzing in her ears still, she took hold of his shoulders and shook him, feeling no resistance. Nothing. And a whole train of consequences unfurled in an instant. It was as if they were already in there, bodies piling into her shop and an ambulance outside in the lane, people staring through the window. Men in fluorescent jackets kneeling over him, looking up at her and asking questions.

Police. If he was dead – police.

The images beat against her, meaningless as rain, set against the thought of him dead. It flooded her with a great sudden rush of warmth, like ecstasy, it coursed through her body, warm and fast as fire.

And if he lived.

As she stood staring down Finn and Matt were there then, in her head, filling it. Finn turning over in bed that morning, mumbling that he had no lessons to go to; Matt saying, *leave him*. Matt's wide smile, his arms around her, the smell of him – and the smell of this man, at her feet, something had happened, piss on his trousers and the wool coat stained with blood. She heard a sound rise in her throat, a hoarse panting breath that someone would hear. *Stop*. She stood up, numb and silent.

Stop.

Make sure, then. Watching, looking in from outside, from behind the glass, Bridget saw herself. Practical Bridget, methodical Bridget. Quiet, steady, useful Bridget. She stepped over him, she didn't need to put out a hand to keep herself upright, and she walked away, calmly, into the stockroom. She took hold of an armful of polythene that had been covering the clothes and she walked back. It was as if she knew what to do. As if she had been a long time rehearsing this, in the dark dreams that shifted under her everyday life.

Looked down at him. Was he dead? As she looked, watching for movement, something rang in her ears, high-pitched, almost beyond her range. It sang to her. She knew how this worked. She knelt down and in one smooth, unhesitating movement she pulled a length of plastic over his head and tied it tight around his neck. She held on.

She pulled tight enough that she could feel the plastic cut into her hands: it seemed important that she should be quite aware of what she was doing, on her own here, no one telling her to do this. No going back and undoing it.

Good.

It sang to her, high and piercing, threnody: it sang and whispered and listening, she looked down as if from a great

73

height. Glazed under the polythene was his ear, like a pig's bristly with hairs. She held on. There was a drumming in some part of his body, a tension under her hands, then he was gone. He had stopped breathing.

He was dead.

If anyone looked through the window, between the back-boards to her display, they might see part of her shoulder. His body was almost all crumpled inside the kitchen. Bridget didn't know how long it was until the sound in her ears receded, and she let go and got stiffly to her feet, but once upright she worked quickly. To and fro from the stockroom: she wrapped him in plastic first. There was plenty after her unpacking session, heaps, layer after layer. Then the duct tape. Round and round. He was trussed like a mummy, he was smaller than she had thought.

More plastic, more tape: Bridget worked on steadily until at last, feeling the heat under her arms and across her forehead, she sat back on her heels: done. How long had it taken? No more than twenty minutes. But quick, *quick*. She dragged him fast, before he could look like anything but a roll of plastic should anyone glimpse anything from outside, knowing that the world was used to her humping furniture around the place, boxes of clothing, rolled carpets. Across her freshly painted floor, carefully around the pale, silky rug and through the stockroom door to where an empty cardboard hanging box stood, ready to be flattened and recycled. She laid it on its side and taped him into it, rolled it right around his body. Shoved the wadded shape under the stock rails that lined one wall of the little room, until it was hidden.

74

She went back for the remains of the log, wrapping them round with newspaper carefully and heaving them piece by piece into the organic rubbish bin that would be collected tomorrow. If Laura noticed the wood was gone she'd only be pleased, wouldn't she? Bridget rehearsed her reasons. *It kept dropping bits on the kitchen floor, bark and moss, unhygienic.* And back inside, making herself walk into the stockroom as if nothing had happened.

The first thing she saw was the awkward corner of cardboard still protruding, but would anyone else see it? No one else would come in. She could come back for him later, when—

With that thought it loomed, gigantic, a vast dark wave about to crash down over her. And then what? Then what?

As if on cue she heard the bell over the door jangle, and voices. She heard footsteps. And someone called her name.

Chapter Nine

She wasn't even ten minutes later than usual getting home: the kitchen clock as she let herself in said five past six.

No one else was home yet: a relief. Bridget went straight upstairs to brush her teeth.

It had been Justine from the jeweller's, asking if someone would be there to receive a parcel the next morning, she couldn't get in early enough herself. Bridget had stared at her just a fraction too long, but she didn't seem to notice. 'Sure,' she'd said, willing herself not to look round, to check what might or might not be visible through the stockroom door. Just shifting, one step over, to block Justine's view.

Leaving the shop, locking the door behind her in the gathering dark she had found herself desperate for something, a drink, a pill. As she unlocked her bike a lad had walked past smoking and on impulse she called after him.

'Sorry,' he turned, wary, and she was conscious of not knowing the etiquette, after all this time, and they'd got so expensive. 'Can you spare one of those?'

He hesitated, shrugged, took a step back toward her, fishing in his pocket. She hadn't smoked in twenty years: more. Skinny and coughing behind the bike sheds at school. Matt hated it.

The lad – more of a young man, skinny himself and wearing a cheap narrow-cut suit, on his first job after school, she guessed, automatically – didn't seem to notice the state she was in, only shifting from foot to foot in the cold as he lit it for her and impatient to be gone.

She wished she could start again. Be young again. Be a different person. She drew on the cigarette too deeply and began to cough. Too late to start this all over again.

And there was Finn. There was Matt.

The cigarette had gone to her head, made her woozy in the dark street. But at least she hadn't gone into a pub, got drunk. Chaos would ensue: she needed to stay in control now. She needed to move Carmichael's body.

But not tonight. With a fumbling hand she fixed the lights on to her bike and set off shakily, the nicotine still buzzing her, the long-ago drug. Tonight Matt would ask why she had taken the van out, Finn would ask why she wasn't home when he got back, no groundwork had been laid for her absence, with the van.

And there was Phoebe. She'd forgotten about Phoebe.

By the time Bridget had got to the edge of town, the red lights of the towers on Rose Hill dead ahead and above her, she'd re-estimated. Tomorrow. She could keep Laura from seeing, somehow, during the day. Keep her out of the stockroom altogether. Distract her with talk of Moses baskets and Nick.

Now standing in front of the bathroom mirror Bridget didn't dare look at herself in it, just scrubbed and scrubbed at her teeth until she spat blood because Matt would notice cigarette smoke on her breath, on her fingers, before she even walked into the room. But as she tugged on the bathroom light pull before the light went out she caught a fleeting glimpse of her face, ghost-white in the mirror. She had to stop that, sort that. Because Matt was never going to know: she couldn't run and ask him to look after her, to sort this out. Never.

Around her the house was cool and dark. Bridget went into the dim utility room to turn up the heating and stood there a moment in among the hum of machines they'd bought and installed: freezer, washing machine, overhead the airer and the cupboard full of cleaning stuff. If she stood here long enough would everything beyond these walls disappear? The box on its side in the stockroom. She knew it wouldn't: she could feel the scale of what she'd done, shifting huge just out of sight, like the sea. It wasn't going to go away on its own.

But one thing at a time. Cleaning stuff: she'd need that. One thing at a time: Phoebe was coming for tea.

Reaching for the tap in the kitchen to fill a pan for vegetables she saw a mark on her shirt cuff and the world tilted: she made herself stop and examine it. Brownish, a smear of green, the bark and lichen from the log – and some blood. Quite a lot of blood. Bridget set the pan on the stove, went upstairs, stood on the bathmat in the bath-room and removed everything she had on: grey skirt, white cotton blouse, cardigan, underwear, shoes, and rolled it in the bathmat. She thought of the boy with his narrow, pale face and cheap suit, impatient to get somewhere else, who'd stopped all the same to give her a cigarette. Would he remember her, the woman white with fear, shaky: would he have seen blood on her cuff as she leaned down to get a light?

Take care, now. Watch out for the detail.

She put on a dress. Dark blue silk: she knew the designer, she knew how much it had cost her at trade price but for a second Bridget couldn't remember how to get dressed, what came next. She told herself: this is shock. Get over it, or live with it. You can't go back.

How long did she have? It was six fifteen now. She made a calculation and went downstairs, into the sitting room. They'd made a fuss, offplan, saying they wanted a working fireplace, but it had never been quite big enough. But she laid and lit the fire and walked back into the kitchen to prepare the chicken. She opened the cellophane and braced herself against the smell of the pale flesh, the clammy feel of it. Salt, pepper, butter, half a lemon inside. Bridget was putting it in the oven when her phone made a sound in her handbag and her heart started up again, pattering.

back by seven sorry. From Matt.

Taking the stairs three at a time she grabbed the rolled bathmat. The shirt and skirt and underwear – unwired bra, she was grateful for that – she put on the fire, one piece at a time: the underwear flared and sputtered. There'd be buttons, there'd be hooks and eyes. The rubber-backed bathmat and the shoes she took out to the garage, running

79

swift and barefoot in the blue silk dress: the door made a loud rattle in the quiet close as she heaved it over her head. She stowed the roll in the darkest corner, beyond the van. Hauling the heavy garage door back down in the dark she heard something. The trudge of feet, very close.

Finn came out of the dark. 'Mum?' He was wheeling his bike, shoulders down, preoccupied. His mind was clearly somewhere else because it took a moment to take in her appearance.

'Did you get a puncture?' Bridget said, groping for the everyday, something normal. He stared at her blankly.

'What?' he said, then registered her. 'No – no – I— Aren't you freezing?' he said and Bridget almost laughed because it was the kind of thing she said to him, in another life, as he cycled off without gloves in a hard frost.

'Oh, just had to – something I'd forgotten to put away, you know what Dad's like—'

He shrugged, not paying attention and she felt herself unwind, just a fraction. People didn't see things.

'Nice dress,' he said vaguely as she lifted the door again for him to wheel the bike in, then put an arm round him.

'Well—' she hesitated, 'You know. For Phoebe? We want to make a good impression, Dad's—'

But he was shaking his shaggy head, side to side, gloomy.

'What's the matter?' Opening the door they were inside. Finn was just standing there looking down at the cycle helmet dangling from his wrist. She could hear the fire crackling in the sitting room. She resisted going in there, resisted even glancing towards the sitting-room door.

'Oh, nothing – well. She can't come tonight after all,' Finn said, in a monotone, head down. 'Phoebe.' And then at last with her name he lifted his head and she looked into his sad brown eyes.

'Oh, Finn, that's—' But she felt only relief.

'Mum, don't. It's fine,' and he dropped his helmet and was on the stairs. 'She's – it's fine.' Mumbled as he went.

Then Matt's key was in the front door behind her. 'You lit a fire,' he said immediately.

'Yes, I—' and his eyes were on the dress, her damp bare feet.

She made herself grimace. 'Yes, I thought – well, Phoebe, you know she's well, *was*—' She made herself start again. 'I was trying to get ready for Phoebe but it looks like she's not coming after all.'

'Oh,' said Matt. 'Oh well—' turning to put his stuff down, bike pannier, backpack, hanging up his weatherproof jacket and knowing him as well as she did, knowing every droop of his shoulders, she could see where his mind was going. It made him nervous, this stuff: not Finn having a girlfriend exactly but the complications it introduced, the pain of it, the upset, if it went wrong. It wasn't something he would necessarily be able to fix.

'I could smell the fire,' Matt said instead, his back to her as he hung his weatherproof jacket up. 'Coming into the close I thought someone was burning something. Did you—'

'I'll just check on it,' she said. And flew. Flew.

By the time Finn trudged back downstairs she'd changed into jeans and sweatshirt, laid the table for three, and the chicken was on the side, waiting for Matt to carve it. Mashed potatoes because she hadn't had time to do roast. Would they notice? They didn't seem to.

Matt would have known something had been put on

the fire: fires were his responsibility, which was why he'd been unnerved by her lighting it. The underwear had disappeared, melted into the ash although it had left a smell, and the skirt she had poked under, but the blouse had been visible on top, a papery black ghost of itself, its edges glowing. She prodded until it was gone too and set another log on top.

Finn loped in, in a T-shirt and pyjama bottoms. 'All right?' said Matt, warily. Sitting down Finn nodded.

'We'll rearrange it,' he said, certain. 'We decided.'

'You haven't had a row with her or anything?' asked Bridget. 'You got in very late last night.' Wondering if she could take the van tonight after all, deciding she couldn't. Matt looked up from his plate, his eyes warning her not to pry.

'We didn't have a row, Mum,' said Finn patiently.

'So what was – what was—' But Bridget caught Matt's frown, warning her off the subject but Finn still didn't seem put out.

'She had maths tutoring tonight and her dad wouldn't let her skip it. He's very strict.' His spirits not quite undented but determined.

'Well, that's—' 'I think—' Matt and Bridget both spoke at once, both relieved.

'Fair enough.' Matt finished for both of them.

'We'll make another date,' said Bridget.

Just not tomorrow.

Bridget cleaned her teeth again before bed: Matt had gone up early, tired, he'd said, though she would have to ask questions if she wanted to know why. He was lying there, next door, the light still on and the thought of being alone with him was suddenly frightening. Was this what it was like, having an affair? The dread. Bridget turned off the light but she didn't leave the bathroom: instead she stood at the small window that looked out down a dark field to the estuary. There was a dull sheen on the water, shed by a moon blurred behind cloud. She could make out the slope of the hill, the dark clumped hedges. If it was just her, she could walk out of this little close-walled house that had seemed so safe for so long, walk out of the back door into the wide darkness and never be found again. Walk into the muddy river and disappear.

From across the landing Matt cleared his throat.

He was looking at something on his phone – it was usually the news – propped in the bed, his glasses on his forehead. She would be blurred to him as she came through the door: she placed a kiss on his cheek as she climbed in and he sighed. She took the book from her bedside table and opened it on her knee: she couldn't remember how long ago she'd begun it, but she hadn't looked at it in weeks. It was a history of Paris under the Occupation, with old photographs she liked to look at, turning page after page to see how people had lived. What they put up with, got on with: a woman scrubbing a doorstep, one with bad teeth, laughing in a bar while she danced lop-sidedly with a man. Another world.

'You're tired,' she said, nudging Matt, gently. 'Hard day?'

'Oh, well—' He hesitated.

Bridget stayed quiet. He sighed again. 'We're installing new software,' he said, letting his glasses fall back on to his nose, turning to look at her. 'It's no big deal. Well, it is, in fact – the internet, you know – the university isn't really prepared for how quickly this stuff changes, not many universities are.'

'What kind of software?' But she could guess.

'Anti-virus and screening software. To protect the university server. And to stop the students streaming stuff illegally, or downloading porn.' Turning to look back at his phone, uncomfortable. 'The students or the lecturers for that matter,' he said, frowning down.

'Is Finn OK?' she said, urgently needing to say something else. To change the subject.

Bridget was familiar with the silence that followed: Matt was giving it some thought. 'You need to give him some space,' he said, eventually. 'Who knows what they got up to last night. It might not be the right time for her to come round.'

She stared down at the book on her lap, open at a page of text now, but it was a blur. 'I'm going to need the van tomorrow to move some stock,' she said, quick and matter of fact. 'Is that all right? I might be back later than usual.'

'You need a hand with it?' Vaguely, still preoccupied.

'Oh, no,' she said, lightly. 'No, no. I can manage fine.'

But she had to put the book back on the table then, carefully, she had to lie down on her side, her back to him, for fear he'd hear it, her heart banging away inside her chest.

The light went out and she began to listen for his breathing: it was her old habit, but it didn't get her to sleep this time. What got her to sleep was remembering standing at the bathroom window in the dark; it was imagining herself dissolving, the flesh off her bones, the gristle and sinew softened, every knobbed joint of her spine loosening to wash out with the tide; sinking to the muddy floor of the sea.

Chapter Ten

Wednesday

Bridget woke at four with a gasp – out of a dream of a man in a box, hammering to be let out. It was perfectly dark, perfectly quiet all around her: Matt didn't even shift at the sound that escaped from her.

How could she have done it? For a second she couldn't breathe.

She was going to get caught.

What if there was someone waiting for him – waiting for him to come home? The thing unravelled in the dark, running busily ahead of her: the police alerted, hospitals phoned, CCTV replayed. Someone had seen him come into the shop. The last sighting.

Yesterday – only yesterday – Bridget could have walked away from him and, four, five steps, no more, across the shop floor to the telephone, she could have called an ambulance, she could have gone to the police and told them everything. She still could.

She knew she wouldn't.

His wife was dead. And somehow she knew, there *was* no one waiting at home for him. Carmichael had told her

86

his wife was dead himself. Only yesterday, he had been alive and he'd told Bridget that his wife was dead, smiling into her face as if to say, *There's no one to stop me.* Bridget thought of him, at her feet, the groan as he rolled over, and in that moment she had seen what it would be like, to leave him alive, to see him sit up, to know that she would never get satisfaction from him, as long as he was breathing. And at the knowledge of what she'd done, she felt something from so long ago she hardly knew what it was. Free.

So *plan*. Make a plan. Prepare.

Around the window the dark was turning to grey, a misty dawn leaking past the curtains.

Carmichael had been a visiting fellow: two years but that wasn't long, people wouldn't bother forming alliances, and not so early, he'd only been there six weeks. Two years had seemed for ever, yesterday.

Easing herself upright on the pillow she dared a glance at Matt, his face relaxed in sleep, unclouded. She'd heard him say in the past, nettled, how little work visiting fellows had to do, how much work they made for him, setting up their connections, troubleshooting their software glitches. Stopping them being high-handed with the secretaries: that seemed to be Matt's self-appointed task. He hated arrogance: it occurred to her that he already didn't like Anthony Carmichael, and the thought set up an anxiety – something he'd said? What had he said to her about Carmichael? – and Bridget had to bat it away. Focus.

A visiting fellow, lightweight, temporary.

So no classes, no office hours, a couple of PhD students to monitor and only the occasional one-off lecture, a law unto himself. No one to miss him, for a while at least. And in the meantime . . .

Isabel? Anxiety pattered, insistent, setting up a hum. Would Isabel miss him? Isabel was a child, who could be fobbed off, no one knew better than Bridget, how easy that was. And she *was* still a child. In her body language, her innocence, the simple freedom of her movements across the shop floor, peering round the curtain, turning in front of the mirror.

You know what you mean. A voice in her head. Say it. You mean he hadn't – Carmichael hadn't. Not yet.

A sound, in her throat. Stop it. Bridget sat very still, feeling herself sweat.

What had she begun to consider, when Isabel broke in on her train of thought? Something. While she worked out what to do next, Bridget needed to look further down the line. She needed a reason for his disappearance. A reason for when people did start to wonder: a reason other than the truth.

Matt rolled over beside her and without opening his eyes brought her into his arms.

There was a slow queue in the station toilets that allowed the women in it a long opportunity to gaze at their grey morning faces, a row of grimy chipboard doors their backdrop, the smell of disinfectant in the air.

Trying to avoid the sight of her own reflection Gill Lawson lugged her battered wheelie suitcase closer: the case, like her, veteran of a hundred horrible provincial railway stations like this one, another train, another city, never been a war correspondent, no foreign travel, not

Lebanon or Paris for her. She'd done the rounds. Basingstoke, Taunton, Carlisle, Chelmsford. The places victims washed up.

There'd been talk of Thailand to follow up a lead three, four years back but there'd been no money for the flights, in the end, and questions had begun to be asked about where it was all going so Gill had backed down. Done it by email, which hadn't really worked out, what with language difficulties and no faces to look into and not enough detail. Not enough detail: it was how you knew truth from lies, the detail. The suburbs of Oxford had been as good as it got for glamour, rows of comfortable semis and a woman pouring Gill a cup of tea while her daughter refused to come out of her room.

In the queue she must have pulled the suitcase carelessly because the woman in front turned sharply and glared, and shifting apologetically Gill did catch a glimpse of herself. Untidy: roots showing and a wisp of speckled hair escaping at the crown; her suit was crumpled, her shirt collar skew-whiff. She'd managed to get make-up on but it didn't quite disguise the fact that she'd been dragged out of bed too early and had, over the course of a lifetime, drunk too many coffees and too much red wine, spent too many late nights trying to get information out of people or drinking with other sad journalists with no home to go to.

Gill Lawson loved her job.

She needed a coffee.

There was a chain café on the station concourse, busy with the morning rush. Gill ordered a double shot cappuccino and a bacon sandwich: she tried not to think about what she should have had instead, if she valued her health

89

and what was left of her complexion. Maybe a year ago she remembered Steve pausing mid-briefing to give her a perplexed look that said, *Where did it all go wrong?* He'd hired her because he fancied her, seven years ago, well, that'll teach you. Sod it.

And last week, as she hesitated on the threshold of the lift, Steve had shaken his head in an echo of that bewilderment. He had led her from the lift, across the foyer and round the corner to a coffee shop: not that it was too early for a drink, ever, but they both knew they had to have a clear head. 'You can go,' he said straight off. 'But you do what you say you're doing, right? And nothing else.'

He didn't know what she knew, that Carmichael could at a pinch be en route for Sandringham, but he also knew she didn't tell him everything. He got from the way she'd phrased the email that there was wiggle room in five days away. Some hacks would use the time to live it up on the mini-bar, but he knew her better than that.

'Legal won't stand for any more monkey business,' Steve said, over his cup of fancy coffee, the pattern in the foam undisturbed as it went cold. 'If you get evidence, it's hard evidence. It's victims prepared to show their faces. Prepared to testify.' He stared at her with that, to make sure she got it. What he was saying was, you've got to break into their lives and smash them up all over again: if you do that, you'll get awards; if you do that, we'll halt the tanking sales figures and we'll all hang on to our jobs.

Not necessarily, Gill wanted to say back. *And if I did, wouldn't they let me, if it meant dragging him out into the open? If it meant he'd never do it again?*

Neither of them had said any of it, not out loud, but

seven years was long enough to read each other's mind. 'Don't overdo it on the expenses, then,' was all Steve did say, pushing his chair back and standing. Looking down at her and their untouched coffees.

Now as the girl behind the café counter wrapped a napkin round the plastic cup and pushed it towards her she smiled, not even pityingly (probably foreign, thought Gill, she'll learn), and the bacon tasted like it had been cooked in living memory. Small mercies. She kept the receipt.

Settling herself on a high stool in the window Gill felt the sun come out, weakly, behind her. Sipping the coffee, feeling it do the job, synapses coming out of their coma. The world sharpening around her.

A young woman pushed her way through the glass doors, silhouetted against the lemon-pale morning. Short, battered leather jacket, cropped hair, dead white face: you look like I feel, thought Gill. Watched her count out coins, saw her look in the paper cup they had there for tips a long moment before dropping one in carefully. For some reason this made Gill feel better.

The sun was out and Gill was going somewhere called Rose Hill. She had a lecture to attend, on Bach.

The delivery man had been waiting on the doorstep with Justine's parcel and Bridget, who had forgotten all about it, grabbed it with relief. The last thing she wanted was Justine musing on how weird she'd seemed last night.

She'd got in early and scrubbed the tiny kitchen down with bleach, fishing a shred of moss out from between floorboards. She hadn't been into the stockroom yet. She would – just not yet.

Bridget had seen Laura wrinkle her nose, coming in to the shop half an hour after she'd finished scrubbing, her hands still raw. But everything seemed to offend Laura's senses at the moment, Chips, coffee, mayonnaise. Her first baby: had Bridget talked like this when she was expecting Finn, a constant stream of wondering, of contemplating the changes in her body, her relationship, what would happen next, planning, planning, planning, planning names and paint colours and blue eyes or brown, boy or girl? No. Bridget had hardly dared think about it, let alone open her mouth. Bridget had expected the worst. She had expected punishment and cataclysm, fistula and stillbirth and haemorrhage. She had said nothing to anyone. And he'd been born perfect, and she had waited for catastrophe and depression but she'd put him to the breast and something had worked. For once, something had worked: her body. Something was normal.

A self-seal plastic bag of fresh mint had been brought by Laura. Bridget poured hot water on it and the smell filled the little kitchen, sharp and sweet and strange. She stepped into the doorway holding the mug and Laura was opening the jewellery cabinet for a squat middle-aged man, extracting a necklace. She heard him sigh, bad-tempered. 'She's got very specific tastes, you see.'

Christmas present buying for the wife. Jewellery was always the safe bet. Carefully she set the tea down for Laura on the counter and left them to it. Laura had set the necklace carefully back and gone for a bracelet. Their two heads close together, a scattering of dandruff on the man's beefy shoulders. Some men felt safe with a pregnant woman, didn't they? Nothing expected of them but a bit of opening doors and offering their seat.

Stepping back from them was the closest Bridget had come to the stockroom all morning. Was there a smell? Something. She didn't turn her head to the doorway. A sweetness. The images were there in her head, she couldn't keep them out: the box on its side oozing, blood pooling. Him, shrouded stiff in the woollen coat.

Beyond the window two police officers appeared, strolling by in the street. Bridget heard a siren, a long way off.

Something had happened between Laura and the customer, abruptly he had reached his decision and was fumbling for his wallet at the counter: she could hear his heavy breathing, as if getting the money out was hard labour. Laura was behind the till finding a box for the bracelet and he glanced sideways, just a second. Had that been a funny look? Was she behaving strangely? Bridget made herself smile, and his expression cleared, he smiled back.

When he'd gone Laura reached for her mint tea, wincing as the desk pressed into her belly. 'I saw that girl yesterday,' she said, thoughtful.

Immediately Bridget knew who she was talking about: she meant Isabel. Laura eyed her over the mug, her eyes clear and blue and Bridget got a glimpse of the old Laura, the pre-pregnancy Laura, the pre-Nick Laura. That Laura had never been dim or unobservant: Bridget had to play it cool. 'What girl?' she said mildly.

'Came in with an old guy?' Meditative, not meeting Bridget's eye. 'Couple of weeks ago.'

'Right.' Bridget half turned to busy herself with straightening a rail, checking a sleeve for an imaginary snag. Laura talked to her back.

93

'Wearing a school uniform, in town. I hadn't really worked out how young she was. Fifteen? At most.' What was Laura wondering?

'She goes to Finn's school,' said Bridget, turning back, shifting the conversation sideways. 'You didn't see *him*, did you?'

Laura looked nonplussed. 'She wasn't at school when I saw her,' she said patiently.

'Oh, no, it's just – he's got a girlfriend, he's being a bit cagey about her—'

Was he? Not really. Bridget pushed on, though. She needed to know more about Isabel. 'We bumped into her at the country park. And I did wonder – if it was her. The girlfriend.'

'She was on her own,' said Laura. 'Carrying a violin case.' And suddenly Bridget knew she had to get off the subject. Her heart was beating too fast, her face felt strange, stiff, hot: mercifully the door pinged and a woman was pushing her way inside.

A violin case? Off for private lessons with Carmichael. She tried to picture the parents, upset on her behalf, that he'd let their daughter down, wasn't to be contacted. Would they go round to his house, bang on his door? His phone going unanswered. Her heart raced, anxious.

The customer, a big, fussy woman was already talking, loudly, fierce dark eyebrows that made her look angry – she *was* angry – was having a go at Laura, asking about the fur trim on something in the window. Bridget stepped in, grateful for the diversion, and Laura shifted on the sofa, keeping out of it. Bridget explained that the fur wasn't real but the woman wasn't to be placated. She moved around the rails tugging at things. She was talking about wool now, rambling, she couldn't wear wool, saying something about the process of shearing being cruel to animals.

Following her at a careful distance, Bridget let her talk. There were customers like this, she reminded herself, they just wanted to talk, to rant, to complain, you had to let them. This was people skills, this was retail: she had to deal with the world – but it was hard. The woman's aggressiveness was having a dangerous effect on her: she could feel herself having to control her responses. She had to stop herself losing her temper.

Carmichael had been a vegetarian: could she have forgotten that until this moment? Finicky. Staying behind the woman Bridget remembered him taking her for a meal, at a vegetarian café somewhere. A plate full of brownish stuff. Panic jumped inside her, at the memory of his face, peering at her, talking to her about battery farms and abattoirs, watching for her reaction. Remembered going home and refusing to eat, mumbling something about being vegetarian and her mother sitting, sobbing at the table, her head low over the plate, the last straw.

The woman's mouth was opening and closing, her head turning mechanically, from the clothes, to Bridget, and back. Ranting, uninterrupted. Bridget could see Laura staring from the sofa but she wasn't sure if it was at her or at the madwoman.

She felt a pulse of dislike for her younger self, she couldn't stop it. Her poor mother, her face looking up from the table, full of despair: poor old Mum. They'd sat either side of her when she died, her and Carrie, holding a hand each, blank with unarticulated grief.

'Look,' Bridget cleared her throat and the big, dark-eyed woman paused, outraged at the interruption. Laura watching.

You were just a kid, Bridget had to remind herself: you didn't know how to manage any of it. It seemed to her so dangerous, that phase. When you tried to get away from your parents, hide things from them. When you want to be grown up. Isabel – she's safe now. That's something to hold on to.

'Is there something in particular you're looking for?' Gently.

And as abruptly as she'd blown in, the woman marched to the door, as if she'd been insulted, and was gone.

Laura made a sound as the door closed then said, something like, *Well,* walking heavily back to the kitchen with her cup, and though Bridget was ready for the conversation, about *some people* when she came back Laura said nothing more. She looked suddenly exhausted, as if it was all too much for her. With the shop empty Bridget seized her chance, and told her to go home. Get some rest.

Laura didn't put up any resistance, though on the door-step she hesitated, looking round momentarily bewildered as if she knew something was wrong but needed time to put her finger on it. Bridget rested a hand on her shoulder, not quite a warning, and then the moment passed. Laura moved on, out, she was walking slowly away past the jeweller's, newly slow, newly awkward, newly tentative with the weight suddenly shifted out ahead of her.

Bridget walked straight into the stockroom, before she could think about it. The corner of the box was visible, but the cardboard was still unmarked, as far as she could see. She didn't know how long – but then she heard the door, and retreated.

A couple: retired but not old, but all the same Bridget's heart sank. She longed for a couple of girls on their lunch break, or young women at least, noisy and excited, to fill the place up with something that was alive, growing. The man sat down on the sofa, clearing his throat irritably.

'I need a dress for Christmas.' Daring a glance at her husband who didn't look back, she was bravely determined. She wore no make-up, hair neat, thin. In a daze Bridget found her four dresses, and shut her in the changing room, managing an encouraging glance as she pulled the curtain to.

He sat on the sofa with the newspaper open on his lap, looking up only to criticise. Ignoring Bridget who turned her back, or she might crown him.

'Is this—' The woman was peering round the curtain. The dress sat on her as though she was a child dressing up.

'It's a bit too big,' said Bridget, 'I've got the smaller one.' And was hurrying into the stockroom for it, clumsy. To get to the back rail she had to push the garments at the front aside and step over the box. She could smell it. She could. Sweetish, rank, combining with the mint to make her feel sick, sick. She grabbed the dress she needed and stepped back so hurriedly she almost fell, groping blindly; something fell, a stack of brochures slithered to the ground with a slap.

There was air freshener in the cupboard under the little kitchen sink: from the sofa the man was watching her now, alerted by the sound. She walked slowly, she smiled: she ignored the man, as he had ignored her. She stripped the polythene from the dress and handed it to the woman, unzipped before walking on to the kitchen, coming back with the air freshener. The man was looking around, wondering: alone in here, she's alone. What kind of operation is this?

Inside the stockroom Bridget closed the door and sprayed all around the box, into the room's corners. She could hear the mumble of voices beyond the closed door. She leaned against it. Her back was bathed in sweat.

Almost every day now there would be a new revelation about child abuse, young women. Bridget had to avert her eyes, turn off the radio, each time it stuck a pin into her. Watching the news with Matt only, what, a couple of weeks before, a woman had sat on a sofa with her hands obedient in her lap, recounting what had happened to her, *he put his hands* . . . a woman who had waived her anonymity: a middle-aged woman like her. Bridget remembered consciously breathing, telling herself this had nothing to do with her. This didn't happen to her. The angry faces of women demonstrating.

But it did happen to her. The evidence was in here, with her, he had polythene around his head, his pale, bristly cheek inside the plastic, boxed inside the cardboard.

'Hello?' The woman's voice piped up from behind the door. Bridget straightened herself and walked out.

The small, mousy woman stood, turning, frowning a little, excited. The dress fitted her, it was the right length: beyond that Bridget's judgement failed her completely. The woman standing there might have been a tree or a chair, but then Bridget saw her face, pleading, complicit.

She wanted the dress. Let her have it. Get them out of here.

'Lovely,' Bridget said, forcing herself. 'Isn't it?' Turning to the husband on the sofa, smiling, encouraging. She felt as if her face was made of wood. For a long moment the man looked at her, expressionless, then let out a sigh. Got to his feet.

'All right then, let's get on with it.' Fishing out his wallet.

She kept the smile on as she processed the transaction for the couple over the till, a couple not happy, resigned, years ahead together. Would that be her and Matt?

And they were gone, too.

She was patient: she made herself go through the motions, doing her paperwork, placing an order for next year by email. Not in the stockroom, though, where she would usually do it, but at the front desk, her head raised every time someone paused in front of the window, expecting him.

The hours passed, slowly, slowly. Bridget monitored the street: she saw Justine opposite come up to her glazed door and look out, bored, blank. Business wasn't good. She didn't look across at Bridget though, her gaze was indifferent, not even grateful for the parcel. Bridget had sent Laura over with it to be on the safe side. It looked like nothing had roused her suspicions.

And then it was five, five fifteen, five twenty. Bridget went outside and brought in the little box bushes in tubs, she turned out the lights. The lights in the jeweller's were still on, but the music from the gallery had been turned off. A Wednesday evening, in November, and quiet. At last, she walked slowly back into the stockroom. She knelt and pulled the long box out from under the rails.

One of the men they had interviewed on the news had said, it was normal back then. Charges dropped.

It wasn't normal. Had never been. Not normal. It was just a kind of – trap, like an animal in a trap that can't go forwards or backwards without tearing itself. Alone in the music room with him, him nodding and moving, putting his hand there and you froze. Your mouth wouldn't open, it wouldn't say, *No*.

On her knees Bridget slid the box around and shoved it ahead of her, out into the shop. It was heavy.

So if you didn't say *no*? If you only said *no* in your head.

Bridget knelt back up, resting on her heels. Paused. Examining what it was that she was feeling, the muscles in her arms and shoulders aching; her back, her neck, her forehead, all warm with the activity. She was alive.

He'd known she was saying *no*, whether she opened her mouth or not; when he had stood there in the shop's tiny kitchen, looked into her eyes and talked about her as though she belonged to him, her half-grown body, the parts of it she had hardly known herself, he had known exactly what he was doing. With a great rush that came to her: of course he had known. And hadn't cared.

So get it done. Before they catch you.

The box was heavy, though. And rigid, which made it easier, unbending as experimentally she lifted one end. Rigor mortis: what did she know about that? Nothing. She didn't know anything about DNA traces, or – any of this. His computer record? His address book, his message history. All the things she didn't know about buzzed, like flies on the edge of her vision.

Traces, witnesses – if they begin to look at his last

movements. He had not contacted Bridget, except in person, walking through the door. He came in once with Isabel, but she had not been aware of any connection between them, he'd said nothing. At least, not while they were in the shop. Laura – well. Laura had picked something up, that much was certain, but she could handle Laura. Laura had enough on her plate, soon she'd be staying home with a baby, soon any vibration of something not quite right between Isabel and Carmichael would have faded. So they were the only witnesses.

His small shiny car parked on the corner of the close? The memory jumped. The other residents of the quiet little cul-de-sac all worked, the place was empty in the day. And Matt had missed him, hadn't he? It hadn't been Matt, after all, that she'd imagined turning in as Carmichael left. Not that Matt – she had to stop thinking about Matt. The lad she took a cigarette off in the street. Long gone. Repeat after me: no one knows. Just get on with it.

The van was two blocks away, where there was free parking. She walked to get it, past dark shop fronts, trying to look normal, trying not to look too hard for CCTV cameras. She saw none and was pretty sure, anyway, that there weren't any in the little lanes this end of town: the other end round the multi-storey, maybe, at the big junction of roads. The pavements were wet and empty, though the pubs were filling up. There was a big old Victorian one on the corner, its windows frosted and engraved and golden with light. The door opened as she came past and a gust of warm beery air came out, a glimpse of oak panelling: a man getting out his packet of cigarettes and his lighter, but not the same man. Older, heavier. As the door closed behind him a face turned from the bar to look out, the glimpse of familiar features that gave her a jolt and she kept going, no. Your imagination, seeing things.

Driving carefully, the wet hissing under her tyres, lights reflected in puddles, she gripped the steering wheel. Her phone rang in her pocket, but she held on tight, didn't look and it stopped. Nothing can happen. Go slow. Careful. She turned into the narrow lane.

Leaving the hazards flashing in the empty cobbled lane Bridget climbed out, and unlocked the shop. Knowing she would be straight back she hadn't set the alarm: for a second the thought of what might have happened, if she had crashed the car, if someone had broken in, ballooned in her chest and she had to stop, just for a second, to catch her breath.

The box sat there, waiting for her in the middle of the shop. The yellow streetlight shone through on the long, narrow, dark shape, a solemn shape. Kneeling, she began to tug at it: she couldn't do this on her own: it would tear on the threshold. As far as the back threshold, it stuck on the step and she had to get behind it and shove. The cardboard could soften in the wet, it could rip open on the lip of the doorstep, on a hinge: she had to go slow.

There was someone coming up the lane.

A car: it revved angrily. She stopped still, crouched over the box. A horn blared, loud, again. A man's voice, shouting.

'Oi! Oi! The fuck—' A car door slammed. 'Oi!'

Hurriedly, awkwardly, she came around the box, half hunched over still, as though caught in searchlights and trying to hide. She came out into the lane and he was right there, a big man in a jacket too small for his shoulders, his arms forced out by muscle, a bald head shining.

'This you?' Thrusting his face into hers. 'Get that heap of shit out my way.'

'I'm sorry, I'm just—' she stammered, trying to sound reasonable, calm, when in her head it screamed at her, quick. *Quick*. Before he looks. Before he sees. His jaw set, threatening, small eyes darting.

'Just fucking do it,' he said, '*Now.*'

Was he trying to look over her shoulder? 'Sure,' she said. The box behind her was inescapably like a coffin. 'Let me just – I was – let me get my keys.' She ran back inside, grabbed her keys. The alarm? Hesitated a fraction of a second: careful. That's what this is about now: taking care. She set the alarm, ran for the door before it went off.

When she got back out he hadn't moved, arms crossed, shoulders bulging.

And as he fell back, just a fraction, Bridget sidestepped him. Climbing hurriedly into the van she saw him shamble back, dangerous still, a gorilla in a too-tight suit, and wrench open his own car door. She set off, bumping slowly over the cobbles, feeling his aggression. Round the back: that was what it would have to be.

Squinting against the glare of the man's headlights in her rearview mirror Bridget told herself she'd never seen him before, would never see him again. She was pretty sure he had no idea who she was. The car behind her barely waited for her to emerge at the end of the lane before squealing angrily past in the wet street – and he was gone.

There was an alley behind the shop where there was a line of lock-ups and rear entry to some of the shops. They'd been lived in, once upon a time: not much more than cottages, with back yards and outdoor privies. Bridget hardly used the back access: it involved going through the yard next door was damp and slimy, and she wasn't sure if the door would even open. Creeping along, she squeezed the van along the narrow space, stopped and sat there, hands on the steering wheel, waiting for her heart to slow.

All right. It's all right. He was just an angry man: the world was full of them. She locked the van, and hurried back down the alley, into the road, heading for the lane again. Quiet still, but not dead, not empty, the sound of footsteps echoing: up ahead a couple were walking, arms round each other. Across the street a skinny little lad leaning against a lamp post for support: a bit early for that, was the first automatic thought she had, then, *Finn* – does Finn? – stop it. She'd never seen Finn drunk and the boy leaning against the lamp post had the wrong hair, a buzz cut; anyway, he was too small to be Finn. She turned into the silent lane, looking both sides now as she hurried – this way, then that way, listening for footsteps, soft sounds just out of earshot – until a thought brought her to a halt.

The jeweller's opposite had CCTV inside – she had it too, though it had broken months ago and she hadn't got it fixed, the monitors were enough of a deterrent, though Laura was always grumbling. Would their CCTV have picked her up, loading a long box into the van at night? She put her hand to her chest, felt the running hurry of her heart. Just as well, then – she set off again, not wanting to think, not wanting to dwell. Narrow escape.

Just get him out of there.

★   ★   ★

104

She couldn't seem to get the key in the lock, her fingers like sausages, transfixed too by the shape beyond the glass, monumental at the centre of the shop: the long box, not quite regular, bulging in the thin, flat light and a shadow at one corner. Was it leaking? Was he— The key turned.

In the same moment as Bridget stepped across the threshold she knew she wasn't alone, *shit* – the word, not usual for her, sounding the alarm in her head – *shit, shit, shit* – you should have looked. There was someone behind her, beside her in the doorway, jostling her. A smell of spirits.

White-faced, cropped hair, skinny, cheerful: it was the boy she'd seen leaning against the lamp post, except it wasn't. The world skewed, righted itself, anger coming up behind fear.

It was Carrie. Pissed. Bridget staggered as her little sister pushed past her into the shop.

'Jesus, Carrie,' she said flinching as Carrie elaborately sidestepped the box to collapse on the sofa, aiming a kick at the corner that missed as she went down. Then her sister's little chalk-white face upturned in defiant mock-apology, eyes almost closed.

'Sis,' she said, drunkenly deliberate. '*Shish*. Not like you to take the Lord's name in vain.' Reaching up a hand, small and blunt-nailed like a kid's, swaying on the sofa. 'Pleased to see me?'

And then the alarm went off.

For a second Bridget held out a hand to meet Carrie's, hearing the awful, deafening iron clatter of the alarm and all its consequences spilling out in her head – and doing

105

nothing. The alarm was connected to the alarm company and the police station. She needed to call them immediately or they would send a police car. But she only held out her hand, her fingers barely met Carrie's. Then she turned away, smooth and quick and calm although inside she was dissolving, she was jelly and water.

She punched in the code, pressed the switch and the sound stopped as abruptly as it had begun, only the echo hanging in the air, and Carrie's dark eyes looking up at her, accepting both the panic and the resolution equally: Bridget would sort it out. Bridget dialled the police first, then the alarm company and she explained it to them. Rueful and apologetic and self-deprecating, *stupid, sorry*. The policewoman brisk, a couple of words and no more, the password and identification given, time noted, done. The alarm company only bored, making her get the account number, jobsworth. She went through it, quelling the tic of frustration. When Bridget turned back into the shop Carrie was leaning back on the sofa with her eyes closed, arms out, a little beatific saintly smile on her face.

'Coffee,' Bridget said distinctly and on the sofa Carrie murmured something up at her, eyelids flickering.

Black, strong, instant, no fuss, a dash of cold in it or she'd slurp and burn herself but this needed to be done quickly. All the time – as she crossed the floor, stepped into the kitchenette – checking, for anything. A stain or a shred of fabric or a smell. Carrie had sharp eyes even when drunk, Carrie saw things, asked questions, Carrie didn't care who she wound up. Bridget had to be tough, not frightened, she had to be big sister: if Carrie smelled fear, she'd know. And there was the box to deal with.

'Here.' She held out the mug and Carrie swung upright, reached for it. Looked around the room.

'What's going on?' she said, staring at the box.

'How much have you had?' said Bridget in answer. Tough. 'You been in the pub all day?' Exasperated.

'Just a couple of beers on the train.' But she was looking down into the coffee now, not meeting Bridget's eye.

'Well, you can make yourself useful now you're here,' said Bridget. 'Drink up. I need some help getting this into the van.'

Carrie wriggled to the edge of the sofa, elbows on her knees in heavy trousers that were like an old man's, chin in her hands. And looked at the box again, harder, frowning.

Skinny white forearms emerged from her jacket but she was strong in the shoulder: Carrie had always worked out: weights, gym, boxing training was her favourite. Carrie squinting over a boxing glove, in a singlet, thinking she was Marlon Brando. Bridget had picked her up at a boxing gym once, a long time ago, and seen the old guys tousling her short hair, it was obvious what the appeal was. She was too smart ever to actually go into the ring, though, which was just as well because Bridget would have had to plead with her then and they'd fall out for the hundredth time.

'Dunno,' she said. 'What is it?'

'Old stock,' said Bridget now, improvising, 'I was going to load it up through the backyard but it's too heavy.' Eyeing her, strategic. 'Maybe it can wait.'

Carrie hunched, bristling for a second, then she bounced up on to the balls of her feet to sway right in front of Bridget. Still a couple of inches shorter and always would be, now. 'No good to you, am I?' she said, defiant. 'Get out of it.' Insisting. Bridget stepped back, almost smiling. Her kid sister.

It's just a box, she told herself, squatting, Carrie at the other end. It still felt rigid, she tried not to think about it sagging, bending, the cardboard giving in their arms. Just a box.

They edged backward out of the shop, Carrie frowning with the effort at the other end. Across the yard of the shop next door, staggering briefly as Bridget paused to unlatch the back gate. The neighbour was a little newsagent, old guy who'd been there donkey's years. He grumbled about how much his stock cost him: with that thought Bridget did look up, thinking she caught the flash of something high on the back of the house, a security camera. But it was a circular ventilation pane set in a bathroom window up there, turning like a windmill – and she kept moving without a break in her step. The van was where she'd left it.

It wasn't until they were unloading at the other end that Carrie seemed to notice how heavy the box was.

On the way through the wet, empty streets she'd hardly seemed awake, head leaning back, eyes half closed, light falling in stripes on her pale face.

In the garage, the big door half down, Carrie stopped, bending her knees to get a better grip. Pausing to shake her head as the hangover kicked in, and it all seemed to come into focus, where she was, what they were doing. Bridget waited, holding her end, blowing the hair out of her face.

'Fuck,' said Carrie, and abruptly she let her end fall, lurching back so it wouldn't land on her feet. 'What've you got in there?' Staring down.

'Well, not china, fortunately,' said Bridget, marvelling at how she could sound dry, how she could just lower her end to the floor. 'Just shoes and bags,' and put a hand on Carrie's shoulder, gently turning her away and towards the wide garage entrance.

'You staying, then?' Pulling the door down with a clang. Standing on the grass Carrie looked small and lost suddenly, staring around at the neat little houses in the close like she'd landed on the moon.

The sound of the garage door had brought Matt to the back door. 'Hey, bro,' said Carrie, stumbling towards him and Bridget's heart gave a lurch as he smiled in the side light.

Matt had already laid the table and something was in the oven. Shepherd's pie, she guessed, a meaty, savoury smell and it was his other speciality. Matt liked cooking, he did it slowly and carefully and precisely, always following recipes to the letter, washing everything up afterwards. She glanced into the kitchen and sure enough, it was clean and tidy. A pan for peas on the stove: Matt always made peas with shepherd's pie. She leaned against him with gratitude, and he patted her on the shoulder, awkwardly. He cleared his throat as if he was about to say something, but then Finn was on the stairs, thundering down, holding the shaggy curtain of his hair to one side to peer, delighted, at Carrie.

They danced clumsily around each other, Finn like a big bear suddenly since they last hugged, dwarfing Carrie. It was always mysterious to Bridget how a relationship as complicated and prickly as hers with her sister could emerge as something so blithe and sunny when it came to Finn.

'Let's go to the pub,' he said, eager. 'Can we, Mum? Me and Carrie?' Looking from one adult to another.

Carrie's cheeks were pink, spots of colour, and she scowled: Bridget knew to disguise her happiness.

'After tea, maybe,' said Matt quickly, before Bridget had to, and then they were all shuffling, grateful, into the kitchen.

At table Carrie had an appetite, wolfing down the pie. She always had had, maybe in reaction to Bridget, refusing to play the same game of pushing food round her plate. 'How long do you want to stay?' said Bridget, hungry herself for the first time in what seemed like weeks. Having Carrie at the table seemed to loosen everything up: Matt relaxed, Finn bouncing with happiness. In spite of everything. In spite of the box in the dusty dark of the garage, behind a rolled carpet beyond the van.

'Dunno.' Carrie forked in more potato, taking a long drink of water.

'You can stay as long as you like, Auntie Carrie,' said Finn confidently.

'Yes,' said Bridget, and meant it though in her head it whirred. *How. When.* 'How's Ella?'

Bridget hadn't intended to probe, but that was how Carrie heard it, Bridget knew her sister's body language well enough. 'All right,' said Carrie warily, laying her fork and knife carefully side by side, on the defensive straight out of the gate.

'You've had a fight.' Bridget couldn't help herself.

'Just a little one.' Carrie pale again but winking at Finn – who had got anxious, instantly, scenting a row. Like Matt, he hated raised voices and drama: they both always managed to forget that that was what Carrie brought with her. Finn looked from Carrie to Bridget and back, uncertain.

'It'll be all right,' said Carrie. 'We need a bit of space.'

Scowling again, this time at the cliché. Carrie fought the idea of any relationship at all, let alone one that was starting to look like a cliché. 'Couple of days? Week, max.'

'So are we going, Auntie Carrie?' Finn had cleared his plate and was pushing his chair back. He didn't wait for an answer. 'I'll get my jacket.'

'You know he can't drink,' said Bridget to Carrie when he was out of the room.

'Sure, sure,' she said rolling her eyes. Matt paused, plates in hand and she went on meekly. 'Yes, *Dad*. I'll keep him out of trouble.' He moved on into the kitchen.

'You all right, then?' It seemed like a casual question, maybe it was, Carrie leaning back in her seat replete and smiling. 'You and old *dad* there?'

Bridget smiled, widening it, it was easy to let it move on up to her eyes, looking at Carrie. 'It's nice to have you,' she said and that was easy too because it was true. Whatever complications it introduced.

When they'd gone – kitted out in warm jackets because it was half a mile and freezing out there – Bridget and Matt sat on the sofa, leaning against each other, the news on TV. Nine o'clock: she guessed Carrie and Finn would stay till closing time. Talking about computer games, and Carrie's exploits. DJing and the dodgy companies she did websites for.

She felt something, though, at the point where their bodies touched, at the shoulder, a restlessness. Matt was usually calm and still and focused. One knee jiggled and she felt a silence growing that was never there before. Then Matt spoke.

'Oh, something happened at work today.'

Bridget sensed it coming, a truck the other side of the blind bend.

'That guy that came into your shop?' Matt wasn't waiting for her to respond, and she kept still. On the TV there was a march, blue starred flags waving against a grey sky: it blurred as she stared. 'He was supposed to be giving a big lecture this afternoon and he didn't show up.'

Bridget felt the bottom fall out of her stomach. This is how it begins: these are the consequences. 'Really?' she said. Mild surprise in her voice.

Matt took a breath and let it out, a big sigh. Picked up the remote from beside him on the arm of the sofa and turned it in his hands. 'Fortunately only a handful of students came so no big deal. Lazy, these visiting fellows.' He sounded exasperated. That was all. Not curious. Not intrigued.

'Maybe he just – forgot,' she offered. The marchers continued their progress across the screen, waving their banners.

'Maybe he's losing his marbles,' said Matt. 'It happens. Dementia.'

'Really?' said Bridget, because there was something in the explanation, a spark of hope. And a memory of someone, on a TV report, when charges couldn't be brought because he had developed Alzheimer's: the powdery skin of an elderly man, his face distorted in outrage as a camera turned to follow him.

Carmichael hadn't had Alzheimer's. He could remember: she knew he could remember. But that had been long ago. Dementia sufferers could remember the faraway past, couldn't they? She liked the explanation anyway, even if it

112

wasn't true: something about it fitted with what she'd done. Erased: he was gone, and all his memories with him.

Matt was still talking. 'Academics — actually, some of them get away with dementia for longer than most because they're smart and they can cover up, I've seen it. Remember Nilsson?' She didn't. 'Physicist. He could still lecture but couldn't tell you what he'd had for breakfast. And as for the disinhibition, people are used to the big brains being anti-social, rude.'

Quite a long speech from Matt. 'Was he rude?' she asked.

Matt thought a minute. 'Yes,' he said, thoughtfully. 'Yes, he was. Arrogant and rude.'

Something must have happened between him and Carmichael and with the understanding a pulse set up, a chain of questions. But she had to be careful. She couldn't ask, not directly, how much he knew about Anthony Carmichael, however much she wanted Matt to be on her side.

He'd always been on her side, without her telling him anything, because that was how it had to be. Only now it was all different, their steady life, it was all tipped and tilted like a sinking ship. One wrong step and he would see. He would see right inside her.

Matt was weighing the TV remote in his hand, but looking at a point above the screen. The weather had come on, a man with a pointer gesturing at the map and in one corner an inset picture of trees blowing flat. She pointed. 'Not another storm,' she said and on cue he turned up the sound.

She had to get Matt off the subject before Carrie got back. Even pissed, especially when pissed, her little sister

113

was too sharp: she had ears like a bat for trouble. No patience with secrets, Carrie saw it as her duty to expose them.

And Carrie knew Carmichael.

Would she remember his name? Of course she would. And a music fellow, gone missing, came into the shop?

They hadn't talked about it, ever. Carrie didn't know what he'd done to her. Or at least that's what Bridget always told herself. She felt herself go still: beside her, fortunately, Matt had leaned forwards to watch the news. Storm Janet heading their way. If their shoulders had been touching he would have known, just like she had known, that something was up.

Ninety mile an hour winds.

And it came into her head, a flash photograph, a fuzzy image on an old screen. Carrie, ten, eleven years old and standing on one leg in the doorway of Bridget's bedroom, Bridget trying to close the door on her. 'I know you've got one. Does he look like Dean or does he look like Jess?' Characters on a TV show they watched together.

Boyfriend.

What had been in Carrie's own head, back then? Bridget had been too busy to care. Getting into scraps at school, coming home with her school shirt ripped, defiant. Carrie had always been good at fighting people off, being stroppy. Fighting her corner. Bridget felt a tightness in her chest, a painful hard squeeze at the thought.

Carrie picking up the violin, setting it on her shoulder, making a soppy, moony face. It would ring bells, all right, if Matt started talking about the new music fellow who'd been into the shop.

114

'Looks like it won't get over here for a while,' he said, leaning back against the sofa. 'Finn and Carrie should manage to get back from the pub – or at least storm Janet isn't going to be what stops them.'

Bridget sighed. 'She'd already had a few when she turned up at the shop,' she said.

After they'd moved Carrie had stuck it out at school for six months before leaving home, aged sixteen. Sleeping rough for a while then shacking up with another girl in a squat. Bridget still didn't really know what had gone on, how she'd kept body and soul together. She'd gone down to London one time to talk to her, their mother beside herself worrying, to try and make it up. Carrie cold and impervious at the door to the squat, some place in south London, a big, sunlit, scruffy square. 'What do *you* want?'

She'd come out in the end, they'd sat on the mismatched chairs of the square's cooperative vegan café and raged at each other. Carrie pretending she didn't care for the longest time before lurching forward and shouting, 'Where the fuck were you when I needed you? Where the fuck were you? In fucking hospital refusing to eat. Shunting us to the middle of fucking nowhere.'

And Bridget in despair had blurted out, 'I was trying to protect you.' Carrie had got angry then, demanding to know what she meant. And Bridget had found herself unable to say.

'Ah well, Finn'll keep her on the straight and narrow,' Matt said, getting to his feet and reluctantly Bridget smiled up at him. Law-abiding Finn, who'd spent the last party he went to kicking out the drunks and helping clean up.

'Cup of tea?' And cheerfully he was off to the kitchen.

They would ask, *why didn't you say anything?* She didn't have an answer. Who to tell? Mum, working three jobs by then? Her kid sister? Teachers at school? Bridget had always been little Miss Goody Two Shoes at school, head down, work hard, take the flak from other kids for being a swot.

And where had it got her? She'd gone back to school after hospitalisation but her grades dropped. The teacher training course had made her feel uneasy and she'd started work instead, among adults, in shops. Among women. Matt had tried to persuade her to stick with it. He had believed in her. But he'd seemed to understand: he'd come up with some money for the initial investment in the shop and the bank had put in some more and against all the odds, slowly, slowly, she'd made it work. Hard graft, careful choosing of stock, second guessing what women wanted, keeping on top of the VAT, dressing windows. Non-stop. But it had worked.

He came back in with two mugs: she looked up at him. She had always relied on him understanding, without her having to say. Now she wanted to evade him.

They drank their tea, they watched a bit of a movie, she made up a bed for Carrie in the spare room. It would have been for another child, if she'd dared have one. She'd needed to work.

It must have lingered in Matt's mind, though, unsolved: Carmichael. They were in bed and about to turn out the light when he made an impatient sound, and Bridget set down the book about wartime France she had been failing to focus on, again. 'What?'

'There was a journalist came, though,' he said, jumping back to the conversation without explanation as if she

116

knew what he was talking about, what he had been thinking about through the news and the movie.

'Journalist,' she said, blankly. Though she did know, somehow.

'She turned up for the lecture,' said Matt, tipping his head back against the pillow, thinking. 'She was a bit pissed off.'

'So you were there?' Bridget asked. 'Actually at the lecture?' The thought of it set up a panicked flutter in her chest.

Matt snorted. 'He wanted PowerPoint and slides and he requested me as backup. Just a couple of days ago.'

So around the time he came to the house. He had known. Carmichael knew Matt was her husband, and he had deliberately involved him, brought him into the circle. She understood why immediately: he had wanted her to be frightened. It occurred to her that somehow she was acting as if Carmichael was still alive, was still threatening her. But her heart didn't slow, calm at the realisation, it seemed to swell, pumped with brief euphoria. She had to control that too.

'Was she a local journalist?' She had to ask anything she wanted to know now: if she waited till the morning Matt would look at her oddly, he'd wonder why she was still interested. And this was important: she seized on that.

He shrugged, pondering. 'I don't think so,' he said. 'She said she'd followed his career. Gillian something? She'd come specially. Asked how he was settling in, all that, was he part of the community.'

'What did you tell her?' That Carmichael was fitting in so well he had already visited a local boutique?

117

He was frowning, pushed his glasses up his nose. 'Told her I had no idea.' Then sighed. 'I figured I ought to make his excuses so I said I'd heard he hadn't been well.'

And suddenly she was angry. 'Is that your job? To cover up for him? There didn't seem to be much wrong with him when he came into the shop.' Shut up, shut up. That was weeks ago, as far as Matt knew, stop talking about him. Too late: Matt had turned his head and was looking at her. She blustered, 'Well, if I just didn't turn up to work one day . . .' tailing off.

'There've been incidents,' said Matt mildly. 'You do hear stuff. He hasn't turned up for tutorials, and said he'd forgotten and gone to London, to take auditions. Left his mobile at home.' It swirled, shapeless, in her head. All the ramifications, all the loose ends she must tie. Had she really done it? Had she just imagined it? No. The box was in her garage.

And Matt was still musing. 'It could be he's just forgetful. Could be arrogance.' Still watching her, absently, perplexed. Something was bothering him. It was all bothering him.

'Oh, well—' she said, wanting to get out from under his eyes, not knowing how.

And then the door was opening downstairs, the sound of Carrie's giggling stage whisper, Finn's deeper rumble, and she was off the hook. Rolling her eyes at the noise they were making, Matt smiling, turning away on the pillow. Book down, lights out.

Chapter Eleven

Thursday

At two, or three, in the dark dead of night, it came to her in a dream. Another dream. Matt's face, his mouth moving, smiling, his kind eyes on her. His mouth opening and closing, talking about Carmichael and she could see that his mouth was black inside, as if it had filled up with tar. Tilting his head as he said it, and Bridget unable to look away from the black inside his mouth. And what was it he had been saying? *Carmichael went to London, auditioning, said he'd forgotten. Left his phone at home.*

And she gasped, out loud, jerked up on the pillow and immediately she knew: his mobile phone. Shit, shit, shit. Once they knew he'd disappeared. Isn't that the first thing they'd do? See where he went. To her shop. And then to her garage. They'd track his phone, in his pocket, or wherever it was, the phone she hadn't looked for, she'd been so busy winding him around and around, mummified in polythene so she didn't have to look at him.

Bridget couldn't sleep, she couldn't do anything.

She had to get the mobile phone from his body. She

formulated a plan, an explanation. For when they came and asked.

He came to the shop, he left his phone behind, she didn't know who it belonged to, she brought it home and left it in the car.

It would implicate her. It would link her to the body. She would be the last one to have seen him. They would search the shop, they would swab out her bins.

She would have to take it to the police station. She would have to retrieve it from the body.

What choice did she have? She lay and waited, for dawn.

The hotel room Gill woke up in – in a Premier Inn on the ring road – was purple. Lilac or lavender they might call it, she supposed: curtains, shiny headboard, feature wall. Silver and purple. She half closed her eyes in case that might stop her head hurting. It didn't.

The student bar last night. Gill turned in the bed and pressed her face into the pillow, stifling a groan.

The lecture – scheduled for mid-afternoon which said a lot about Anthony Carmichael's timetable – had been on Bach and mathematical theory. Five students had turned up and they didn't seem very bothered by the great man's failure to appear. Gill had been looking forward to it on a number of levels, herself. Looking forward to seeing his face when he saw how few of them there were in the big auditorium, four lads and a girl with a twitch and thick glasses all sitting with respectful distance between them. To that wondering look when he tried to place Gillian Lawson, who had, you might say, followed his career with interest.

120

She'd thought it would be harder to get in. Students came in all shapes and sizes, these days, though, there were plenty of hairy types – masters' students – her age and older, and a university like this was more catholic than most. Of course: that would be why he had come here. Camouflage.

She sat at the back, trying not to be noticed. After ten minutes passed, then twenty, and there was still no show, it occurred to her that he might have peered round the door, seen how small his audience was and fucked off home. Not considering it worth his very valuable time. Gillian Lawson knew him. He didn't know she knew him, but she did.

The girl with glasses, two rows below Gill, might have been his type. His tastes weren't catholic but neither were they based on any specific look, only on vulnerability. The chattering grew louder as he didn't appear, and next to the girl someone took out a bag of crisps. Gill leaned forwards in her seat and said, 'Is he usually this late?', trying to engage with them but no one answered, and the looks she caught represented more or less contempt. As if she was the pervert. A lanky boy just stared and edged along his row and off without a word.

In the lobby where they gravitated Gill approached the girl, apologetic. 'I've come to interview Dr Carmichael,' she said, hoping she wouldn't have to name the paper, because you could rely on this lot to put the word about and it would get back to Steve even if it only appeared on page nine of the *Socialist Worker*. She wasn't sure any more if the *Socialist Worker* had as many as nine pages.

The girl was fiercer than she looked, a lapel full of

incomprehensible badges. One of them had just read, *Fish?* Question mark.

'Who are you, then?' she said to Gill rudely. 'Gutter press?' And turned on her heel. The lads sniggering, although it hadn't been clear if at her or the girl or just because human interaction brought that out in them. Mouth breathers to a man. How was the human race to survive if this was what kids were like, these days? Gill thought. Scuttling back off to their screens to interact, rather than IRL.

Not that Gill could talk. No kids, and plenty of screen action.

The tech guy shifting the projector when she went back in to the lecture theatre had been as wary, leading her away from the students to a dim office at the foot of one of the towers. A photograph of a wife and son on the desk: something had made her look at the woman, but then he had gently steered her away, not touching her, just stepping between her and the desk. She had taken his name: Matt Webster. Seemed like a nice bloke, but very correct, very guarded, you'd think universities were nuclear power plants, full of dangerous material and official secrets. You couldn't tell, straight off, if they were hiding something or if they just didn't trust journalists.

So the college bar it would have to be. Gill had seen them across the piazza between the towers when she came back out of Webster's office, the girl hunched over her folders hurrying ahead of the boys, and then she had killed the rest of the afternoon drinking buckets of nasty tea at a chain café with wifi, computer open, for 'research'. Not the research she was supposed to be here for – well, not here, exactly, given that the Royals' Christmas story was forty miles north. Could you even call it research? Staring at the signage in a Starbucks that was probably for the chop for lack of custom – not much call for an almond milk latte in the shadow of Rose Hill, it would appear – and turning Google search terms over and over in her head. *Anthony Carmichael. Tony. Self-harm. Talented young musician.* She could hear Steve's voice, torn between knowing what a story it would be and wondering about her mental health. *It's a compulsion. It'll get you into trouble.*

It had got dark quickly. The bar sat at the foot of one of the big ugly towers, rammed inside, a glimpse of orange walls beyond packed tables and figures between them. Big doors opening and closing on the windswept darkness outside and a handful of smokers standing on the doorstep. And then one of them had turned in the orange light and seen her.

In the corridor beyond her purple room now someone laughed a machine-gun laugh and there was an exchange in a foreign language she didn't recognise, followed by the high buzz of a hoover coming on. Gill groped on the side table, found the blister pack of paracetamol with caffeine: her drug of choice. That and horrible white wine. There were two left in the packet: she sat up and necked them with the glass of water she'd left helpfully beside the bed and had then promptly ignored. It tasted dusty. She leaned back against the shiny lavender headboard and let her eyes close again.

You couldn't get anything useful out of students. Sober they were self-righteous, drunk they were kids. Had Gill ever been that young? Affirmative action, she remembered that. Collecting for the miners, rent strike. They thought they had all the answers, but they were headed down the wrong road, somehow. Boycotting lectures at the drop of a hat – no platforming, it was called. Whatever happened to free speech? Bleary with the hangover Gill thought she believed in that, and she'd better, hadn't she? She was a journalist.

They were all about big, colourful issues, kids were. Massive injustices, their right to their sexuality. Safe spaces for transvestites – well, fine. But there were little grey issues too. Muddy, dirty issues, places where there wasn't much in the way of safe space. It was called the home. It was called childhood. They got to university and they thought they could leave all that behind.

It had been the girl from the lecture with the bottle-bottom glasses – a smoker, it turned out, hunched against a concrete pillar out of the wind and nervously dragging on a roll-up like her mother might catch her at it – who'd recognised Gill. *Well, that's it, then*, Gill had thought, as the girl, squinting round the smoke, launched herself off the pillar towards her. And said, just as Gill was about to back off and go home – if you could call a Premier Inn home, and sometimes you had to – *Want a drink?* A turn-up for the books: you couldn't always tell, it turned out, when someone liked you. Or perhaps the kid had just been lonely.

In the corridor the loud hoover – something stuck in its intake, whining – knocked carelessly into the door. Housekeeping: a term so old-fashioned it didn't seem to fit in this place, with the faceted mirrors and acrylic carpet. They'd want to be in here in a minute, and Gill hadn't hung the *Do Not Disturb* on the handle. She threw back the purple covers.

See if she could get his home address out of the office. Look over someone's shoulder.

None of them round here really seemed to know who Carmichael was, was the point. Did his colleagues know? Someone must: someone must have given him the job. Must know about the legendary career as a virtuoso violinist that began by performing Ravel's *Tzigane* in front of the Queen when he was eleven and ended abruptly and without explanation when he was twenty-five, regularly put down as a sign of his genius; the celebrated monograph on Bartok; the essays for the *TLS*.

She needed to get out of here. Places to go, people to see. Someone rattled the door handle.

'Give me a minute,' said Gill wearily and reached for the shirt she'd worn yesterday and saw a grimy line at the collar and the sad thought it put in her head, of her washing machine, lonely and unloved in her flat in Eltham, almost brought a tear to her eye. There was another life out there, where home smelled of freshly washed sheets and Windolene and even dinner, at a pinch.

Not even the students who'd turned up for the lecture seemed to have much of a clue any more who Anthony Carmichael was. Perhaps that was why he was here.

If he was here.

Chapter Twelve

Breakfast had been accomplished downstairs without Bridget: a normal Thursday. Matt and Finn moving in the kitchen downstairs, the rattle of cereal into a bowl.

She had pretended to be sleepy, turning over in bed when Matt set down the mug of tea so that he wouldn't turn the light on. She wasn't sleepy: she was bone-tired but wired at the same time, she had to concentrate very hard on keeping still or she might start to tremble. The time when she would be able to rest and catch up on sleep seemed impossibly distant. She didn't trust herself to sit up and look him in the eye.

By the time they had left the house, Matt and Finn together, she had migrated to the bathroom. 'Bye, darling,' she called down through the locked door and there had been a little pause, tiny but significant, before Matt had called back up the stairs, 'Have a good day.' She could hear them on the front porch, talking in lowered voices as they set up their bikes, adjusted backpacks, zipped their outdoor jackets, same brand, Matt's dark green, Finn's pale blue. Matt pausing to check something for Finn, a loose chain or a bottom bracket. Their morning ritual.

There had been a hard frost: looking out of the bathroom's little window Bridget could see a sparkle on the long winter grass, the field sloping down to the estuary where the water was grey as pewter in the early light. She remembered waking up here, their first morning and looking out of this window heavily pregnant with Finn and she had stopped, her toothbrush half raised to her mouth as she had felt a bubble of unexpected joy expand inside her. For a second it was as if it had been yesterday: if she closed her eyes she would remember the weight of him inside her, the way you had to adjust for balance. Watching her belly move as she lay in the bath, bubbles sliding off it, a wonder. A miracle.

Unlocking the bathroom door and stepping cautiously out on to the landing she saw the spare room's door closed and with a small shock she remembered Carrie. She listened: a small, snoring breath. Bridget's little sister might be lean and wiry but Carrie always had snored: she'd broken her nose falling out of a tree aged eight and had been a snuffler and nose-bleeder and snorer ever since. Bridget wondered if Ella knew how to deal with the nosebleeds: sometimes they went on for an hour. She leaned her cheek against the door a second, listening to that sound: the sound of her childhood.

Back across the landing Bridget got dressed quickly, pulling on jeans, fleece, thermal socks. Trainers. Not work-wear but then she couldn't do what she had to do in a silk blouse and pencil skirt. Softly down the stairs, she paused in the kitchen for a sharp knife and rubber gloves. Hesitating with the knife in her hands, but all she needed to think about was, would it do the job? She came out through the kitchen door because it was on the opposite side of the house to where Carrie slept. There wasn't much she could do about the noise the garage door made beyond pulling as gently as she could on it and stopping when it was up enough for her to edge under at a crouch. The garage door was at right angles to the house, facing along the front gardens of the neighbouring houses. She didn't open it fully also because she didn't want anyone looking in at her inside.

Once inside she straightened in the cold half-dark, feeling her heart pound: the light from outside only illuminated a little way in, up to her knees, but she didn't turn the light on that Matt had installed, a bare bulb hanging at the far end. There were Matt's tools along the wall beyond the van, the shelving unit he had got out of a skip. It was bitterly cold and Bridget shivered, not just at the cold but at the thought that came into her head: good. The body wouldn't have deteriorated.

As she edged around the van her fleece caught on the wing mirror: looking down at the shred of fabric, all the other traces she might have left unfolded in her head, multiplying. She'd have to burn it all, everything she was wearing. Or boil wash? That would do.

The box was still there, half hidden under the old carpet. it came as a small shock to Bridget to realise it was not, after all, something she had imagined, or dreamed. Though she had had that dream, too, of shoving him, watching him disappear into a hole that opened up for him, a cesspit, a well, a sinkhole. Bridget paused a moment, leaning against the van, working out where that hole might be found, now. Then she knelt, set down the knife, put on the gloves and pulled back the carpet.

Nothing smelled: warily she lowered her head to sniff. Dust, oil, damp: there *was* something else, after all, under it. A denser smell, more complex, more animal, a sour cheese smell, salty, sweet. She felt her throat contract. The cardboard of the clothing box had softened, its corners collapsed a little, a bulge at one side. Bridget took the knife and quickly drew it down one edge, prising open staples. That animal scent bloomed under her nose, rotten: methodically she kept on, unpicking, pulling open. She was used to this: she had to dismantle these boxes for recycling. It came open: layers of polythene underneath and something pressed against the transparent plastic. Skin.

Quickly Bridget turned her head a moment to look somewhere else, her eyes searching the shelves for something, anything. Paint cans, tools hung in orderly rows, jamjars full of screws. Breathe.

Inside her it reset, as she had known it to in the past; she knew a panic attack when she felt it, and she knew how to dodge it, quick. Go through the motions: when it happened in the supermarket you just kept pushing the trolley, packing the bag at the checkout.

She lifted his arm. The limbs weren't stiff any more, they were heavy, but that needn't slow her down. All she needed to do was check his pockets: she was looking for the phone. That was all. Trousers, front and back: as she pushed him up she felt his deadweight. Cold.

The jacket was easier, one, two: start with that. Wallet – she didn't bother to examine it. Handkerchief, folded: she remembered his handkerchiefs. Used to wipe himself, dropped for his wife to wash. Who washed for him now? The handkerchief was ironed. She pulled him over, on his face. A stain on the trousers at the back, spread almost the width – she turned him back over, heaving.

His face was there, a blur.

And then suddenly she needed to stop. The smell seemed like a cloud around her head suddenly, a cloud full of bees. She heard the humming, she saw it, it had a colour. It was black and sparkled. She heard voices.

They murmured, talking to her. Were the voices in her head? Then something whirled, the light changing and the glittering cloud was gone: Bridget shifted on her haunches, turning her head towards the garage door.

It was Carrie talking, it wasn't in her head, after all. Bridget heard the challenge that was always present in her little sister's voice, the scrappy little dog in her. And the low murmur of an answer: Bridget knew that voice too. Their postman, mild-mannered Keith, bright and early.

Bridget almost laughed, hysterical: scrappy little dog meets postman. Five yards from her. Between her and them was the van's bonnet and the half-open garage door. The light was brighter through it, the sun higher in the sky. How long had she been in here? She couldn't tell.

She couldn't move.

Thanks, then. That was Keith. She heard the slam of his door as he climbed back into the van. Keith over whose shoulder she had seen the little black car and Carmichael beside it. *Call me Tony.* Had Keith seen him?

'Bridge?' Carrie was calling her name, carelessly loud. People would come, people would come out. Carrie called again, her voice lower, questioning but that wasn't good, because it meant she'd seen something. She'd seen the open door, the van through it. She was coming closer. A shadow passed across the light shed inside the garage.

Bridget heard Keith start his van's engine and the sound brought her to her feet, she could move, after all. Stiff, stumbling, she came round the van just as Carrie tugged the door up high in one careless movement and Bridget stood there, blinking in the light. As she raised a hand to shield her eyes she realised the knife was still in it. Saw Carrie look at the knife, and the gloves and sidestepped vainly, trying to block her path.

'*What?*' said Carrie, standing there in a frowsty old track-suit, bare feet in the frosty morning. Carrie didn't do slippers. Staring at her, the gloves, the knife.

Pushing past her.

There were explanations: recycling. Cutting up carpet to get it in the car. As long as Carrie didn't walk around the van.

But in the early morning frosty garage it was as if Carrie's passage from the light into the dark had created a vacuum, a wormhole – out of nowhere Bridget was somewhere else.

She heard an intake of breath.

She was at her mother's bedside. Their mother's: she was dying. Herself and Carrie in the dim room. And for a second Bridget stared out through the open door with the knife in her hand, into the world outside, where postmen delivered parcels and cars got cleaned on Sundays and lawns got mowed, but she was in here, in the dark.

131

'Bridge, what the— Bridge, what the *fuck*—'

And Bridget turned at last, from the sight of the empty, early, outside world and Keith's van disappearing round the corner.

Too late.

The two of them had sat at their mother's bedside in hospital, avoiding each other in the corridors. Their mother no longer able to speak, just looking at them imploring. Carrie stony and dry-eyed, Bridget faffing around trying to make her comfortable, to persuade her to eat, pleading with the nurses, the doctor to adjust her drugs.

Carrie snapping at her outside: *it's too late*. Bridget losing it and shouting back. *Who are you angry with? She did her best.*

Sometimes it isn't good enough.

And now Carrie was beside her, grabbing her arm, shouting in her ear. Her hands were strong, her grip was so tight it hurt and Bridget pulled away. Her mind was blank.

'She's dying,' she'd said to Carrie, in that hospital corridor. 'Come back in and pretend, if you have to.' Carrie's face closed and angry. 'Come back in or I'll never forgive you.'

And then they'd both gone back in. Staring at each other across their mother's body.

Carrie wasn't shouting now, her voice was low and trembling, close to Bridget's ear and Bridget could smell the fear on her. 'Bridge, please. Talk to me.'

Without saying anything Bridget stepped to the garage door and pulled it back to where it had been, half closed. When she turned back Carrie was there on the ground, half kneeling, her face pale, upturned, pleading.

As she walked back towards Carrie, it was as if she was walking on air or water, and it came to Bridget with a revelation made up not of the here and now but from out of the past that was concentrated now in this damp dark space, a hundred clues she hadn't seen: something had happened to Carrie, too. Not him, but someone else, some other time, some other place. Why hadn't she seen before? She came down beside her, feeling grit under her knees.

'What the fuck?' said Carrie reverently, still gazing at her, head moving to follow her sister's. She was pale, drawn, hungover: the drinking was getting to her, thought Bridget, miles away, floating.

'Bridget?' said Carrie. 'Sis?' Then she looked back at the body, leaning a little way over him, a hand coming to her mouth. 'I know him,' she said slowly.

And then the world crashed back in on Bridget, the stink, the feel of his wool trousers under her hand. 'No,' she said urgently, pulling Carrie away, trying to block her. Trying to get between her and him, lying there in his stained trousers.

Carrie shook her off, leaning over him still. 'It's that pervy violin teacher. Jesus, how long is it? Twenty-odd years.'

Pervy. Had she known, all along? Bridget let her go. It must be only guessing. What good would knowing it all do her? It was enough that Bridget knew: the detail of it crowded her head, it had found a chink and flooded inside. The light through the curtains he'd drawn before turning to her, smiling, the silver frames on his mantelpiece, the smell of his breath. Stubble on his chin and the gasp she had had to suppress when she was taken hold of, rough, splayed like a chicken on a butcher's counter. Chop, chop, chop.

'He came after me,' was all that came out of Bridget's mouth. 'It was – it was an accident—' Carrie's eyes on her. Tell the truth. 'I did it,' she said, the words sitting there. 'He came after me. I couldn't do anything else.'

Dust motes hung in the air between them, dancing in the sparkling light under the garage door. Pale in the dark Carrie examined her and then, slowly, she nodded.

'I helped you carry him,' she said, chewing her lip, calculating. No questions about when, how. Why.

A sweat broke over Bridget, up her back, her neck. 'I'm sorry,' she said. 'You came along at the wrong time. What could I do? There's no CCTV, no one will have seen. I'll burn the box in case there's any of your—'

Carrie just shook her head, impatient, palms up to block her. 'All right,' she said. 'What next? What the fuck do we do next?'

We. 'You need to keep out of this now,' Bridget said, keeping her voice as steady as she could make it. 'I'm not involving you. Go back home to Ella, you haven't seen anything.'

'Are you fucking kidding me?' said Carrie, hissing the words, pushing herself back on her haunches in the half dark, ready for a fight. The body between them. 'I'm not leaving you alone with this. My law-abiding fucking sister? You haven't got a fucking clue.'

'You can't,' said Bridget. But Carrie just shook her head, finished.

'Try and fucking stop me. Look—' and as Bridget tried again the sound of a car starting up beyond the garage

134

door silenced them both. They held very still, waiting. It moved off, receded. 'Get Matt?' said Carrie, searching her face. Matt who sorted everything. Fixed the bikes, the car, the guttering. 'Bridget. Tell Matt?'

'No,' said Bridget, and at last she was certain, instantly. She could unblock a toilet, plumb in a washing machine, schlep boxes of stock: she could do this. 'Never. Not Matt. Not Finn. I mean you've got to promise—' *Never.* 'This happened so they wouldn't know. About – about—' she stopped. 'Do you understand?'

'No,' said Carrie, rethinking. But still not asking for explanations. Know about what?

'All right,' Carrie said, her kid sister, who ran on adrenaline. 'Let's start from the beginning.' And Bridget began to shake her head but it turned out she was asking a different question.

'What were you doing? When I came in.'

Subsiding, Bridget told her quickly. About the mobile phone, about lying awake wondering what the phone might tell anyone who was looking for him. Anyone like the police.

'Yes,' said Carrie, serious now. 'I get that. OK then. You want me to do it? To look?'

They did it together. It was easier, with someone else. With Carrie across from her, so matter of fact, moving and turning him, thrusting her hands in one pocket after another without even a change of expression. Looking at the swirl of hair at her cropped crown, the white tips of her small ears, Bridget remembered something she'd long since forgotten: Carrie working in a care home as a teenager one Christmas and just shrugging about the gross aspects, the arse-wiping and spoon-feeding, the visits from the funeral home. And she'd always been a bit like this. Curious, nerveless, bold.

And in the end, ten years ago, Carrie had come back in from the corridor to that hospital bedroom where Mum lay: she'd sat the other side of the bed from Bridget and had taken Mum's limp hand from where it rested on the sheet and kissed it. Their mother had opened her eyes and smiled at her, a lopsided smile. Had Carrie meant it? Bridget hadn't known: it only mattered, after all, that their mother thought she had.

Methodically they searched in the dark: it probably only took five, six minutes, and the only sound their breathing. His trousers were old fashioned, with buttoned pockets at the back. A small pocket she'd missed inside the jacket.

The rigor had gone off, his body was showing signs. Blood pooling black where he had been left to lie.

He had once been alive. He was someone's son. Bridget tried out the thought: it left her cold. He'd gone. That was all that mattered.

Who had loved him? No one loved him.

There was no mobile phone.

In the kitchen the mugs still sat there on the draining board, Finn's cereal bowl, congealing in the sun.

Their rubber gloves were in a bucket at the back door. Bridget had made Carrie wash her hands, anyway, then she had washed hers. What the hell did they know about DNA traces? Bridget was standing at the table unable to sit or settle, her mind running, round and round.

All they could do was minimise the chances. Be thorough.

Carrie was filling the kettle: Bridget saw her head lift

as she eyed the bottles, ranged along the top of the cabinets: a dusty bottle of something bright green; gin, vodka. Matt drank the odd beer, he wasn't a spirits man. Bridget drank gin and tonic when they went to the pub, but she always made herself stop at one. It seemed safer. Safe, though, was a concept whose meaning now eluded her. Maybe she should have gone Carrie's route: run straight at what scared her. Run at it shouting and waving your arms. 'Everything's got a risk attached,' said Carrie, as if she knew what Bridget was thinking. 'What we did—' and she paused, not looking round, looking down. Changed tack. 'Everything's got risk. You've got to just keep going.'

What we did.

'It could have fallen out in the shop,' said Bridget.

'You'd have seen it,' said Carrie, looking back over her shoulder now, and Bridget knew she was right. She slowed her thoughts down: why? What had made her think of the phone, in the middle of the night? Because of something Matt had said. The secretaries up at Rose Hill saying, of Carmichael, that his excuse for not returning calls had been, he left his phone at home.

He had been of an age not to be dependent on it. *Maybe* – and as she had the thought, Carrie spoke it. Slopping boiling water on top of teabags with her back to Bridget. Turning to stand, casual against the counter and a spoon in her hand bearing an unsqueezed teabag. It dripped.

'He was an old codger,' Carrie said, shrugging. 'He'd have left it at home, wouldn't he?'

She set the mugs on the table, grey and unappetising. Carrie was many things, but domestic angel wasn't one of them: once upon a time they'd have bickered over the dripping teabag, the scum on the tea. Bridget scolding her. Back in fairyland.

'D'you know where he lived?' Carrie pulled out a chair and sat across the table from her.

Shocked, Bridget shook her head, staring down at the mug, tightening her hands around it. Shocked at the thought that she would have wanted to know where Carmichael lived. It felt as though Carrie was asking her if she had a relationship with him. 'No,' she said, in a low voice. 'He'd only just turned up, but I wouldn't have – wouldn't have wanted—' A house somewhere, with all his stuff in it. She swerved the thought, stopped. Changed direction.

'Look,' said Bridget. 'I can handle it now.' It. The body lying in the dust, behind the van. 'I want you to go home.'

Carrie just shook her head, merry in the sunlit kitchen. They might have been having a coffee morning, if anyone looked through the window. 'Isn't that how you got into this crap?' she said cheerfully. 'Not telling? Not involving other people?'

'I'm not going to the police,' said Bridget immediately.

'No,' said Carrie. 'You're not. We have to think about this.' She was calm.

Not a word, still, about why he died. Bridget didn't mind that: let it be just a fact. An animal dead on the veldt, one of those nature documentaries. 'We've got to get rid of him,' she said. 'Quickly. Find somewhere—' she searched for the place, news reports, true crime. Where? The ones you read about, the body had been found. The pale sun filled the kitchen window, lighting every corner. 'But – maybe we should wait till dark.'

'Yeah.' Carrie nodded, lifted the tea to her lips, scowled.

'We can't go off on one, panicking, can we?' She leaned back in the chair. 'You were always the methodical one,' she said. 'You were the one who fussed around getting the detail right, doing my plaits for school, making sure the parting was completely straight.'

'I didn't want everything to fall apart,' said Bridget, helpless now. 'Back then.' Getting Carrie ready for school seemed another life. Hanging on to the detail, let the big stuff take care of itself. But the big stuff got bigger

'No,' said Carrie. 'You took care of the big stuff. That's what you did here. Now we have to make sure you don't get caught. What time does Matt get home?'

'Six thirty,' said Bridget. 'Well, usually. Finn – well a bit earlier. If he's not out with—'

'I can handle Finn,' said Carrie. 'He's away with the fairies at the moment, anyway, isn't he? The important thing is to do it before Matt gets back.' And suddenly she yawned, a yawn so wide it split her little pale face. 'I'm knackered,' she said, and stood up abruptly. 'I'm going to go upstairs and sleep this off.'

On cue Bridget got up too, began to clear the mugs, opened the dishwasher, mechanically beginning to restack after Finn. Already thinking about it. Build a bonfire, plenty of leaves after all, burn the gloves, the fleece, the trainers: before or after? Keep them in a bin bag.

Get to work.

But when she turned around Carrie was still in the doorway, motionless, and her face was different. Closed.

And then suddenly Bridget knew why. And she hadn't seen it. Too busy not eating. Too busy hiding up her own backside.

'That's how you know,' said Bridget. 'Isn't it? It's why you didn't need to ask me – about him.' The merest jerk of her head in the direction of the garage. The big door pulled down now, and locked for good measure.

Carrie's mouth turned tough. She said nothing. 'You believed me, straight off, you understood why I did it,' said Bridget, intent now. 'About him. Without asking.'

There was a silence and then a long sigh broke it. 'Do you remember Doug?' said her little sister, and moved at last, tipping her head to rest against the doorframe. Leaning there as casual as if they'd dreamed it all: the light slanting into the dark garage, the smell in their nostrils as they worked. They'd taped the debris of the polythene and cardboard back around him with duct tape and rolled him in the length of old carpet Matt had been saving to keep weeds down, and put him back in the van.

Doug. Did she? 'The guy who went out with Mum? That Doug?'

Why?

Carrie nodded, the mug to her lips.

'Fat bloke, bald head, red face?' said Bridget.

'Like he'd been boiled,' said Carrie, expressionless.

And suddenly Bridget did remember. Doug came sharply into focus: his red face behind Mum's at the hospital bedside. Bridget had been in hospital most of that year, the mental hospital, though they didn't call it that now. Juvenile psych unit, where the anorexics and self-harmers go.

'You remember he just disappeared?' Bridget shook her head, ashamed. 'I stabbed him,' said Carrie, meditatively. 'Just through the hand, defending myself: he came into my room after Mum had gone to work. I saw it coming, I had hidden a knife under my pillow. She'd asked him to give me a lift to school. I said I would go to the police unless he fucked off.' And then she stood up, and yawned again. She crossed to the door, then paused. 'Get someone to close up for you, say you have an errand,' she said. 'Think of somewhere to get rid of him, permanently. Somewhere he won't be found by a dog walker.'

'He could have killed you,' said Bridget, thinking: my kid sister. Don't hurt her.

'I could have killed *him*,' said Carrie. And she was on the stairs and climbing them as steadily as if she'd just said goodnight.

Chapter Thirteen

As she turned into the lane on her bike Bridget could see Laura up there grumpy on the doorstep, shapeless in pink layers against the cold. She could only have been waiting ten minutes – but Bridget was never late.

She locked the bicycle and hurried towards Laura, starting to apologise. Registering how different the girl looked when she was unhappy: everything seemed to change, even her fine golden hair sat flatter and duller. She was unmade-up too, which wasn't like her.

'Is everything all right?' said Bridget, reaching past her with the key, poised to kill the alarm, peering through the glass. Last night. *What if—* For a mad moment she thought, she imagined him still in there, lying on the floor.

'That man was here,' said Laura, arms folded indignantly on top of her pink-muffled belly. Bridget paused, key still raised. The dark shop interior was empty, just the rug was slightly askew on the pale-painted floor.

'Man?' she said, not quite trusting herself to say more than the single word.

'Customer, yesterday?' Laura's neat little mouth pursed. 'Old bloke buying something for his wife. Or was it the day before?' Crossly. 'I don't know. Anyway, he wanted to bring it back. Changed his mind.'

And conspiratorially Laura rolled her eyes: their favourite topic. The customer who changed her mind. *It's just not me*, they'd chant in unison as the door closed behind her. Or her husband didn't like it. What could you do but smile? Never mind. Bridget tried to remember the man, and couldn't.

The key went into the lock and Bridget punched in the numbers. Remembering last night and the alarm going off: three strikes – false alarms – and you lost your police call-out. And your insurance. Least of her problems, though: the last thing Bridget wanted was a police call-out. The door opened and they were inside.

Turning on the lights, one after the other, Bridget paced out the space, trying not to actually sniff. The days when she and Laura used to moan about fussy customers seemed such a long time ago.

'Why didn't he wait?' she said, leaning into the tiny kitchen, down to search the corners. No phone. She looked back at Laura over her shoulder, the girl standing beside the sofa unwinding a long scarf disconsolately.

'He wanted to talk to the owner,' Laura said. The scarf, a pink mohair poncho, a coat: the layers came off and were discarded impatiently on to the sofa. Emerging from them she looked flushed.

'But he didn't wait for me?'

'He didn't seem like he was in a hurry,' said Laura, frowning. 'Just passing, he said.' She scooped up the bundle of her stuff and began to walk – ungainly now if not quite a waddle, she was too dignified for that – to the stockroom. It was hard, the end of pregnancy: Bridget remembered that much. Heaving yourself around, always untidy. Laura loved to be neat and tidy.

Her due date was less than a month away. Bridget didn't know much about her husband, the sainted Nick, only that she met him on Match.com, they got all lovey dovey straight away, he wanted babies as much as she did. A dream of a man, no commitment-phobe, liked things just so, just like Laura. Bridget followed her cautiously to the stock-room.

'Let me,' she said, taking the bundle off her and Laura brightened finally.

'Why don't you nip next door for a paper,' said Bridget encouragingly to shift her, only belatedly thinking, she's not going to be nipping, exactly, poor Laura. But she needn't have worried: the stockroom was innocently tidy.

Bridget was grateful, really, for Laura going on about him for most of the rest of the morning, her sainted Nick. Her pale face softening, settling back into its blithe pink smoothness. Cooing.

He didn't make her tea in the morning, though. 'Oh, *no*,' Laura had said, almost horrified when Bridget had ventured Matt's morning tea as evidence of his love. 'I do kitchen things.'

It was soothing, the babble. Where Nick would be today, the new company car, the birth plan. The sainted Nick, she'd known for all of a year, was it now? Closer to two.

Did you have to mistrust everyone? Maybe you did. Bridget thought Matt had cured her of that.

But a baby always changed something, didn't it? Bridget had been lucky. It had been like a counterweight holding her down, a washing line safely tethered, the small sandbag-weight of Finn in her arms. She felt a pang at that thought, Finn slipping in and out of the house these days, and one day he wouldn't come back.

A big delivery came in before lunchtime, Christmas knitwear, and Bridget still hadn't broached the subject with Laura of leaving early. Every time she thought she saw an opening Laura seemed to change the subject, from nursery colours to what she was making for tea, or waterbirths.

Hauling boxes across the floor while Laura sat, Bridget set to clearing the stockroom to make space, scanning the dusty floor as she did it. Still no phone – but when she pushed the rolling rail aside, she saw a stain.

It was like, one time, she'd found a little lump in her breast: for a moment her mind jumped to, *well, no, of course it isn't* – before forcing herself to make a doctor's appointment at which it had turned out to be something called a breast mouse. She hadn't told Matt. She knelt, leaned closer, made herself examine the stain. Head down, among the swinging garments in their plastic covers. It was blood. Brownish.

Steadily she crossed the shop floor to the kitchen and got out bleach and disinfectant: from the sofa Laura's head moved, her mouth opened. 'No,' said Bridget, making herself smile. 'It's.' Keeping on walking, reduced to monosyllables and nonsense.

She was kneeling again and scrubbing when she heard

the phone go in the shop, and Laura taking an agonising four rings to get to it, across from the sofa. Why did everything have to get her heart racing? And then Laura was talking, she was bright, talking easily. Chatty. It would be an agency, ad sales.

It was Matt.

He wasn't at work; he had gone home.

Bridget smiled at Laura as she passed over the handset, to make her go away.

He was in the garage.

'Bridge?' He sounded bewildered; worried, almost. It was what she had always loved about Matt – one of the things, one of the many things – that he was consistent, reliable, everything in its place. But when things weren't—

'Sorry, I came home for a tool, this kid, student, needed a hand with his bike—'

Had Bridget even breathed, since he had begun to speak?

'Have you seen my needlenose pliers?' There it was again, that edge of anxiety.

Needlenose, needlenose, the silly word went round in her head. 'I—'

'I know they're here somewhere,' he went on, not waiting. 'Have you moved the van?'

Quick. Quick. She knew Matt, thorough to a fault, brilliant at finding things. Methodical doesn't come near it, and obsessive.

She heard a voice in the background, Matt's hand over the receiver. Carrie?

In her head it was like a landslip, all tumbling out at once: his face, if he found out. All of it. The ramifications. In a way she was more terrified of saying the words: he raped me. That old man raped me. She was more frightened of that than of him finding the body. Matt made me clean, Matt saved me. She could picture Matt taking a step back from her. That would be all it took.

She made herself breathe. *If you faint, we're all fucked*, said Carrie in her head.

'Hold on,' said Matt and his hand was over the receiver. But she could hear Carrie's voice, not the words but the tone. Carrie trying to distract him; but Carrie didn't know him well enough, she could say the wrong thing. They had to think of something to stop him searching.

'Matt?' Raising her voice – across the room Laura, straightening the rails, a dark red party dress under her hand, paused to look over – and he was back, and in the same moment the idea came to her.

'I've got them here,' Bridget said quickly.

'What?' His surprise was more than that, it was on the edge of disbelief, he would push her if she couldn't think fast.

'I borrowed them, something got stuck in a light fitting, tweezers would have done, but—' Bridget stopped herself, babbling. 'I'll track them down and bring them over to the university this afternoon.'

He sounded faintly bewildered now. 'Sure,' he said. 'Sure.'

She'd never lied to him before. Or did omission count as lying? Was it all a lie? It occurred to her that she had to find them now, or buy a new pair, and he would know the difference if she did that. 'See you later, then.'

She hung up and Laura was staring at her, her hand still on the soft dark dress, what was that colour, ruby red?

'Could you stay this afternoon after all, Laura?' she said,

lightly. Laura shrugged, curious. Bridget had to remain calm: she pulled a face. 'Men and their tools,' she said. 'I lost his precious pliers, brought them here and can't think for the life of me where I put them.' Treachery upon treachery, Matt would never have a go at her for such a thing and here she was pretending he was one of those husbands, inviting complicity.

And Laura smiled, absently agreeing, starting on some long, boring story about Nick's shed and her not being allowed in, but she wasn't interested in Bridget any more, she was back to gazing down at the rails, dreaming past pregnancy to a day when she would be out to dinner with Nick and dressed in strapless red.

Back on her knees in the stockroom to finish putting away the knitwear, hasty but efficient, it had to be done right or they'd never be able to find anything again – but what if it's all over? Why do I still care about where the Christmas cashmere is? – Bridget worked out a plan: like she said to Laura. She'd borrowed the pliers, then she lost them.

On the doorstep, standing in the doorway with her arms folded over the bump as Bridget climbed on the bike, Laura said, 'What if the man comes back, about his wife's present?'

'Give him a refund,' said Bridget, seeing Laura's eyes widen at the recklessness. 'I authorise it.'

Laura pulled her plump lower lip between her teeth, unsure. 'He was very insistent,' she said, 'About talking to the manager.'

Bridget remembered only the man's shoulders, beefy, the way he had moved, a kind of shuffle. He'd made the decision too abruptly, and was going to blame it on them.

148

Stepping across the bike, itching to get going, she made herself smile. 'He'll have to come back tomorrow.' And she was off, with Laura's eyes on her back: Bridget was fifty yards away when she heard the ping of the door that meant Laura had gone back inside.

Where were they, though? The pliers. She didn't want to think of those long minutes she and Carrie had spent kneeling in the dust. They'd wrapped him in the old carpet. Had the pliers got knocked on to the floor?

The bike bumped on the cobbles: Justine from the jeweller's was on her doorstep, watching her pass. There seemed to be a face in every window, and all of them peering out at her. Traffic roared past at the foot of the lane and Bridget had to brake outside the music shop. She turned her head away so as not to see the window display, the gold flash of brass, sheet music on stands. Would he have been in there? Might he have stopped in there with Isabel on the way to buy that dress – or to pay that last call on Bridget? A bus squeaked to a halt in front of her, blocking her path and she gave in, and turned her head.

It looked down at heel, the sheet music dog-eared, a lot of cheap guitars hanging along the top of the window, a couple of trumpets and a banjo. Not his kind of place: he'd hated folk musicians. *Dirt under their fingernails.* She tried to block the memory, thinking sideways, upwards, anywhere but there. He wouldn't have gone in there, and that's the end of it.

The tool shop was on the way out of town towards Rose Hill, on a busy corner with a trade stationer's. It was a cheerful place, a smell of rubber and oil and neat rows of tools. A shuffling queue of builders and painter and decorators, chatting easily, taking time off the job: it felt so safe. Another world, a treasure house, a place where all problems could be fixed. She flagged down an old bloke with nostril hair and fingers seamed with black and asked him about needlenose pliers. Looking round the big, dark storeroom as he talked she saw rolls of heavy polythene, saws, zip ties, duct tape. Gallons of paintstripper. And then quite abruptly her head was crowded with images of body disposal, cutting, binding – maybe while she was here she should – she sensed something. Was the old man looking at her strangely, drawing bushy eyebrows together? There were news reports about that, too, weren't there? CCTV images of stocky men leaving hardware stores equipped with knives and saws. *No. Don't.*

The needlenose pliers were expensive, and Bridget hesitated with the credit card in her hand, then paid in cash. As she mounted the bike the towers of Rose Hill were far off, beyond their quiet little close, looming misty in the pale blue November light.

When she got home Bridget called up the stairs, but there was no answer, and cautious on the stairs she peered into Carrie's room to see it empty, the duvet hanging off the bed. She stuck her bike in the garage and got into the van, for speed. She stuck to the limit, though, all the way. Don't get a ticket, don't attract anyone's attention.

As she drove Bridget tried not to think too hard about her story: he would know if it sounded rehearsed. Just be upset that you lost them, and he won't notice the rest. He hated her to be upset. And it wasn't hard: just seeing his kind, anxious face at the door to his office (on the ground floor, she'd always been grateful she didn't have to brave

150

the cramped lifts and never more so than now) almost made her cry.

'Couldn't find them,' she said, on the edge of tears, holding out the paper package from the hardware store. 'I drove via the hardware shop. I know how much you use them so I—'

The furrows in his forehead deepened and Matt ushered her into his small, tidy office. The last thing she needed: give her an inch and she'd be sobbing, sobbing, she'd say it all. He sighed, took her by the shoulders and sat her down. 'I'll make you a coffee,' he said. 'You didn't need to come out, you know.' Regarding her, then the pliers, perplexed.

'I think Laura might have chucked them away by accident,' she said, fiddling with a scrap of tissue in her lap. Treacherous: she didn't look up until he had turned away.

Matt had an eccentric old coffee machine in the corner, his pride and joy, a thing that bubbled, with a glass balloon and snaking tubes. Bridget sat, obedient, looking out through the big window while he cranked and loaded it. The window, a blessing in the dim hessian-walled room, whose décor was unchanged since the seventies, extended across one wall of the office: Matt washed it himself, because the budget didn't extend that far and he liked his view. And today Bridget agreed with him: from its circle of scrubby grass the brutalist fountain burbled and sparkled in a shaft of clean light falling between the towers. She couldn't remember when she had last come out here. It had felt like a place of safety, once upon a time: a modest, quiet English oasis on a hill, just light and water and shelter. The perfect setting for Matt.

He set down the coffee in a Perspex cup and saucer. 'How long is Carrie planning on staying, d'you think?' he said, easily.

Bridget sipped. Remembered how surprised she always was that the machine produced nice coffee. 'A couple of days?' she said cautiously.

Matt nodded, leaning against the window frame with his cup. 'Nice for Finn,' he said. 'They get along. It *can* be hard to get through to him these days, you're right. Is it just his age?'

Even distracted, she heard worry in Matt's voice and for the first time since she'd sat down, Bridget looked up at him properly. The murmur of their voices at the back door that early, getting ready to get on their bikes, came back to her.

'He's online a lot,' said Matt meditatively. 'Playing with gamers all over the place.' Shook his head a little. 'I mean – I see that here. That stuff. There's some students – well. Some of them I have to warn over the amount of data they're using and when they come in, asking for more bandwidth – for some of them it's an addiction.'

'Not Finn, though?' She searched Matt's face.

He shrugged. 'I don't think so, no. No. But – it's – well, it's an unknown quantity, isn't it? How that stuff works on the brain.'

'Yes,' said Bridget and nodded, and for a second everything cleared: what else mattered, after all? Finn was what mattered.

'There's the girlfriend, though,' she offered, the cup between her hands and Matt smiled, nodded, and at last sighed and turned to set his cup down.

'Sure,' he said. 'It's just his age.'

Finn and her and Matt, the steady little tripod of their lives.

In the piazza, striped with light and shade, there was movement. Bridget stood up, slowly, reaching for her cup and took a step close to the window. 'Pretty out there today,' she said, her back to Matt. A slight figure, pushing a bicycle, came out of the shadow and into the shaft of light and stopped. A girl, wandering, a girl too young to be on the campus.

It was Isabel.

She looked fragile, lost, her pale spun hair like a halo in the sun. She was staring up at the towers.

In the same moment the question and its answer came into Bridget's head. *What is she doing here? She must have come to find him.*

Slowly Bridget made herself turn her back on the window, looking into the room.

Bridget couldn't say anything about Carmichael, however much she wanted to know. She couldn't betray any interest, or point to Isabel and say, I know that girl.

She held out the cup. Something was still bothering him: she made herself smile up into his face. 'Better get back,' she said. He took the cup and set it down carefully and when he turned back – knowing as she did it that it would puzzle him even more but unable to stop herself – Bridget put her arms around him, just for a second, just to touch him, to breathe him in. She felt him go still inside her embrace: his hand patting her shoulder, helpless.

'Sorry,' she said, breaking away, making herself laugh. *Stay here*, she thought, inside this room, with him. But she walked to the door, instead.

153

Matt was behind her, but to her relief there was no sign of the bike, or Isabel. 'Thanks for the coffee,' she said, but Matt shifted a fraction to look over her shoulder. Then reluctantly – frowning – lifted a hand to greet someone, and she dared turn to look and see, who it was.

No one. A door closing across the piazza, in the base of the tower opposite.

'I'll walk you to the van.'

The car park sat a way off from the towers, set into the hill with more levels dug out below. She'd found a space in the open air, though and they were almost there, she was almost home free, the towers above them now and the clean, smooth hill sloping down to the gatehouse, when Matt said his name. Standing with his back to the van and to her, looking down the hill toward the elegant, slate-roofed building behind its neatly trimmed hedging. A Victorian rectory marooned in a seventies landscape.

And then, just as she thought the danger had passed there was his name, on Matt's lips.

'He still hasn't turned up,' said Matt, without turning, hands in his pockets. 'Dr Carmichael.'

'Really?' Did she have to sound so strangled? 'What makes you think of him?'

Matt turned round then, and he looked surprised, as though he'd thought he was alone. 'Oh,' he said vaguely, 'the bloke I waved to, across the piazza? That was Alan Timpson. Carmichael's mate.'

The white van was driving too fast on the single-track road and Gill had to sidestep on to the verge in a hurry. She swivelled with forefinger raised but the van was long

154

gone. White van man, except she was pretty sure it had been a woman.

Half a mile ahead of her the towers sat black against the sky, the nearest of them glinting down one side, light refracted at angles off the glass: Gill had got off the bus too soon. She'd asked the driver if he stopped at Rose Hill and he'd grunted: that should have told her, he couldn't be arsed one way or the other.

Not very investigative, failing to ask the bus driver where her stop was. Not very hardboiled, mistaking him for someone who could give a toss, out here in the middle of fucking nowhere. But Gill couldn't afford to take any more taxis: yesterday had been the luxury. There were, she thought wistfully, journalists with expense accounts out there somewhere, and fearless reporters whose editors sighed and said, *I'll give you twenty-four hours.* Reporters with their own cars, yet. Her arse was in the grinder if Steve even found out she was here.

The sun wasn't warm but it was bright, bleaching out the expanse of grass ahead of her as she trudged, and the figure just disappearing into the shadow of the towers was a little stick man, a Giacometti. Her phone blipped with an incoming text: she cursed, most of her alerts were turned off, but she looked anyway. It was from a Tinder date from two weeks back who'd just walked away from her on the pavement outside the wine bar he'd chosen when she said, Thanks but no thanks.

He'd been good-looking. The Tinder date. Proper job, a barrister. Not too old. Witty. She couldn't have identified exactly why she'd turned him down but she'd known she was right then and she certainly knew now. She'd meant to block and delete his number, but her mind had been somewhere else. She deleted the message but not before she'd seen what it said.

Frigid bitch.

It was two, three in the afternoon, so he was unlikely to be pissed. He had drunk one glass of wine in the bar when they met, and only that one so that he could have an erudite conversation with the maître d' about vineyards in Stellenbosch, or wherever. A man who sat at his privileged little desk in the middle of the day, his leather-topped desk in his panelled chambers, and typed in those words. She sighed. *Great.*

She liked Giacometti. And Modigliani: something about the way their heads tilted and the long necks. You couldn't say that to a Tinder date. I've got two nieces and I like Modigliani. *And actually I like fucking with the lights on and my legs over your shoulders but you're not going to find that out.* Psycho.

The walk was doing her good, though. That's what she told herself. Gill had been walking a lot since she gave up the gym – to the newspaper from Kensal Rise on the days she went in, a good four miles each way and time to think, watching kids on their way to school, people's faces on buses. It had suddenly made her feel sick, everything about the gym. The woman with a stringy neck running, running, running on the treadmill beside her at seven in the morning and giving Gill a wild-eyed look when she tried to smile. The men's eyes ranging round the room, settling on their own reflection in the big mirror, for preference.

Her nieces were three and five. They climbed on top of

Gill on the settee when she visited, laying their hot little heads on her belly, making her do funny voices.

She was at the towers, now, and it was cold in the shade. She stood a moment beside the fountain, orientating herself, working the place out a bit. The ground floor of each tower would be occupied by communal areas and admin, she calculated, on the evidence. Janitor, bar, the computer geek's office at the foot of one of these. Had that been him, the Giacometti? Students up high, so they'd have something to stare out of the window at when they were pretending to work.

Gill's own university years – down on the South Coast, rowdy, scruffy campus on the edge of a party town, nothing like this place – were a bit of a blur, it had to be said. History and French: she couldn't remember much of the French but she still had friends from back then. One of them had made a lot of money in magazines – enough to retire to some island in the Caribbean – and he still asked her to marry him every couple of years. In a jokey sort of way.

The trouble was, single blokes her age were mostly single for a reason. The same, of course, must apply to women. Too busy: too busy having fun, or not having fun, or working or hiding. Too busy on a crusade no one wants you on, not even the victims.

A door opened in the dark glass at the foot of one of the towers and she saw inside. A little, crowded, scruffy office – and a white-faced kid on work experience. Bingo.

Chapter Fourteen

It had got dark very fast: driving inland one minute the sky had been a vivid cold green at the wooded horizon ahead of them, then grey, then black. It was freezing outside. Three of them in the van: her and Carrie in the front, silent. Carmichael's body was in the back.

Bridget had been sitting in the van in the lane behind the shop staring at her phone when Carrie had called her, home from an afternoon in the pub, it sounded like.

Bridget had just decided it wasn't sensible to google his name. They could check that stuff.

Carrie's voice was tense and dead. 'It's freaking me out being here with him,' she said. This was how Carrie panicked: she froze.

'OK,' said Bridget. 'I'm on my way.'

She had to go into the shop first, though, or Laura would worry: wearily she had locked the van and hurried inside. The shop was quiet – empty, actually – and Laura looking up from her magazine on the sofa but Bridget didn't even have the time to care: another bad day, and so close to Christmas. VAT due next week.

'Something's come up,' Bridget said, smiling carefully.

Laura looked up at her quite composed then: she'd had time to do her make-up in the lull, because she was all pink and white and starry-lashed again. 'Sure,' she said.

'Lock up and bring the keys back tomorrow?' said Bridget. 'I'll use the spares in the morning.'

Carrie had been waiting for her in the front garden, hugging herself, lips bloodless in the cold. She was wearing some punk T-shirt and a cheap fake leather jacket over her ripped jeans. Not enough clothes to keep a cat warm. Bridget found herself rubbing her sister's arms, exasperated, the two of them standing out in the middle of the close, arms round each other. It was four o'clock. They had two hours before Matt got home. It came to her that seeing that man, the friend of Carmichael's, had made him angry: he'd been angry when she saw him last.

Alan Timpson. The name refused to go away, lodged in her gut like something that would make her vomit.

Standing there in the shadow of the towers beside the van that afternoon, Bridget had stopped still at Matt's words. *Carmichael's mate*: he didn't have mates. 'Timpson,' she repeated, numbly.

'He was going into Tower Two?' said Matt, turning to look up at them.

The towers had names as well, but no one used them. It was Tower One the girl had jumped from, all that time ago. It was the tower where Matt had his office: no one had jumped since, Matt often said that, disapproving, when

159

people mentioned it. He had refused to be superstitious too, when they allocated his office.

'I didn't see him,' Bridget mumbled, but Matt hadn't seemed to notice that she couldn't get the words out properly.

'Yeah, well, he waved, I nodded.' Matt was cool. 'People can't just disappear whenever they fancy it. He got Carmichael the job, he's taking a bit of flak.'

'Doesn't anyone . . .' Her voice silly and high now, hoping he couldn't hear the falseness. 'Hasn't anyone got any idea where he's gone?'

'Probably swanned off to Salzburg or Glyndebourne,' Matt said. Still apparently indifferent, but she knew when he was angry. *He's on my side*, the hope sprang, foolish, for a fraction of a second. *No.* He can't know. Never.

'Timpson was the one who recruited him,' Matt had gone on, hands in his pockets, looking back at his place of work up the hill. 'They're old mates. From way back. Oxford, probably.' There was still something in his voice that wasn't like Matt, and the longer it went on the more anxious it made her. As if there was something he wasn't saying: but Matt was always upfront. Her Matt.

She pushed it, despite herself. 'What?' she said. 'You don't like him.'

Matt, still staring away from her, had shrugged. 'He's rude to the secretaries. Carmichael was too. You can always tell an arsehole when they blame the secretaries for their fuckups.'

She'd fumbled, stupidly grateful that that was all there was to it, just Matt's chivalry, with the key in the van's lock then. A quick peck, and he started back to his office.

160

Almost at the foot of the hill in the van, Bridget had passed Isabel, on her bike, recognisable even in the uncertain light: the flossy hair, the little colt legs freewheeling. As she overtook, slowly, Bridget had seen the girl's face, pale and set and as she looked in her rearview mirror she saw she had no lights on the bicycle. With a tight feeling in her chest she hesitated, reluctant, then something took over, a fierce need to know what the girl knew. She indicated and pulled in. Wound down her window and stuck her head out.

'Isabel?' she called backwards, her voice high and anxious. Isabel wobbled to a halt and looked at her uncertainly, not quite recognising her.

'You came into the shop,' she said. 'Do you remember? The dress?' She didn't need to mention Carmichael. This was between her and Isabel. Isabel nodded slowly. 'Haven't you got any lights?' she asked. Isabel hung her head, fiddling with a bit of tape on her handlebars. 'Can I give you a lift?' The girl looked worried now. Hanging back. A woman in a van. 'You do remember me?' said Bridget gently, winding the window down further. 'From the shop. My husband works at the university, I saw you there. It's fine if you don't want a lift. Have you got far to go?'

Isabel hesitated and in that moment Bridget willed her to get back on her bike and freewheel away. But she nodded, frowning. 'Thank you,' she said.

They put the bike in the back, Bridget laying it down gently on the metal floor. Thinking, *she shouldn't be doing this. She's too easily led. Too eager not to offend.* Too late now, she'd made the offer, it had been accepted. Bridget had to remind herself she wasn't the predator, but the chime it set up still jangled.

'Where to?' Isabel named an affluent suburb, a couple of miles on, and sat back, silent, her hands folded, obedient, in her lap.

It would have been better to drive past. Everything she did seemed to stick her tighter to Carmichael. Whose body had been in the back, where Isabel's bike was.

The silence grew: sensing anxiety, Bridget asked Isabel if she was all right. A moment of quiet before she answered, in an undertone. 'I have to take the dress back,' she said. 'My mum and dad said so.'

Good for them, thought Bridget, that tall, lean serious pair, good for them. 'That's fine,' she said. 'That's nothing to worry about. I can take it back, Isabel.'

Out of the corner of her eye she saw Isabel fidget, 'Yes, but—' still hesitant, still wary, and for all Bridget approved that instinct the other side of her wanted to know what she was going to say. 'Don't worry,' she said again, gently. Hating herself, because the gentleness was a trick. She waited a beat, and another. 'But what?' Glancing quickly sideways, a mild look or inquiry.

'I – I haven't managed to get hold of him yet.' Looking straight ahead. 'I have tried,' pleading, and she could hear it in Isabel's voice, a tiny echo of her own younger self. *She's anxious, she wants to know she hasn't done something to offend him. She wants to please everyone. Him, her parents, even me, even me, even this woman in the shop she hardly knows.* 'I sent an email. His colleague Alan – his colleague said he was unwell.' And it was still in her voice, that wounded note, trembling on the brink of rejection, not knowing how to be good.

'Alan?' said Bridget, hearing a kind of roar in her ears, 'Who—' but she managed to stop herself, to change tack.

'Never mind,' she said again. 'Just bring the dress back, any time.' Isabel just nodded, mutely and Bridget looked back at the road.

'Drop me here,' said Isabel suddenly: they were not quite there as far as Bridget understood, but it was a good part of town, big houses, tall trees. Christmas trees in big bay windows. 'I'm nearly home,' unclipping her seat belt as Bridget pulled up. 'Mum would kill me if she thought I'd taken a lift.'

'Sure,' said Bridget, turning off the engine. 'I'd be the same.' Wanting only to reassure her. 'You know my son,' she said. 'Finn? He's in the year above you, isn't he? Or is it two years?'

'One year.' Isabel seemed uncomfortable. Yes she knew Finn. They climbed out together and Bridget hauled the bike out for her. Dusting it off.

'And this girlfriend of his?' Trying just to sound like the friendly mum.

'Yes, yes,' said Isabel.

'Phoebe, right?' Bridget handed the bike over to her.

'Oh, yes, she's really pretty.'

She seemed embarrassed now. Pushing her bike away, suddenly in a hurry, and in a moment of revelation as she watched Isabel struggle to get the heavy, old-fashioned frame on to the kerb, Bridget knew why that was – from somewhere, way back, aged thirteen or whatever. Before violin lessons, before periods, a time so innocent she felt herself on the brink of tears at the memory. You fancied a boy, you gazed at him – then he came round a corner with a girl on his arm. Older, prettier, longer legs, a *girl-friend*. And you felt like you'd never be a *girlfriend*.

Isabel fancied Finn. The girl paused, hand raised quick and awkward, not even looking back and said, 'Thanks.' And hurried off, on those delicate bird's legs.

Pulling away, it had seemed to Bridget a good sign: it meant, though she couldn't say exactly why, that Carmichael hadn't yet done anything to Isabel. And that was good. That was wonderful. She had driven on to the shop, fixing on that. Hadn't *yet*. She realised that in her head he was still alive. She veered away from the thought.

Sitting parked in the lane had been when she'd thought to google him: Carmichael. Timpson, too, while she was at it. Where they'd been, what they'd done. And stopped herself. The phone wasn't just how they knew where you'd been it was where they found messages, searches.

The police.

She would look, but some other way. Some other time.

She didn't need to look him up, not yet. What she needed was to get rid of him. And on cue, that was when Carrie had called. *He's freaking me out.* Even dead, he could do that. Not for much longer.

Bridget could feel Carrie's thin shoulders under her arms now, and released her.

'Right,' she said, looking into Carrie's eyes and Carrie nodded, shivering.

Chapter Fifteen

Inside the garage, together they lugged the carpet containing Carmichael's dead body into the van. Deadweight. Carrie's morale seemed to improve with just the physical activity: Bridget remembered her as a kid, hyperactive, fidgeting at her desk, always in trouble. Mum just at her wits' end: Carrie had been nothing like Bridget, not quiet, submissive, patient. But was that what had saved her? She'd have never had the patience for violin practice.

They sat, hunched in the van at the kerb, with the engine running.

'Where are we going?' Carrie said, not shivering any more but her face pale and set: outside it was dusk. 'What? Bury him?' Insistent. 'Chuck him off a tall building? Drop him in the sea?'

Bridget engaged gear but her mind was a blank, terrified. Pulled away from the kerb.

'Drop him in the sea,' she said, peering both ways at

the junction but she didn't know. She clicked the indicator left, down to the estuary. Where?

There was a place where they went walking. But what if there was someone there, parked for a twilight walk. And there was the tide: the thought of the body washed back in, turning up on a beach, haunted her. The movements of the water and the shallow channels snaking inland were something she knew nothing about.

'Somewhere to wash him clean of the DNA, though, of carpet fibres, all that,' she said. She still hadn't moved off from the junction: soon someone would see. 'I can't—' her voice broke. 'How can we be — how can I be thinking like this?'

'Stop it,' said Carrie, beside her, her voice rising, panicked. 'It's done.'

Then Bridget remembered the reservoir. Where she'd gone with Matt to look at the dinghy.

Reservoirs were deep and cold and empty. She clicked the indicator the other way.

A half hour's drive inland. She remembered the route from the journey with Matt. They passed a pub he'd pointed out to her. 'Nice Sunday lunch, I've heard.' Matt and Finn, diving in to roast beef and Yorkshires, happiest moment of the week.

About halfway she'd taken her foot off the accelerator and said, 'This is nuts, isn't it? The sea is right there on the doorstep.'

'I don't think so,' said Carrie, unexpectedly calm. She'd been just sitting there, staring out into the dark. The headlights on the frozen grass of the verge, a rabbit hurtling across a narrow lane, ears flat on its back.

'I think that's why it isn't crazy,' she went on slowly. 'And if we do it right – they'll never find him. Or – not much of him.'

As they got closer, a sign for the sailing club appeared and Bridget made herself think. Not there: people there. So where?

She and Matt had stood at the edge of the water, looking. A tufted island at the centre, some people walking along the eastern edge. On the far side, opposite, there'd been a kind of rock cliff and a stand of trees above it. And then, miraculously, before they got to the sailing club there was a turning, a narrow lane between high, bare hedges, to where the sun was just a lemon glow on the horizon. West.

They were skirting the reservoir now: the lane ran close to it then receded and more than once they almost stopped but didn't. They went slower now, and silent, both of them leaning forward and searching, searching, for the right place. And then it came into view: a slight semicircle of gravel on a bend, the gleam of water glimpsed between a scruffy stand of pines. They came to a halt and turned off the engine.

A motionless second as the engine ticked into silence, then another. Then Bridget looked at her watch. 'Let's get going,' she said. It was five fifteen. They climbed out.

It was quiet, a wintry evening: no birds. A faint smell of pine. Thank God, thought Bridget, it isn't summer. People walking. Did they come here? Picnics. Swimming. She hoped fervently that it was as deep as she imagined. She opened the van's rear doors, and there it was, a misshapen roll, diagonally across the metal floor.

He was heavy, or the carpet was. They lugged at the

rolled shape, one on either side, fruitlessly for a second, until Carrie was ready to climb inside and shove from the other end – but then it shifted, scraped over the lip and thudded at their feet, already beginning to unroll. Something fell out, a gleam in the thin moon, a little something. Carrie leaned down and when she straightened she had it in her hand: she held it out. Matt's pliers, tape wound round one of the handles. Bridget took them from her quickly and set them inside the van, out of sight. The tape round the handles made her want to cry, and she couldn't afford the time.

Carrie was already leaning over the rolled carpet, shoulders swaying as Bridget looked down. A foot was visible at Bridget's end, an ugly shoe, worn down at the back, an ankle that looked blotchy in the thin light. Everything in her head screamed for them to just haul him through the trees, shove him into the water and drive away. Quick, quick, quick.

Instead Bridget took a deep breath. 'Hold on,' she said, steady. 'Let's get him closer still rolled up. Then we search him again.'

They hauled him as near as they could get to the cliff-edge, between two pines where the soil dropped away. The water was about five feet below them, black, wavelets lapping a little in the sharp wind. 'You all right?' Bridget said to Carrie, who was squatting with her back against one of the trunks. She nodded, but her face was in shadow. 'I've got a torch,' said Bridget. It was in the van's glovebox.

They got to work. Bridget found it was all right if she just focused on the cloth under her hand, not what lay beneath it, inanimate now. Into one pocket then another.

Dust. There was still no phone. Carrie sat back on her heels.

'Do you think,' she said, her face uplit by the torch, set and determined, 'we should get his clothes off? Like, so he can't be identified, or, or,' she wavered. 'I don't know.'

'I don't, I don't—' Bridget stiffened, rigid. She didn't want to do it. But the more she didn't want to do it the more she told herself, it had to be done. It wasn't the time to be squeamish.

'It won't take long,' said Carrie roughly. 'You hold the torch.'

She started to unbutton his trousers: Bridget looked off into the dark but the torch beam wavered, and she had to look back. Carrie made a sound. 'Jesus,' she said.

'What?' She couldn't seem to make her eyes focus.

'The old bastard liked to go commando,' said Carrie, disgusted and for a moment although she knew the phrase – who didn't? – Bridget didn't understand what she was saying. She made herself focus and saw an inch of greying pubic hair against pale, flabby skin. A misshapen mole. She stood up, swaying, and for a moment she thought she was going to vomit.

No. No. If she vomited here—

'He didn't – he wasn't—' And then suddenly it was rage Bridget was feeling. 'Button him back up,' she said, her voice shaking with it. 'Go on.' An order, and Carrie obeyed, fumbling. 'They could identify him by his teeth, anyway, couldn't they?' Bridget said.

'Do you mean—' Carrie sounded afraid now. 'You want me to—'

'No,' said Bridget, stiffly, and it was as if her whole body had turned cold as iron, she could taste it in her mouth. 'What I mean is, we can't cover all the options.' And now trying to locate the trembling: where was it? At her knees, her thighs, turning her spine to jelly.

She swallowed. 'The most we can do is make sure they don't find him at all until we're all dead and gone. Or even just gone.' Then she stood up, because if she didn't move she would start to shake, she would fall on the ground beside him and shake like an animal.

Taking a hasty stumbling step backward, she nearly tripped over something. A tree root. Think. *Think.* She turned away.

'What are you doing?' Carrie's voice was high. Bridget stopped, holding on to the nearest trunk: she couldn't bear the sound of Carrie frightened.

Think of something.

'It's all right,' she said, although it wasn't, then it came to her.

'I'm going to find something heavy,' she said. 'To put in his pockets. To hold him down.' And then Carrie was on her feet beside her. Behind them he lay, exposed in the moonlight.

The earth was dusty, powdery: every time they found something that looked like a rock it crumbled. Carrie broke away from her, wandering. Bridget was about to stop her when she called, low.

'Here.' Excited.

A little sweep of stones, beyond the van, dusty, all different sizes. Bits of concrete were in among them: Bridget calculated, not wanting to remove something that would be missed and decided the stones were hardcore, an attempt at shoring up the verge. There were plenty of them. Carrie ran back for some of the polythene and they scooped handfuls of the stuff into it, dragging the bundle back to where he lay.

They filled his pockets and sat back. 'That's not going to be enough,' said Carrie, on the edge of frightened again.

'Hold on,' said Bridget. She went back to the van and got the roll of packing tape she kept in the side pocket, for when boxes split. Could you trace packing tape? She doubted it. Think – but don't think too hard. You can't control everything. When she came back she saw Carrie, looking down at him from where she sat with her back against the tree, motionless, on guard. It had got darker: there was no more than a sliver of moon, high behind them.

'We've got to be quick, now,' Bridget said. 'I don't want anyone seeing the torch.' And they had to be quick for Matt, cycling peacefully home from work. She blinked to get rid of the image.

Kneeling, she began to tape around the trousers at the ankle, and Carrie, understanding immediately, began to scoop up more of the hardcore and shovel it down his trousers, still unbuttoned. Carrie had angled herself so she blocked Bridget's view and by the time she moved back out of the way it was done.

His head was furthest from them, hanging back a little over the cliff-edge. Bridget could see his chin, tilted upwards. She could see stubble: it went on growing, didn't it? She'd read that somewhere. Hair, skin, nails, they go on growing after you're dead. How long for?

'Now,' said Bridget and they positioned themselves on either side of him without any further communication passing between them, and heaved.

He went over without a sound. What sound had she expected? A cry, an accusation, a plea? And then the splash, loud. A gurgling sound that pinned them to the spot for a second then they both looked over. The sliver of moon illuminated something, the monstrous mounded shape of his coat ballooned with air and bobbed. One minute passed. Another.

'Oh, my God,' Carrie almost groaned, and scrambled for the edge, reaching for a root to hang on to, ready to lash out and kick him down. Just in time Bridget grabbed her back.

'No,' she hissed. 'Just wait. Wait.'

And as they watched, holding on to each other, at last there was a swirl in the black water below them, and he went down.

The silence that followed seemed vast. Bridget felt a great, peaceful emptiness, like space, as if she closed her eyes she might float, weightless, away from the earth.

Along the bank something rustled.

'We've got to go,' said Carrie urgently. And the world rushed in again.

There was always a wine bar, and Gill was sitting in it, nursing a large glass of red.

Pubs were noisier, you couldn't sit quiet and think, you couldn't shape your sentences, for what that was worth. Not even these days when every other pub had been made over with scrubbed tables and wifi – well, not here they hadn't. The gastropub and the hipster coffee shop had yet to flourish in the shadow of Rose Hill.

Identify the older part of town: Gill had spotted it from

the bus, heading back downhill from the towers. Her hotel was off to the north, a modern tower with purple lettering, and on the opposite side she'd seen the cluster of red-tiled roofs, nicely tumbling over each other. No more than a couple of old streets, but there'd have to be something. And there was: seventies French-café style with a long bar, tealights on the tables, a big window looking out on to dark cobbles.

And it had been a reasonable day. Not outstanding, but time with the university admin office had been well spent: they'd been short-staffed, not the usual row of eagle-eyed middle-aged women who would have busted her straight off. There was one woman but she was on the phone, walking up and down between her desk and a corridor. The work experience kid had turned to Gill, hopeful, as she edged through the door. A boy, flustered. She introduced herself as Dr Somebody, randomly. Had she even said, Dr Finlay? The kid would have been too young to know who Dr Finlay was, anyway. She had smiled at him, kindly. Could he remind her of the number of Dr Carmichael's house, she needed to get a book to him for review and he wasn't in his office. Use the right tone of voice and an inexperienced kid will just obey.

He had looked, panicked, across to the boss, but she was still on the mobile, one hand clutching at her forehead and a glare hovering, just ready to be activated.

Use the right tone of voice, like you're his mum. Gill had had a mum, after all, even if she wasn't one, and Chloe was enough mum for both of them. Supermum. The girls liked their auntie, though. You needed a respite from Supermum once in a while.

173

Gill took a leisurely sip of her red, and found it to be not too bad. House red: she wasn't the *little-South-African-vineyard-I-know* type, after all, and this wouldn't have been the place for it if she had been. Maybe it was her kind of town, in some ways, even if she still didn't believe it was Anthony Carmichael's. He had travelled, done stints in Dijon and Chicago, conducting. And Bangkok, and São Paulo, too.

Whatever: Gill must have got her tone of voice right because the work experience boy had scrabbled through a pile on the desk he was at and found a laminated list. He had held it out to her and there he was, top of the Cs, Dr A. Carmichael. An honorary doctorate, from the university of arseholes.

'Why do you hate him so much?' Charlie had asked her that. Charlie with the sad eyes, her last editor: she'd left that job because of Charlie, who had been married. Why she hated Carmichael was a long story, beginning with that girl, hanging herself. A promising violin student, and Gill had gone back to see the man who had taken her under his wing, encouraged her musical talent: Dr Anthony Carmichael, Mr, back then, before the university of arseholes singled him out for their special honour. She'd gone back to ask him for a quote, but mostly to confirm the feeling she'd had when first she met him, standing while he was photographed with the dead girl on one side of him, her friend Bess on the other.

He'd been offhand about the girl, platitudes expressing sorrow and sympathy insultingly thin. *Really I hardly knew her, a handful of lessons.* Eyeing Gill, trying to place her.

When Gill tracked her down, Bess had said different.

Piercings all up one ear now with a death-metal boyfriend and a ripped Metallica T-shirt, she had said, glancing quickly at the boyfriend sitting frowning in the corner of their bedsit, he played us off against each other and she was his favourite. Took her on days out in his car. But she had shaken her head when Gill had asked if she'd go on the record, looking uneasy, and the boyfriend had got threateningly to his feet.

In the office at the base of the tower as the light outside faded and the work experience kid shuffled from foot to foot at her shoulder, she'd taken down the address and phone number – a landline – and the computer guy's number while she was at it. Matthew Webster.

It had been late by then, and a twenty-five-minute wait for the bus on the windswept slope pondering, for the twentieth time, what would have brought Anthony Carmichael to this place. By the time Gill had got back to her hotel it was after seven and she was knackered. Exposure to Carmichael, even at this distance, drained her. She showered, poured some peanuts from the mini-bar down her throat and was off out.

'Twenty-four-hour reception,' chirruped the girl behind the desk in an Eastern European accent Gill couldn't identify more precisely. Dyed blonde hair, pretty, tired: her skin beginning to go. Was she happy, out here, far from home? The resilience of young people never ceased to amaze Gill: she remembered, belatedly, as she pushed through the door and out into the darkness that she'd been young once, and ready to travel. She was about ready to go home, these days.

Enough Carmichael for one day: save that home visit

for tomorrow. Would he remember her this time? She walked, down the hill towards where she calculated the old town should be. There was a distant gleam from the estuary, and at her shoulder, blinking, the red lights on top of the towers.

The lights were still visible from the window seat of the wine bar: Gill moved so she couldn't see them. A man was eyeing her up from the corner of the room but Gill paid no attention.

Taking another sip of the wine, Gill shifted back to look out at the cobbles and something eased, just enough. The bits of evidence she had accumulated over ten years – the rooms, the faces, the sounds, images that spent all day cramped in a corner of her head – began to spread themselves out, for her perusal. She'd been through this before. Her routine.

She was thinking of faces, the other faces she'd known. The faces on the wall of a front room, a girl in school uniform, reception, first year at big school, hair in bunches, hair hiding her face, braces on, braces off. A girl and her mother from a school Carmichael taught at in his spare time, the mother desperate to believe there had been nothing in the accusation, the girl hiding her face. The police deciding there wasn't enough evidence and the school closing ranks.

Persecution of a great talent and public-spirited man who couldn't do enough for his community, the lawyers' letter had read. The girl and her mother hiding behind net curtains after that while journalists – Gill still in there – camped out on the doorstep on a night like this one, bitter cold, and tried to get them to talk.

176

She'd interviewed him again, only months before, about an ex-pupil who'd made it big. He hadn't remembered her when she went back: when he did the same trick of holding her hand softly and looking into her face she thought he had, but there'd been no recognition in his eyes, it was just what he did. She'd felt his finger in her palm. Gill had listened to him saying that was what it was all about, bringing on young talent, not about ego. She had loathed him.

The way he looked her up and down, like he'd remember her next time. A hard-faced wife patrolling the room while they talked. And Gill had believed the accusations, every word. She'd convinced the mother and girl she believed them too, only when the police dropped the case they wouldn't talk to her any more. As if it had been she who'd betrayed them.

Unstable, vulnerable, those were the words used of the girl who'd killed herself, the first one. Until he came on the scene she hadn't been, only unprotected. No father and a mother run ragged: predators from top to bottom of the scale target those. No doubt Carmichael thought himself a cut above but he was the same as an uneducated taxi driver from Oldham who gets together with his mates to groom girls in care for sex. They identify an opportunity. They pick off the weak.

She had started to dig, then.

First Charlie, then Steve: both of them interested to start with, in the story. Just another story, the gleam of excitement at the chase. Then – stupidly, stupidly – she had slept with Charlie, just the once, *stupid*, *wrong*, and he felt that had given him the right to make it personal, to question

177

her motives. *Were you, you weren't ever . . . ?* And started to tell her, it wasn't safe, she was too close to the story. She'd walked out, so angry she hadn't been able to trust herself to speak. More angry than was reasonable, because there was a germ of outrage in it — *she* wasn't damaged, thank you very much — that made her understand the bind they were in, those girls hiding in their bedrooms, their fierce mothers. *Don't call me damaged.* But most of all because: did you have to have been abused yourself to know this was wrong? Maybe that was how men saw it.

Then Steve. Gill wasn't going to make the same mistake again, this time their relationship was strictly professional, or close enough. And gradually the focus was on those issues, it wasn't called a witch hunt any more, it was mainstream, it was big news. And Steve had said, *Go with it*, that gleam in his eye. But Gill didn't bring him what he wanted. She didn't bring him the victims, she just got the newspaper threatened with legal action. She was close to the edge, and she knew it.

Gill took another swig of the wine and got out her laptop: at the bar the man who'd eyed her up adjusted his position on his stool and she sighed: couldn't help herself. She brought up the search page. She was supposed to be in Sandringham at the weekend some time, interviewing the Queen's butcher about what she was going to have for her Christmas dinner.

Anthony Carmichael. She varied the search terms every time. Dr Anthony Carmichael. *Violin prodigy gifted student suicide.* And she looked, for the thousandth time at where he'd been, who he'd taught. These were the faces she saw, from school yearbooks and class outings and local newspaper cuttings: a handful, no more. They populated her dreams, sat on buses with her, kept their heads lowered in a crowded street. She noted patterns of drug abuse, repeat offending, self-harm. And there would be others who simply disappeared, melting into the background. Passing for normal.

She saw them everywhere. She saw them yesterday, she'd seen them today.

A shy girl, accepting a prize in a long, loose dress that didn't disguise how thin she was. Mother and sister in chairs beside her. The man giving the prize – for effort in music, year nine, *effort*, Jesus preserve her – was Anthony Carmichael, in a sports jacket, hair just beginning to go. Thought himself God's gift. A middle-aged sleaze but they're all gazing at him like it's the second coming.

A school hall full of cross-legged kids, knickers showing. Wouldn't be allowed these days. What's wrong with me? Gill thought.

The girl accepting the prize was one of the ones Gill looked for, pursued, and came up with nothing: she had disappeared into thin air. Except. Except. She'd know that face anywhere. She'd seen that face. She leaned closer to look at the younger sister, front row next to her mother. Primary school age, little white chin set and angry. And that face, too. She frowned, as it bothered her. Was it that she saw them everywhere, like ghosts?

The man at the bar was coming over: her glass on the table seemed to be empty, suddenly.

'Get you another?' His voice diffident, polite. He's her type, close up: dark hair, stocky, not too polished. Gill bookmarked the page and closed her computer.

'Go on then,' she said, weary.

Chapter Sixteen

Friday

Some of the things that woke her, at half hour intervals through the night, were real.

His bloated body had risen to the surface and was bobbing there as the sun rose, turning slowly to face the sky.

Not true.

It had all been an accident, a mistake, a misunderstanding and the police were letting her go home. A kind face looked at her, nodding, as she explained.

Not true.

Someone had seen them.

That one was true; that one started her fully awake.

Staring in the bedroom dark until her eyes hurt Bridget had to lie very still otherwise she thought her heart might accelerate out of her chest. Every chemical in her body felt toxic. She'd die, and the carpet and cardboard and polythene with his DNA on it still in the back of the van would be found and – *and*. And nothing: then it would all go away.

But she didn't want to die. Not any more. The thought came to Bridget as a revelation.

So think: there had been a man.

He hadn't seen them doing anything, but he had seen them. He had been standing at the verge as they came back along the lane, close to the turning to the sailing club where a single streetlight stood guard. A youngish bloke with hair sticking up, in overalls. He must have recognised Bridget, her and her little white van because he raised a cheery hand, peering in as they slowed. The lane had been narrow.

Carrie had gasped beside her. Out of nowhere Bridget had managed to smile at him. And to gesture, down the turning, to indicate as she passed him.

'What are you doing?' Carrie had hissed, white-faced.

'I'm giving them a reason we're here,' Bridget had said, not sure where she found the calm. She hadn't recognised the man at all. But she calculated: it must have been when she came with Matt to look at the dinghy, he must have been someone they talked to. And of course, they always remembered a newcomer, round here.

As she and Carrie crunched along the unkempt gravel lane the little clapboard building came into view. Six thirty, the time illuminated on her dashboard jumped at her. They'd both left their phones at home, so Bridget couldn't call Matt to say they'd be late. There was a glow in the window of the clubhouse's bar, where the die-hards were having a leisurely drink after a winter sail, or a spot of maintenance, just Matt's cup of tea. The innocence of it.

Climbing out Bridget paused a minute to look over the water. The temperature seemed to have dropped ten degrees. The light had gone from the sky but the uneven tree line bordering the reservoir was just about visible. Could you

181

see the light of a small pocket torch from this far off? And if you did, would you make anything of it?

Carrie climbed out. 'Jesus, it's cold,' she said. Looking around. 'Anyone with any sense'll have been holed up in there all afternoon,' she said, nodding towards the clubhouse. As if she knew what Bridget was thinking.

Bridget put an arm through hers to stop her shivering and steered her toward the steps. 'We're buying Matt a boat,' she said.

There'd been a brief lull in the hum of talk when they came through the door but it soon picked up again. A handful of men round a table and an apple-cheeked woman in dungarees with wiry hair at the bar. The old man selling the dinghy was there in the corner, merry with a pint in front of him and hadn't shown any surprise when Bridget had approached him. A Christmas present, she said, sitting down beside him, offering to buy him a drink and he had nodded, nodding even harder when she'd said, 'Cash all right?'

She'd given him what she had in her wallet, a couple of hundred, as deposit while Carrie stood quiet, looking round the warm room. There was a bit of discussion about the trailer, and when she'd be back with the balance. Carrie always seemed in her natural habitat in a bar, any kind of bar. They'd slipped out again, the hum of conversation resuming behind them.

'Respect,' Carrie had said as they climbed back into the van. There was colour in her cheeks. 'That was quick thinking.'

It wasn't until they rejoined the road, Carrie apparently so relaxed now that she had sat back, eyes closed, that it all began to clamour in Bridget's head. What if they'd looked in the back of the van? What if anyone asked the young bloke in dungarees which direction they'd been coming from?

They wouldn't. That was the mantra that had got her through the evening. That, and the glass of wine before dinner. She'd drunk another, quickly, in the kitchen while Carrie played a computer game with Finn in the living room, while Matt read the paper. The whoosh and crump of virtual weaponry.

And it was Carrie who had made it work, as they came through the door. 'Where have you two been?' Matt had said, ready, Bridget could see even as she hung back, to be anxious. Carrie mischievous, tapping the side of her nose. 'Christmas shopping,' she said cheerfully.

The wine was supposed to help her sleep, and it had put her under, at least, so quickly she had barely managed to get her clothes off. Struggling out of the jeans, the sweatshirt: they had smelled strange to her and she had pushed them away, into a little heap. She must have been asleep when Matt came up. She reached for her phone in the dark to check the time: it was twenty past three.

No one had suspected anything. Not the man on the verge, nor the sailors in their clubhouse, not Matt, not Finn. By infinitesimal degrees the dark of her bedroom felt warmer, more protective, and Matt's breathing beside her told her, all right. All right.

The next thing Bridget knew the light was hurting her eyes and Matt was sitting on the side of the bed holding a mug carefully in both hands, examining her. She sat up in a hurry.

'What?' she said, taking the mug.

'What was up with you last night?' he said, worried. He put a hand to her forehead.

'Well, I—'

He thought she was still ill, she realised with relief. And she did feel it, queasy with the lack of sleep, and flushed from last night's wine, and somewhere far back in her head, locked in its own little box, was what they'd done, her and Carrie. Their hands on his contaminated body. Bridget looked into Matt's worried face.

'Dodgy sandwich at lunch yesterday, I think,' she said, grimacing apologetically. 'Tea'll sort me out.' Smiling, grateful, ridiculously grateful, when the frown disappeared and Matt nodded. He stood up, relieved, then leaned to plant a quick kiss on her cheek.

'I'm off, then,' he said. 'See you this evening,' and clattered downstairs, suddenly cheerful. The back door banged.

It wasn't even eight: early, even for Matt. Bridget could hear Carrie and Finn downstairs in the wake of his departure: no one was lying in bed today, she should get up too – but her body felt heavy, still, after the sleepless night, her head felt thick. She leaned back against the headboard and before she knew it, she was asleep again.

Something woke her less than half an hour later, but sitting up Bridget couldn't identify what it had been. Someone was talking quietly downstairs, but that wasn't it. She got up. The small pile of clothes from last night was half hidden under the little chair beside the bed: ignoring it she went to the window, leaning her cheek against the cool glass. Looking down the soft, silvery field to the estuary; she couldn't see the towers from here. There was only the grey water, embroidered by muddy inlets and creeks, a sandy point gleaming far off where the estuary opened to the sea and for a second a bubble of something almost like euphoria was there in Bridget's chest, before she squeezed it small. The towers would still be there, when she came out of the front door. Towers One, Two, Three.

Where Carmichael had friends. And where a journalist had come to listen to him speak.

She heard Finn coming up the stairs: she knew his cheerful clump.

'Mum?' Peering anxiously round the door. 'Dad said—' he didn't finish the sentence but came in and sat on the unmade bed, fidgeting. He had his waterproof jacket on and his bag on his shoulder.

'You off?' said Bridget, trying not to look at the pile of clothes half under the chair. She'd have to burn them. 'Made your sandwich?'

'Dad said you weren't feeling great,' he said. He seemed nervous.

'I'm fine,' she said, pulling her dressing gown together, cheerful for Finn. 'How are things with Phoebe, anyway?'

Just to change the subject: on the bed Finn studied his hands, uneasy. 'I think she's worried about meeting you,' he said eventually, looking up. 'Like you might – not like her.'

'Of course I'll like her,' said Bridget, giving him a little shove. He smiled uncertainly. 'If you like her she must be lovely.' Hoping she sounded convincing.

'I told her about your shop and she thought that was cool,' said Finn, sheepish, fiddling with the lanyard of his backpack on his lap. She wanted to take him and squeeze him and tell him not to worry, even though the thought of him telling Phoebe about her shop made her unaccountably anxious herself.

Why? How many times had Matt sighed when she said, *No, I don't want to sell online.* He knew why – at least Bridget thought he did, without ever having been told. Finn looked up at her from under his eyebrows and she smiled.

'I saw Isabel yesterday,' she said. 'She told me how pretty Phoebe was.'

Finn looked blank and Bridget thought, Mistake.

'Isabel?' She made herself speak patiently. 'Fluffy hair, slim? Year below you at school? We saw her the other Sunday with her mum and dad, out walking.' Leaving out the bit about her coming into the shop with Anthony Carmichael.

'Oh,' Finn said, still bewildered.

'I think she likes you,' said Bridget and he frowned, uncomfortable.

'She's just a kid,' he said and Bridget made herself laugh.

'Oh, a whole year younger?' And thought with resignation, if she wanted the part of bothersome nosy mum, she was playing a blinder. Change the subject. 'Was that the landline?' she said, and she realised why it had taken her a while to register it. No one used it these days, only occasionally the university secretaries and the sound of it had become unfamiliar, exotic. 'That woke me up?'

Finn shrugged, uninterested, halfway through the door now. 'Auntie Carrie answered it,' he said. 'I think it was for her.'

And then he was off, clumping back down the staircase:

she thought about calling after him for a kiss but there was the heap of clothes at her feet. There'd be Carrie's too. And the cardboard. And the rest.

When she got downstairs Carrie was at the kitchen table with a mug of black coffee, pale but steady. The room was startlingly tidy.

'You're going,' said Bridget immediately. 'Good, that's good. I want you out of this.'

Carrie didn't move, but her knuckles were white around the mug. And suddenly Bridget felt like she was on the edge of a cliff: all the tools she had used to get herself here didn't seem to work. Be practical, be good, be polite. And now she had to fight.

'Carrie?' she said. 'Did you hear me?'

'I'm going nowhere,' Carrie said, and then as if the word had broken a spell she lifted the mug to her lips. 'You can't make me.'

Bridget sat down and sighed. 'You need me,' said Carrie. Then, 'He raped you, didn't he?' Then. 'Was it just him?'

It was as if the words hadn't been spoken. 'Who was that on the phone?' said Bridget, her head full of white noise. Carrie stared at her a moment, then shook her head once, twice, as if she needed to clear it, then said, 'She wanted Matt.'

She pushed the mug away, her mouth set. Bridget recognised that stubborn mouth, it was so familiar it made her want to grab Carrie's head and press it hard against her chest, like she used to, somewhere between a hug and a fight.

'Something to do with work.' Staring down at the mug. 'A woman. Gillian something? I said he was on his way in. She asked if I was his wife. *Are you Bridget*, she said.'

'It'll be one of the secretaries,' Bridget said automatically but she could feel her heart step up, faster. She couldn't remember the last time she'd spoken to one of the admin staff.

'Don't think so,' said Carrie, indifferent.

The hairs rose on Bridget's neck. 'But she knew my name?'

Carrie looked at her, getting up to stash her mug in the dishwasher. 'Come on,' she said over her shoulder, 'every school leaver who calls trying to sell you solar panels or cheap internet knows your first name. It's a ploy. There's a word for it, probably. Personalisation or whatever.'

Bridget stood, abruptly from the table.

'We've got to get rid of some stuff,' she said. 'You up for that? Carrie nodded, waiting. Bridget reached for her coat. 'And we've to get to an internet café.'

In the lavender light of her hotel bedroom, Gillian Lawson hung up and chucked her mobile on the bed.

It had come to her in the small hours, four o'clock or thereabouts, when she always woke up when she was like this. Her mind running even while she slept, asking questions, answering them. A hunch? A face in a frame on a desk. Could it be? One way to find out, because she had his number. Matthew Webster.

If she wanted to, Matthew Webster's wife could call back: Gill never withheld her number. But something told her that wasn't going to happen. There would be a way of Gill getting to her: for the moment through her husband looked like the quickest route: her nice husband who happened to be the computer officer at Rose Hill. There was

188

something Gill didn't like, about that coincidence, it ticked away in her head, implications stacking up.

A coincidence – unless it wasn't. Had Carmichael come after her? Got a job on the same campus as her husband? She doubted it. But abuser and victim could wash up in the same sort of backwater, a place like this.

She got out her phone and googled Bridget Webster, and the town's name. Nothing, nothing, nothing. Tried images – and there she was. Small businesswoman, looking strained at a civic gathering.

The bed was untidy, a man's tie forgotten over the back of a chair. She stared at it, cursing: she'd already forgotten him. The stocky bloke who'd been in the back of a taxi with her last night, arm careless along the back of the seat and her shoulders. He hadn't groped her, though, and he'd paid for the taxi. And when she'd woken up at first light through those vile polyester curtains he was still there on the pillow beside her, just the hint of a snore: he hadn't scuttled off before she woke up, they did that often enough. They didn't always leave their tie behind. He had been crumpled, cheery. Nice enough. She'd kicked him out when, with his back to her and blearily fumbling with the little plastic pots of horrible milk at the tea tray, he had started to ask her about herself.

Gill jumped out of bed, twitchy at the memory, tugged perfunctorily at the bedclothes. Why did you do that, when someone was being paid to make your bed? Still worried about what people thought of you, after all these years: a bit late for that. She refilled the kettle from the bath tap.

Clicking it on to boil, Gill sighed, reset. It was bad for

your sex life, having an obsession with a predatory paedo-phile. Sometimes you needed a bit of mindless normal sex to clear things out a bit. He hadn't distracted her for long from the faces in her head, though. He hadn't got her to sleep. Could she ever live with someone, listen to them breathe or snore beside her without it driving her nuts?

Not all men are the same. You couldn't suspect them all. He hadn't complained that she hadn't had a Brazilian or tied her to the bedposts. There were no bedposts, she registered with the same thought. The kettle hissed and creaked to a boil.

Matthew Webster, now. Was he normal? (And what was normal anyway? Not her, not Gillian Lawson.) Men who married victims of abuse were practically a secondary industry, clearing up the mess, or feeding off it. She poured the water on top of the teabag in the too-small, too-thick china cup. Why didn't they ever give you a bloody mug in these places? Burned her fingers trying to extract the bag: she could hear Chloe tutting, her mother tutting, whole generations of Lawson females sighing over her.

At which point Gill had to tell herself, *Stop it.* You're pissed off because you're lying to your editor, you're living out of a suitcase like a slob, and you can't see a bloke without suspecting him of being a pervert. But nobody made you do it. *You* made you do it.

Besides, Matthew Webster had seemed like a genuinely nice man, and her radar was set pretty high for sleazebag husbands. He had looked tired, there in the big auditorium with the handful of students whispering to each other, with his laptop in his arms, the overhead projector set up and unused, exasperated and bemused by the waste of his

190

time. She could have told him, Carmichael never did care about the little people. Disdaining the UHT milk thimble Gill raised the thick china cup gingerly to her lips, and burned her mouth. She thought perhaps she would go back and find Matthew Webster today, after all.

Was she putting off Carmichael, or saving him up? The thought of seeing him made her flesh crawl. When had the last time been? Four, five years back.

The wife, though. Matthew Webster's wife. Had that been her on the phone, pretending to be someone else? The voice had been rough and suspicious. Just answering, no, when Gill had asked, is that Bridget? Confirmation though that Bridget *was* who it was, Bridget in the picture frame. Bridget Webster, Bridget O'Neill as was.

Had Anthony Carmichael come after her? All the way over here from his gleaming spires, to hang out among what he'd no doubt classify as inbreds and provincials, just to track a child he had once taken under his wing, a one-time violin student who had turned out – and so many of them had – not to have made the grade and who would, besides, now be pushing forty. And therefore no longer his type.

It would depend on whether he was more a predator than a paedophile, and that one, on the evidence Gill had, was a toss-up. Could it be coincidence? Another depressing explanation, of course, would be the statistics. That Anthony Carmichael had abused so many of his pre-pubescent protégées – nervy, skinny, vulnerable girls, girls with a weak point, needy, hopeful, romantic children – that there were simply so many of them that, wherever he pitched up, there would likely enough be one. One grown to anxious adulthood, in hiding. Passing for normal.

191

Shit. Shit. Had she – she panicked, on her knees, not left it in the wine bar? The bulging nylon briefcase that held her laptop, her notebooks, her life. *Back of the taxi?* – no. She crawled towards it. On its side under the TV table. And in it, Carmichael's address. She pulled out the note-book to look at it.

He'd refuse to talk to her, of course he would – if he was even there.

Webster had said Carmichael wasn't well. Sitting on the floor with her briefcase clutched against her chest Gill's imagination leaped, spiralled, wishful thinking: on his deathbed. Something horrible, I hope.

She set down the cup with its dusty dregs, and walked into the shower. Time to get clean, just so you can get dirty all over again.

Chapter Seventeen

The town's last internet café was behind the bus station, between a boarded-up gaming arcade and a print shop. Once there'd been ten at least, but now everyone did everything on their phones. Most people didn't wonder how safe their phones were. A bearded man was begging outside it, hunched over his knees. He could have been any age from twenty-five to fifty. He had a card, *homeless*, it read, and a greasy cap with some coppers in it. Bridget hesitated, then dropped in a pound coin. As she always did: they could see her coming. She and Carrie pushed their way inside.

It was empty, except for the guy with his feet up on a computer console playing *Call of Duty* who had no interest in anything but the two pounds fifty that bought them an hour on a computer. Bridget couldn't spare more than half an hour. Laura was opening up but sooner or later even she would think, *what is all this?*

They started with just his name plus *musician*. A row of pictures: intellectual at a podium with glasses on; hands raised to conduct a quintet; leaning down over the shoulder of a girl whose face you couldn't see, only the violin in her hands, her bowed head, her shiny hair, her centre parting. Quickly Bridget scrolled down and the pictures were gone.

There was nothing about his disappearance. Nor was there anything to indicate he might ever have been involved in any kind of scandal. Bridget shifted on the office chair, Carrie pulled up on an identical one beside her.

'Fucker,' said Bridget, the word escaping her. And Carrie's eyebrows raised.

'Why is there nothing?' Bridget said, feeling her chest tight.

After a moment Carrie shrugged. 'People don't stick their necks out,' she said. 'It's intimidation. Bloke like that. People are scared of getting in trouble.' She leaned forward and scrolled back up to the row of photographs, and Bridget didn't try to stop her.

'Look at him,' said Carrie, sitting back in her cheap office chair. 'Thinks he's fucking God.'

And there he was, filling the screen leaning on a lectern with one elbow, a half smile on his face at some question.

Bridget felt her throat close: leaning quick past Carrie, she typed in the name of the music school she'd seen reported on all those years back. The one where there had been the beginnings of a scandal, swiftly quashed. The time Bridget had gone up to the police station in town, with Finn in his buggy. But because the school had been far away, because this station was the place where she'd reported

194

her bike stolen once, where they knew her as a member of the local independent retailers' organisation, contributor to the Christmas lights fund, she had just stood there, feeling her heart pound, before walking away.

Why did Bridget need this? She knew what had happened. She knew what he had done.

But still.

Some bland pieces on the music school's European tours, a student shortlisted for a prize. Photographs of landscaped grounds, a semi-stately home, a cedar tree. It was twenty miles from where Bridget had grown up.

She typed in his name, plus the school's name.

And there, on page two, buried away, she found it. An investigative piece, five years old, on a national newspaper, about the deaths of two students from the school, a year apart, promising students who also happened to be slim, gawky pre-pubescent girls, one fair, one dark, one with braces, both shy in their yearbook photographs. Anthony Carmichael's name was mentioned but carefully, judiciously. Only reading between the lines was it possible to infer that the writer suspected him of involvement.

The piece was written by a small investigative team: Carrie pointed at the lead name. 'That's her,' she said. 'That's the woman who phoned.'

Bridget stared at the name. Gillian Lawson.

'Shit,' said Bridget, feeling language escape her, good manners and everything, going. 'Shit.' But under her breath now. 'She called the house.' She felt cold with terror. '*Carrie.* She knows. She asked for me by name. She knows who I am.' Her hand on Carrie's wiry shoulder, shaking it. '*Carrie.*' Breathless. *Help me.*

'Not necessarily,' said Carrie, putting a hand up to hers, speaking levelly with one eye on the man with his feet up on the table. He hadn't moved, except for his thumbs a blur on the console. 'Stay calm.' But Carrie spoke in an undertone too. 'Matt might have mentioned your name to her, I don't know, or to a colleague. It's like cold callers, trying to sell you something, it's their foot in the door, knowing your name. Same for journalists.'

But what if she does know? Staring at Carrie, Bridget didn't say it: neither of them did. The panic subsided, gradually: she needed to stop this. She needed to stay calm. All she knows is Matt has a wife called Bridget. Plenty of Bridgets: Bridget Webster isn't Bridget O'Neill.

The man didn't look up when they left.

The shop was empty when they arrived and Laura was in the kitchen, at the tap with the little watering can they used for the plants beside the door in her hand. She had paused and was looking up at the space where the log had been, but the question hadn't yet formed, her mind elsewhere. She looked pale, violet shadows under her eyes. Bridget had her explanation ready but it seemed to stick in her throat. A lie: what if she fumbled it?

But then Laura looked past her, at Carrie and the moment was gone. Bridget had forgotten, the effect her sister had on people. Her white face, cropped hair, the line of studs up one ear. They didn't expect Bridget to have a sister like that.

'This is my sister Carrie, Laura,' she said and saw Carrie's deadpan look settle on Laura's smile.

Laura nodded, weary. Her hair straggled at the collar of her cardigan. Bridget remembered how that was: too tired

196

at the end of pregnancy to do anything, Matt hovering, waiting for her to explode. She took the watering can from her and crossed to the plants, Laura following obediently. 'Sit down,' she said, and Laura hoisted herself on to the stool next to her at the desk. Carrie took the sofa, elbows on her knees, watchful.

'He didn't come back,' she said.

Carrie's head lifted, inquiring. Bridget pressed her fingers into the soil of the plants.

'Who didn't?' Carefully, head down.

'The one with the present for his wife who wanted to talk to you.'

'Right,' said Bridget, and only then did she look up, everything slowing, back to normal.

'I could have sworn I saw him looking in the window but when I got to the door he had disappeared.' And then Laura was struggling to get down off the stool and Bridget moved to help but by the time she was on her feet she had moved on to varicose veins. 'I thought it was old ladies got them,' despondent. 'And Nick—' Bridget smiled and nodded, zoning out. Something about him telling her to get the veins done, about him going drinking when he should be home decorating the nursery. When she came to a standstill, Bridget told her to go for lunch.

'Where'd you find her?' said Carrie when the door had closed behind her. 'The Stepford wife?'

Bridget found herself defending her. 'She's all right,' she said, stopping herself saying, *you don't know what it's like, being pregnant.* All the hormones, that slow, heavy feeling, that anxiety. She wondered if it would ever happen to Carrie.

But Carrie had moved on: she was on her knees extracting cleaning products from the little kitchen cupboard. 'Right,' she said. 'Let's get started.' Looking up. 'So it happened in here, right?'

Where she knelt there was some bark Bridget hadn't seen, round the side of the cupboard under the little sink. Kneeling she began to prise it out, scraping, scraping, reaching for the cloth Carrie held out to her, wiping. It was easier to say the words if she didn't have to look at anyone.

'It fell. It fell. I hadn't realised how heavy it was but when I saw—' she paused and did look up then – and found Carrie was watching her, not shocked, not angry, just nodding.

'So he could have been already dead,' Carrie said. She was squatting, balancing on the balls of her feet like a kid ready to sprint. 'You – it might not have been you, at all.'

Bridget sat back on her heels. 'He was still alive,' she said, and as the words bloomed between them in the cramped space, quite suddenly she was calm. 'I could have phoned the ambulance, I could have phoned the police.'

Carrie straightened, leaning against the doorframe and listening, sombre, arms folded across her taut little belly. She had rolled up her sleeves and Bridget could see a tattoo, of a heart and the last girlfriend but one's name, on her forearm.

'He could be alive now in a hospital bed and I could be telling the police what happened,' said Bridget. 'But I'm not.' Still calm: not happy, exactly, but certain at least. 'I'm not glad I killed him,' she said. 'But I'm glad he's dead.

And there was a long pause before Carrie exhaled and said with a quick nod, 'And then you took the body next door.'

Going through it again for Carrie's benefit Bridget found she could think about it fairly clearly: how long it had taken her, where she had paused, dragging him across the floor. She remembered checking she had been obscured from the street by the window display. The stockroom took longer than the kitchen to examine: there were rails to remove and boxes of stock to look over. By the time they were sure it was clean, Laura had been gone almost an hour.

'Could anyone have seen him come into the shop?' said Carrie. They were both hot, sweating with the exertion, washing their hands together in the sink by the tiny toilet.

'It's possible,' said Bridget, thinking. 'The lane was fairly quiet, though. A November Tuesday is quiet. And—' she hesitated, forcing herself to be rational. 'It would have to have been someone he knew, wouldn't it? Someone who recognised him. For it to be a worry.'

She'd need to remember to take the hand towel home to wash.

'I told Matt he'd been in,' she said slowly. 'A fortnight before.'

'All right, all right,' said Carrie, dismissive. Jamming her hands in her pockets. 'I know Matt. He won't think it's relevant. Will he? The guy's just gone AWOL but it sounds like he never took the job seriously anyway. It's just if – they have any way of retracing his steps. How did he get into town? He must have left his car somewhere?'

'I don't know,' said Bridget, hearing her own anxiety. Something beginning to sound, all the possibilities, fuzzy images on a camera screen, *last seen*. She needed to think clearly, be methodical. Like Matt. Remembering the little car parked on the kerb opposite her house, the smart little black car. Did anyone see? Carrie was leaning against the door of the little toilet.

'Parking's a nightmare in town,' Bridget said, thinking hard. 'You'd walk if you could. If you lived—'

Then she remembered.

'I have got his address,' she said. 'He wrote it down.' And she was behind the till, and flipping the pages of the big exercise book they used for notes and customer details, back, back, and Carrie looking over her shoulder.

'Look,' she said, at last, and pointing. His handwriting: it was vivid now in her memory. How could she have forgotten how it felt when he smiled across the desk at her in the shop that evening with Isabel waiting, uncomfortable, at the door. He had taken the biro from Bridget's hand to write it down. As if she couldn't manage.

'He lives in town,' said Bridget now, staring at the address. Near where she'd dropped Isabel. 'He would have walked.' She raised her head and someone was there in the street, a youngish woman standing looking at the window display. She smiled, automatically and the woman moved for the door. 'Must have.'

'It'll be OK,' said Carrie, nodding. 'No car – that's good.' The door pinged and the customer was coming inside. A woman on her lunch hour, in a skirt suit, with earphones in listening to music. *Tschkk tschkk*, they could hear, her head moving a little to the sound as her eyes travelled over the rails. Paying them no attention.

Carrie moved away to the sofa and shouldered her little backpack. 'I'll do the food shopping for this evening,' she said cheerfully, one eye on the newcomer. 'I'll cook, even. All right?' Bridget nodded.

Watching her profile as she moved off in the lane Bridget felt suddenly stupidly protective of her, her small white face out here in the sticks. Anything might happen to her, and she looked so brave, so tough.

Across the shop floor the woman in the suit had taken a long, dark, chiffon dress off the rail and was waving it at Bridget, earbuds still in. Reluctantly she pulled one out only when Bridget was in front of her. 'Anything more like this?' she said, in a voice too loud.

The customer was barely installed in the cubicle when the door opened again, and then again. Lunch hour was often like this, too busy for Bridget to think, and she was grateful for it, even though she was alone. The phone rang and, rooting in the stockroom for sizes she had to ignore it.

When finally the door pinged to admit Laura, a customer Bridget hadn't even seen come in was standing with one shoe in her hand in the middle of the floor demanding attention. Her husband was already on the sofa opening his local paper.

The phone rang again. 'You get it,' said Laura comfortably, taking off her coat and reaching for the single shoe. Bridget lifted the receiver.

'Hello?' she said. A crackle on the line.

The headline on the man's paper was about a missing teenager. A blurred photograph of a laughing boy. It set her nerves jangling.

'Hello?' she said again. Laura was on her knees hauling shoeboxes out from their cupboard, and Bridget wanted to get over there and tell her to stop it.

'Hey.' It was Carrie, and her voice was full of something suppressed.

'I'm at his house,' she said.

He was sitting in the hotel lobby when Gill came out of the lift. When he saw her he half hovered to his feet, peering sheepishly down at his own shirt open at the neck. He had come back for his tie. Gill's heart sank. She stopped.

She couldn't remember what he did for a living. Engineer? She couldn't remember his name, even. Did he know hers? She'd rather he didn't. Google made finding out names all too easy.

Messed up: this is messed up, she told herself. She smiled stiffly.

He was properly on his feet now and heading towards her as she stood there like a lemon.

'Sorry,' he said, 'sorry, it's just – well, I haven't got another tie and the conference starts in—' He held out his wrist to examine a battered watch. 'Ten minutes ago.' The trace of a cheeky smile.

She sighed. 'OK,' she said, turning sharply and marching back to the lift, not waiting to see if he was following. He stood in the lift next to her with his hands folded at his crotch like a naughty schoolboy. She said nothing.

At the door he followed her into the room and Gill stopped immediately, holding up a hand. 'Wait there,' she said.

She whisked the tie off the chair and came straight back with it and he made a little lurch towards her, trying for a kiss. 'No!' she said, outraged.

He subsided. 'Sorry.' Tucked the tie in his pocket but didn't move. 'Can I see you again?' he said promptly.

'No,' said Gill, just standing there. What else was there to say?

Slowly he nodded, backing out of the door. Jack, she thought. That was his name. Stopping just a second with his hand on the frame, then he fished in his pocket and brought out a business card, shrugged, apologetic, and was gone.

With the card in her hand — why had she even taken it? — Gill waited: she didn't want to go back down with him. She watched him turn the corner and only when she heard the *shoosh* of the lift doors did she lock the room back up and walk after him.

He had slowed her down. That was all she knew. As she was walking out though the purple lobby she was dialling Matthew Webster's number at the university: he picked up immediately.

No one had given him any message. Well, surprise, surprise. But he covered for his wife, loyally: Gill pretending he'd spoken to her. 'Bridget's not my secretary,' he said mildly, 'and besides, she's got a lot on her plate at the moment. Christmas and all that.' Hearing the name on his lips Gill could still hardly believe it but there it was: Bridget O'Neill, married, normal, housewife and businesswoman. Matt Webster was her hiding place.

She held the phone to her head: the receptionist was signalling for her room key and she walked back and slapped it on the desk.

'Sure,' she said. 'Sorry to have called you at home, it was just—'

'It's fine,' said Matt Webster, easy.

Nice guys, though, could you trust any of them to be what they say? The engineer giving her his card: Christ, he'd almost bowed when he did. He'd looked at her like she might be about to slap him but he was going to do it anyway.

'I'd like to come back up and ask you one or two more things,' she said.

'I could see you at the end of the day,' said Webster, hesitating. 'Six-ish? Though, honestly, I don't know what help I can be. I hardly know Mr Carmichael.'

Carmichael wouldn't like that, his honorary doctorate dispensed with so carelessly: either Webster was an innocent or there was no love lost between them. There was something there: Gill hadn't got this far without being able to hear that tiny pause that meant something wasn't being said. Then he said it. 'What's it about, really?' he said.

She hesitated. Because now it was a bit different, wasn't it? Now she knew he was married to Bridget O'Neill. One of Carmichael's little prodigies, a girl who looked scared in that picture from twenty-five years ago, a girl who might be scared still.

It was a complication that had been in the equation almost since the beginning. Do no harm, was that the phrase? These were girls, women, just about hanging on, struggling to climb out of the shithole he left them in. The last thing they wanted was to have a camera trained on them, a microphone shoved in their faces. She could hear Steve's voice. *That's for doctors, that do no harm crap. You're a journalist, Gillian Lawson.* And Matt Webster could be a goldmine, to a journalist. Matt Webster knew all about who was doing what, on the university server.

204

An edited version was what she gave him. Controversy, she'd been following Carmichael's career, such a talented man who gives to the community. Blah, blah. She couldn't come out and say it, of course. 'I'd like to talk to some of the people who work with him.' A silence: he could laugh, in that silence. *Say, what? Like the computer guy?* She had an instinct Matthew Webster knew what she was after. And knew he shouldn't talk to her, all right. But he was going to. 'Five thirty, six ish, then,' he said. 'It'll have to be quick.'

'Thank you, that's really kind,' she said, 'Honestly.' Laying it on so he wouldn't bail on her. But she had to get back on track: she had most of the day still then. 'I'll be there.' And hailing a cab as she hung up. Sod the expense, her head hurt.

There were things she could be getting on with.

Chapter Eighteen

Bridget was driving, hunched over the wheel. Up the hill towards the corner where she'd dropped Isabel: she could see the big trees, bare now. The street was mercifully empty.

Laura had stared at her: it had felt as though everyone in the shop was staring at her.

'I don't think that's a good idea,' Bridget had said into the mobile, turning a little so they couldn't see her face. Walking to the door, out into the street with all their eyes on her back. Once out there she said, 'Stay right where you are.'

Looking up and down the narrow, cobbled lane. In the window opposite Justine was peering at her over her glittering display. Bridget found herself registering the detail of this street as if she'd never seen it before. How many people there were out shopping this lunchtime. The other shops: a shoe repair man, a shop that sold home stuff, mirrors and lamps and linen, a newsagent's. She knew them all by sight, some for longer than others, the feeble independent retailers' organisation that put on the Christmas lights and petitioned the council over business rates.

Through the glass Laura was still staring at her: Bridget waved cheerily. 'Don't, Carrie,' she said. 'Just, don't. I'll call you back.' She hung up. When she walked back in the customer was at the desk: Bridget held out her hand for the card.

When the woman had gone – the husband took an age to get up off the sofa, folding his paper, tutting – Bridget made herself turn to Laura, smile.

'How you feeling now?' Solicitous. But Laura was bright-eyed; she liked work. Bridget turned away.

Before she had shifted two steps she could hear Laura on the phone to her husband, half listening to her droning on, *Yes darling, no darling, comfortable, no, I'll leave it in the oven for you.* She went into the kitchen, to text Carrie. *What the hell do you think you're doing? Wait for me. Wait.*

'Who was that on the phone?' said Laura when she emerged, looking across the counter at her mildly. On cue. 'Do you need to get off again? It's fine if you do.'

'Family stuff,' said Bridget, grimacing cheerfully. 'You know the kind of thing,' though she knew Laura was an only child, and probably didn't. 'My sister, a bit of a black sheep, you know. She's—' she improvised. 'She's gone off in search of an old girlfriend.' Laura still nodding helpfully. 'Trouble is she's got tanked up first and—'

'Oh, go on then,' said Laura, flapping her hand complacently. And Bridget didn't wait to be told a third time: she grabbed her coat and was off.

She'd dialled Carrie again as she headed up the alley: the phone rang and rang but Carrie wasn't answering.

Finn's school came into sight on the wide ring road. The lunch break seemed to be still on, a handful of lanky sixth formers were milling at the gates eating chips. She was almost past them on the other side of the road when she spotted Finn, talking to a girl, head down. The girl was smoking. He didn't see her; the van was small, white and anonymous, and there were three lanes of traffic between them. Gazing back at him in the rearview mirror Bridget remembered a serial killer of children who used his white van to abduct them. White van man.

And then the slow incline appeared and the rooflines of big houses between tall bare trees.

The harder her heart pounded the more carefully Bridget drove. She indicated. She knew why Carrie was there: it was almost a game to her. Find out about this man. Carrie was fearless, but it had always been Bridget's job to be careful.

She'd just turned into Carmichael's road and had time to register it was a short, discreet street, no more than five or six big houses, when her mobile rang in her lap. She pulled in abruptly. It was Matt.

He was asking if someone called this morning, a woman called Gillian. He sounded on the alert.

'Sorry?' she said. 'Oh, yes, Carrie answered the phone just as I was heading off to work, she did say something but – I'm sorry. Was it important?'

'Not sure,' he said, distant. 'Well, she got hold of me, anyway. She – I wanted to check how you were feeling.'

The engine ticked quietly and she sat, hands on the

steering wheel. 'I—' Bridget realised she was about to tell him she just saw Finn with a girl but realised in time that then she would have had to go into an explanation of where she was and why. 'I'm fine,' she said. Hearing a hesitation in his voice. 'Why?'

A sigh. 'She's coming to see me. I might be a bit late home,' he said.

'That's all right,' she said quickly, relieved. The later he got back the more breathing space. Only— 'Who is this Gillian, then?' she asked, airy. *The one who knows my name.*

'The journalist,' said Matt with a sigh. 'She wants to come and talk to me about Carmichael again.' *Again.* And then Bridget remembered: the journalist who'd been at the lecture that Carmichael hadn't turned up to.

'Oh, him,' said Bridget, and tried to put a whole world of possibilities into the two words, some flaky, arrogant academic she hardly knew from Adam who'd missed a lecture, gone up to London to audition or socialise.

When would this be over? She sat back in the driver's seat, thought about the police, about prison: it looked like an option, suddenly. The peace, the calm. No more toxic fear in her system.

She thought about Finn. Finding out. A courtroom.

Just hold your nerve. She realised she could identify Carmichael's house: he was number five and she was parked outside number three. A tall, solid Victorian house, a garden with shrubs neatly tended. There was no sign of Carrie.

Something had to happen. To explode, somehow. So she wouldn't have to live feeling this way.

'What's she after, this Gillian? Any idea?'

'She didn't really say,' he said shortly. 'A lot of stuff about how eminent he is, what an interesting figure. But the questions – well, does he do private music teaching, do I know why he left his previous position.' A silence. 'I probably shouldn't talk to her, but—' *But you're too straight, you're too kind, you're too honest.* He'd never say that stuff.

His previous position at a prestigious collegiate university. Organ scholar. Bridget knew all about that, all those fruity-voiced middle-aged men protecting each other. '*Do you know why?*' she asked. Matt never gossiped, it hadn't occurred to her that he would know stuff, would hear stuff.

'No,' said Matt, shortly. But Bridget wasn't sure about the way his voice sounded.

'What's she hinting at?' she asked, persistent. This was dangerous: it wasn't like her and Matt knew it. In a moment she was going to have to say the word. But Matt did it for her.

'Paedophilia,' he said, clearing his throat. 'I think she's after him for abusing girls.'

Isabel, thought Bridget, poor little Isabel. Her own self she didn't think about. Her other self, little Bridget in her flowered dresses to hide how skinny she was getting. If she thought about that girl, it was as if she was someone else. An almost-stranger.

There was still no sign of Carrie in the wide, quiet street. The gate between the hedges, though, was ajar.

'She asked about his internet use, his computer history,' said Matt. 'If I'd noticed anything suspicious.'

'You didn't tell me all this,' said Bridget.

Matt sighed. 'Of course I told her, no way. No way could I talk to a journalist about a colleague.' Or his wife either.

'But is there anything?' The words escaped her. She tried to sound unruffled, merely interested.

'I haven't looked,' he said calmly.

'Right,' said Bridget uncertainly and then, hurriedly, she was pretending to be distracted. 'I'd better go,' she said, 'I'm at the post office, Laura's on her own.' At the end of the road an old woman had come out of her gate. She had a small dog with her and was fussing with a lead.

'Anyway,' said Matt, 'I only wondered if she was telling the truth about calling the house. She seemed suspicious. Talked about people closing ranks.'

'I'm sorry,' said Bridget. 'Like I said, I – we – just forgot.'

After she'd hung up she sat a second, trying to sense what the conversation meant. What it had told her. Gillian Lawson the journalist thought Carmichael was a paedophile: well, she was right, wasn't she? And now she was suspicious of Matt, too. At the far end of the pavement the old woman was making her way slowly towards the main road, the dog zigzagging joyfully at her feet. She'd have to come past the van. Bridget kept very still, head down.

How could you know about anyone? How had Bridget known Matt wasn't threatening when she first met him? Geeky with his bike, awkward but determined. She just did. Matt was her touchstone. Matt bringing her tea on a tray, Matt worrying over Finn. The old woman was level with the van now and Bridget could hear her muttering, she could hear the click of the dog's nails on the pavement: she held her breath, and then the woman was past and receding in the rearview mirror.

When she was out of sight Bridget opened the door quietly.

211

She hurried along the pavement. The hedges were high here, the houses were quiet. No windows visible but these places were too grand for net curtains, anyway.

Inside her it sat like lead: the journalist and her suspicions. That they were closing ranks. There were things she'd wondered, on and off, sometimes sparked by those news reports, sometimes flowering out of the dark spaces in her own head. The abused go on to abuse their children. Memories of motherhood surfaced, but they seemed only to hold love, her hand stroking his head while he slept but what if she was no judge? Her thoughts zigzagged, terrified.

Slowly she walked past the house then turned and walked back: on the return she spotted an alley, narrow between laurel hedges, and turned down it.

'Carrie?' High and nervous.

A sound, almost a laugh, suppressed. 'Bridge?' It was Carrie's voice, low and excited, and then her face appeared between the leaves overhanging a low wall. She was in his back garden.

'Come out of there,' hissed Bridget. 'What d'you think you're doing?' Agonised. 'It's bloody trespassing.' Carrie disappeared and a little further along the alley a wooden door opened and her head peered round.

'Come on, Bridge,' she said. 'It's not like he's going to catch us, is it?'

Just to get out of the alley – what if anyone came along? – Bridget pushed her back through the door and followed, pulling it shut behind her. She could feel her heart patter as she set her back against it. The garden was lush, even for November: money had been spent on it. Trimmed evergreens mounded against a soft grey brick wall, the grass trimmed and bright. A long, handsome window with fresh paint was set in the side that faced them, and a wide porch at the back. It was a version of the same house he'd had when Bridget had been fourteen and his student. She could still remember the feeling of standing at his front door, hand raised to a big brass knocker.

'Nice place, right?' said Carrie, scornful. Taking Bridget by the shoulders, giving her a little shake. 'Look, soon people will know he's properly missing,' she said. 'And then they'll come to the house looking for him, the police even, maybe. I don't know why they aren't already, do you?'

Bridget felt numb with panic: they were trespassing. She made herself focus. 'No,' she said. 'He's got friends, after all. Or a friend, anyway.'

'Right,' said Carrie, eagerly. 'So soon it'll be too late.'

'Too late for what?' said Bridget, but even before Carrie spoke she knew. Daredevil bloody Carrie.

'To go in there.' Eyes wide with excitement.

Bridget almost groaned. 'It's not a game, Carrie,' she said, agonised, again. 'They'll know. Break in? It's illegal.' Carrie dropped her hands, took a step back, and smiled.

'I've got his keys,' said Carrie. Then her head whipped round and she put a finger to her lips.

Someone was coming along the alley.

They ducked to a squat under the laurels and waited, hardly daring to breathe. Slow footsteps and an excited bark, a voice grumbling tiredly. The old woman with her dog, or another one. After what seemed like an age the dog had exhausted its snuffling and had moved on, and they got up and made their way across the soft winter grass towards the back porch.

It was neat, orderly: he had a gardener. They edged round a stack of garden chairs, a compost heap and a mound of leaves ready for burning. She'd made a bonfire of hers that morning, only there'd been barely enough leaves to cover the small pile of clothes, hers and Carrie's. They'd caught quickly, the smoke rising in the cold blue morning, and she had been grateful for the seclusion of their garden, on the outer curve of the close. They'd offloaded the carpet in a skip they'd passed on the way back in the dark. It had already been overflowing with flytipped rubbish, old kids' toys and takeaway wrappers.

She'd need to make sure the ashes were swept up before Matt got home. Matt saw everything.

Carrie was on the porch, crouched, and Bridget joined her. 'Carrie, what if— look, the police could—'

'We've got to find his mobile,' said Carrie impatiently. 'I'll go in, you don't have to.'

Bridget patted the pockets of her coat and to her relief found her leather gloves stuffed down in one of them. 'We'll both go in,' she said. 'Just don't – don't touch anything.'

The back door, flanked with etched panels of red and blue Victorian glass, opened on to the back of a wide, bright, double-height hall with a grand staircase. The floor was polished wood with a strip of pale thick carpet. Bridget put a hand on Carrie's arm to stop her.

'Wait,' she said. 'Take off your shoes.'

Not even feeling foolish, they hid them behind a big ceramic jar holding an umbrella. Would that help anything, if the police came and knocked on the door, or the gardener? The house was hoovered, tidy, the woodwork freshly painted and impeccable. A raincoat on a rack and a vase of big white lilies standing on a console table halfway down the hall.

It gave Bridget the creeps.

Carrie was ahead of her, padding on men's woollen socks she must have pinched from Matt's drawer. She disappeared through a panelled door, leaving Bridget alone in the bright hallway that smelled of wax polish and lilies. She took a step closer and saw the big flowers were on the turn, one or two of them edged with brown.

It was warm, stifling in the house. Those flowers would need changing soon, thought Bridget, a little smoke spiral of anxiety rising inside her.

'Hey!' Carrie's hiss of excitement came from round the corner. When Bridget got to the door she was standing by a long bookshelf in one corner of a big, square room where a piano stood in the window, and holding something up triumphantly. Without gloves.

A mobile phone, plugged in and charging.

'All right, all right,' said Bridget, relief mixed with fear. 'So we found it. So it can't – he can't be traced to me, to us. Now, look, wipe it down and leave it where it was and let's go now, Carrie. Please.' But Carrie had that smile on.

'No, Carrie,' Bridget pleaded. 'This isn't stealing apples. This isn't safe.'

'Come on, Bridge,' said Carrie, quite relaxed, defiant. 'Don't you want just a bit of a poke around? It's not like we're going to get this chance again.' Looking around the room, up at the shelves. Bridget was beside her now: she took the mobile and wiped it carefully with her gloves, set it back down. Carrie moved off, restless, and Bridget followed her. It wasn't safe to leave her alone.

215

The books on the floor-to-ceiling shelves seemed to be all about music – a whole shelf on Bach, two – rows and rows of CDs. A stacked music system was in the far corner, with tall, elegant speakers that looked like some kind of artwork.

Carrie came to a stop at a fancy side table polished to a high shine that looked like it might be used as a desk.

'He'll have a computer somewhere,' said Bridget, her heart sinking.

'No doubt,' said Carrie. 'But – it'll be password protected,' tapping her teeth. 'That might not be a problem. It's more—'

'More, what?' said Bridget.

Carrie tapped her fingers against her lips. 'Well, if we find it, take it, it sounds alarm bells, doesn't it? If we get into it and look – well.'

'Look for—'

'Look for anything about you.' Carrie was blunt.

'Like emails.'

Carrie shrugged. 'Or – whatever.' Nodding. 'But you know what? He left his mobile at home. He's old school, right? He's going to be wary of keeping things on the computer. He'll do his thing in person, one to one – he—'

'He might have photographs of me,' said Bridget, inter-rupting.

There was a silence, Carrie looking at her. Nodding, like this didn't surprise her. 'Like I say,' she said, 'I think he's not going to put that stuff on the computer. Prints, negatives? People have known that stuff was safer kept off the laptop for a long time now. And if he has been looking at – paedo websites online, that's different. If the police look on his laptop and find that – bingo. He's busted.'

Bridget stared, feeling sick.

'Don't you want him to be busted?' Carrie's hands on her hips. 'Like, can you think of a better reason for him to just – disappear?' And there it was, the tiniest crystallisation of hope.

'And if I'm identifiable?' said Bridget. 'If I can be connected to him?'

Carrie nodded. 'It's a risk,' she said. 'But—'

'But everything's got risk attached, right?'

'I was going to say, but you won't be the only one,' said Carrie.' Not smiling, serious. 'And straight up I think if he's kept actual pictures they'll be hidden away somewhere.' Looking around the big pale tasteful room. 'Give me the gloves,' said Carrie.

She began to open drawers, Bridget looking with her, but everything was innocuous. A stack of bank statements, bills, some gold-edged invitations. A handful of yellowing cuttings of reviews. They stopped, frustrated.

'It's all right,' said Bridget, edgy. 'I – we've got to get out of here, Carrie.' She backed out of the room into the hall and Carrie followed her. They were at the foot of the wide, carpeted stairwell that led up to a gallery, doors off it.

Carrie looked up the stairs. 'It'd be somewhere a cleaner wouldn't find them, right? So not under the bed, probably.'

The panic spiralled: Bridget put her hands to her face and in the sudden dark it came to her. She'd been in his bedroom. Not this one, not off a gallery, another bedroom. He'd turned to her and said, 'Let me show you something.' Wordless now, she pointed up the stairs.

There were three bedrooms off the gallery but she knew which one was his without knowing.

217

She stopped in the doorway so abruptly Carrie ran into her. It spoke to her out of another place, out of the dark in her head. An old oil painting, of a man in a wig at a spinet or some antique instrument above, a table with silver-backed brushes, a leather-padded headboard. A big, dark wood wardrobe.

'Gloves,' said Bridget, holding out her hand for them. This was for her to find. As the wardrobe door swung open she almost gagged, the smell coming back to her out of the past, his smell. The most imperishable of the senses, unrecordable, yours and yours alone. Leather and aftershave and sweat: he didn't like deodorants. He had told her that. She tried not to breathe, her head in the swinging clothes, suits, jackets, slacks. Horrible, old man slacks. It was dark, but there seemed to be sparks behind her eyes. She fumbled, one way then the other, into the wardrobe's corners.

He'd taken it out and set it on the bed, all that time ago. Bridget could remember what she was wearing when she'd walked up those other stairs, a shirt with a peter-pan collar Mum had bought from Marks. A round-necked, pale blue jumper. He'd already done it to her twice by then. He'd put the box down on the bed and held a finger to his lips, because his wife had been downstairs. He had lifted off the lid.

Carrie wasn't at her shoulder, Carrie knew. Carrie was way back by the door.

Then suddenly Carrie was there, Carrie was holding on to her. Everything seemed to have gone black on the edges of her vision.

The first picture had been a girl giving him a blowjob. Her fringe. Her eyes. She'd known it was him because of the pooled trousers at his feet. The shoes.

218

Her eyes. Bridget hadn't known her. There had been two men in the next picture but you couldn't see their faces.

There was no box in this wardrobe. Turning to Carrie, Bridget's mouth moved but she couldn't say anything, she swayed. There was a high-pitched sound in her ears, and the next thing she knew she was on the floor. Not lying down, sitting. Carrie was still holding on to her.

'All right,' said Carrie, gently peeling the gloves off her and putting them on. 'We're going now.'

She closed the wardrobe door, then the bedroom door, then shepherded Bridget down the stairs. Bridget could sense her looking right and left, checking things: was incapable of doing it herself. She felt as though if she looked anywhere but straight ahead something terrible would happen. The underworld. It was the underworld, and she was being led out of it by her little sister, padding on soft carpet.

At the back door Carrie knelt at her feet, putting her shoes on for her, then whispered, 'Wait. Got to make sure we didn't leave any of those drawers open.' Bridget waited, leaning against the door, while she closed the door on the big sitting room again and put on her own shoes.

Carrie had her hand on the back door's brass doorknob, when they heard something. The adrenaline sharpened everything instantly: Bridget understood in that second what a powerful thing it was, and dangerous. She saw Carrie's pale face, in stripes of blue and red light that shone through the old door. They turned, and looking down the long hall saw a shadow through the front door's stained glass. A key moving in the lock.

Then the sound stopped: it changed. There were voices. The shadow divided, a pale, larger shape behind the first one.

'Quick.' And then they were back out, Carrie turning the key carefully in the lock, pocketing the bunch again while Bridget waited, taking the porch stairs two at a time and running, running, soundless across the grass.

The back door latch creaked and then they were in the alley, holding each other's hand tightly as they crept forwards. The voices murmured, on the house's front steps, louder as they made their way back to the road. One voice foreign, the other insistently English, not loud but determined. Both female.

Bridget stopped a little way back, where the laurels thinned out, and Carrie with her. Peering, they kept very still so as not to be seen. A young woman in cheap tight stonewashed jeans and an overall under her coat was standing in front of Carmichael's front door, looking grimly suspicious. The woman talking to her had her back to them and all they could see of her was thick untidy hair, collar length and a dark coat. She sounded English.

Carrie was frowning, listening. Holding up a finger.

Half a profile as the woman talking turned to fish something out of her bag. Cheap bag. A notebook or something like that. From the profile Bridget saw she was older. Forty-something, maybe.

They heard snatches. *No idea when—*

The other one, the foreign one – Bridget could have told you she was foreign, she found herself thinking, mindless, just by the clothes – was shaking her head tightly. Meaning, *No I wouldn't tell you if I did know.*

Ducking, Carrie gestured towards the end of the alley: hidden by the front hedge they slipped past and let themselves into the van. Sitting there, not daring to start the engine. The two women on the doorstep were just visible behind a large cypress.

'That's the journalist,' said Carrie, suddenly. Staring through the wide window at them. The young, foreign woman in overalls was holding up both hands, palms out, shaking her head. 'The older one. The English one.' Swivelling to take in Bridget's bewilderment. 'I recognise her voice,' she explained patiently. 'Off the phone.'

Bridget leaned forward to get a better look at her. 'She's on the case, then,' she said. 'Asking where he's gone.' The woman who was the journalist stood back then, looking up at the windows. 'She'd like to get a look in there, wouldn't she?'

'No doubt,' said Carrie, drily.

Bridget stared at her hands on the wheel. 'He told me there were photographs,' she said. 'Carmichael did, when he came back. If anyone – if they—'

Carrie rubbed her hands through her short hair, jittery now, evasive.

'Maybe he was bluffing,' she said. 'I mean – he would need something, wouldn't he? Leverage? To keep you quiet.'

Bridget looked at her, dumbfounded. She hadn't thought of that. She had been a danger to him. It hadn't felt like that, never felt like that.

'Maybe he got rid of them a long time ago,' said Carrie. 'No one would recognise you, anyway,' she said finally. 'Back then you were – you were so ill. No one would know you.' Uncertain.

'I would,' said Bridget. 'I would know.' Silence.

The voices on the doorstep were raised, now, and the older woman was gesticulating.

'Let's go,' said Carrie, 'While they're busy, OK?'

Bridget turned the key in the ignition and they moved off. They hadn't got to the end of the road when she saw it, in Carrie's lap. As if by magic, spirited there: Carmichael's mobile.

'What? What are you – *Carrie!*' A jab on the brakes, she couldn't help herself. They were stationary in the middle of the empty road. In the passenger seat beside her Carrie shrugged, sheepish. Bridget looked, right to left, for witnesses.

'I was careful,' Carrie insisted. 'I used the gloves, didn't I?'

'No,' said Bridget, frantic. Pulling back into the kerb beside the peeling trunk of a big plane tree, checking they were out of sight.

They were parked behind a shiny little black car. 'Can't you see they'll trace it, that's the whole point?'

'They,' said Carrie, sullenly. 'You keep talking about they.'

'The police.' Carrie shrugged, obstinate. 'We're going to have to put it back,' said Bridget.

'I want to keep it.' Carrie's hands were curled around it. 'Aren't you curious? There could be anything on it. We could find out stuff. Useful stuff. Messages, I mean, if someone wants to know where he is. What he's been up to.'

'It'll be locked,' Bridget was pleading, now, because she knew Carrie had something. The germ of something. But the last thing she wanted was to see inside Carmichael's life. What if there were pictures on it? She didn't want to know. They sat, deadlocked side by side in the wide, peaceful street, the big handsome trees with their splotched and speckled trunks standing at regular intervals, the well-tended gardens. Bridget put out her hand: Carrie hesitated then put the small silver phone into it.

Old-school, maybe five years old. Not a smartphone – that was good. It meant there'd be less on it. Less technology. No email or Facebook or anything like that, no location services. It occurred to Bridget that he might have another phone somewhere, for that kind of thing. But she didn't need to see that.

'We're going to have to put it back in the house.' She stared through the windscreen blankly.

The little black car in front of them had sheet music on the back shelf.

'Look,' Carrie began.

'Wait,' said Bridget. Turning to her. 'You've got his keys.'

She took them from Carrie, no more than the briefest tremble in her fingers, and there it was. A little leather fob, a car key. 'That's his car,' said Bridget.

'What are you—' Carrie began, bewildered. Bridget pointed the key through the windscreen and pressed: the car's indicators flipped jauntily.

'I've got an idea,' said Bridget.

Chapter Nineteen

When Bridget pushed her way inside, at first she could only see Laura's back: she was on her knees on the carpet re-packing boxes of stock. Then she heard a throat being cleared and turned to see a man in a suit on the sofa, hands clasped in his lap. It took her a moment to recognise him: she'd only met him once. Nick.

'Oh, Laura, I'm sorry, sweetheart,' said Bridget with a pang of guilt. Distracted. 'Get up, you don't have to do that.' She couldn't work out why the man was just sitting there.

Laura turned, scrambled round, flushed. 'Oh,' she said. 'Oh. I'm sorry.' Her eyes darted to Nick. 'This is my – do you remember my – he just came to see—'

And then Nick shifted on the sofa at last, forwards, smiling, getting to his feet. 'We *have* met,' he said. Something faintly belligerent in his tone, challenging her not to remember him. He was about to hold out his hand to her and Bridget stepped back abruptly, on instinct.

'Yes, it's Nick,' she said hastily. 'Of course,' then turned away from him to help Laura to her feet. She seemed uncomfortable, short of breath.

'Nick came to, came to—'

'She left her phone at home,' said Nick. 'Forget her head if it wasn't screwed on. Pregnancy brain, isn't it?' His smile didn't reach his eyes.

Behind her Laura made a sound of assent, but Bridget was fairly sure she'd had the phone when she got in, remembered her checking it as she removed her coat. She opened her mouth to say so, frowning, but Nick was moving off, quick and easy, heading for the door. 'Don't keep her late, now,' he said, and was gone.

'Laura?' she said, the bell over the door still tinging in his wake, but Laura waved her off.

'Just need the—' She was heading for the toilet.

Bridget stood, staring down at the half-packed boxes on the floor. Knelt.

Carrie had tried to persuade Bridget to leave her at the pub but Bridget dropped her at the house. 'You said you'd buy stuff for tea, remember?' she said, fishing some cash out of her pocket. 'You know where the supermarket is. Borrow the bike.' Carrie had pouted but she hadn't said no. The plan was for later.

There were things she would need to do. Clean everything all over again. The shop and the garage and the back of the van. Would there be an end to it? She had no idea.

Go back to Carmichael's house. The thought of it, of the wide hall and the smell of lilies, made her feel sick, and worse than sick. Frightened.

From behind the toilet door came the sound of water

running and Bridget sat back on her heels. When eventually Laura reappeared, her nose was red and she was fiddling with a sodden bit of tissue.

'What is it?' said Bridget, but she knew. If not what, then who. 'Is it him? Is it Nick?' Laura subsided on to the sofa, an ungainly heap. Bridget got her some water. 'Tell me, Laura,' she said.

He'd come in late, he'd been drinking, she could smell it on him. Sniffing, the limp shredded tissue at her nose again.

Re-stacking the stock, Bridget listened, although there was so much else to think about. She was going to have to get hold of Carrie straight out of work, they'd need two hours at least. But Laura's voice kept tugging at her.

Voice raised, querulous. *And not just that.* Standing on a stool as she pushed the box of T-shirts on to a high shelf behind the till, Bridget paused, hands over her head. She hadn't liked him the first time she met him, the sharpsuited salesman, too beefy for his jacket. Too smooth for Bridget's liking – smooth and edgy at the same time. Bouncing on the balls of his feet. But it took all sorts, she'd told herself then, you can't judge a book by its cover.

All that rubbish people say.

Laura looked up at her now from the sofa with her big blue eyes brimming, her little sharp red nose, shoulders hunched miserably over her knees. She'd been twenty, when she came to work for Bridget, carefree, pretty. Wore the teenage uniform, tight tops, jeans, boots with heels clomping around, flicking through the stock carelessly like she could take it or leave it: that had changed since the sainted Nick. More ladylike, now, more careful, and pregnancy – or something – had made her quieter.

As Bridget watched she rocked a little and there it was: a little wince of physical pain.

'Are you all right?' And then Bridget was off the stool and kneeling beside her.

'It's nothing,' said Laura, head down, pulling at the shredded tissue.

'Is it the baby?' Laura shook her head, sniffing. But she wouldn't look up. Bridget took her gently by the shoulders. 'Laura?' And at last Laura looked back up, her mouth trembled, open. She didn't know how to say it.

Bridget knew. 'Did someone hurt you?'

'He – I don't think he meant—' Searching Bridget's face for understanding, so she didn't have to say.

Nick. 'What happened?' said Bridget. 'Nick came home late. You said that.'

Nodding, head back down. 'He wanted to – to have sex with me.' So quiet she was almost inaudible but Bridget just leaned close and listened to her whisper. Their heads together, and Laura's words a mumbled litany, once sharpening to a shocked whisper. *I told him I didn't want to. I told him.* Then Laura raised her head, her face blank and bewildered.

'He isn't what I thought he was going to be,' she said, lips pale. 'He was never like this. He said all these things about putting me on a pedestal, when we first, when he—' She broke off, trembling. 'And he was just disgusting.'

Nick, who'd been sitting there when she walked in. Just sitting watching his wife work.

Bridget took her by the shoulders so she wouldn't look away. 'Did he force you?' she said. 'You said to him you didn't want it?'

Laura ducked, evasive, she let her hair fall over her face. 'I don't know,' she said. 'It's not his fault. He said sorry.' Looking toward the door, the outside world, looking for escape. Then back at Bridget, pale and frightened. 'It's just – what if he's hurt the baby.' Mumbling.

'Is there bleeding? Pain? Cramps?' Laura shook her head stiffly. Bridget took her gently by the wrist. 'Babies are tough,' she said. 'I think the baby is fine.' Laura looking down. 'I think it's you he's hurt.' Laura pulled her wrist away.

'You should talk to someone,' said Bridget. 'The doctor. The midwife? What if it happens again?' Then, not having the faintest idea how it would actually work, but determined: 'Look. You can come and live with me and besides—'

But Laura was on her feet then, shaking her head, stepping back from her as if she was the dangerous one. 'No, no, no – really.' And smoothing the wool of her maternity dress down, brushing at herself, dabbing below her eyes. 'It's fine. We're fine.'

Bridget stood, helpless, watching Laura compose herself. She folded her arms, holding herself by the elbows. Had she overreacted? But she'd said it. Laura had. *He was just disgusting.*

She knew about that. The things they did that seemed to come from a different place: the grunting, the forcing her under him. In love. Bridget hated *in love*. And the way she'd felt afterwards.

Matt didn't do *in love*. Not flowers or dates. He did tea in bed and bikes and knowing when she was sad. Knowing when she was frightened.

She and Laura weren't the same: she needed to remember that.

'As long as you know,' Bridget said, clearing her throat and Laura glanced at her sideways, then looked away. 'There's helplines.' Nothing. 'As long as you know there's somewhere you can go if you need it. You can come to me.' Standing behind the desk with her hands flat on the day book, Laura didn't look at her. 'All right?' And slowly Laura nodded.

A couple were outside the window, holding hands. Middle-aged. He pointed, she smiled.

Bridget sighed. 'So how was the day?'

Laura looked blank, a frown chasing across her face, then she shrugged. 'OK. A few customers. Sold—' she looked down in the book. 'A white blouse.' The frown deepened. 'She was a pain. I don't even think she wanted – well. She came in right after you left.' She shrugged again. 'And he came back. The man.' Tapping with a fingernail on the big exercise book where they wrote everything down, the customer requests, the email addresses, sales, and Bridget came round beside her to look. 'What man?' Running her finger down the page.

The door pinged and one half of the middle-aged couple came in. The woman, still smiling and flushed, shyly expectant. As if they all should know what she was here for.

In Laura's handwriting Bridget saw a name carefully written. A mobile number. An address. 'Laura, when did you—' But Laura wasn't listening. The woman was standing right on the other side of the desk now and Bridget had to look up. She had to smile.

'I'm getting married next week,' said the woman, breathless. Sixty if she was a day, and so happy.

'Yes,' said Bridget, in a daze. 'How lovely.' Automatically. 'Let's – well we have—'

Mechanically she led the woman through the rails, as though she was sleepwalking, sleeptalking. Sometimes the shop *was* in her dreams, more and more: clothes stained, boxes full of hands where shoes should be. Moving down the rail Bridget just kept talking. 'Do you want sleeves?' They always wanted sleeves, as though a bare arm was shameful.

The woman – Marie, she confided, her second marriage, the first had been a disaster and she thought she'd never find anyone else, *But Gerry was, well, he was* – took about an hour and a half to decide on a pale grey suit. And then the door pinged shut behind her and the quiet settled, terrifying, in the room.

Bridget stepped back behind the desk and looked down at the book again.

'Laura?' she said, and she knew it had crept into her voice – a little too high, a little too light – because of the way Laura's head lifted sharply.

'Who is this, did you say?' Tap, tap on the book.

Laura moving slowly, a hand gingerly on each side of her belly, neat and contained now in her navy wool. 'When did you write this?

'It's the man who wanted to talk to you about the present for his wife,' she said straight away, obedient. 'You served him the first time, he's been back twice. That man.'

The name written in the book. Alan Timpson.

Carmichael's friend at the university, the man who had recruited him, the man who was covering for him, the man Matt hated. Matt never hated someone for no reason.

Laura seemed quite composed again. She wouldn't call any helpline, Bridget was suddenly sure of it. She was pretending it had never happened.

At her shoulder Laura said, 'Yes. Professor Timpson. He said would you call him maybe.'

Fuck it, thought Gill gloomily, staring at her emails as a girl tried laboriously to work a spluttering espresso machine behind the grubby counter. Running out of time.

Six hundred words? See if you can get a photograph while you're there, striped apron, big smile, all right? We can use stock pictures for Sandringham.

It was how the world worked. Did people think journalism was about righting wrongs? Maybe they did, but what they wanted to read was how low the Duchess of Cambridge's neckline was going to be on Christmas morning. Or how she liked her three-bird roast. Sitting on the tube she'd seen them turn the page quickly when it was another story about celebrity abusers or grooming gangs. Making a disapproving noise under their breath: *not decent.*

She sighed and began to type. *On it. Should be able to file by Sunday evening.*

She could always make it up. The thought sprang outrageous into Gill's head and all the consequences it would trail after it. No shame greater than faking a royal story: her journalistic career would be over, dead and buried. For some reason the prospect left her unmoved. She could always work in a coffee shop.

The school-leaver working the machine flashed a mouthful of metal in an apologetic smile as she set the cappuccino gingerly down in front of her. Gill smiled wearily at her.

The other girl, the one on Carmichael's doorstep had

been a tough cookie, not giving an inch. His cleaner, chipped nails, overall, thousand-yard stare. Presumably that was why he'd chosen her: someone who knew exactly what her job was worth and was going to defend it tooth and nail. Did she turn a blind eye to her employer's private life? Or had he got too old? Abusers went on and on, particularly now they could get it up till they were ninety but even before. It wasn't about sex, after all. It was about hurting someone. It was about power.

The cleaner had been young, too: Gill guessed she was nineteen or twenty, under the thick layer of slap. Girls did that – always had, always would, in defiance of a mother saying, *Get that rubbish off your face* – but there would be an advantage to looking older than your years if your employer was Anthony Carmichael.

But the fact remained, Gill hadn't gained access. 'Can I come in and wait maybe?' No joy. The girl standing there holding her gaze till she had to just turn round and walk away. 'He is not here,' she said, jaw jutting. The girl foreign but pretending to have worse English than she did have.

Closing ranks. Why would anyone want to protect Carmichael? People whose job it was. People who didn't know. People who did know, and were part of it.

He had a big house. So he had money, from somewhere. His wife's will had made the paper, wills and announcements, four million. Less tax. Which is why he had hung on in there. Had she known she was cover? Her musical evenings, standing next to him on podiums. Nice bit of town, maybe he planned on staying, maybe not.

Not exactly net curtain territory, hedges and shrubberies

and people minding their own business. Up to a point. Gill had thought she was being watched all right.

The girl had stood there, though, till she'd had to go.

Gill pushed the cup away across the table. Time to head back up the hill.

Chapter Twenty

'Sorry, darling,' she said, on the phone to Matt. Holding her breath when he didn't respond. 'The stuff needs to go back this evening to their depot. It's only a half-hour drive and we can just make it.'

A story she'd cooked up about mis-delivered stock that was worth a lot of money. The insurance wouldn't cover it if it was left in the shop overnight.

'It's fine,' Matt said, distant. 'I told you, I might be a bit late anyway.'

'Oh,' said Bridget evenly. Was he just distracted? 'Yes. The journalist.' Matt made a sound of impatience in his throat but Bridget couldn't tell if it was with her or the prospect of talking to the journalist. 'I'll get home as quick as I can,' he said. 'I really – I wish I hadn't said I'd talk to her but—'

'Well, just be polite,' she said, to reassure him. 'Make sure you don't give her our home address, all right?' Trying to make it sound like a joke. 'Oh – and Laura found your pliers after all. So now you've got two pairs.' Regretting it almost as soon as she'd said it, in the silence that followed.

'Sure, right,' said Matt after a long moment. Bemused. There was a sound in the background, and he said, 'Got to go. See you later.' And hung up.

No *love you*. The desire for the words was irrational: it would have been so out of character they would have freaked her out. But she felt as though she was on the brink, about to fall, she needed something to grab.

'Bye,' she said into the dead phone.

Finn and Carrie had been in the garage when she got back from work, thick as thieves. Finn had his bike up on the stand and was explaining something to Carrie about his gear set. She was looking interested, even.

Standing there in the garage Bridget remembered Carrie had been a cycle courier, once upon a time, when Finn had been five or six. Bridget had begged her to stop when she found out but she did it for a year, in defiance. She remembered Matt looking up from his paper when Bridget had hung up after that conversation and pondering how odd it was that they were sisters, one of them with a deathwish, the other one so risk-averse she turned the gas off at the mains when she left the house. 'I like you that way,' he'd said gruffly, from behind his newspaper when she'd stood there anxious.

Peering at his bike in the dim garage Finn had been upbeat, happy. Excitable. He even mentioned Isabel, darting a glance at Bridget across the bike frame, Carrie looking away.

'I bumped into her after school,' he said, nodding. 'I like her, she's nice.' Obediently, as if he knew that would please her. He didn't mention the girl she saw him talking to in the lunch hour but then why should he?

'That's good,' Bridget said. He had wiped his hands on a rag.

'Right,' he said. 'I'm making tea, am I?'

She and Laura had locked up the shop together, Laura restored to being calmly feminine, pretty, her pale pink lipstick carefully applied. Back at the other end of the spectrum, suddenly, with Bridget and Carrie at the sweaty, bloodstained end of being women, as if what Nick had done had never happened. And Laura went home to him.

It was impossible to know what actually had happened between two people, without witnesses. Was Laura so easily shocked that it had been in fact something innocuous, just something he said, or a drunken fumble? It hadn't felt that way. Should Bridget have told her: go to the police? She wouldn't have gone – but still. But still. It ticked away inside Bridget as she followed Finn inside.

'Dad said he'd be home in about an hour,' Bridget said to Finn's back as he knelt in front of the fridge, fishing things out. Carrie had bought tuna steaks and green beans and some tubs of prepared things.

'Sure,' he said, peering at a box of potato salad, and Bridget had jerked her head to Carrie. *Upstairs.*

They sat side by side on Bridget's bed. Bridget pulled her phone out of her pocket and slipped it under the pillow. 'We've got to leave them behind.' Carrie rolled her eyes. 'And yours,' said Bridget, holding out her hand. Taking hold of her by the shoulder and pinching: *it's the whole point*. Carrie wriggling under her grip and it was like they were ten and five again. If only.

Standing, she sorted through the drawer where she kept gloves and scarves and found some fine-knit gloves for Carrie. Carrie shifting from foot to foot, looking around at her neat dressing table, the photograph of Finn on the wall, the dresses hanging in the open wardrobe as if she was in a foreign country. Daredevil excitable Carrie, raring to go.

Bridget left calling goodbye until the front door was closing behind them, and got a mumble in return. A pan clattered on the stove.

Carmichael's wide, peaceful street looked quite different by night. It was well-lit and the tall, bare trees shed ghostly shadow-patterns on the pavements. Big windows glowed behind neat hedges as Bridget pulled in to park around the corner.

The phone was still there in the glove compartment of his car, where Bridget had left it.

'Right,' she said, handing the van's keys to Carrie. 'You can remember how to drive, right?'

Carrie's eyes glittered, mischievous in the streetlights. She shrugged. 'More or less.'

'I'm serious,' said Bridget, under her breath. The street was empty and quiet, but she heard a burst of chatter from a couple of houses down as a window or door was opened. 'Take it easy. No clipping anyone's wing mirror, even. No speeding, no dazzling people with headlights, no drawing attention to yourself. No punctures: if we get into trouble we've got no phone to call for help.' Carrie just nodded. 'Let's go then.'

She climbed into his car. There was air freshener in it, a little pine tree hanging from the rearview mirror that made her want to be sick: she had known she didn't want Carrie in here, and now she knew why. He was in here, inside the expensive padded space, his backside on this seat, his hands on the wheel. His smell. His smell. She indicated and pulled away smoothly from the kerb, monitoring the rearview mirror to check Carrie was following.

He'd had a bigger car before, a flashier one. He had leaned over her to recline the seat. He's too old for that now.

All right. All right. It ticked away in the back of her mind, *not old, not old any more.* You killed him, remember?

They'd talked about it, she and Carrie, in whispers outside his house. Take the car to where his body is. He'll have committed suicide. When they find stuff in his house, on his computer, they'll understand why. The police. The car needs to be in the right place and the mobile in the glove compartment to help them trace it. His last movements.

It was a plan. It was all they had.

The luck of it, Carmichael's leaving the phone at home when he came to the shop that last time, almost took her breath away. Bridget indicated to join the ring road. A sheen on the road, of wet or frost. Carrie was still there in the rearview mirror. The junction loomed, too many lanes, two sets of traffic lights and then with headlights coming at her from all directions, bouncing off the road, the yellow glow of streetlight: it jumped into her head and abruptly everything inside her accelerated, screaming.

Don't panic. Smoothly Bridget crossed the traffic, left the ring road, out of nowhere a layby appeared and she indicated, *mirror signal,* pulled off and turned off the engine. Her heart beating like a deranged machine, faster, faster, faster. She sat. Carrie's face appeared in the window, angry, confused but for a moment Bridget couldn't talk.

Carrie came round the other side and tugged open the door.

'What the fuck, Bridge,' she said, white-faced. Wordless Bridget shook her head, *No.* She climbed out and stood there, holding on to the small black car. Her legs were jelly. They stood there in the dark. The sea was still visible, an inky gleam, the other way the red lights on the towers of the university.

Bridget spoke. 'We can't leave the car at the quarry.'

'All right,' said Carrie, warily. 'Why not?'

'Because that will lead the police to his body and if they find his body they'll know he was dead before he went in to the water.' Something eased, the thundering in her ears ebbed just fractionally.

'I don't understand,' said Carrie, obstinate.

'I read it somewhere.' She was certain. 'If you drown your lungs are full of water. They'll know he died of something else. Somewhere else. And someone put him in the water.'

Blunt head trauma: the words jumped into her head.

Slowly Carrie began to nod. 'Right,' she said, obedient at last. 'OK. So what do we do?'

A heartbeat, another. Bridget couldn't say, I don't know. She couldn't scream and shout and bang and run. She'd got them into this. Think. The next step came to her only as she opened her mouth to speak. She said, 'We'll leave the car by the sea. And the phone in it.'

She knew the way, even in the dark: when Finn had been small they used to come here for long days, at the first hint of sun. A half hour to the north, a stretch of velvet greensward on those summer days, breakwaters and beach huts. They hadn't been in five years, more: it had changed, or perhaps it was out of season. The down-at-heel high street where they bought buckets and spades and fish and chips was deserted in the cold: in convoy Bridget and Carrie drove down it at a snail's pace, obedient to the speed limit.

Bridget knew there was a camera, on the front. She turned off before they reached it and parked on an unlit street at right angles to the sea, where small, dark, Victorian houses crowded against each other. When Bridget climbed out she could hear the waves, shushing softly in the dark at the end of the street. She could smell seaweed and ozone and had a vivid memory of those long days, sheltering against the greenish-black slimed supports to the beach huts, Finn stamping on bladderwrack with his small bare feet.

Would Carmichael come here to kill himself? He might. If he had been the kind ever to contemplate suicide, and they weren't to know he wasn't. She knew. His mate Timpson probably knew.

This was a quiet place, unfashionable, unpicturesque, a blunt parade of modern flats beyond the terrace where they stood. A windfarm's array out to sea, tens then hundreds of little red lights at the horizon. No music festivals, no gourmet pubs.

Carrie stood beside her, shivering. There was a damp, cold wind off the sea. Bridget took Carmichael's phone out of her pocket.

'Right,' she said, hesitating. Once this was done, it was done. 'We'll leave this in the car.'

A silver bullet, heavy in her hand. It was too old to be code-locked but she hadn't wanted to look at it. She didn't want to see messages, or pictures.

They'd follow it, that was the point. Eventually. Wouldn't they? They'd find the car, in this down-at-heel little back-street, in this dead out-of-season place, the closest access point to the open sea. They'd think—

'But why would he disappear?' asked Carrie, rubbing her upper arms in the cold. As if she knew what Bridget was thinking; she always used to have that knack, of asking the question Bridget didn't want to answer, doggedly, the grit in the wheel. 'Why, though? Why would he walk into the sea?'

'We'll work that one out,' said Bridget, as stubborn in return. She could only think of his arrogance, his certainty that he could bluff anything out. He would never kill himself.

Carrie had her hands in her armpits, pacing on the dark pavement. Marching back to stand in front of Bridget. 'Can't I have a look first?' she said. 'After all, once we lock it in there—' Hand out. 'I bet you I can get into it.'

Bridget contemplated her, the little chin thrust out. 'Get in the van,' was all she said. Once inside she handed the phone over without a word.

Carrie frowned down at it in her hands. 'It's a piece of shit,' she said, looking up cheerfully. 'I suppose they'll be able to track it from the signal but it hasn't got location services, any of that.' She flipped it open.

'No—' said Bridget. 'Don't—'

'Keep your hair on,' said Carrie. 'Just making sure there's nothing that will lead to us, that's all.' Swallowing, Bridget looked away, out of the window, down the dreary, dark little street. One light on in an upstairs window, far from the sea.

After five minutes Carrie nudged her to turn round and handed the phone back to her, folding her arms across her front. Bridget didn't ask her anything. She just climbed out, wiped it down, put it in Carmichael's car's glove compartment and locked the car.

'OK,' she said to Carrie at the passenger door to the van. Held out the keys by their fob. 'Your turn.'

She stood at the end of the street and watched as Carrie ran, wheeling across the cropped grass that was more black than green in the dark. She disappeared down between the beach huts' pointed roofs.

Alan Timpson had wanted to talk to her. Did he know? Could it be a coincidence? Her heart beat steadily, but too fast, too fast. She knew she was grasping at straws: this was no coincidence. Why did he think his friend had disappeared? She wouldn't call him.

Carrie reappeared, panting, smelling of the sea. Her jeans were splashed with water. 'Gone,' she said, climbing in.

As they turned for home Bridget took one last look in the rearview mirror, at the car sitting there in a strange street, ending in shifting darkness.

At the base of the towers the campus was deserted in the early dark. Lights had come on against the electric blue dusk, higher up in the student rooms, where there were floor-length windows. Gill saw a figure hunched over a desk halfway up the nearest one – sixth, seventh floor? – push back the chair and stand suddenly, stretching. Looking out down the hill towards the town where more lights twinkled. It looked almost welcoming from up here.

In the cold, grey piazza the fountain dribbled and spat and the low-lit student bar was empty, except for a tattooed girl wiping tables. It was still only just after five and Gill had time to kill. A bit early for drinking, but the sun was no more than a distant glow inland, and to the east the estuary was dark. Gill knew which tower held the music department, and drifted that way, quickly past the windows of the admin office, although its blinds were down and the lights were out behind them.

At the base of Tower Three, she hovered, diffident, monitoring movement. Across the piazza she could see the light on in Matthew Webster's office but she didn't want to be early. Never look desperate. The campus wasn't quite deserted after all, figures came out and flitted quickly across the chilly space between the big buildings, heads down in the wind, disappearing back inside as quickly as they had emerged. It wasn't a place to hang out, not in November. Perhaps summer was different, though Gill couldn't imagine it.

Something moved from out of the shadows, lumbering, a big, awkward shape she couldn't quite work out straight away, and then it came into focus, a gangly boy lugging some big instrument. Cello? Bigger than that, double bass maybe, though Gill was ignorant, still, maybe wilfully not wanting to be in his world, of orchestral instruments. The boy held a card to the entry panel and as the door opened she was behind him, holding the door for him, so helpful. He didn't make eye contact as he mumbled thanks and

Gill hung back, pretending to look at the noticeboard as he waited for the lift.

There was a handwritten page pinned up. *Dr Carmichael will not be available this week.* No more than that, no explanation, no signature, no substitutions.

The lift door shushed behind the boy and his coffin-sized instrument. What a pain, lugging that thing around: Gill, with not a musical qualification to her name though she'd had her share of misspent youth on the dancefloor, felt a grudging admiration for the sheer physical effort. Their world was different, wasn't it? A secret language, listening for different sounds, their private music playing in their heads. And the rehearsal rooms, with doors closed against the philistines. The chippy kids like Gill. She took the stairs.

Carmichael's office was on the fifth floor and Gill was wheezing as she got there. A little lobby with two uphol-stered chairs in it and an engraving of Beethoven or someone. It was warm up here: stuffy, even. Although Carmichael's door was locked, of course, it had a glass panel in it, and she could look inside. The room was dark but a wide window was uncurtained and there was a gleam from somewhere, an invisible moon. It looked neat, not as though anyone had left in a hurry. There was a view out across the estuary.

They installed glass in the doors and open-plan offices for student protection. Gill knew very well what steps educational institutions had implemented, and why. The institutions themselves liked to keep it all very vague, very positive: they didn't talk about what might or might not have happened, why certain staff had taken early retirement, they just talked about student welfare, and openness and feedback.

So Anthony Carmichael had to put up with an office anyone could peer into, at any time. No green baize here, no sandstone college room with double doors for extra privacy. She bet he didn't like that much. But he had a job, didn't he? A job where people covered for him when he got bored and headed off somewhere where more reverence was paid to him perhaps, and where the doors didn't have windows in them. He had a job, when he should be in prison.

The little lobby felt stifling suddenly, the stiff mustard-coloured fabric on the chairs, the rug, and Gill pushed her way back out on to the concrete stairwell and down. There was an institutional smell here, and the cold air whistled up from the ground, but she could keep moving.

She'd talked to the police, over the years, she'd talked to teachers and social services and the body that provided police checks on all those working with young people. There were still so many cracks for them to fall through, though. Children's brains didn't work like hers, like the standard reasonably adjusted adult brain. She had seen that in the half dozen victims she'd seen, girls hiding in their rooms, skinny adolescents crushed into a corner of the settee in their mum's sitting room, under the framed photographs of them holding the instrument, blank and awkward. They could be moulded, they could be lied to, they believed in stories.

Gill clattered on the stairs, in a hurry now. Uneasy. She was a storyteller herself. She'd lied, hadn't she? She'd lied only this afternoon, more than once, to get what she wanted.

Carmichael's cleaner had been a tougher nut to crack than an English blonde in a backstreet boutique, rushed off her feet, even if she did have a few instincts left, a wariness, a nail bitten down to the quick on one hand. A bit late to be wary of strangers once you're pregnant. Too much to lose.

And then Gill was outside, in the damp, cold, fresh air, breathing it in in great gulps. Rose Hill was nothing like its name. It was dark and cold and windswept, it was concrete and glass. Suddenly across the piazza students were crowded into the bar now, in the twenty minutes that had passed the place had filled up. There was light and warmth in there but Gill couldn't go in again. It would be to draw attention to herself and she needed to take this carefully.

A girl broke off from the crowd, opened a door and came towards her. Bottle-bottom glasses and a centre parting, hair fluffy in the wind. Gill had ten minutes before she was due to meet Matt Webster, and she waited for the girl to come to her.

Chapter Twenty-One

In silence on the way back they didn't mention it: just her and Carrie side by side, staring ahead through the windscreen into the dark. They talked about Finn, and it shifted in Bridget's head, further and further back. The flashy little black car incongruous on the back street; the seaside town's high street decked with union jack bunting, celebrating freedom: a place he'd never have gone, with the windfarm and the charity shops.

'He's turned out so lovely,' said Carrie with wonder. 'Little Finny.' They'd got past Rose Hill, and were descending towards the town that twinkled against the dark estuary. This must be how you do it, thought Bridget, just don't look round. 'I hope that girl looks after him. Whoever she is.'

'She's got to,' said Bridget, indicating, turning into the close. Her Finn. Their safe little place, houses at their neat respectful distance, all with lights on now. Only downstairs at theirs, so she calculated Matt still wasn't home. 'He'll be all right, won't he?' she said, coming to a halt. She turned off the engine.

Carrie turned in her seat to look at her, sardonic. 'You mean with a pair of screw-ups like you and Matt for parents?' She shrugged, shoving the door open with her shoulder. 'Well, you never know. He might overcome his disadvantages.'

The table was laid, at the centre of it a vast salad with everything Finn had found in the fridge, it looked like: peppers and onions and lettuce, and chunks of grilled tuna. He peered round the door from the living room, proud and sheepish at once.

Carrie was already leaning over the table to filch a bit of tuna with grubby fingers and they both descended on her at once, slapping her away.

'Where's Dad?' said Bridget. Carrie had got herself a beer, rooting in the drawer for the opener, and was off for the living room. They heard the TV come on.

Finn shrugged. 'You told me he was going to be late,' he said. They both looked at the kitchen clock together: it was just after eight. It was a long time since Matt had been home anything like that late.

'I'm going to have a quick shower, then,' said Bridget, to cover the silence, and he just nodded, giving her the Finn frown that no longer told her anything, if he was happy, or sad, or worried, that just covered his thoughts. Did he sense anything? Was she different, to him?

She showered in five minutes flat then left the water running as she dialled Laura's number.

It took six rings for her to answer, but she sounded bright when she did, and determined.

'Bridget.' She used the name as if she was announcing it to someone else.

'Just checking timings for tomorrow, you're in at eleven, right?' said Bridget. Clearing her throat. 'Everything OK?'

There was a tiny intake of breath before Laura spoke. 'Oh yes, yes—' Then she broke off and there was a man's voice in the background, muffled. Bridget didn't like that: what kind of person interrupted someone when they were on the phone? She didn't like it.

She didn't like her own anxiety either, though. It was as if everything was getting tangled up: her and Laura; her and Carmichael; Laura and Nick. And if she got too involved she might give herself away.

But still. Nick had made Laura have sex. That hadn't been her imagination, that hadn't been Bridget projecting anything. Maybe he hadn't known she didn't want it. Maybe it was a one-off, maybe he's a good guy, maybe it will settle down.

It was still rape.

If you say it over and over. Carmichael gone, nothing to do with her, the world should be a safe place after all.

It was still rape.

'You need to ring that helpline,' she said. 'You're frightened. He could do it again.'

And Laura was speaking again, her voice calm and level. 'Sure, that's fine. I'll open up again if you like.' Was that an answer? Maybe it was all the answer she was going to get.

'OK,' she said, hesitant. 'As long as you're sure you're OK.' A pause. 'With that.'

'See you tomorrow morning,' said Laura, and hung up.

* * *

249

When Bridget got back downstairs towelling her hair Matt still wasn't home, Finn was on the sofa with his feet up, and Carrie was outside, on the phone. Bridget could hear an intense mumble advancing and receding as if she was pacing up and down in front of the living room window. Bridget looked inquiringly at Finn as she plumped herself down next to him. 'Ella, I think,' he said. 'She's been out there ages.'

'You OK?' she asked and his head dipped a little towards her, leaning on her shoulder. He nodded against her. 'Let's eat, then, shall we?' she said, resting her chin on his head, smelling his boy smell. 'I bet Dad'll turn up the minute we start.'

Carrie came back in as they were sitting down. She looked miserable. 'Sorry,' she said, pocketing her mobile. 'That was Ella.'

'What is it?' asked Bridget. Carrie just shook her head, and pulled the salad towards her. Bridget looked at her sister's shorn head, bowed over the plate, the sharp angle of her white chin. Wishing she could just beam Carrie back to Ella, get her out of all this. But that didn't look like it was on the cards.

Their plates were still full when Bridget heard the sound she'd been waiting for, and felt something inside her that had been running too fast subside, at last. The creak and rattle of the garage door, up, then slowly down.

She didn't know if Carrie or Finn noticed that Matt had been drinking, but she did, before he even came in. It might not even be much, just something fractionally off about his footsteps down the side of the house, the rattle of the door handle, the way he looked around the room and smiled as he came in, setting his backpack down inside the door.

Beer: she smelled it as she leaned up to kiss him. 'Look what Finn made!' she said.

It wasn't that he was pissed, nothing like. It was probably just one beer: that would be his limit. But one wasn't normal.

Matt smiled, tiredly, and sat. 'Thanks, Finn,' he said, but he was pale and preoccupied. They ate quickly: Carrie recovered herself enough to praise Finn's cooking and talk to him about the game they'd been playing together, and Bridget stood quickly to clear, ushering them out so Finn wouldn't notice how little they'd eaten. He seemed eager to return to his computer, anyway, a quick squeeze round Carrie's shoulders and he was on the stairs back to his room.

As she put the leftover salad in the fridge she heard Matt go up after him, slow and weary and for the first time since she'd met him, for the first time in almost twenty years, she was afraid to follow him.

Carrie just nodded from the sofa when she put her head round the door, raising another beer to her lips, Arnold Schwarzenegger on the screen popping muscles. ''S'all right,' she said, tipping her head back. 'Don't worry, sis.' The glaze of booze over her.

All right. As if.

The light was already out and Matt a humped shape on his side, unmoving. Bridget took off her clothes and slid into bed beside him, her hair still damp, everything suddenly unfamiliar. Her own body, on the verge of trembling because she didn't want to get it wrong. To give anything away.

251

'Are you OK?' she whispered, her hand creeping over his chest. He made an indistinct sound: his back was to her. Always lean, he felt skinny to her now. She laid her cheek against his back: she could feel the beat of her own heart, too loud, but came closer anyway. Raised his T-shirt and pressed her breasts against his bare back. His hand came up quickly and took hers across his body: not asleep, then, or anything like it.

A murmur from Finn's room across the landing as he talked online. Downstairs the TV sound, the thumping crash of film explosions.

It would be safer to do nothing: safer to pretend to sleep, as he had been doing. But Bridget put her mouth to the back of his neck, she breathed his smell, familiar with an edge of something new. The beer, or something else, a sharp sour smell. Kissed the delicate skin, pressing closer to get back to what she knew, to Matt's sweet smell, of sweat and soap. At his chest she extracted her hand gently from his and moved it down, across his abdomen: she bypassed his cock, not daring. She stroked his thigh, down between his legs where she felt him warm and strong, and he moved. This was new. Rhythmically she stroked, she knew this was deliberate, but she didn't want it to be calculating, she wanted it to be them, to be theirs: she wanted love.

But if she got it wrong.

Her fingers feathered between his legs and then, moving a little she felt his erection, surprising against her wrist, hot and hard. She made a sound, in spite of herself, and with the sound he moved with sudden, quick ease and was over her. He was inside her. Not rough but determined,

252

and saying nothing: this was different. Matt always said something. *All right? Is that — do you?* They always did this to be in touch with each other. But this was the opposite: she could only hear the regular pant of his breathing, quite separate from her, telling her nothing.

Her Matt, the Matt she knew who was so safe and kind and good.

She had started this. Had she thought it would lull him, quiet him? That wasn't what was happening. And then as she was on the verge of panic something else happened: he thrust hard into her, so hard he grunted and she came, gasping loud before she could stifle it. He paused for just a second and then he came too, with his own sound that she knew. They hung there a second, his face over hers in the darkness. Then he rolled off. She stayed in stunned silence for a heartbeat, another that stretched into minutes waiting for him to say something. Then she realised he was asleep.

Numbly she understood what this meant. It wasn't just for her that things had changed. Matt was different too.

Her Matt. Safe and kind and good.

Listening to him breathe in the darkness with weird detachment Bridget turned the thought over that there was something wrong with them, her and Matt both. Had it always been going to come out like this, because she was damaged? But her body disagreed. It hummed with pleasure, a steady warm feeling. From downstairs came the crackle of gunfire on the TV, music rising, and somehow it all receded, her head motionless on the pillow, her thoughts diffused to nothing.

Sometime later she heard the front door, a soft click

and after that small sound the house fell quite silent at last. She slept.

In dreams things came to her, she imagined whole scenarios unspooling, the man from the boat club by the quarry, the girl in cleaner's overalls on Carmichael's doorstep. A man called Timpson, peering in through the window of her shop with his hands cupped either side of his face.

Chapter Twenty-Two

Saturday

Matt was beside her on his back with an arm flung across his face, dead to the world and Bridget was sitting upright beside him, barely awake but her mind already spinning, spinning.

He'd be at home all day: the thought set up a hammering. If they hadn't got rid of the body, if they hadn't taken the car last night – Matt at home all day, pottering about, in and out of the garage, he would have found something.

Beside her his chest rose and fell gently, but she couldn't see his face.

They'd got rid of the carpet, too. She'd burned the clothes in the little incinerator, she'd put it back where it belonged. Except Matt saw everything in such detail: if a question occurred to him, he needed it answered. Swiftly Bridget scrambled out of the bed and ran downstairs. She put on the kettle. Why shouldn't she bring him breakfast in bed, once in a while?

When she got back up with the tray Matt was sitting up, bleary, frowning at the news on his mobile. He looked up in mild surprise to see her but no question seemed to occur to him, after all. Nothing about last night. He looked pale but otherwise it was Matt. She handed him his tea, apologetic because it was still too weak.

'This is nice,' he said, frowning down at the cup, looking at her, frowning and smiling at once, rain and sunshine. Every day, even Saturday when he didn't have to be up, Matt made the tea. If she wanted to show him something was different, this was the way to do it.

'Well, you seemed so worn out last night,' she said, the words covering the anxiety in her voice.

Matt nodded, took a sip of the tea. 'Yeah,' he said, thoughtful.

Maybe the sex was something they had dreamed, both of them together. Cautiously, Bridget experimented with that thought. Let it lie.

'The journalist, was that it? So she did come and see you? Did you go to the pub with her?' Letting herself sound a bit put-out.

She'd never been that kind of wife – but then she'd never had to be. The worst she could complain of was Matt out on a bike ride on a Sunday when he could have been in bed with her. She felt a warmth at the thought, rising up her neck.

He eyed her a moment then sighed. 'Gillian Lawson. Yes, she came.'

'What's she like?' Stubborn as a jealous wife.

Cautiously Matt eyed her over his tea. She heard Finn emerge on to the landing, heard the bathroom door close behind him.

'She's all right, actually.' He was pondering. 'A bit – you know. Pushy. A bit tough. I think she's on the level, though.

And yes—' He sighed again, rubbing his chin. 'She persuaded me to go to the pub. Maybe I shouldn't have gone, but too late now.' He reached for the toast, crunching it cheerfully.

'Did she tell you anything about – this bloke? Carmichael?'

Matt set the toast back down, not quite looking at her, and pushed the plate away. He shrugged. 'She's got a bee in her bonnet about him, that's for sure. She's been following him for ten, fifteen years? Talking to students. She's got theories – well, I told you. That he grooms girls. Abuses them. But she can't pin it on him.' He rubbed his chin, thoughtfully. 'I really shouldn't have talked to her, I mean, from the point of view of the university, I'm sure I shouldn't.'

'They wouldn't want to *know*?' She didn't need to conceal her outrage. She needed to keep it down, though. Matt lifted the tray off himself and set it on the floor, then sat on the edge of the bed with his elbows on his knees, rubbing his head between his hands.

'Well, it's complicated,' he said, straightening, his hair sticking up. 'I said – I told her if I knew anything at all I'd tell her.'

'But you don't know anything?' She couldn't help it: she needed to understand.

Matt stood and stretched. Boxers on his hips, a vulnerable strip of belly revealed as the T-shirt lifted and on impulse she leaned forward and put her arms around him quickly, her face against his skin. He took hold of her shoulders and made her look up.

'You were a while in the pub, though,' she said, obstinate.

Matt sighed. 'I went back to the office after,' he said. 'I wanted a look at his internet history.' And then he turned away, out of her reach, he didn't see her put her hand to her mouth. Looking for his trousers on the chair, tugging them on. Across the landing the shower was running, on and on.

'And?' she said.

Matt turned, buttoning the trousers, pulling open a drawer and getting out two of his many identical T-shirts, one short sleeved, one long, the long under the short. Same every day. He put them on carefully and only when he had tugged his sleeves down did he turn to her, nodding. 'I think she's right,' he said.

She was on her feet in an instant, but in the same moment the drumming of the shower ended and Matt held up a hand to stop her, shaking his head. 'I'll do a supermarket shop this morning,' he said. 'If you'll make me a list.'

When she got down to the kitchen Finn was standing at the kitchen table, spooning cereal into his mouth. He looked cleaner than she'd ever seen him, scrubbed and smelling sweet. Matt was still upstairs, shaving carefully in the steamy bathroom. She sat and tried to write a list. *Eggs, milk, pasta.*

'Are you off somewhere?' she asked Finn, looking at the clock. *Tomatoes, apples,* she wrote. It was only nine still. Looking down at her Finn wiped his milky mouth with the back of his hand. 'Got to get a present for Phoebe,' he said happily. 'It's her birthday. I'm seeing her tomorrow.'

'Really?' Bridget was taken aback. Had he mentioned a birthday?

Finn nodded, looking at her from under his eyebrows. 'Isabel said she'd help me.'

'Oh, well, well—' Ridiculously pleased at the thought, the two of them out shopping, nothing safer, nothing more innocent. 'That's great, Finn,' she ended lamely, seeing him begin to shake his head at her.

'Anyway,' he said cheerfully. 'She said ten at the shopping centre so I'm off.'

As Bridget waved him off at the back door – head down, legs pumping – behind her she could hear Matt moving round the kitchen, collecting carrier bags, a backpack, for the supermarket shop, methodical. Alone together, she thought with a qualm, but then she remembered.

'You seen Carrie?' she asked and he'd only begun to shake his head when she was up and off, on the stairs, with a funny feeling in her legs.

'Carrie?' she said, on the landing. Remembering the soft click of the front door last night. Leaning in to knock. 'Caz?' Pushing the door open

The bed hadn't been slept in.

Matt, at the foot of the stairs, saw her expression. He started up towards her and she stopped, forcing herself back down from frightened to just impatient. Tetchy. Big sister.

'She's stopped out,' she said, curt. 'You know Carrie. She'll have gone on a bender. A Friday night wild one.' Below her on the stairs after a second's hesitation Matt went into reverse, backing into the kitchen. When she got to the door he was head down and busying himself with stuffing carriers into his backpack. *Whatever.* But he was uneasy too, she could tell from the speed of his movements.

'She'll roll back in in time for tea. I hope she took a key, is all.' He said nothing. 'Matt?' He looked up and she was next to him, a quick hug. 'I've got to get going,' she said and in that moment she wished she could stay, safe in his orbit. But she couldn't. He nodded, head still down. 'See you later.'

She sent the text quickly, standing astride her bike in the lee of the garage. *Where the hell are you?*

She slowed as she passed the pub but it was closed up and silent. It was a clear morning again, and bitterly cold, the air stung her exposed skin as she descended into town. Carrie wouldn't have been out in it, she told herself, she'd have ended up at an all-night party or something – but all the same. How long did you leave it? To say someone hadn't come home.

Consequences unreeled in her head. What happened with a missing person, go to the police, what did they do next?

Had anyone reported *him* missing yet? She came to a halt at the lights, her hands frozen even through her old gloves: of course, she'd burned two pairs now. The town gleamed pale below her after the frost, roofs white with it and the light steely.

She thought not: she thought there would have been something on the news, or in the papers.

Matt had been looking at the news on his phone. Behind her someone bipped his horn, tetchy because the lights were changing, and she moved off, her heart speeding. He would have told her. They'd just been talking about Carmichael – he would have told her.

If Carrie got drunk. If she talked to anyone.

Town was still quiet, early morning traffic was light on a Saturday. Bridget rattled up the lane, early for the shop. She'd be in before Laura for the first time in days. She locked up her bike round the back, glancing up at the rear of the shop, the tilted roofs, the grimy windows, the place she'd hunkered down to hide. And now it had turned into the place Carmichael had died. And in that moment there seemed a kind of exhilarating inevitability about it. He had followed her there, maybe not initially, but eventually, he had seen her, he had come back for her. And he had died. Serve him right.

Carrie, though.

When had she last been in a pub with Carrie, years ago – ten years? Somewhere in London and Carrie out and proud, drinking steadily. Chatting up girls, saying outrageous things to get their attention. Showing them her piercings. Laughing at Bridget, my straight sister, straight as a die, surprised she hasn't got her pinny on.

Kissing a girl Goth for so long the pub started clapping them, and then off they went together and that was the last Bridget had seen of Carrie for a year or more. No goodbye, Bridget left there with her gin and tonic. She'd had to laugh: the pub crowd were friendly to her, sympathising. *That's Carrie*, they'd said.

This wasn't Soho, though. The bike ride to work had seemed to be saying that to her, all the way down; it said this was a funny old place for anyone to end up. Pale and bleak in the winter light, rolling down to the grey estuary, the houses only scattered, then the town feeling closed up, net curtained.

More gay-friendly than it had been, she tells herself, things had changed, loosened up. Girls holding hands in the street was OK, she had a few gay customers, and a trans regular that Laura rolled her eyes at, giggling when she'd gone. But underneath had much really changed? Their local was a quiet place, old-fashioned. Carrie wouldn't have got hurt, would she? Being outrageous.

As Bridget unlocked on her own in the quiet lane – disabling the alarm, flipping the sign – her mind ran on. Then as she turned from switching on the lights there he was in the window. Just as she'd dreamed, hands cupped, face so close to the glass she could see his breath. Moving towards the door, his hand on the latch.

And suddenly, vividly, she remembered him. The man Carmichael's age buying a Christmas present for his wife, side by side with Laura at the jewellery cabinet. Had she known, even then, had he made her uneasy? He had stood a little too close to her, she remembered his heavy breathing.

He pushed the door open now, squeezed through. His belly overhung brown trousers.

'Hello there,' he said. And he stood in the middle of the shop, looking around like he owned the place, in his jacket that strained over his shoulders. Craning his neck to look back out through the glass a second, but the jeweller's opposite was still dark. Supposed to be open at ten thirty but she was always late. 'Remember me?'

She nodded stiffly. 'Mr Timpson,' she said. 'Yes, Laura told me.'

He raised his eyebrows. 'That your girl? Laura? They do say pregnancy makes women ditsy but there are limits.' More hair than Carmichael, down to his collar and maybe he thought it made him look younger but it was greasy. He looked at her with arrogance. She hated him violently.

'I do hope Laura didn't upset you,' Bridget said with hostility.

He frowned, considering anger. 'She doesn't like the earrings,' he said, jutting his rolls of chin at her aggressively.

'Your wife?' Thinking hard, trying not to let it show. Why had Timpson come, before, when he'd bought the earrings? To have a look at her. Get the lie of the land. Carmichael must have said something to him about her. When he disappeared – Timpson thought she must have scared him off. Her? She felt a nervous laugh rise. *Did more than that.*

'Girlfriend, actually,' said Timpson, his fingers splayed against the cabinet now, she could see every hair on his knuckles. The trace of a leer on his face. 'She thought it was an older woman's choice, is the truth of the matter.' The leer trying to look like a kind smile.

'I think Laura told you that you could have a refund,' said Bridget, moving behind the till. 'We can do that now.' The earrings had cost less than fifty pounds. Cheapskate. She hated him. 'I don't know what else I can do for you,' she said, smiling blandly.

Timpson pushed himself off the tall jewellery cabinet and wandered to a rail, flipping the clothes carelessly. A flowered dress, a red ruffled skirt; she loved that skirt. She wanted to shove him. He reached up to a scarf displayed on a higher shelf and pulled it down, examining it with a frown.

'Maybe we could talk about alternatives,' he said. As if he was a Saudi billionaire or an oligarch. 'I told the pregnant one, I needed your *expertise.*' He smiled. 'I want to get it right. It's a new relationship, you see,' and he put a hand up to his heart, he winked. 'A much younger woman.' Bridget had to look away.

'How old is your girlfriend exactly?' she asked, insolent almost: making herself look, making herself take in every detail of him, every pore. No woman would come near this man, unless she was forced, no man either. There was no girlfriend, no younger woman; he had come to warn her off. To scare her. He thought she had threatened Carmichael with going to the police, and if *Tony* went down, so would he.

He looked her up and down openly now. 'Younger than you,' he said. Smiling. 'A lot younger.' He took a step to the side of the desk and reached a hand to the collar of her blouse, rubbing the silk between finger and thumb as if testing the quality.

She held very still.

'It *is* you,' Timpson said, sneering. 'After all. I wouldn't have recognised you.'

'Do I know you?' She looked into his face, one eyebrow raised then down at his hand and he dropped it but nothing more, no stepping back, apologetic. *You don't scare me.* It was bigger than being scared, though. It was as if she was standing at an open door and beyond and below it was nothing, a white roaring emptiness. She stood very still, suddenly certain that she had to pretend absolute ignorance – of all of it. Her own life drifted, like smoke, away from her. The rooms she had been in, the ceiling cornice she had stared up at past a jacketed shoulder, how his finger-nails had looked as he fumbled to unbutton his trousers.

'Tony said he thought it was you.' He looked at her wedding ring. 'Different name, of course.'

Bridget informed herself that she didn't know this man. She had never seen this man before. She made herself smile, uncomprehending, hands flat on the glass top of the desk.

Alan Timpson shook his head. 'No,' he said, 'I would never have recognised you.'

'I don't know what you're talking about,' she said. Acting cool, bemused, as though her life depended on it. But she was burning, a white flame that lit this man in her memory, his fat shoulder pressed against her face, his fumbling fingers. *I killed him*, was the mantra in her head. She said quietly, 'Get out of my shop, you creep, or I will call the police.' Her head moved, just slightly, she glimpsed a face peering round the window display. White-faced, dark eyes, desperate. Was it Carrie?

Suddenly there was sourness in her throat, his smell of mothballs and sweat and bad breath and with a violent movement she stepped away. She couldn't stand Carrie to see this, for Carrie to know that her sister submitted to the thing she had fought off on her own, little wildcat Carrie. Irrational, in the light of what she'd done: so irrational she almost laughed, wildly, because if he only knew— He turned to see where she was looking but there was only Justine, trudging up the alley in her heavy coat, key already in hand to open up across the street.

'You'll excuse me while I get on,' she said, turning her back on him, walking across to the kitchen. Out of sight of the street there, as she knew. Laura would need a cup of tea when she arrived.

Timpson followed her. 'I don't like what you've done,' he said, leaning down, and he was letting anger into his voice now even though he spoke in an undertone, thick and salty as blood. 'What did you say to him? A man of his standing. With his gifts.' She took the kettle, filled it, saying nothing.

He kept talking. 'Don't you see, no one would believe anything you said? You know what happens to you. You've seen them on the television, sad, middle-aged women wanting the world to believe they were attractive enough once for a famous man to fuck them. Riding on his coat-tails. Or did you want him back?'

She would have killed him if she could. At that moment she couldn't see anything wrong with it − except that she would get caught. Laura would walk in − and with that thought a little bright second gave her a glimpse of the three of them, she and Laura and Carrie, battering him to nothing.

Be rational. Be clever. You couldn't kill them all. And with that thought something cleared and she saw how the see-saw balanced, the power hesitating, between her and him. It slid her way, fractionally but with certainty. Alan Timpson had no idea that harm might have come to Carmichael − to *Tony*. All he thought was that she had said something that had scared him off. He thought she could do that: *he* was the one who was scared.

Clicking the kettle on Bridget turned and forced him to back out of her way, into the centre of the room. She leaned to straighten the rug and when she was standing again put bewilderment on her face. 'Honestly?' she said brightly. 'I don't know what you're talking about. This is harassment. I'm going to call the police if you don't leave right now.'

The two of them must have talked about her. She didn't let the thought show.

'We'll have to get together when Tony reappears, won't we?' said Timpson, tipping his head. It was almost eleven. Behind her the kettle was coming to the boil and she turned away from him again. Where did he think Carmichael had gone? Somewhere he couldn't be found: that would make sense. Alan Timpson was still talking, he followed her, she could smell him. She wished she could block out what he was saying, but she couldn't.

'Just like old times,' he said. 'We were looking at some old photographs just the other day.'

In her hand the kettle trembled, a splash of boiling water hit her wrist but the ping of the door covered the sound she made.

Photographs. The world narrowed, to that battered box in a wardrobe somewhere, or gathering dust in an attic. Who would clear his house, when it came to it? Some distant relative? This man? Or the police.

She turned with the kettle in her hand, the scald on her wrist startlingly painful, and looked past him to Laura. She was standing in the doorway and looking at them, her coat half off. She looked pale and tired, and there was a tiny look of puzzlement on her face, as if the scene didn't quite make sense to her. And then distraction replaced whatever that look had been and Laura dropped her bag on the sofa, moving off painfully to the stockroom to put her coat away.

Timpson glanced at her then back to Bridget and smiled, his fleshy face dividing into rolls. 'Old times,' he said, softly. Bridget wished he would talk louder, the timbre of his voice suggested too much, it would get Laura pricking up her ears. 'Perhaps Tony didn't tell you about the pictures?'

She heard the rattle of a hanger as Laura hung up her coat. 'Of course not everything we got up to when we're young should go on Facebook, should it?'

Bridget had two mugs in her hand now. She could resist the urge to throw the hot liquid in his face: she steered a course past him to the till.

'Let's see about that refund,' she said, setting the mugs down.

'Credit note will do,' Timpson said, loud now, cheerful, hoisting his trousers under the overhang of his gut. 'I'm bound to be back in. These girls, always wanting something new.' Looking around, his eyes sliding over Laura as she emerged, pale in black knit. 'Perhaps you'll have something more appropriate for her age group, when I'm next in.'

And at last he was gone. Laura seemed barely to register the exchange now, gazing at herself in the mirror, tucking a tendril of blonde hair behind an ear, anxious. Bridget pulled herself together.

'Are you all right, Laura?' she said. 'When you came in, you looked—'

Laura turned from the mirror, focusing with difficulty on Bridget. 'No, no,' she said vaguely, 'I'm just not sleeping, it's so hard at this stage. Nick's being great. Doesn't mind me sleeping in the spare room at all. Doing a lot of working late.'

So in twenty-four hours the story had changed. Being great? She thought of the man sitting there motionless on the sofa while Laura knelt over boxes at his feet. Hardly the hardworking type. Still she told herself, this was OK. Was it? Spare room, no confrontation, *Nick's being great*. It wasn't OK.

'Only two weeks to go,' she said.

'Yes,' said Laura, quietly. 'I'm just focusing on getting the baby born safely at the moment.'

Bridget searched her face for what she wasn't saying, she couldn't help herself. 'But if you—'

'It's all right,' said Laura sharply. 'Really. I've got it under control.' She frowned, then said abruptly, 'There was something weird about him, wasn't there? Something not very nice. That man Timpson. What was he on about, Facebook?'

This time Bridget couldn't control her face, and she knew it. And then the door blew inwards and Carrie was inside the shop, breathless, startling them both.

Sandringham was a neat little place, even in November, pretty if you liked that kind of thing. Floral displays and trimmed hedges and old brick: self-important and why not? Not every village got Her Majesty for Christmas. Gill didn't go near the royal estate, out of republican stroppiness, but it sat there just out of sight, impervious, unassailable. The royal warrant all over the place in case she needed reminding. Grocer's, garage, railway line.

Gill had liked the drive better, but she had to admit most people would disagree. Most people would call it a nightmare of B roads and blind bends and country drivers with mud flying off their Land Rovers and red faces glaring at her as they passed, little townie in her hire car. It had given her something else to think about. Three days with more or less only Anthony Carmichael in her head had not been good: it felt as if her brain was waterlogged, or gestating something horrible, swelling against her skull.

The hire car had gone on Gill's own overloaded credit

269

card: she couldn't charge it as it was her own fault she was in the wrong place, and it was cheaper than the train. She'd stood there behind the plastic counter with its bright signs – a photograph of a young, good-looking couple off on a mini break, cheers for that – a good thirty seconds while the payment was processed, not sure if the card would be rejected. Not only was the train more expensive, but the times were hopeless. And her editor wasn't just impatient, he was firing her.

She'd been sitting against the shiny headboard cradling a plastic half bottle from the mini-bar when she'd emailed him from the purple hotel bedroom last night.

Listen, Steve.

Had that been her mistake, insufficient respect? Excessive familiarity? Although it had been him made a move on *her*, back in the day, and she'd been nice about it, hadn't said, *You're married Steve, you sleaze*, just squeezed out a tear about an imaginary previous relationship and that had seen him off. Men didn't like tears.

I'm not going to get you the Queen's butcher, I'm going to get you Carmichael. I'm so close, Steve . . .

He'd called at seven to say that if she didn't get him the Queen's butcher she didn't have a job. Flat and tired and angry. It wasn't even light: she'd scrambled upright in the bed, feeling sick. The banging head so normal she didn't even bother to call it a hangover.

And now Gill was parked up next to a church in the nearest village, on the phone, listening to canned music. No word from her admirer the engineer, for which she was grateful. The Queen's butcher was refusing to talk without permission from the Royal Warrants Office, and that was who she was waiting for. She was fifth in the queue.

The churchyard was also nice if you liked that kind of thing and Gill grudgingly had to admit she did, old lichened stone wall, pollarded limes, gravestones leaning at all angles in long grass. Where will I be buried? she wondered, before telling herself almost with relief, Don't be daft, it's all ashes scattered from the Shard these days. Mourners are so last year.

The thought that at barely forty – well, forty-five, all right – she shouldn't be thinking about her own death with something approaching pleasure, flitted across the back of Gill's mind, and then someone picked up the phone.

It was tough enough to sound not angry – because where did they get off, the Royals, like the bloody Mafia – and Gill knew something a bit more than non-rage was required. Respect and deference and enthusiasm. You're in the wrong job. But then she thought about her credit card bill, the wrong job better than no job, and injected just enough of whatever was necessary into her voice. Christ, she even made herself believe it. Can't be that much fun, anyway, can it, opening daycare centres twice a week, at her age, and not even the most rabid republican could blame her for Anthony Carmichael.

Permission granted. And Gill's gratitude at least was sincere.

She started the engine and drove away from the old stone wall and the soft grey peaceful shape of the church. There was a grain of truth, of course, in what Steve had said, or else she would have walked, well, somewhere. But this was a job. You didn't get to do what you want.

The butcher was a decent bloke, in the end, plus he had a female assistant, cheerful, youngish woman in her bloodied white coat and lipstick, so there was a bit of a story there. Gill's mind almost wiped clean of Anthony Carmichael as she talked to a woman briskly dissecting a pig into joints, leg, loin, spare ribs, and admired the skill. An honest day's work – well, unless you were the pig, of course.

And she felt almost cheerful herself as she climbed back into the car, at the thought that sometimes her job was just a job, too, a reasonably honest day's work. A feeling that lasted all of twenty minutes and the first sign to the A road that would lead her laboriously south to the towers on Rose Hill. To the lit windows where students paced up and down in their tiny rooms, the grey estuary, to the tangle of houses and lanes, shops and houses and families and somewhere in there was a woman who'd once been Bridget O'Neill.

I'm going to get him for you, Steve.

Chapter Twenty-Three

Carrie and Bridget were in a greasy spoon on the main road: elderly clientele, neon lighting and a big pot of tea and two cups in thick china in front of them on the red formica tables. Carrie had looked round the décor and said it'd go down great in Hoxton. She was halfway through two rounds of toast and on her third cup of dark brown tea. 'Liquids,' she said, lifting it to her mouth and draining it. 'Already had a can of Fanta, but it's tea you want, really.'

She had spent the night with a girl. Of course she had.

Bridget took a triangle of toast. Sliced bread, dripping with salted butter. Salty butter, marmalade sweet and bitter at the same time. She'd forgotten how good it tasted, especially when you were relieved your sister was still alive.

'You didn't find her at the Green Man?' Bridget was confused. Their local pub hosted middle-aged couples holding hands over their ploughman's, the occasional well-scrubbed teenager. Of course Carrie had already been in there with Finn, but they knew Finn, they'd have tolerated Carrie the wild auntie with her sleeves rolled down to cover her tattoos but not Carrie on the loose. Carrie offering to buy a good-looking girl a drink.

Not just any girl.

'Nah,' said Carrie, pushing her empty plate away, replete. 'One drink there then I hitched down here, into town. I can take care of myself,' she said, avoiding Bridget's fierce look.

'Not necessarily,' said Bridget, thinking of the truck driver who'd murdered women and left their bodies discarded on a heath, no more than thirty miles away, to the north. Carrie shook her head.

'Like I'd get in a car with a man,' she said, patiently. 'It's not rocket science. Only get a lift off a woman.' Their eyes met a moment then glanced off each other, both thinking the same thing. We'd never. A woman wouldn't. Carrie almost smiling.

She'd met the girl in a gay club. Magdalena, she was called.

'I didn't even know there were any gay clubs,' said Bridget.

'A lot you don't know,' said Carrie merrily.

So Bridget had been here twenty years, with her eyes closed, it felt like. Her little shop, the cobbled lane, the bike ride home. Scared of everything.

'Magdalena,' she said blankly. 'So – who's Magdalena?' Because Carrie had said it with meaning, leaning across the table with her little pointed chin on her fists, eyes dancing. And now she sat back.

'You know Magdalena,' she said, 'or you've seen her at

least. You saw her yesterday standing on Carmichael's door-step.' She smiled. 'Magdalena from the Ukraine. Very good family, she tells me, very religious.'

'Oh,' said Bridget, stupidly, because it felt like a thump to the solar plexus. 'So she's – does she—' Stopped then started again. 'What does she know? What have you told her?'

Carrie's eyes roamed the room, restless, a combination of hungover and excited, dangerous, volatile. It occurred to Bridget that she could still be pissed.

'*Carrie*,' she said, taking her by the wrist across the formica. On the next table an old man in a smelly over-coat shook out his paper, clearing his throat. Bridget took her hand away, and tried to sound calm. 'You haven't told her?'

'No,' said Carrie, rolling her eyes. 'Course not.' But Bridget remembered her as a child, lying, secretive. Reckless. And she pushed. 'Nothing?'

Carrie shook her head. 'I didn't even need to mention his name. She said her employer was away and if we wanted to go and have some fun in his super kingsize bed . . .'

'You *didn't*—'

'Nope,' said Carrie, adopting a serious expression. 'I didn't think that would be safe.'

Bridget breathed. 'She thinks he's gone abroad,' Carrie went on. 'She said, that was what had happened last time *his friend* came round calling for him.'

'The man.' She'd told Carrie about Timpson, as they ran through the spitting rain for the café. Spilling it out, the opaque threats. The photographs. *He and Carmichael go way back.* 'Him? Timpson?'

275

'That would be my guess, she seems to know him, although Christ knows there might—' Carrie stopped.

'There might be others?' And something *went*, in Bridget's head, a snowstorm, her brain a room filled with flying feathers and static, like a TV on the blink. A room with others in it, circling while she lay face down on a sofa with her knickers cutting into the backs of her legs.

Carrie stared at her. 'Sis, you—' and her hands were held up, fending something off. Her bravado gone.

Bridget shook her head. Her face felt as though it was frozen. 'She only mentioned one man?' she said stiffly. 'Magdalena did.'

Carrie nodded, subdued. 'Fat man from the university,' she said. She didn't say his name.'

'And that time, he'd been abroad, and not told this man.'

'A week in Thailand,' said Carrie leaning back, arms folded. 'He came back with pictures on his phone. He showed them to her.' Her voice was level.

The old man on the next table got up reluctantly, patting his pockets, and shuffled for the door, peering out into the wet street. The waitress was on his tail, clearing the table before he'd even gone.

'Pictures of what?' Carrie shrugged, uneasy. But Bridget knew what. Him with girls.

The waitress was loading her tray impossibly slowly, her square backside facing them with its apron tail. Was she listening?

'Magdalena hates him,' said Carrie quietly. 'We could tell her.'

And instantly Bridget was sitting up. 'No,' she hissed. 'You didn't say anything? You can't, Carrie. You *can't*. No one can know. If anyone knows, the risks – she tells someone, they tell someone else.' She was shaking her head in disbelief.

'Keep your hair on.' Carrie was frowning, rocking on the back legs of the chair. 'I didn't tell her. But I did think maybe, with what she knows about him, if she went to the police, it might be a good story. Cover story, paedo on the run. Shame she hates the coppers as much as she hates him.'

At last the waitress turned, eyed their empties, looked at them then decided to move off.

'And it might just alert them to what's happened,' said Bridget, focused now. 'Is she legal? Here legally, I mean?'

Carrie shrugged. 'Ish,' she said. 'Ukraine isn't Europe.'

The thought that there was someone else who hated him – who knew him – sat there, a temptation. Bridget hesitated. 'Can you trust her, do you think?' she said care-fully. 'In general? I mean, without telling her what we'd done, could you trust her?' Carrie was saying nothing, thinking. 'We can't get pissed and tell strangers,' Bridget pleaded. 'You get that? However much we want to.'

Carrie nodded. 'She could tell I was interested,' she said. 'In him. But she doesn't care.' Bridget could see she was holding something back. A sudden gust of wind rattled the café's windows, and a scattershot of rain hit the glass. The old man in his overcoat had gone from the pavement outside: he'd have got wet, thought Bridget, her thoughts veering, wild, away from all this.

'But what's she like?' It was important: it was the most important thing.

Carrie narrowed her eyes, wondering whether to get serious or not. Then leaned forward. 'She's had a shit life,' she said. 'She doesn't trust anyone, she looks after herself.' Shrugged. 'I guess we have to take that into account.'

'You got to her, though,' said Bridget, because she could see it, suddenly, the two of them, tough as nails, in each other's arms. 'Didn't you?' Carrie pulled back a little and shrugged, surly. Silence. 'Carrie?'

'Maybe,' she mumbled. Then her hands across the table were moving towards Bridget's until their fingertips touched. 'She knows all about him,' she said.

'*All* about him?' said Bridget.

The gleam in Carrie's eye told her: there was more.

'Magdalena told me there were photographs,' she said. 'And she knows where he keeps them.'

Had it been there, all along?

Bridget had had her eyes closed, for twenty years. That feather-filled room that was the inside of her head. That memory of the elastic cutting into the backs of her legs as they were tugged down. Of course, it must have been there all that time.

She thought about those people interviewed on TV with their faces blacked out in shadow but you'd see their hands, trembling hands, or a trail of smoke from a cigarette held out of shot. Experts talked about false memories, about PTSD. Someone took them into an interview room and asked them questions. And sometimes they weren't believed. It was their word against his: it was down to their credibility, as a witness, and their damage might muddy the waters. Sometimes charges were dropped.

The precious thing you carried around, all your life. The dark, precious thing – precious because if you broke it open your life would fall away around it in pieces, if you broke it open the black swarm it released would cover the sun – imagine taking that precious thing to a police interview room only to be told to put it back where it came from except now it is bigger and darker and heavier. Now it is a black hole, so dense it sucks you inside after it, and there is no more you.

They weren't allowed to name the things he'd done on television. The things that he and the others had done in the feather-filled room, the snowglobe shaken, shaken, the picture obscured. Not before nine o'clock. The *acts*.

They called them sex acts. There was a watershed, after which the words could be spoken. When children had gone to bed, children in soft pyjamas, their covers turned down, their nightlights on.

She can feel the callous on her forefinger, the rubbed place on her shoulder where the violin has rested, they are the only sensations she allows. The room is dim, his sofa, his piano is gleaming in lamplight, flowers on his mantelpiece.

His wife is out.

They have laid a towel beneath her. She saw him do it and wondered why: that she didn't know raises the hair on her head now. Shame bathes her.

She comes home and walks to her room, her legs are shaking. Her body belongs to someone else, it has been broken into pieces and reassembled. She vomits until there is only bile. She feels that she will never be able to eat again, to put anything in her mouth. She is disgusting, the tract that leads through her body from mouth to anus is all she is. It wasn't love. There was no love. She had thought there would be love. She wants to die. She will die.

She has a violin lesson two days later, at his house. She goes to it.

Chapter Twenty-Four

The sky was black as she hurried back, and the rain coming in sheets, blown sideways.

'I want to meet her,' she said to Carrie, holding her arm to keep her a minute longer. They were standing on the pavement outside the steamed-up window of the café, in the rain. Behind it the stocky figure of the waitress moving between tables in the yellow light and the smell of bacon frying. Would that light, that smell, always be associated with this feeling? Everything had changed: the light had changed, sounds were different. A hole had opened up and something was rushing in, icy water. Smoke and feathers.

'I want to meet Magdalena.'

It was a risk. But Bridget needed to see someone else who knew. Carrie hugged her, quick, in the rain, smelling of last night's booze and cigarettes, and was gone.

Anyone out in the rain was hurrying like her, head down, ducking into doorways. Coming round a corner

Bridget hit a gust, it knocked her sideways and she had to steady herself before moving on.

How could she have thought she would have a life? That it had been anything but pretend, all of it. She thought about twenty years of sex with Matt, whom she loved, who loved her, of his hand careful on her, gentle, the whispered words. It had been like something children do, tentative, cautious. She wanted it back. The last time had been dangerous. Had that been her, or him? Something had climbed into the bed with them, and she had brought it.

Finn wasn't pretend, was he? Big, good, loving Finn. She hadn't invented him. But she could lose him. Head down. Keep going.

On the threshold of the shop Bridget hesitated, peering in: it was busy. Took a breath and was inside, shaking the raindrops from her coat on the mat, parking her umbrella. Surveying the room.

Three sets of Saturday shoppers. A husband on the sofa with a fidgety small child either side of him – looked like twins, one girl, one boy – while he read the paper. Laura who was moving between the curtained changing room and a man and woman frowning together over a choice of two outfits in the far corner. Dark red knit versus black velvet: talking about Christmas Day.

'But can you imagine getting the turkey out of the oven in it?' Laura was saying earnestly. 'That's the key.' The man peered at his wife, hopeless.

Christmas Day. Only a month away. Was it going to happen, ever again?

'Darling?' A youngish red-haired woman, frazzled, soft,

had emerged from the cubicle in a pale green party dress in a gleaming satiny fabric: the children bounced off the sofa and ran to clutch at her, *mummymummymummy*.

She stood at the centre of the room and looked at her husband, anxious. The fabric rippled on her, showing a little bit of baby belly. 'Mummy, you are a princess,' said the small girl, pressing a cheek against the satin. Her husband – ironed shirt under a jumper, big ears – set the newspaper aside and for a second she only saw his smile. And then she saw the newspaper open on the cushion beside him, where a child had sat.

Laura would have brought it in with her, she always did on Saturdays. The magazine sections on the mirrored cube.

Police widen search for missing boy. She leaned to look, despite herself. There was a picture of a small, curtained house on a bleak but tidy estate: the boy's home. He had gone out to meet mates and never come back. The estate was four miles from where she stood, in this small space with a happy family.

The world he had disappeared into was so much bigger than the safe spaces they thought they could make.

And abruptly she remembered. He was fatter now but she'd known his smell, the thick sound of his voice turning his head to say something to someone else that had made her twist to hide herself, her face, in the sofa in Anthony Carmichael's music room. Something about the Greeks. And then, *There's nothing like a boy, for pleasure.* And then he had hurt her.

They had been younger then, Timpson and Carmichael. They'd have been in their forties. What had they done since? The internet had happened since. Paedophile networks. All of this had been the background radiation to her adult life, growing in the dark where she didn't look, turning her face away from the newspaper, walking out of the room when the news came on. The internet: the big, wide world.

Matt hadn't wanted to tell her what he'd found that made him think Gill Lawson was right about Carmichael.

Someone was saying something to her now, and she turned, making herself focus. The red-haired mother was talking to her and Bridget recognised her after all, from a while ago. She was looking down at her little belly in dismay and tugging at the fabric and they were all looking at Bridget, waiting for her to say something.

'You're beautiful,' Bridget said, plucking the words from the air and the little girl began to jump up and down in delight.

They had seemed the right words at the time but she modified them, because they were all looking at her, it wasn't quite what they had expected. 'It's perfect on you,' she said, politely enthusiastic, turning the woman in front of her to look at herself in the mirror.

Adjusting the lie on the shoulders the fabric loosened, skimmed, and the redhead nodded at last. The Christmas Day wife was in the second cubicle with her husband outside, the older woman got up off the footstool to button her coat and the focus shifted, everything subsided back to the everyday.

There was a lull at about two and Bridget picked up the paper quickly on the pretext of tidying, folding it very slowly. A photograph of the boy: no one she recognised. Not a child, maybe seventeen, eighteen. Alan Timpson had always liked boys: she had been low on his list, but he'd taken what Carmichael had offered.

Laura was pink-cheeked and cheerful again, carrying her pregnancy lightly today, it seemed. She'd even been moving things around in the kitchen: going in after her Bridget had seen a box sitting on the shelf where the log had been. Nothing heavy: the Easter decorations, painted cardboard eggs and sprays of paper cherry blossom. Nothing had been said; nor, it seemed from her blithe smiling composure, would it need to be. Nest-building had taken care of it, perhaps, and it occurred to Bridget that it covered a multitude of – what? Sins? Some women's instinct to arrange, to tidy, to present an orderly face to the world. To conceal.

Only when Laura subsided into the chair in the stock-room, balancing a Tupperware box of salad on her belly, could Bridget see how close she was to term. She leaned down into the box, seeking out avocado and looking up caught Bridget watching her. She seemed calm and un-troubled but Bridget glimpsed, in that second, the tiniest adjustment, as if her every effort was to eliminate worry.

Had Bridget done that? She'd been anxious throughout her pregnancy with Finn, terrified. Matt had got her through it. Stayed calm for her, protected her, at scans, with every twinge, every Braxton Hicks. His face when Finn was born: startled, joyful. She had to do this without him, now.

Then the bell pinged, not once but again and again and a hen party was trooping through the door, deely boppers and tinsel sashes, one of them lifting a pair of high heels from the window and brandishing them overhead, another one – pissed, Bridget calculated from the way she was teetering on heels – cheerfully holding a five hundred quid

285

ballgown up against herself in the mirror. When Bridget next checked her phone an hour later, there was a message from Carrie.

They'd just finished clearing the changing rooms and Laura was walking along the rails straightening everything to a regulation two centimetres apart, humming to herself.

Magdalena can do coffee this afternoon.

Laura was looking at her and Bridget cocked a thumb at the door. 'I'm just – can I—' She slipped out into the lane, pacing in the drizzle. Carrie answered on the first ring.

'Hey.' She was eager, excitable. 'Magdalena says, why don't we meet at the house? Like, Carmichael's house.'

It took a minute for the implications to register.

'She's not worried about being caught?' Bridget was hunched in the rain and Justine peering at her across a customer in the jeweller's opposite. 'If he came back?' Justine's customer was a man in late middle-age, sandy-haired, for a second, she thought, for a mad second – then he turned. No one she knew.

'She's pretty sure he isn't coming back,' said Carrie.

'So she knows – something?' She'd turned her back on Justine and instead could see Laura standing in the empty shop, both hands on her belly, feet apart, looking down at herself. Then her head lifted: Bridget could hear it too, the ring of the shop phone. Behind the glass Laura moved off to pick it up.

'All right,' said Bridget. 'At six, then.'

She looked up and down the lane: it occurred to her that she'd thought maybe Finn, out in town looking for a present with Isabel, might have dropped in to say hello.

He used to do that, Saturday mornings, to ask for a fiver for lunch. Saturday afternoons was mountain biking with friends, he was never home early, not even on a wet November Saturday. As a small boy he'd needed running, like a dog, shaggy head bouncing ahead of them in rain or shine, to the swings, in the park, down the field towards the estuary. Since he'd got the bike he could roam free and come home with raindrops sparkling in his hair and soggy trainers, to crash on the sofa and eat a whole packet of biscuits before dinner.

'I'll be there,' she said. Laura was lifting a hand to her through the glass, beckoning her in.

Bridget felt numb: the cleaner might know already, somehow. Magdalena: neither of them knew anything about her. She might go to the police, she might blackmail them. But she slipped the phone into her pocket and pushed her way back inside: Laura had hung up by the time she got back in.

'It was Matt on the phone,' said Laura. 'He's trying to get hold of you, you were on the mobile.' She grimaced. 'Sorry, pregnancy brain, you know that, obviously.'

'No such thing as pregnancy brain,' said Bridget, frowning: hearing Nick's voice – and Timpson's. 'Thanks, Laura.' She dialled him straight back but it went to answerphone, tried again straight away but still no joy. *This is Matt, sorry, I'm not able to answer the phone*, just the sound of his voice made her throat close, but the message she left was quick and quiet. *Home at seven, hope everything's OK.*

The rain set in and the shop stayed empty. No word from Matt, however often she looked at her phone. Just her and Laura, walking past each other, avoiding each other's eye. At five fifteen Bridget turned the sign to closed, locked the door.

When she turned Laura was standing there in her coat, arms folded over the bump, submissive – and something else. Bridget took hold of her by the elbows. 'What is it?' she said. 'What's wrong, Laura?'

Laura's lower lip was between her teeth, like a kid. 'There's something I didn't tell you yesterday.' She faltered. Bridget took her hands away but Laura stayed hunched, so still and small the unwieldy bump looked almost grotesque.

'A woman came in, just after you went off to the post office,' she said, avoiding Bridget's eye. 'The one – that bought a white shirt. I told you that, didn't I?'

Bridget did remember. 'You said she was a pain.'

Laura chewed her lip. 'Yes. I didn't – well, I wasn't sure if I should have talked to her so I didn't tell you. But it – the more I thought about it the more it seemed you should know.'

'So,' said Bridget cautiously. 'What should I know? I don't know her, this woman?'

Laura shook her head.

'She said she was a writer,' she went on, frowning down at the bump. 'She said she was writing a piece about small out-of-town boutiques. I think – there was something funny about her. She didn't ask about what brands we stock or anything. Asking lots of questions about working here. I should have mentioned it but I – I had a lot on my mind, you know. And it's not like she was a shoplifter. There was nothing missing.' And only then she lifted her head, her shoulders dropped a little. She exhaled.

'Questions about working here,' said Bridget flatly. 'About working for me?'

Laura tipped her head side to side. 'Not really. She did say it was you she wanted to see but when I told her you were out she just smiled and said she'd ask me some background and come back.'

'Background?'

Laura shrugged, uncomfortable. 'Just stuff like, how long I'd been here, what hours did I work. All sort of – friendly. But persistent.'

'What did she look like?' The two of them standing there in the middle of the empty shop, lights still on, and Bridget had to be at Carmichael's for six – but this seemed important.

'A bit older than you. Like she hadn't combed her hair. She pretended to be looking for an outfit too but she hadn't got a clue. Obviously, she was wearing—' and Laura gesticulated, almost distressed. That might just mean, Bridget knew, that the woman had on bad shoes. 'I think she only asked me to find her the white shirt so she could poke about while I was in the stockroom.'

'You left her alone?' said Bridget, aghast. 'She could have been a shoplifter.' Although that wasn't why. The idea of someone wandering unmonitored round the shop frightened her. Laura tugged her coat around herself defensively, but it didn't come anywhere near covering the bump.

'Only for a minute or two,' she said. 'But she wasn't – I'm sure – she didn't seem the kind.' Lamely. Hesitant. 'She did seem to be interested in that, though, she asked what did we do if someone dodgy came in, she asked that. Dodgy guys.'

289

'And what did you say?'

But instead of answering Laura moved her head, quick, a panicked look on her face.

There was someone at the door. Someone out there in the dark, shuffling from foot to foot. A pale face with stubble. Laura took a step, then stopped. Bridget looked closer.

Talking of dodgy guys. It was Nick, his eyes dark against white skin, sliding over Bridget's and away. Laura was patting her pockets, looking round for her bag, her umbrella. Bridget could hear her breathing.

Laura raised a hand to him through the glass. 'I told her everything was on CCTV,' she said. 'I mean, no harm in mentioning it, is there?'

'Even though ours is out of action,' said Bridget, but panic was beginning to hammer at her.

'No,' said Laura, peering into her face bewildered. 'The guy came to fix it. Didn't I tell you? I was sure I'd told you. Couple of weeks ago.'

And pointed up at the screen. Bridget stood there staring up at it not quite able to respond as if winded by the information. How could she not have noticed? All that wondering about cameras in the street.

Laura was looking properly alarmed now. 'She wanted to see how it worked,' she said, her voice rising.

Nick is tapping at the door now and she crossed to open it, head turning to monitor Laura just standing there. She stood back, reluctant, to let him across the threshold and then he stood there, hands in his pockets, looking around airily. 'All right, girls?' he said cheerfully.

Bridget didn't answer, but Laura mumbled something,

she had her handbag on her shoulder, a carrier of shopping in each hand, already shuffling toward the door with her head down. Nick didn't offer to take the bags.

Bridget put up a hand to keep her back a moment. 'Did you show her?' she asked. 'How it worked?'

The CCTV sent images to the laptop, but she hadn't looked at it in days. She had been neglecting everything, orders, the mailshots, the on-off blog they'd started to advertise the shop. Everything. What if. What if.

Nick was pretending interest in the jewellery cabinet.

Laura looked relieved. 'Oh, no. I told her, but I'm not going to show our things to any old reporter, am I? No way. I did go on to the laptop after she'd gone to have a look at the footage – just in case I'd been wrong about her being a shoplifter but then I couldn't find it.'

'Couldn't find it? Couldn't find what? The – the footage?' The thought of what she might have seen.

Laura's shoulders were sagging now. 'The laptop,' she said, anxious again. 'It wasn't where it usually is. On that shelf under the till.'

Thank God, was Bridget's first thought, and then she saw Nick crossing shamelessly to the till, to the desk, leaning to peer round under it to the shelf, stuffed with invoices, a pincushion, a jar of pens, stuff customers weren't supposed to see.

Bridget glared at him and he withdrew, amiably. Wandering the rails now.

She saw Laura's face. 'It's all right, Laura, you've done nothing wrong.' She took a deep breath. 'You get off now. It's Saturday night, you've been on your feet all week.' And as if on cue Nick moved nimbly to reach her, solicitous.

'Let me take those sweetheart,' he said, and Bridget saw the surprise on Laura's face, that softened into pleasure. She held the door open stiffly.

She paused a moment with her face to the glass to make sure they were gone. Laura and Nick walking away, Laura's head down and his arm heavy on her shoulder.

Laura was right, the laptop wasn't there. She tried to think, but her head was too full. Had she taken it home? She did that sometimes. She took it into the back room to check stock sometimes too. She headed for the stockroom, glancing up at the cameras, watching herself move on the fuzzy screen, divided into four shots. Checking the angles: till, front door, back rail, stockroom door.

What could the cameras see? Not the tiny kitchen, but they would have seen him follow her in there, they would have seen him fail to emerge. If someone had dragged a body, however quickly, across the shop floor. The thought of replaying that moment in slow motion, over and over, made her feel dizzy.

The cameras would have seen her at the desk when Timpson came close to her, and that thought, *that* thought propelled her, hot with shame, flushed from the roots of her hair to the backs of her legs, to the stockroom door.

Her phone blipped as she got to the door. It was Carrie. *You're on your way, right?*

The stockroom was a mess. Two boxes of shirts in cellophane on the floor and some paperwork sliding off the tiny desk.

Yes five minutes

There was no time to look for it now. Lights off, lock up. The rain had stopped. Bridget had to make herself be careful, Matt's voice in her head, *bike lights on*. Then she thought of something and removed the battery from her phone, grateful for once that Matt had made her buy the other kind of smartphone, the cheaper kind, the more modest kind. Whose battery could be removed. Did that mean they couldn't trace her movements? She had no idea, but it was her only option. Battery in one pocket, phone in the other. But every moment she delayed, leaning over the bike in the dark and the bike frame slippery under her fingers with the wet, the world seemed to tighten and close around her. When she straightened up she thought she heard something, she thought she saw something move beyond the lockups and made herself wait, heart pounding.

She rode fast and fierce in the wet dark, raised in the saddle and her handbag slung across her, bumping the small of her back. Calm down, she told herself, you can wipe it. First you find it, then you wipe the images.

A car turned out of a lane behind her, slow, cautious, refusing to overtake. The rain had begun again, soft and steady and the road gleamed.

The car didn't pass her all the way, it was there at her back until she was almost at Carmichael's place. Then it turned off, down the next street.

The house was dark and quiet as she locked her bike.

The street looked so safe. The warm glow of lit windows, the broad speckled trunks of the plane trees. Did these people know? Behind their curtains.

She paused at the entrance to the alley that ran alongside the house, in a pool of shade out of the reach of the streetlights. She heard a murmur of voices and took a step down the alley, listening until she identified Carrie, gravelly from the cigarettes, amused.

'Hey,' she hissed.

A face appeared at the side gate: not Carrie. Magdalena. Close to she was strikingly attractive, black hair, blue eyes. And younger than Bridget had thought, closer to twenty than thirty, even when sallow from the night before. A thick Eastern European accent. What had Carrie said? Ukrainian. That was Russia, more or less, wasn't it? All she knew about Russians from the shop was that they bargained hard.

The garden was dark and wet, shrubs brushing against Bridget as she followed them up on to the back porch, Magdalena ahead of them. She flicked on a light at the back door, getting out a bunch of keys.

'What makes you think your employer isn't coming back?' The pretence seemed suddenly laughable, that they had any reason for interrogating her other than the true one. But she mustn't admit it. She was after the pictures: he had disappeared and she was after the pictures.

Magdalena paused, the key in the lock, and looked up at her amused. Under the light she could see Magdalena's skin was not quite flawless, her eyes flat and dark and in that instant Bridget could imagine her in a court room or an interview room, just shrugging, *Sure. Yes, she told me he was dead. She told me she killed him.*

'Maybe something happen to him,' she said, her mouth curving upwards. 'Maybe the police want him, maybe is all over for him and his friend.' The key turned and she gave the door a little push. Inside the wide hallway was dark.

'His friend?'

'Alan,' said Magdalena, in her accent that made everything sound a joke. *Al-lan.*

Then she stepped inside, reaching back to extinguish the light behind them and they were inside, in the dark. 'Why you want to know? Why you want these photographs?' Closing the door behind them.

'If you've seen them, you'll know,' said Bridget, emboldened by the dark.

'I told you why, Magdalena,' said Carrie, and Magdalena let out a harsh little laugh. 'I told her,' said Carrie again, but to Bridget now. 'We're vigilantes.' It sounded like bravado, Carrie making up her own Wonder Woman adventure. 'We want to expose paedophiles.'

Magdalena said nothing. It wasn't quite dark, after all: the streetlight shone through the etched glass of the front door, where sunlight had streamed in the last time they were here. Magdalena leaned against the wide, sloping staircase and the flat planes of her face gave little away. Tough, hostile – and evasive. How could they trust her? Just because she'd spent a night with Carrie? They couldn't.

'We can get money from him,' she said, languorous. 'Maybe. We can threaten?'

Bridget felt the situation getting desperate. The girl might be just interested in money. You could hardly blame her. And if no Carmichael to blackmail – who else? The other person who didn't want anyone to see those pictures was Bridget. But she had no choice.

'Please,' she said, and she heard herself: low, broken. Turned to look at Carrie, pleading. Magdalena frowned, looking from one to the other.

'Sisters, huh,' she said. 'I have also a sister. Don't know where she is.' She made a sound with the words, half a laugh, but unhappy, and as they went on watching at last she nodded, and pushed herself off the carved wood of the wide staircase.

'Upstairs,' she said.

There was a glass cupola in the ceiling above the gallery: Bridget hadn't noticed that the first time. The cloud must have cleared because there was a moon somewhere, a soft, diffused light that shone on the walkway, the doors dark in shadow all around the gallery. Magdalena led them, all padding quietly. They'd left their shoes at the back door. Her shoulders were narrow and skinny, but Magdalena walked as if she owned the place: she passed one door, then another, then the door to his bedroom and it was the next door she stopped at. Pushed, reached in for the light switch.

It was a dressing room, big-panelled, softly lit. Ties hanging in rows, mahogany drawers, a round polished table and low velvet chair. It might be in a magazine spread. Unhesitating Magdalena crossed the room and pulled open a deep, wide drawer under a pair of heavy brass-inlaid doors.

Bridget was beside her: she wasn't sure how she'd even got there. Carrie was still at the door: Bridget looked back but Carrie, white-lipped, didn't move.

The drawer contained shirts. All folded, ironed. 'You do his ironing?' she said to Magdalena, not even knowing why except it was what she did for Matt and the thought made her sick. Magdalena shrugged. She leaned forwards and reached past the shirts, fiddled with something, there was a click and the drawer shifted forwards another foot, as if under its own weight.

296

The box was in a compartment that must have been designed for the purpose of concealing things. Those dark, precious things.

It was the same box she remembered, secured with thick rubber bands, an old cardboard box from an old-fashioned haberdasher's, a gentleman's supplier, a place where they sold tweeds and pale brown slacks and rubber boots and collar studs. Magdalena stepped back, and for the first time Bridget felt a chink in her suspicions of the girl, with her flat eyes and thick pale skin. Magdalena didn't want to watch, she didn't want to gloat.

'Can you—' Bridget's voice was thick, hoarse. 'Would you mind—' But they were gone, anyway, she could hear them pad away around the gallery, down the stairs.

But she didn't look. She stepped away from the box to the tall, handsome window and looked down, into the back garden, across the thick, dark trees, silvered here and there in the moonlight. The wide navy-blue sky, already speckled with stars. She could stand here all night, or she could pull up the sash and jump.

The little house seemed far away, their safe, bright little house could have been like something she'd dreamed. A husband and son, not hers. She blinked because unbidden she could see more, she could see too much. But they *were* hers, she thought, almost to her surprise. Matt would be watching the football highlights and Finn would be on his computer. They were waiting for her to come home. She pulled the curtains and went back to the box.

The pictures of her were on the top. As if he had been looking at them.

Her mouth opened and with it, it felt as if her whole

body split like a fruit, when you opened a peach and found the kernel black inside. Everything black inside, and spoiled and rotted, the room spinning with a dark, silent whoosh around her as she stared down, at her own face. Her own eyes, her ears flattened against her skull like a frightened dog's, her eyes black and bottomless. Little Bridge.

She blinked her eyes shut, and felt her mother's hand, on her cheek, her father's warm side as she had leaned on him when she was small. The two of them watching TV. A sound escaped her, incomprehensible. She opened her eyes and looked.

There were others. Many others, the box was stuffed, they began to spill out. Other girls. A boy. Two boys. She didn't know any of them: they were all about the same age, the age she had been, the age just before you grew, when your body was smooth and small. Twelve, thirteen, fourteen. The men's faces weren't shown, but she saw things she knew: a mole on a man's hand. A cufflink. A mantelpiece.

She was on her knees and she didn't know how she'd got there: on her knees with the box hugged against her. She released it and began to put the photographs back in, carefully, smoothing their corners. She put the lid on, she replaced the rubber bands.

She didn't touch anything, not the drawer, not the light switch, when she walked back out on to the gallery. Down in the wide hall below her Carrie and Magdalena stood in the moonlight with their arms around each other. With one hand Magdalena was stroking Carrie's hair: when she heard Bridget on the stairs she looked up, her face a pale oval, her eyes dark, but made no move to disentangle herself.

298

Carrie's head was on Magdalena's shoulder when she got to the bottom of the stairs. How could you be sure you could trust someone? You couldn't.

'What about his computer?' she said, and then Magdalena slipped a little out of Carrie's arms, and gave a small shrug.

'I don't know where it is. Don't know where he keep it.'

Bridget didn't know if it was true: she thought it probably wasn't. If she accused Magdalena of lying, everything would change. Carrie shifted, uncomfortable.

Magdalena could be hanging on to it for reasons of her own.

It occurred to Bridget as Magdalena stared her out in the half-dark that there was a possibility Carmichael had been having sex with her. Not, she imagined, consensually.

'Magdalena—' she hesitated.

How old was she? Maybe twenty. Which would have been too old for him, when Bridget knew him, but maybe he had fewer options now, even with the internet. But there was something she wasn't coming clean about.

'Did you see any friends of his coming over to the house?'

Magdalena stood alone now, rubbing her arms, skinny and small in the moonlight. 'Sometimes,' she said.

'More than one person?'

She shrugged: 'Sometimes, like I say. I don't look. I don't live here.' Following Carrie's head, trying to make her look back. 'I don't see everything that happens.'

'Would you go to the police? About what you know about him.' She made herself say it. 'About what he does to girls?'

Magdalena made a contemptuous sound. 'Other thing I do first,' she said.

Bridget stepped in front of her, taking her arms, trying to be gentle but to make her understand, too. 'Don't do anything,' she said. 'For the moment, don't do anything. As far as you know, he's gone on holiday like he did before.'

Magdalena pulled away. Obstinately silent. Then at last she cleared her throat. 'OK,' she said grudgingly.

Bridget turned to Carrie, standing there looking away from both of them.

'You coming?' Bridget said.

Carrie turned back, shook her head. 'I'll be back later,' she said.

The sky was almost completely clear when she emerged, made her way through the wet undergrowth to the gate. It creaked rustily in the dripping quiet: she could hear her own steps in the dark alley. She held the box to her chest, her heart beating against it, until she reached her bike and set it down in the basket.

She had time, she thought, if she was fast she had time to cycle back to the shop and look for the laptop.

She heard the sound as she leaned down to unlock the chain, a footstep then a soft, diffident clearing of the throat, and when she stood and turned under the shifting shadow of the plane tree, there he was.

He stood in front of her. 'Bridget,' he said, and his voice fell away in the dark.

Chapter Twenty-Five

Gill was almost there.

The wet night had slowed her down, the unfamiliar roads and this town. This nasty town, with its ring roads and mini-roundabouts and one-way systems and all the time the red lights up on Rose Hill blinking at her from this side then from that side, leading her astray.

Back up somewhere in Cambridgeshire it had almost been all over. She'd finally got on to something resembling a motorway and her foot hard down when a striped barrier appeared, gleaming red and white in her headlights, a lane closed off for flooding. She had veered into the path of a truck behind her, its horn blaring, water hissing out under her tyres and the thing almost bloody aquaplaning. For a moment she'd felt the machine slip her control and thought, not *now*. Not fucking *now* after all this time. And wrenched the car back on to solid tarmac, watched the dazzle of the truck's headlights recede.

That was part of the problem, of course. Her mind on other things, when she should have been watching the road.

There were things Gillian Lawson had done as a journalist of which she was not proud. Could she really stand on the moral high ground? She had lied and stolen and bullied to get to the people she wanted. She wasn't going to think of that, not right now.

Had it all been worth it? Had she done – did she still do – harm as well as good? Even the butcher had looked anxious as she left his shop, as if she might lose him his job, his female assistant eyeing her over his shoulder. Gill had got a photograph on her phone of her with cleaver raised, one saucy eyebrow up.

Matthew Webster yesterday had been a harder nut to crack. Not necessarily cannier, just immovable. Slight but determined in his all-weather trousers and T-shirt, waiting for her in the office whose modest dinginess had not really struck her before. He didn't have any fancy furniture, no walnut-topped desk, just a battered filing cabinet and a scuffed desk and a glass contraption for making coffee. And that picture in its frame that she could no longer see because it had been turned face down.

Completely calm, completely unimpressed by journalistic credentials. Matthew Webster had waited until she was close. 'Look,' she'd said, leaning across the desk and appealing, without calculation, direct. 'Look, I *know* what this man has done, all right? I've talked to the people he's damaged. I know.' A flicker of something, his broad hands on the table top and his glance just skating towards the photograph face down on the desk. 'And I think you know, too,' Gill said then, sitting back in the plastic chair.

302

And then, with a funny little movement, it was done: he was going to let her in. She still didn't know why but he had been ready. He hadn't spilled, though. Nothing hasty: that wasn't, she had worked out by then, in Matt Webster's make-up.

He'd given out information, he told her a name. Told her she couldn't ever quote him but he knew what she was looking for. He knew who.

'I have to respect the privacy of the teaching staff. But monitoring internet usage is part of the job, yes.'

'The job must have grown, since you've been doing it, how long, twenty years?'

'Almost,' he said, raising his head to meet her eye. 'You couldn't use it to stream *Lord of the Rings* when I started, or for gaming.'

'Or downloading porn, or accessing dodgy sites.'

'Nor that.' He nodded, calm enough but his face was in shadow. 'So. I have to protect individuals – but my job is also to protect the integrity of the server. So under certain circumstances I have to look.'

'Am I right in thinking,' Gill said carefully, 'that you can tell if someone had accessed the dark web.' She didn't need to ask him if he knew what the dark web was: the flip side of the internet, where snuff movies and suicide sites and bomb instructions and child pornography lived, invisible to the ordinary man. A collection of websites that existed on an encrypted network and couldn't be found using traditional search engines. Matt Webster would know. And he did.

'There are clues, yes,' he said. 'Proxy servers, special search engines that get you in there. You have to download them – there are certain visible sites that lead you there.

Yes. I mean . . .' and he paused, looking up again, his face clear and untroubled. 'If you really know what you're doing you can cover your traces completely. But he doesn't. They don't.'

He struck her then and even more forcibly now, as a man who knew what he thought. A man who was certain. They were sometimes dangerous, they very often rubbed Gill up the wrong way, being told things by a man did tend to get her goat automatically – but she had stopped herself, looking at Matt Webster, listening to the way he talked. Quiet. Considered.

The name he gave her was Alan Timpson.

'I think – well, in Dr Carmichael's absence, anyway – you could find him useful. They're very good friends. Go back a long way.'

Her satnav diverted her, the line of her route suddenly doing a loop the loop on the little screen: she cursed. Had enough of this. She sat back and examined her surroundings. Tall trees, a hedge, a little way on, a street sign she couldn't read but looking up she recognised it vaguely, even in the dripping dark. This was where he lived, wasn't it? Somewhere close by. In her lap, her phone rang.

Shouldn't have it there, dangerous, looking down when driving, assuming the police wouldn't be able to see. Just another one of her lifestyle choices, along with fags and coffee and fast food and red wine and loneliness. She pulled in at random.

It was Steve, and she'd done something right for once.

'Great piece, Gilly. Very happy with it. Very happy. Love the girl.'

Girl. The female butcher had been thirty-five if she was a day. *And don't call me Gilly.*

The piece had been written in a layby, juggling her laptop and a sandwich while simultaneously googling Alan Timpson, with a styrofoam cup of horrible burger bar coffee to wash it all down. Nasty taste in her mouth.

Timpson had connections in Thailand. A school out there that Carmichael had visited, an orchestra. Another one in Brazil. There had been a photograph of Timpson a couple of years back in a crowd of grinning olive-skinned boys.

The engine ticked down, quiet, but Steve was still talking. He'd had too much coffee, if he was getting this excited. Or maybe he was back on the sauce. 'You see what you can do when you put your mind to it? You're the business. A pro. You're a trouper, love.'

Don't call me 'love'.

Gill turned off the headlights. The person she really wanted to see though – now more than ever – was Bridget Webster. The woman she'd only seen in photographs: a yellowing cutting from the nineties, the picture on Webster's desk, a google image search. Gill had updated her information: now she knew Bridget Webster's taste, that shop where she'd felt uneasy: neat rows of expensive things, a scent in the air, of money. A flickering image on a screen.

She'd bought a white shirt from Bridget Webster's shop, astonished at the price. But then the last shirt Gill had bought had been from Marks five years ago, they'd come in packs of five.

Matt Webster had had no idea, had he? Of his wife's previous connection with Carmichael, of the two years

305

she'd spent in the psych unit. Gill knew. Gill, who'd never met her but had unearthed an old school friend, pierced and tattooed, who'd told her what she remembered about Bridget O'Neill. Her getting a prize for violin in front of the whole school. Her passing out in the lunch break, her legs like twigs, taken off in an ambulance, rambling and slurring.

Did he know now? He didn't seem stupid. And looking up, looking up into the dark striped with yellow streetlight, there she was. Under a tree a figure bending over a bicycle and when her head tilted into the light Gill knew it was her, as sure as if it was a mugshot.

Unlocking her bicycle, no more than a hundred yards from Carmichael's house. Why? Why?

Of course, she knew where he lived. Of course. He'd been back in touch with her, of course.

And then, out of nowhere a man was standing there, too, holding Bridget Webster steady, not embracing her, keeping her where she was. One hand on each arm. A man in a hooded sweatshirt.

In the darkened car Steve was talking into Gill's ear, saying things she couldn't focus on: she tried to shut him up as she saw the man lead Bridget Webster to a van, saw her stand docile as he loaded her bicycle into the back and opened the passenger door for her.

'Steve, Steve, I— look can you, can I call you back.' But as she hung up she could only watch, helpless, as they drove away.

Then she saw that the lights were on in Carmichael's house.

★   ★   ★

306

He looked like a stranger. His eyes were in deep shadow under the hoodie, his cheekbones showing yellow in the streetlighting: she stared at him. Her Matt.

Bridget. He sounded so sad.

'What are you doing here?' They both spoke at once, then were both silent.

Matt spoke first. 'It's raining,' he said, tense. 'I'll give you a lift back.'

'I—' She faltered, not daring to look at the box sitting in her basket, but Matt didn't seem to have noticed it. Her mind raced, round and round, all the things she mustn't say: she was trapped. All she wanted was to go back to the shop and find the laptop. She had already thought she could hide the photographs there. Think; think. If he asked, *what's in that box, why are you here?* She needed an answer.

But Matt was talking; he had pushed the hood back from his face and he was her Matt again, or something more like it.

'I was driving back from town and I saw you, I thought you'd want a lift. You didn't go the way I expected. You seemed to be in a hurry.' Quiet, reasonable, curious. 'Whose house is that?'

She stared at him hypnotised. Stuttered, scrabbled. Get close enough to the truth, she had learned that much, if you want a lie to be believed. And then it came to her.

'Carrie's met someone,' she said, making herself sigh, weary. Jaded. 'Her new girlfriend lives there, she wanted to meet me. Asked me for a drink.'

He reached across her for the handlebars. 'Let's get this in the van, shall we?'

And in a quick, swift movement, before he could touch

307

it, Bridget plucked the box out of the basket, holding it against her. It was already damp from the rain. He walked in front of her, wheeling the bike.

Bridget suddenly wanted a drink. Desperately. Anything to loosen this feeling. She followed him obediently, then round to the passenger seat.

The box felt heavy on her lap. The smell of the van reminded her of him, the old smell of air freshener, a hint of rust from the rear, and a new note, something muddier, dirtier.

'All right?' Matt turned to her, the key in the ignition. There was something wrong with this, Matt almost never drove, he hadn't said why, where he had been going – but her thoughts kept turning back, pulled by the weight. Go to the shop, find the laptop, find somewhere to hide the box of pictures.

'Sure,' she said, hesitating, making herself smile. 'This rain, I just wondered if—'

Or maybe it wasn't safe? Her hands tightened on the box in her lap: safer to keep the photographs with her, to take them home. Because how was it going to work? Pictured herself carrying them into the shop, Matt asking questions, but she couldn't leave them in the car with him, either.

The thought of the laptop tormented her. Part of her was fascinated, too: she wanted to see it from outside. See what happened, the grainy images, she would have the power to slow it all down, slower, slower, *stop*. Rewind.

All she could remember was what she'd been wearing that day, the skirt that had got his blood on it, the tights that were snagged. She'd burned them all – but even that could incriminate her. If the police asked her to hand over the clothes to them, what would she say?

She had to remind herself, there were no police. There was no search. Carmichael had gone to Thailand or Brazil, he wasn't coming back.

'What?' said Matt, indicating, pulling out into the quiet street.

'Nothing.' She subsided into quiet beside him. All she had to do was delete the footage. Whatever it showed. Tomorrow, she'd find an excuse to go in even though it was Sunday, she'd done that before, something left behind, a light left on. She couldn't bring it home, though, where Matt and Finn, both techno savvy, could look at it. The laptop had been Matt's once, handed down to her. A new-old piece of kit in the house, neither of them would be able to resist, flipping the lid, *hey, remember this?*

They were on the main road, heading home. The towers were up ahead, blinking red against the night sky. Think of something to say, something safe.

'Did Finn get his present? For—' For a moment she couldn't remember the girl's name, her brain mush. 'For Phoebe?' She cleared her throat, hearing the timidity in her voice with the streetlights strobing over them, dark, bright, dark.

'Yes,' said Matt, leaning forwards to turn on the radio. 'He got something. He's happy. He had fun with that girl, Isabel, apparently. He's at home cooking dinner for us now, he's suddenly into it, recipes and everything.' But Bridget was hardly listening, leaning forward in the seat over the box, still calculating. How could she sleep, knowing the laptop was there, where anyone could see it? Could she get him to turn around now, rehearsing in her head, searching for the right tone, light, cross, *shit, I forgot, can we.*

The radio burbled, and Matt turned up the sound, she could tell by the way he cocked his head that something had caught his attention. *Police have called a temporary halt to the search.* 'You hear this?' said Matt, turning to her, serious. 'Just as well Finn's home safe.'

'What—?' The wipers were struggling with a sudden gust of rain that was pelting the windscreen but then Bridget caught the newsreader's voice, a woman, calm but with just the right level of concern. She was talking about the missing boy, the boy whose disappearance had started out in the local paper then moved to the nationals. The report Bridget had been looking at only today. *The weather is expected to improve.*

Divers will focus their attention on Bardleigh reservoir.

Bridget turned, involuntarily, to Matt in the dark, they slowed at the lights, came to a stop under a streetlight that illuminated his face and would have to illuminate hers. Matt shifted and looked at her, just for a second, two, but long enough for them both to know. He said nothing.

They were both lying.

Matt had come out looking for her and followed her to Carmichael's place. All this turning off her phone had been for nothing because there was a witness – more than one. Multiplying witnesses: Carrie, Magdalena, Matt. What about neighbours, the gardener?

The lights changed and Matt engaged first gear, the wipers flogging relentlessly in the steady rain. Let it rain. Let it rain for a week and that would keep them away from the reservoir long enough for her to plan something.

What did he think? That she was having an affair? That would be the usual thing to think. The idea made her sick. An affair in that house. Was that what she had with Carmichael? An affair? A *love affair*? It's what she had wanted it to be, all that time ago, was it? She'd groped blindly for love and could only blame herself. She had wanted it: it had been in his every soft word to her, telling her what she felt, *you can't help yourself, can you?* Everything he had ever said to her was still in her head somewhere. *It's all right, I love you, that's what you want to know, isn't it? Isn't it?*

Bridget sat in the passenger seat in the dark and her body seemed small, soft-shelled. disgusting as a jellied undersea creature. If Matt made her talk she would have to admit that she had never even managed to end it: she had just tried to die rather than break it off. She had never said no.

So she couldn't talk. Wouldn't.

And then at last they were turning into the close, quiet houses, soft lighting.

'God, I'm knackered,' she said, her shoulder against the passenger door and desperate to get out. 'I hope there's time for a shower before dinner.' She heard Matt getting her bike out of the back as she ran.

The house was full of the smell of cooking. Passing Finn in the kitchen Bridget managed a smile but he was too busy in his apron, flour in his hair, to pay any attention and gratefully she was on the stairs. Taking them two at a time with her bag bumping against her side, the box tight in her arms. Because if it fell, spilled, the pictures slithering on the stairs – Her lungs burned with the effort, with not being able to breathe.

311

Once in the bedroom she shoved the box in the bottom of the wardrobe – and then shakily she could exhale at last, subsiding on to the bed. A sweat bloomed, from her armpits to the small of her back to behind her ears. Burn it.

She got her phone out of her pocket and put the battery back in and almost immediately a message pinged. It was from Carrie. *Back tomorrow, be OK.*

'Mum?' Finn was calling her. His face comically anguished at the foot of the stairs. 'Something's gone wrong with the gravy.'

The distraction saved her. Standing at the stove instructing him, ladling boiling water from the beans, telling him to get the gravy boat and asking him about salt. Behind her she heard Matt come into the room making cheerful sounds, a chair moving. Wine uncorked. Happy family.

Halfway through the meal, pushing roast pork and baked potato around her plate, Bridget thought about Matt and his bicycles, alone in the garage. Set her fork down. Was that his distraction? She'd never thought of him as needing it. Something to keep your hands busy.

How many glasses of wine had she drunk? Not too many, three, maybe. She poured herself some water and pushed the wineglass away a little.

'This is lovely, Finn.' He beamed, flour still in his hair. 'So you're seeing Phoebe tomorrow, then?'

They let him talk. Full of it, bubbling over. His Sunday plans: he was going to spend the whole day with Phoebe, her parents were away. A walk in the country park. The present was a bracelet, Isabel had found it in a shop she knew. Matt caught Bridget's eye and smiled: everything felt blurrily good, it felt yielding, as though she was just resting a bit, in a feather bed. Her glass still seemed to have wine in it. Her cheeks were warm. She drank.

Standing at the washing up Bridget knew she'd had too much: she felt it in the way she leaned heavily against the sink, her back to them so they wouldn't see. Just for Finn: this is all for Finn. Her thoughts were slowing to sludge. Clang, went the pans stacked on the draining board.

She turned and smiled uncertainly. 'Just heading off now,' she said, pretending to yawn. ''S been a long day.' Upstairs she tried to do things properly, cleaning her teeth, folding her clothes but gave up. Once between the sheets she fell into sleep too suddenly, in a T-shirt, the light still on.

Dimly she was aware of Matt coming up later and turning it off, then moving around the room softly in the dark and as she lay still, drugged, she could see words behind her eyes, the after-image of a headline. *They're dragging the reservoir.* They pulsed there, the wine still in her system dulling their meaning, and she fell asleep again. The sleep was dark but not restful, with pinpricks like electricity, signalling things she didn't understand.

At one, the phone rang.

Bridget sat bolt upright in the dark, her head suddenly sharply painful and her heart racing as if it might kill her, finally.

Beside her Matt groaned, there was a clatter as he dislodged the receiver. 'Yes?' Groggy with sleep. 'Whass—'

It was the police.

Chapter Twenty-Six

Sunday

The alarm had almost run out of juice by the time they got there, no more than a feeble squawk in the night. Matt stood beside her in the dark, wet street, surveying the scene. There was glass all over the cobbles, forty minutes since the phone call and Bridget still couldn't seem to slow her heart down. She wondered, as if from a distance, how long it could go on running this fast.

She'd reached for the phone the moment Matt held it away from his ear. The moment she understood it wasn't Carmichael, it wasn't Carrie, they were phoning about the shop.

'Let me talk to them.' Matt lay back on the pillow, one hand to his forehead, as she leaned across him.

'Mrs Webster.' The policeman had sounded weary. 'Your alarm's going off, and according to your neighbour—'

Neighbour? What neighbour? They must mean the newsagent. 'Someone's chucked a brick at your shop window.' He sounded reluctant. 'We're dealing with a major road traffic incident just now but we can get someone down there by—'

The CCTV.

Bridget was scrambling out of bed, registering the T-shirt she was wearing, the fact that she still had her bra on. 'No, no,' she said, groping for her jeans, 'I mean, let me go and have a look first, I don't want you to have to—'

The laptop. If someone had—

They agreed she'd call them back. When she hung up, beside her Matt was pulling on his trousers, uncomplaining.

'No,' he said, firmly when she protested. 'I'm coming with you.' She sat, suddenly irresolute beside him on the bed, wanting him with her, knowing she should go alone. Then his arm was round her shoulders and he pressed his lips quick and soft against her cheek and she couldn't stop herself, her head dropped under its own weight to rest against his shoulder.

Across the landing in his room Finn was still up, talking softly to someone online in his room. Laughing. He pulled off his headphones when they appeared in the door: from the crowded split-screen she could see he was gaming. Not Phoebe, but the fuzzy, delayed image of some laughing teenager in Arizona. He was concerned, obedient, when she told him what had happened, but buzzing underneath it, impatient to get back to whatever it was.

Matt drove. They parked round the back. A dim light was on above the newsagent's, under the eaves: she had hardly registered that he lived there, she realised. The windows always so dirty.

Matt had made her put on more clothes, warm socks, a fleece of his. And now standing in the cold dark Bridget was grateful for it: she felt as if something was draining

315

everything out of her, warmth and energy, like her heart was a malfunctioning engine.

'Well,' said Matt mildly at her side. 'Someone did a job on it.' Peering closer. 'Doesn't look like you've been cleaned out, though.'

The jagged remains of a starburst at the edges was all that was left of what had once been the window and the rest of it was lying in shards on the cobbles and winking inside on the shop floor. Reluctantly Bridget peered in.

The dummy in the window had been knocked drunkenly sideways, its skirt rucked up. On the floor behind it there was a big lump of stone, not something you'd find in the street, big enough to have been hauled out of a rockery. The glass was almost completely gone but inside the clothes still hung on the rails, the handbags along the shelving. The jewellery cabinet was untouched.

Pointlessly, because she could have stepped right through the window Bridget unlocked the door, reached in and turned off the alarm. There was a smell of urine. She felt Matt come in after her, more than heard him. Heard him sigh, bewildered.

Saying nothing she walked quickly across the shop floor into the stockroom, turned on the light. Matt didn't follow her: she heard him sigh, bewildered, on the shop floor. She scanned the room: it didn't look as if anyone had been in here, either. The desk with its papers: how to tell if this was new disarray, or how she'd left it? But she couldn't see it. Couldn't see it. She pulled open a drawer in the desk where she would have put it. Peered under the rails, between shoeboxes.

No laptop, anywhere. Behind her in the shop she heard

316

Matt move, the crunch of glass, and she emerged. He looked at her, distraught in the light from the stockroom, nonplussed.

'I don't think anything's gone,' she mumbled. Matt looked at her a second then he walked away, slowly, circling the room.

'Just vandalism, then,' he said, thoughtfully. He didn't sound convinced. But the smell of piss was unignorable and in the next moment he stepped back, wrinkling his nose. 'I'll get the boarding.'

While he was gone – five minutes, less – she ran around, opening shoe cupboards, there was a secret shelf she'd forgotten behind some shelving in the old chimney breast – but there was nothing but dust in it.

They put up the boarding between them: Matt had done it before, he said, when someone smashed a window in the student bar, and he'd brought everything with him; two minutes in the garage as she waited in the van and he'd been equipped, but then that was Matt. All the same Bridget winced as he drove a nail into the window frame and he gave her a sideways glance. An apologetic shrug.

The boarding done, he stood in the doorway, peering in as she re-set the alarm. For a moment she thought he might go back in, exploring. Typical Matt, wanting to gather evidence, to know the reason for things.

'I'll deal with it in the morning,' she said quickly, a hand on his shoulder. 'Don't touch anything, not now.' She didn't have to pretend to be dead tired, her head hurting. He looked at her a second, then nodded.

Bridget was silent in the van as Matt drove home and he seemed suddenly too worn out to ask questions, his face pale and strained. The roads were empty, except one jostling group of lads swaying outside a dark pub, two girls in heels clinging to each other for support. It must be three in the morning, the sky darker than ink. It was impossible to believe summer would ever come back

They wouldn't find who smashed the window. She knew they wouldn't. And if they did – who, though? Who? Just coincidence?

Who might want that laptop? Her head hurt, the booze all gone from her system, the hangover set like concrete.

Who? Matt glanced sideways, said nothing.

She didn't want the police anywhere near her, or the shop. How would she clear that with Matt? The rain had stopped, and the same police would be dragging the reservoir. Too close, too close for comfort.

She climbed out of the van and wearily they made their way up to bed, Matt behind her on the stairs, his hand resting a minute on her hip, patting. He always used to do that, following her up to bed, as if to say, *I'm here.*

Undressing she found the long T-shirt she slept in and went into the bathroom to clean her teeth. She looked at herself in the mirror, white as a sheet, haunted.

They would find her. They would. They would find his body and then they would find her. She was seen there. His car thirty miles from his body? How stupid. How stupid. And the chance was there, right in front of her, she could spill it all out, confess, the police would be right there in the shop, she only had to pick up the phone.

She laid down the toothbrush, pushed her hair out of her face, stared. *Don't you dare.* She heard Carrie's voice in her head. *Don't you fucking dare.*

Behind her in the bedroom Matt turned out the light. Were they coming for her? Then let them come.

The hideous lavender light was beginning to look like home.

Gill didn't need to turn her head on the pillow to know she was on her own. She had wanted nothing more than to crash out face down in clean sheets, last night. She wondered – and it was a thought almost as depressing as finding a purple hotel bedroom a decent substitute for home – if this was down to her age.

Sometimes Gill did still want sex so badly that she felt like flinging open her bedroom window and shouting down into the street for it. But more and more the thought of it only made her feel sad and tired. It had been one in the morning when she walked back into the lobby last night, a handful of men still drinking under the dim mauve downlighting above the bar and for a second she had thought she saw the engineer reading a newspaper in one of the leatherette armchairs and stopped, her first instinct to go into reverse, back out on to the street, back into the taxi, to some other bar, some other town.

And then the man in the chair had shifted, and it was someone else. Getting paranoid, or too convinced of her own charms. Not all men are stalkers.

She had quite liked him, though: that was the thought she woke with, that propelled her out of bed to put on the hotel kettle. Which made a change. She frowned down at the tiny capsule of fake milk.

Today felt different. Like a day when it would all turn around and she could pack the overnight bag back up – the

319

overnight bag that had overnighted three nights now, or was it four, and everything in it grubby – and go home. She could even buy real milk and put it in her own fridge.

Hell, she could clean her own fridge, and then retrain as a butcher. Honest work.

Black tea, that would be the start. Turning with the cup in her hand she looked across at her briefcase leaning casually on the purple velvet chair – too low to sit on, unless you were five years old, or an Edwardian prostitute – and crossed to it. She set the mug down carefully on the desk and pulled the laptop out of the bag.

Gill Lawson had long since known that following her instincts could get her into trouble, but even by her standards, this was madness. And criminal madness into the bargain. She opened the computer and it asked for a password. *Low battery*, it said. Shit: she hadn't thought of that. No charger cable. She closed it again and sat there with her eyes closed.

She wanted to see her. Needed to see little Bridget O'Neill, know how she'd turned out . . .

Was it for Steve? It would help, of course – if she could get Bridget O'Neill to talk. She had a good husband. A decent bloke, and more importantly, a bloke who knew more about Carmichael than most, a bloke who wouldn't doubt her, not for a minute. Gill'd bet anything you like he knew already, somewhere, deep down. People did. They didn't say it out loud, though. Maybe that was what Bridget needed: to say it out loud. Maybe. To her husband – and then to Gill. On the record.

Jittery, nauseated, Gill opened her eyes. Was it late nights and booze giving her this sour feeling in her gut?

Or all the lies she was telling herself? She closed her eyes again.

To be a fly on the wall. Did computers hold everyone's secrets, these days? Some of them. She wanted more than anything to stand in front of her, talk to her, tell her – tell her what? That she understood? That she was there to help? Gill knew how those conversations went: shutters coming down. *Are you all right, Bridget O'Neill?*

The surface of the laptop was smooth under her palms. She didn't know how that girl would have turned out, the prodigy who hanged herself, whose mother, Gill remembered from all that time ago, had said she wanted to be a doctor. A clever girl but that was a long road, wasn't it? Life was a long road. A struggle to keep at it, job, kids, no kids, love, no love. A long road. And all clever had got that girl was as far as the woods with a length of rope and half a bottle of cheap vodka inside her.

Gill heard herself sigh, opened her eyes again and sat up. Set the laptop aside.

Looking through the front window of Anthony Carmichael's house last night as the rain poured relentlessly, she had seen something unexpected. There had been two women inside the music room, with its oil painting of his wife and a vase on the mantelpiece and the big polished piano.

They had been looking at a computer too, cheek to cheek, the cropped head and the one with long, shiny hair, shoulder to shoulder. Time to close the computers, girls. Time to close your eyes, work it out.

One of the women was his cleaner, though she hadn't looked like she was working, six o'clock on a Saturday evening sitting at his shiny mahogany table and making herself at home. The woman with her she'd seen before: pale and angry and with hair so short you could see her scalp through it, she'd got off the same train from London as Gill had taken. That small, white, pointy-chinned face that had seemed somehow familiar then and more familiar now. Gill had to jump back from the window in the dark as the small woman sprang to her feet and began pacing. Talking.

She knew the voice, too. It had answered the phone to her. Not Bridget Webster – but Bridget Webster had had a sister, too. Mentioned in that little local rag piece about her skill as a violinist, sitting in the front row at school prize-giving, next to her mum. Their mum. Aged about ten and the hair a tangled cloud, but the same pointy little chin, the same fierce, dark eyes.

Gill had done her time on local press. Prize-givings, funerals, am dram. Concerts in village halls, charity recitals. Carmichael's bread and butter.

What was Bridget Webster's sister doing inside Carmichael's house? Looking at his computer.

This was getting close to dangerous. This was getting into police territory. Tread carefully, Gill.

Was this the day? The day she nailed him, and all his dirty washing, the day she threw the lot out into the street for the world to see. For the first time in her life, Gill was afraid.

Chapter Twenty-Seven

A message pinged, two messages, three. Bridget's phone on the table beside her head and she jerked awake, fumbling for the light switch.

It was light outside, but grey. Bridget felt hot and confused after no more than three hours' sleep, her face felt flushed. The night rattled around in her head and she couldn't tell what was real, it all seemed like a bad dream. The dummy hanging sideways out of the window, broken glass glittering in the street. A light on behind a dirty window, high up over the newsagent's shop. The laptop.

She reached for the phone. The texts were from Laura, something about Nick being weird. Bridget couldn't work out what she was talking about. As she pulled herself upright on the pillow her head began to hurt.

Beside her Matt had his chin propped on a hand, looking at her: she glanced at him then looked away quickly, back at the phone though she couldn't focus on it.

'Are you going to tell me what's going on?' he said quietly, and it was as if that hole had opened up, she was going to fall.

'What?' she said, the breath leaving her. 'What do you mean? It's just – it was vandalism—'

He shook his head just once, watching. 'It's not last night,' he said. 'Or not just that. Is it?' She didn't answer. He sighed. 'This woman Gillian Lawson,' he said. 'This journalist who came here looking for Dr Carmichael. She has evidence that he has abused young women over a long period. Twenty, thirty years.'

Looking at her steadily, those kind, clever blue eyes that were always on her side. Even when she scraped the van, set the grill on fire, even when she nearly dropped Finn as a baby.

'She thinks he's gone online. She thinks – she is beginning to think he might even have come here because one of his victims, from a long time ago, also lives here.' He paused. 'She wants to talk to the woman.'

The way he was speaking was measured, thoughtful, just a shade of puzzlement. As if she knew more, he was asking her to tell him. He wasn't taking his eyes off her. What was she supposed to say? He was laying it out so carefully, it was pointing in one direction. Was that her imagination?

Don't jump the gun. Keep quiet.

'Anthony Carmichael turns up here,' he said, as if pondering. 'He comes into your shop. He disappears. Do you know what he's been doing? Him and his friend Timpson.'

'Me?' She couldn't get more than the single syllable out.

'He's been on the dark web. You know what that is?' He frowned.

324

She made a small movement with her head. She knew. She didn't want to, but she did, it was in her head like the grainy occluded spot on a scan. Criminals used the dark web: it was where you found drugs, information, porn. It was where you sold them.

'I know,' she said.

And then he moved, raising himself up on the pillows and he was closer, but he wasn't touching her. Making sure not to touch her. She had the sudden, terrible sense that he might never touch her again. Was this Matt? Was this her husband?

'She thinks,' and his voice was soft, 'you might have known him, once upon a time. The journalist does. That you might have recognised him.'

She was frozen, now, mesmerised. Her mouth moved but she couldn't answer.

'*Did* you know him?' he said. To someone else he might seem only puzzled, but she knew Matt, it was a strategy, it was a face he used, patient with students who've fucked up their network connections or downloaded a virus or crashed the server.

'No, I – well—' She couldn't look at him. She had to change the subject somehow. What could she say? 'I wasn't sure—'

And then there was a sudden sharp sound from downstairs, a laugh, a machine-gun laugh, and then Finn talking.

'Carrie's back, then,' Bridget said, wildly, breathless, swinging her legs out of the bed and grabbing clothes off the floor, but before she turned she saw the darkening look on Matt's face, a shutter coming down.

She descended the stairs so quickly she almost slid and

fell, recovering herself automatically, *Keep on. Keep going.*
Matt didn't follow her. She had to think.

Turning at her appearance in the kitchen door, Finn
was standing at the table holding a giant pink stuffed toy,
looking downcast. 'Isabel loved it,' he said, uncertain. Carrie
had her hands on her hips. She and Bridget exchanged a
glance, a tiny shake of Carrie's head said, *later.* 'I thought
she found a bracelet,' she said, hearing the little tremble in
her voice and correcting it.

'And this.' Frowning, Finn looked comically anguished
and Bridget just wanted to hug hum, grab hold of him.
The one who believed in her innocence, without even
knowing he was being asked. She patted him lightly instead.
'What about a bit of breakfast?'

'I'm making pancakes,' he said. 'Isabel gave me a recipe.'
Then Bridget saw the mixer had been pulled out, a bag
of flour and the eggs were on the side.

Isabel and Finn together. It sounded so safe.

Carrie cleared her throat, jerking her head to the door.
'Where's the Tampax?' she said, meaningfully. 'I looked in
the bathroom.' Finn turned his back and reached for the
jug of milk.

Matt was on the stairs coming down as they headed up:
'They're in the bedroom,' said Bridget over her shoulder
to Carrie but she had to look him in the eye as she edged
past and his face made her heart sink.

Carrie closed the bedroom door behind her.

'When did you get in?' said Bridget, breathless.

'God, I don't know,' said Carrie, impatient. 'Eleven?
Something like that. Matt said you'd gone to bed early. We
stayed up talking—'

'Didn't you hear us go out? There was a break-in at the shop.'

Carrie didn't seem to be listening. 'I think you might be right about her, I don't know. There's something she's not being upfront about.'

'About who? Magdalena?' Heart bumping again, almost wearisome now, the new normal. She was tired, and she was frightened.

'She's not telling the truth about something,' said Carrie, her back to the door. 'She's had some involvement with him, Carmichael. And the other one, the one she said came to visit—'

'Timpson.'

'I'm pretty sure – well, she got funny when I asked about him. She knows him all right.'

'Sex,' said Bridget immediately.

Carrie frowned. 'Maybe. I'm not sure.'

'I mean, they don't care about her – her sexual prefer-ences, you know that, right?'

Carrie rubbed her arms, anxious. 'I just don't think we can trust her.'

'What does she know? About – us.' Carrie looked down and Bridget stepped closer, urgent. 'Carrie?'

'I didn't tell her anything,' said Carrie, panicked. 'She showed me his computer – she knows his password.' She chewed the inside of her mouth: when she was frightened she did that, used to do that, Bridget recognised the response. When she was little. 'She showed me the stuff he looks at.'

She'd thought Carrie was unshockable, but her eyes said different.

'I can imagine,' she said and reached for her sister, pulling her roughly, pressing her lips into the soft fur of her head. The box of photographs was upstairs, dangerous. Anyone could look inside it. But it was evidence. It could be used in her defence. Or used against her? Carrie pulled back.

'She hates him,' she said quietly.

'Why?' said Bridget and Carrie stared.

'I can't believe you're asking that,' she said.

'We need to know her motives,' said Bridget, patient. 'To know if we can trust her. We need to be sure it's not just—'

'It's not money,' said Carrie, swift and certain. 'It's—' she hesitated. 'He's made her do things. She didn't say what. She talks tough – she says she doesn't care, she says worse things happen at home, worse things happen to other girls. But she does care. She cares about what he did to her. I haven't told her – what we did. But she said to me, she doesn't care if he's dead. She said, if anyone killed him, I would give them a medal.'

A clatter came from the kitchen downstairs. Bridget sat on the bed abruptly.

'I think Matt knows,' she said, examining her hands. 'Or knows something. There's this journalist, the one we saw on the front porch talking to Magdalena.' Looked up at Carrie. 'And you heard about someone chucking a brick through the shop window?' Carrie nodded. Bridget swallowed, trying to swallow the panic. Her mouth felt dry.

'I think Timpson's taken the laptop,' she said, 'because he thinks it recorded him trying to intimidate me. What if he sees what happened to— What if he sees what I did? To *him*. The images.'

'You mean the CCTV was on and you didn't erase the footage?' Carrie stared in disbelief.

Bridget just shook her head. 'It's been on the blink for more than a year,' she said. 'I got used to not looking at it. Laura forgot to tell me. We're not a high-risk operation at the shop, it's a little backstreet place.' The irony of that wasn't lost on her. It felt pretty high risk now.

Carrie sat beside her. 'So you think it wasn't just vandalism? You think it was someone breaking in to find the computer?'

'That's what's worrying me,' said Bridget. 'He might have seen himself on the CCTV, or he might have worked it out later. Or he might just want to know what I know.'

'And made it look like vandalism? Matt said—' Carrie broke off. She meant the smell of urine. Bridget couldn't imagine Timpson doing that. She didn't want to imagine it.

'Tell me it's password protected,' said Carrie.

If he saw it all, on the laptop.

'The password—' she said, 'I never changed it. It's *password*.'

Carrie raised her eyes to heaven. *'Bridge—'* she began, then gave up. 'I know where he lives,' she said, instead. 'I'll go over there. Not you, me.'

'You know where Alan Timpson lives?' Bridget didn't understand.

'Pancakes!' Matt was calling up the stairs. 'Hey, you two.' Was he angry? She couldn't tell any more. Then his footsteps, he was coming up. Bridget grabbed the box of Tampax, thrust them at Carrie and went out to meet him.

Matt stood there with his hand on the banister, looking

up at her. 'All right?' he said warily. She nodded, and he turned to go back down ahead of her. 'The police say they'll come along to the shop this afternoon,' he said quietly, when they got to the bottom.

'They called?' Bridget hadn't heard the phone. Above them Carrie padded across the landing.

'I called them,' said Matt. 'For the insurance, you need to report it to the police.' There was something in the way he looked at her that made her feel cold. Was he turning her in? He pushed open the kitchen door and there was the bright kitchen, the table laid and Finn with a pan in his hand.

'They wanted to come straight away,' Matt said, easily. 'But I told them this afternoon would be fine.'

Pacing the mauve room, Gill was on her third cup of black tea: all it was doing was making her feel jittery. It certainly didn't feel like a detox. She pulled back the curtains to look over the town's rooftops. Past a block of light-industrial development, past a church spire and the curve of a ring road she could just see a sliver of grey estuary. The big eastern sky was on the same spectrum, watercolour grey smudged with charcoal.

She was trying to guess the password. Hers was the name of her first dog. She'd called him Genius because he was so dim. So Genius72 was her password, the dog plus the year of her birth.

For more than an hour last night she had waited to see if Bridget Webster's sister was going to leave, sitting on the porch to get out of the rain while the cold garden dripped around her. Thinking time: sometimes you needed pointless waiting to get your head together. Waiting for her to leave not because she didn't want to talk to the girl – well, Gill calculated the sister would be more than thirty, no more a girl than Gill was – but because she'd learned from long experience that you had to divide to rule. The two of them together would have clammed up.

One or both of them *would* go, Gill assumed, because after all, this wasn't their house, was it? The cleaner might live in – and if she did there would be plenty of reasons for Gill to talk to her – but Anthony Carmichael wouldn't want her having girlfriends over, that was for sure. Gill had been about to give up when she heard the voices in the hall and had scurried round the back to wait. Bloody soaked, by then, so cold she couldn't feel her feet. She'd waited for five more minutes, to be sure, before knocking. Not ringing, knocking, soft and persistent.

There was something in the cleaner's face as she opened the door that suggested to Gill she'd almost been expecting her. Magdalena: standing at the grey window looking out over the sea, now Gill knew her name, and plenty more. Magdalena had sighed, taking in her dripping hair, her soaked feet, and let her in. Almost immediately she had hissed sharply at Gill to take off her shoes, her coat and leave them at the door, then led her across pale creamy carpet into a big kitchen.

The kitchen was very clean but it smelled. Cleaning products with something nasty underneath. A bachelor's kitchen, where butter goes rancid in the fridge. On the table was a bottle of vodka that looked like it had just come out of a freezer, and a tumbler that looked like it had been emptied at least once already. Saying nothing

Magdalena had reached for another glass and poured two drinks.

The girl drank like she'd been born drinking: it had been hard to keep up. The bottle was two-thirds full when they sat down, and Gill calculated from the way Magdalena started straight in talking, staring down into her glass, that she'd drunk the other third herself. Quite possibly in the five minutes since she said goodbye to Bridget Webster's kid sister.

Sitting there with the glass between her hands, she stared at Gill and said, 'You a journalist, right? Interested in bad things?' Then didn't look at her again, just talked.

Not about Anthony Carmichael, although it was in a way all about him.

Gill knew how to listen. If you didn't know how to do that, you would get nowhere in the job. Plenty of people had never been listened to, and they were just waiting to tell it all, to sound off to another human being. As if it might somehow make sense, that way, what they'd suffered, what they'd had to endure. Some of them never told, they waited and waited for the one who would listen but she – or he – never came along.

And Magdalena had had to endure plenty. Her childhood in the Ukraine, her father casually violent, the boyfriends who had passed her around, the one who'd broken her collar bone and her left arm when he found her with a girl. She reached for another glass of vodka, and drained it. The next boyfriend who'd seemed pretty OK with her being bisexual, or gay: supportive. So enthusiastic, even, that he'd told her about London, how great it was for people who were different, he'd found her a job, all legal.

And brought her over as a sex worker. Another glass of vodka. She had escaped from a house on the edge of London wearing dirty bedroom slippers and a shell suit, the only clothes she'd been given, with twenty quid a punter who'd felt sorry for her had given her. Then Magdalena looked up at her with a smile that came nowhere near her eyes.

'And now I am cleaner for Dr Carmichael.' Eyes flat.

Looking out over the small, grey town Gill wondered, the vodka still numbing certain bits of her, if everything was relative. To Magdalena the abuse of a child was just on a spectrum, so was it down to what you were used to? To what was – or appeared to be – tolerated in your society? As far as Magdalena was concerned it was tolerated here, on this tight-arsed little island where people were so quick to pull their curtains shut. Was it down to Gill to decide what was right and what was wrong? Someone had to.

Magdalena had begun to tell her about Timpson when there was less than an inch of vodka in the bottle. If this had been a police interview none of it would have counted, but she showed no sign of being drunk. She stood and paced in the bright white kitchen, with its sour smell: she paced as far as the fridge door and pulled it open, searching. Peering past her Gill managed to see something wrapped in cling film in a lower drawer. Meat or fish, and probably the source of the smell. 'Maybe we go out and get beer?' said Magdalena thoughtfully. But then she was back at the table sitting down and the last of the vodka was in her glass. Gill hadn't asked her what Bridget Webster's little sister had been doing there yet, but this was interesting. This was what she was after.

'He is the one making the websites,' she said, her voice flat, her eyes flatter. Looking only at the glass, rolling the liquid from side to side. 'Mr Timpson. Dr Carmichael thinks he is too good for that, he is the *intellectual*.' She turned the word into three syllables, contemptuously. 'Also he likes something different. The girl in his house, the power, he makes her impressed with him. She is in his room, that room.' She jerked her head back to the music room.

'Is there one at the moment? A girl now, he brings here?' Gill knew she shouldn't interrupt, first rule of the good listener, but this couldn't wait. Magdalena had the rim of the glass against her teeth. She nodded. 'She came looking for him, last week, when he didn't contact for the next lesson.'

'She's a pupil?'

'I don't think he fuck her yet,' said Magdalena. 'I think he needs long time. He enjoys that, getting her in the right place, so she can't say no.'

'It's called grooming,' said Gill, unable to sound calm, unable to keep the anger down.

'I know,' said Magdalena. And then quick, she darted her head low across the table, resting her chin on her knuckles and staring at the empty glass. Then up at Gill. 'So?' she said, her voice light and dangerous, leaning forward.

Tread carefully, thought Gill.

'So Timpson is the computer man?' she said. 'How do you know all this, Magdalena? What have you seen?' But there was too much accusation in her voice. Magdalena stayed where she was a second, then straightened up. Looked a long moment at Gill's notebook, that had sat on the table all this time, unopened, then at Gill, tilting her head to examine her. Saying nothing, hostile. Then she spoke.

'Listen,' she said, level, but dangerous, rage very near the surface. 'You. Listen. Try to understand. My father was never not drunk. Ne-ver. From six o'clock in the morning. You learn to keep your head down, this is good English phrase. Keep your head down. You wait, and wait, until it makes you sick to wait more.' Stared at Gill. 'I hate this man, Mr Carmichael,' she said. 'I hate his fat friend, Mr Al-lan. You want me to talk to the police, tell them about him? Foreigner? Greedy foreigner, how much is she involved. Sure. Sure.'

Gill held her angry gaze a long moment. 'All right,' she said, at last. 'Yes. I get it. But you can talk to me. If you tell me the truth, I am going to believe you. You understand that?' Magdalena's eyes narrowed, then she shrugged. 'Yes.'

'So where do you think he's gone?' said Gill. 'Mr Carmichael.'

And the dark in Magdalena's eyes turned softer, deeper, a look of satisfaction. She smiled, stood, swiped her coat off the back of a chair. 'I don't think,' she said. 'I know.'

Gill was on her feet too, but Magdalena was at the door and speaking first, cheerful. 'We get the beer, now?'

Now the morning after Gill wondered if it could even be true, any of it. The last fifteen years no more than her own deranged obsession. She'd sat up with a vulnerable girl until midnight feeding her alcohol, encouraging her to dredge up secrets or inventions. And the girl was as crazy as a snake, too, a whole bag of snakes, dangerous, spiky, vicious, funny as well as vulnerable, born to lie just like she was born to drink.

By the time they'd left the bar, Magdalena shouldering a bag and walking off God knew where at long past midnight down gleaming black streets but not, at least, back towards Carmichael's house, Gill had had enough to drink herself to believe in it all, everything Magdalena had said. But that didn't mean it hung together, or made any kind of sense, and Magdalena had been drunk, and she was still a kid, under it all.

All Gill knew for sure, as she gazed beyond the town at that little slice of the real world – the old world, the grey-green sea – the single new piece of solid information that had found its way into her notebook, was Alan Timpson's address. He lived on site, some administrative responsibility in the university. 'Old house,' said Magdalena with a sneer, 'like janitor for the university? That place.' An old house in the shadow of the towers. That place: Rose Hill.

When housekeeping knocked half an hour later Gill was still there, sitting at the flimsy hotel desk in her knickers and a sweater, frowning over the laptop. She looked up at the woman in the door with her little paper cap and apron and trolley full of cleaning things, saw her but didn't see her. Mumbled something then was back at the computer.

Try again. Before the battery dies, try one more time.

Chapter Twenty-Eight

Carrie had gone. Having bolted her pancakes, muttering about people to see, she'd flung open the back door and gone. Jumped on the bike, hissing through a puddle then out on to the road beyond the close without looking.

And now she wasn't answering her phone.

Bridget sent a message. *Don't go near bloody Timpson, all right? Just stay away, he mustn't know any more about us than he does already.*

Matt was in the garage and had been since she'd gone. When Bridget went out with a cup of coffee she found him frowning over his own bicycle in the grey morning light, taking it apart, and he took the coffee from her without a word.

Finn needs me, in the kitchen. That was what she'd have said if Matt had started to ask her anything but he didn't: probably because he knew she'd have an excuse to run.

The kitchen table was covered with green tissue paper

and Finn was grappling with the teddy, trying to make the paper's edges meet around it.

'I can't carry it like this,' he said, sheepish.

'When are you meeting her, did you say?' Making him hold the paper in place she nipped off a bit of sellotape and fastened it deftly. Folded, turned. How many birthdays and Christmas eves had she sat up late, surrounded by ribbons and paper, Matt shaking his head and saying, *you've gone overboard, as usual*.

Only so many of those left before Finn left home. The thought upset her. Frightened her. The single present exchanged, her and Matt, then just a normal day. If they were lucky.

Finn set the present down on a chair, it peered over the table and he regarded it helplessly. 'I'm meeting her at three and we're going for a walk,' he said, and she saw him flush at the thought of walking hand in hand with a giant teddy in between them. 'It was Isabel's idea,' he said again, helpless.

'I like Isabel,' said Bridget, wondering if the teddy was Isabel's attempt to sabotage the relationship, or genuine. All so innocent, just kids with toys. It felt like a distraction from the fluttering panic she could feel rising, rising, always there. 'Did you get along?'

'She's good at music,' said Finn, and she saw him relax at the change of subject, shoulders dropping. 'But she doesn't want to do classical, she wants to be in a band, she's fighting with her parents over it.'

'Good for her,' said Bridget, wonderingly: she'd almost forgotten about Isabel's connection with Carmichael, now she was safe. Forgotten that it had been Isabel, unknowing, who had started all this.

'She asked about you,' said Finn and then the fluttering grew faster, harder, it beat against her chest. 'Did you play the violin once?'

'A long time ago,' said Bridget, turning to gather the detritus of present-wrapping from the table, avoiding his eye. She didn't ask how Isabel knew because there was only one explanation. Carmichael must have said something to her. She felt cold. 'She should do what she wants,' she said. 'Tell her that when you see her next.'

But Finn lost interest: he had his head in the cupboard where they kept plastic bags, had hauled a big crumpled one out and was manhandling the teddy into it. 'She said it would make Phoebe laugh,' he said. 'I mean, I—' he stopped, uncertain and she felt a rush of warmth, love, at the same time so far distant from these two, so young still, so innocent.

'She'll love it,' she said, hugging him awkwardly with the stuffed bag between them.

Would she save him? His Phoebe? When it all went tits up. Like Matt saved me, thought Bridget. Or not quite. Not quite.

You had to save yourself, didn't you? In the end. And now she couldn't afford to panic, or to think that way, in terms of needing saving.

But when she released him there was Matt standing in the kitchen door, watching them, the three of them held in suspension for just a second, two — then Bridget's phone rang on the table and the spell was broken. Matt went to the sink to wash his hands, Bridget released Finn and picked up the phone.

It was Laura, though she didn't know if she would

339

have recognised her voice if the phone hadn't shown the name.

Laura was panicking; she was frightened. 'Did you read my messages?'

'Laura—' Matt heard her alarm and glanced across. 'Hold on, stay calm, Laura,' said Bridget, spreading her hands to him, helplessly, the phone under her chin. 'What – it's been a bit of a hectic night, I only glanced at the messages.' *Shit*, she thought, *shit*, a combination of guilt and alarm. She'd put Laura to one side; she'd thought, that can wait, but it couldn't. It was the same, anyway, wasn't it? Nick abusing Laura, another violent manipulative arsehole wanting his own way. 'What?' she said, keeping her voice level, making sure Laura knew, she was listening. 'Tell me what's happened.'

Finn was edging out of the kitchen; he was gone. She heard him on the stairs.

'We had a row. Me and Nick.' Laura's breathing was ragged. 'He went out, in the middle of the night, he hasn't come back.'

'Did he hurt you?' Laura's breathing was heavy. 'Laura. Did he hurt you?'

'No,' she mumbled. No way of knowing if that was true: Bridget bet it wasn't. Laura was still talking. 'He hasn't come to your house, has he?'

'My house? Why would he come to my house?' Matt stood very still at the sink, his hands in a tea towel.

Laura was making an effort to be rational. 'I don't think he knows your address – but he thinks – he said you were causing trouble.' She sounded strained. 'I – I told him I didn't have to have sex if I didn't want to, there was a

340

number I could call and he knew straight away you would have given it to me, I didn't tell him. He called you a—'

'All right,' said Bridget, looking pleadingly at Matt. 'I think you should call that helpline. Leave the house in case he comes back. You're pretty sure he doesn't know my address, right?'

'Yes,' said Laura, subdued now. 'He's only ever seen you at the shop.'

'Right. So come here. If we're out – it won't be for long, and Finn's here until after lunch.' Matt dropped the tea towel, took a step towards her with his hand out for the phone. But the line went dead. 'Laura?'

Matt stopped, right in front of her. 'It's that nutter of a husband of hers,' she said. 'He's – they've had a row.'

'Is she OK?' Matt was looking at the phone.

'I think so,' said Bridget. She set the phone carefully on the table, face down. 'I told her – well, you heard. I want to go to the shop right now, have a chance of getting back before she gets here. All right?'

'I'm coming with you,' Matt said. Calm.

She hesitated. 'All right,' she said.

She ran upstairs after Finn and caught him in the bath-room, in a cloud of aftershave with a towel wrapped round him.

'Finn,' she said, 'You know Laura, pregnant Laura? She—' then she stopped. Not fair on him. Looked at him, helpless.

'Mum?' he said, puzzled. 'Is everything all right? I don't have to go and see Phoebe till later. I don't have to go at all if you need me to help. Mum.' And for a moment she didn't have a single word to say to him, her big boy. '*Mum.*'

341

He knew her so well. He still had the child's responses under there, when he was small, he used to hold her face on either side and examine her, he always knew when she was sad or anxious. I wished that on him, thought Bridget. Now she only wanted to go back and start again.

What to tell, what to withhold? If her child had been a girl, if she'd had a girl, what would Bridget be telling her? It suddenly seemed important. 'You be careful, Finn,' she said abruptly. 'You need to make sure you end up with the right one.'

He looked startled. 'Never mind,' she said quickly, 'just me being daft. Look – Laura might come over, if she gets here before we're back can you make her a cup of tea?'

'Sure,' he said immediately obedient, happy to be asked.

Matt was waiting in the car, grim-faced. As he drove she felt the fear start up again, shifting like a sea inside her, of the distance between them: of the thought that Matt might ever cease to love her. And as if he couldn't stand the silence either he turned the radio on, midway through a news report.

They were talking about the missing boy. *A body has been found.*

The rain had stopped: the world beyond the windscreen wet and grey. Bridget couldn't talk, she couldn't open her mouth. *Awaiting identification.*

Matt turned and said, 'They called me, you know.' Indicating to turn across the ring road's Sunday traffic, he was pale and focused. 'From the sailing club. About the dinghy. They said you'd been out there, when was it, Tuesday, Wednesday?'

And her terror was complete, it opened like a flower to swallow her up.

'Thursday,' she finally managed. 'I went there on Thursday. It was supposed to be a surprise.'

She could tell him. The cliff edge was there in front of her, the dark water below them.

'You should have told *them* that,' Matt said, calm but still pale. 'They were calling to arrange collection.' He leaned down to turn the sound up.

Bridget sat back against the headrest, the world beyond the windows a grey blur and a weird ringing in her ears, and for a moment or two she couldn't work out what the report was saying. Then she could. *Heathland to the north of the town, a wooded area.*

The body hadn't been found at the reservoir, after all. It had been found in woodland. *Relatives have been informed.*

Relatives. Woodland? Then it dawned on her, in a rush, that the body that had been found was of the missing boy, after all. Not Carmichael. They'd called off the divers at the reservoir. Relief flooded her, quickly followed by shame. A boy was dead. A face in the newspaper.

The dead boy still hadn't been named but they were talking to the neighbours of the missing child. A foregone conclusion. In a daze Bridget listened to the voices, kind, worried, anxious. *A good boy, always on his bike when he was smaller.*

She glanced sideways at Matt, unreadable behind the wheel as they turned into the alley behind the shop, and bumped slowly up to the end. Were they safe? Not by a long chalk.

He pulled up and turned the engine off. They sat a second in silence. 'Aren't you going to get out?' he said quietly. His arms were straight out in front of him, his hands resting on the wheel.

'Will you wait for me here?' Bridget tried to make it sound bright and normal.

'If that's what you want.'

Bridget had her hand on the door handle but she couldn't make herself take the simple action, press the lever, open the door. Because he knew. Because what he was saying was, *Keep me out of it if that's what you want* – but he knew.

'Actually—' she hesitated. 'Can you come in with me?' Not knowing if it was the right thing to do only that it was the only thing. Without him, without Matt and Finn, there was nothing. 'I could do with a hand.'

When they got inside Matt just stood in the middle of the shop looking at the blank monitor, raised on its shelf in the corner of the shop. It was the first thing he looked at. Then the cameras, one, two, three, noting their position.

With a small shock as she looked at the clock on the wall Bridget registered that it was after one o'clock. The police would be here any minute. Half an hour at most.

'The laptop's gone,' said Bridget, and it came out breathless. Then, 'What are you thinking?'

And then he turned and looked at her. 'Someone just threw a brick through the window and ran away,' he said. 'That's what this looks like. Where should the laptop have been?'

'Behind the till,' she said. In the daylight, or what there was of it through the intact window, what she had thought last night was confirmed. The jewellery cabinet hadn't been touched. Clothes still on the rails, handbags on the shelves.

'Why would they just take your laptop?' Matt said, just

344

mild, just curious but there was more, she knew him too well. 'It was old.' He hadn't moved from his position at the centre of the room, watching her. He wasn't letting her off the hook.

'Maybe because — because — it would identify them? It records the CCTV.' The words seemed dangerous, this path was dangerous. And slowly Matt shook his head.

'If that's the reason—' he stopped.

'When — when did the police say they'd be here?' she said, trying to divert, to forestall. But Matt didn't seem to hear.

'The monitor itself has a hard drive,' he said. 'You knew that, right?' She shook her head slowly.

'The images are stored there, too,' he said, carefully. Her face gave her away, she could feel it wobble, dissolve in panic. And then Matt stepped towards her. He took her by the arms.

'This is what we're going to do,' he said.

The Sunday buses were slow and irregular: the one Gill had taken went all around the houses before it made the final climb to Rose Hill, and the town fell away behind them.

It stopped beside a car park at the foot of the hill that was almost empty, but then even if it hadn't been a bleak November Sunday Rose Hill was hardly a tourist destination. As she got out Gill registered that it was starting to rain again, big drops blown sideways by a steady wind.

Standing at the bus stop she looked uphill. Did any of them like it here? Some must, there must be fun going on up in those towers because that was what kids were like. Stick them anywhere and they'd find the fun — unless something had gone wrong, of course. They arrived in places like this with the damage already done, invisible. They got off their trains or out of their parents' cars with their iPod docks and their posters and their baggage, and it was sink or swim.

Perhaps it was just as well, thought Gill gloomily, that I never had any kids. Understatement of the year. *I'd only worry.*

A bit of movement across the piazza, but most of them in their rooms, where she could see lit windows against the sky. The daylight was going already, even though it was barely two o'clock.

Across the grass under a tree a couple was sheltering from the rain, a gawky boy with a mop of black hair, a girl looking up at him. They seemed to be having some kind of a row: the boy was holding a package, awkwardly shaped, wrapped with ribbon. A cluster of trees beyond the towers showed the slate roof of a gatehouse, the warden's house. From way back when there'd been a crumbling manor house whose gates it guarded, torn down in the sixties. The gatehouse was where Alan Timpson lived.

Gill had known about Rose Hill before she came, a vague memory that some places left you with, through newspapers or TV reports, *Isn't that where?* In this case, where a young woman had killed herself, a long time ago, when Gill was a kid. Long before Timpson or Carmichael came but it had made the university notorious, for a while.

Gill had googled Timpson, of course, once Matt had mentioned his name, and again this morning after Magdalena last night – but nothing had come up on his reputation, no rumour. Only she would have seen something sinister in Alan Timpson standing in a crowd of smiling boys in a third world country. She rubbed her shoulders, cold in the patchy rain. Lucky not to have caught her death last night.

One day, Gill thought as she skirted the foot of the hill, the internet would be turned inside out and it would all become public, all their dirty secrets exposed. All it would take was a logarithm and they wouldn't need her any more, no one would need investigative journalists because there would be nowhere for them to hide, no encryption too strong.

She already knew what had happened: she'd only needed a look at Bridget Webster's face for it to be confirmed. Haunted, pale, on her tiptoes to kiss her husband under Rose Hill but still looking over her shoulder for who might be watching.

Gill had seen it. But one look wasn't all she'd got, this time. This time she might have evidence, too.

What must Bridget O'Neill have thought, after all this time, when he turned up? She knew how they responded, just to photographs of their abusers. She'd seen girls run to the toilet, their guts turned to water. She'd seen them begin to shake, while their mothers tried to comfort them.

The young couple with the teddy bear had disappeared – and then she saw the girl, marching away, on her own up the hill in a red raincoat.

The lights appeared to be off at the warden's house. She circled it. The curtains were drawn.

She heard someone behind her.

Chapter Twenty-Nine

'Not much else we can do,' said the uniformed officer, grimacing as he looked round the shop. He was a bit older than Matt, and stockier, wearing a fluorescent gilet with a radio phone attached to it.

He'd knelt to examine the lump of rock first off. Useless for identification purposes, the surface too rough, but after half an hour or so on hands and knees they'd found a shard of glass with a clear fingerprint on it and levered it into an evidence bag.

'You'd be surprised how often this happens,' said the officer, who seemed nice enough but largely indifferent, gesturing at the splintered window. 'And down here,' looking up and down the lane, 'there's no street cameras. The print, well, could be anyone,' he said peering down at the plastic bag. 'Could have been someone leaning up against the window—'

'I washed them yesterday,' said Bridget quickly, and then

he'd smiled at her briefly. Matt had been standing in the doorway, hands in his pockets, frowning down at the floor. She didn't know if he'd ever talked to a police officer before, but she thought probably not. Once upon a time she'd have assumed he'd have told her if he had, now she wasn't so sure. Bridget had, a couple of shoplifting incidents. Both times it had been a woman. Bridget tried as hard as she could just to be the way she'd been on those occasions, upset, but not too upset. Angry.

'Sure, yes, well,' said the policeman, mildly encouraging. 'Like I say, we'll run it through the system. If it's someone with a criminal record then it's a start.'

Not much else we can do. Would Alan Timpson have had a criminal record? If only. She experienced a brief white flash of something she hardly recognised: rage. Violent, passionate: send him down. Put him among the criminals. She just nodded, thoughtful, and smiled back at the policeman.

'Lads, probably,' said the officer, zipping up his gilet, nodding to the other one waiting for him on the cobbles, leaning against their patrol car. 'Even if you had CCTV operational they'd just have had to pull their hoodie over their face.' Peering back into the shop to where the CCTV monitor should have been. 'It was only connected to the laptop, you said? Because you can get it to send the images to your mobile?'

She shook her head. 'It had only just been fixed,' she said, her voice descending to a mumble.

And then Matt stepped forward, head up and he was doing the talking. Quiet and calm, thanking them for their trouble.

The patrol car moved off, slowly, their officer raising a hand through the passenger window, but Matt was already on the shop phone, calling a glazier. Bridget heard him make arrangements for the man to come tomorrow first thing, she remembered as if from long ago that he'd had to do the same for the student bar. Good old Matt.

She began to sweep up the remaining glass, and when he'd hung up without a word Matt got the dustpan.

'A good job no stock was taken,' he said, kneeling, meticulous, picking shards out of the rug. 'Otherwise they might have suspected you of doing it for the insurance.' He was cool, level, practical. Bridget felt cold. She felt sick. Matt had always been practical, preferring to get on but this – this was new. Before – he would have been asking her, Are you OK? Stroking her shoulder, telling her what he thought, what he felt. He'd be angry on her behalf, that someone had done this.

This wasn't accidental. He was refusing to do any of that, just moving things around, sorting things out. Was this what divorce felt like? When you no longer knew each other?

She went to the chimney breast where some glass had flown, the broom in her hand, her head down, and began to sweep it out carefully. All of her life she'd thought she had Carmichael in there, guiding her actions, making her the person she was but it had been Matt all along. Quietly working away to keep the ground level under her feet. It was Matt she was losing.

Three or four times on the drive home Bridget opened her mouth to say something. But she couldn't identify the right words, not even to begin the conversation.

The house was empty: her first thought was relief, then dread. The rest of their life loomed, the silences. Matt pulled into the garage, and only then did he speak. 'I'll unload,' he said.

There was a note on the kitchen table in Finn's big untidy scrawl: *Laura didn't come, see you later, Finn.* No Finn, no Carrie, just the two of them.

And then Matt was at the back door, holding it in his arms wrapped in a dustsheet. They'd put it in the back of the van before the police turned up. The CCTV monitor.

He set it down carefully. Bridget stood there with the note in her hand. 'Finn's gone out,' she said. 'Laura didn't come. Or hasn't yet. I hope she's—'

He interrupted her. 'All right,' he said, and for what seemed the first time since they sat in bed that morning with her stonewalling, he held her gaze. 'All right. Before we look at this. We're going to take it slowly. You think you know who smashed the window already, don't you?'

Bridget didn't know what she could say. 'Yes,' she said finally.

'I'm not the police,' said Matt. And then there was some colour in his face, an emotion she couldn't identify. 'I'm your husband.'

At that moment though he only looked to her like a man. Another man. 'This isn't to do with you,' she said. Silently pleading with him, *understand.* 'This is about me. About things that happened to me.' She could feel it trying to come out – while she tried to keep it inside.

She started again. 'I need to take responsibility for my own life,' she said and it sounded stupid, like something people said on daytime TV. Matt's face was stony in their

351

little brightly lit kitchen. The kitchen she'd paced up and down in with Finn as a baby, where she'd sat with him in his high chair, coaxing him to eat. Why couldn't those days come back? Her life come back. And again, desperate now. 'I don't want to involve you.'

'I *am* involved,' said Matt. Not confrontational, just simple fact. Resting the monitor on the table between them.

'I'm going to ask you some questions,' he said slowly. 'And you only have to tell me the truth and it will be all right. We won't even need to look at the CCTV because I'm going to believe everything you tell me.'

She nodded, but her throat felt constricted.

'But it has to be true,' said Matt. 'You only have to answer what I ask you but it has to be true.' He paused. 'This is your story.'

He was ashen, her fit healthy Matt, as if the effort of confrontation was taking something terrible out of him. He spoke carefully. 'Who do you think broke the window?'

It felt to Bridget as if she was balanced on a knife edge.

'I think—' she hesitated, tried to be accurate. 'I'm frightened it was Alan Timpson.'

Matt nodded. Just once, and he didn't ask why, nor why Timpson would want the laptop. That would be the next stage, wouldn't it? Though he could guess. Matt knew Carmichael, and what kind of man he was. And Timpson was his friend. 'So you think Alan Timpson has your laptop, with the CCTV images on it,' he said.

Bridget could tell him all of it now, it was after all what she had wanted to do so many times, but she hesitated. Once he knew, she wouldn't be able to protect him any more.

352

And then from the sitting room came the sound of the phone ringing.

Matt made a move to go to it but stopped himself, and quickly Bridget moved.

The phone was beside the sofa: the room was dim, indistinct. The sky beyond the sitting-room window was layered grey cloud, purple and black and the sun low behind it somewhere.

It was the policeman. He said his name but it didn't register, just as it hadn't that afternoon, but it was the same man. 'Mrs Webster?' he said, sounding upbeat, energised. 'We got an immediate result on the print,' he said. 'He's on the system, and recently too, eighteen months back.'

Timpson was on the police system? She felt a surge of something, panic and excitement together, at the thought that someone else knew. 'Is it—' she almost said his name, but stopped herself. Matt was one thing, the police were something else. 'It's someone with a criminal record, then?'

'It's a man called Nicholas Barnwell,' said the officer and for a moment Bridget drew a complete blank. Nicholas? Then she realised.

'Oh,' she said, numb. 'That's Nick,' she said, 'he's married to my assistant, Laura.'

'We've got an address for him,' said the man. 'I can't give it you – but does your assistant live in Mason Street?'

'Yes, but he's gone AWOL, Laura phoned me this morning, she was worried about him – I didn't make the connection.'

Stupid. Nick? Nick? Pissing on the shop floor, that made sense, that would be Nick. 'He's got a criminal record?' said Bridget. 'What's he done?'

353

'His ex-wife has an injunction out against him,' said the policeman, and some wariness had crept into his voice. 'It's a matter of record so you can know that. And a conviction for actual bodily harm. Against a girlfriend.'

Shit. Shit, shit, shit. So stupid.

'She didn't come,' said Bridget urgently, almost to herself. Then: 'Look, please would you get someone to her house? She's pregnant. She's nearly due, she's—'

She heard his hand go over the receiver before she'd even finished, she could hear him shouting something across a room. Then he was back. 'It's in hand, Mrs Webster, as a matter of urgency, thank you for your cooperation, that's—' But she was barely listening, and when he'd finished she hung up in a daze.

Matt was standing in the doorway. There was no sign of the CCTV monitor. 'It wasn't Timpson,' she said to him blankly. 'It was Nick.'

Immediately he said, 'Would he have taken the laptop?'

She frowned hard, trying to think. 'I don't think so. I don't know. Why would he? He must have found out I gave her a number for a helpline. A crisis centre, maybe the laptop—'

She thought about when he came for Laura, the way he had looked at Bridget then. The laptop hadn't been behind the till, had it? She tried to arrange things in her head, times, faces – then something else came to her. Laura, apologetic, Laura panicking, something Laura hadn't really wanted to say. She had said she couldn't find the laptop, after the woman had come in asking questions. The woman who'd bought a white shirt, who'd asked about CCTV.

Who had said she was a journalist. She turned and Matt

was sitting beside her on the sofa now. He took her hand, he lifted it and pressed it against his cheek. It was a gesture so unlike him it almost made her head spin, as if she was standing on the edge of a cliff.

'If I retrieved that hard drive from the monitor,' Matt said, so gentle. 'What would I see?'

She couldn't speak, but he didn't move, he was going nowhere. He still had her hand, between his now. 'Did he hurt you?' he said. 'Did they hurt you?'

And there was no safe way to fall. Matt was just another man, Matt was a stranger who wanted to pry through her secrets. Her hand in his felt hot, sweating. Only a pervert would have had her, therefore Matt must be one too. All the details of the room around them – the framed poster above the fireplace, the bowl of fruit, the photographs – seemed to belong to strangers, or someone had come in and put them there for a stage set.

Then the light outside the window changed, the low grey sky split close to the horizon and the sun was there, almost gone but not quite, pale lemon between layers of cloud. And the world shifted, it all spread out below her. Bridget looked past Matt towards the light and in her head she saw Carrie, on her bicycle, riding across the town to Timpson's house, a tiny figure climbing the smooth green hill in the last of the lemon light, towards the towers.

'He lives in the warden's house,' she said. 'Did you tell me that? I can't remember.'

'Timpson?' said Matt, alert, not understanding. His hands were on her shoulders now and she had to look at him, though her eyes seemed reluctant to focus.

'Carrie went to Alan Timpson's house because she

thought he had the laptop,' she said. 'He'll hurt her.' And then she saw Matt in sharp focus at last: she saw the mole on his cheek, the Sunday afternoon stubble with a bit of white in it, the clear, anxious blue eyes.

And Carrie, inside her head, the small fierce Carrie she'd held there for twenty years, her little sister.

'I know he'll hurt her,' she said.

The gatehouse sat surrounded by high hedges, a gate between them, a stone path. It was a little island on the smooth green slope, left behind by the march of progress. If you could call it progress. Gill marched straight up to the front door, her backpack slung from her shoulder and her footsteps loud on the path, and rang the bell. She waited in the silence that followed.

Leaning back to look at the upstairs windows, it seemed to her that the house wasn't empty, though she couldn't have pinned down exactly why. Gill hadn't done much door-stepping but she'd done enough. Downstairs curtains drawn, was a sign. She'd had the impression of movement somewhere upstairs, although it could have been the clouds scudding, reflected in the glass. The light was uncertain, everything dimming to grey, with the occasional low glimpse of sunset from the horizon. She rang again.

Was there a sound, a scuffle from somewhere inside? She peered through the letterbox and saw a dark hallway, light shifting somewhere. 'Hello?' she called. 'Mr Timpson? Dr Timpson?' Nothing. What could you do, bar breaking in? You could do a bit of a recce. She set off across the cut grass, everything neatly kept, at the taxpayers' expense. Wasn't the warden supposed to be available, wasn't that why he got this place, rent-free? She could quite imagine Timpson scorning *that* idea. He was a first-class mind, a superior talent, he and his friend, Carmichael.

The curtains were drawn at the back windows, too, and a blind down in what she took to be the kitchen. She tried to be quiet, tiptoeing, listening, but someone in there knew. Were they both in there? Is this where Carmichael was hiding out?

Carmichael had been to see Bridget Webster, she was sure of that. Been to see her in the shop. Bridget Webster hadn't called back, had she? And Gill was fairly sure, from what she knew of Carmichael's victims in general, and Bridget's face that peered out of that yellowing newspaper cutting, frozen, frightened, that she wouldn't talk to any journalist. So subterfuge was maybe in order. Gill stopped, sighed, the voice in her head insisting *but how hard have you even tried?* It was theft, not subterfuge.

She'd give it back. She would. She wouldn't use anything she found. Unless – well.

She had to know what had happened. And then, there, standing between the neatly labelled wheelie bins in Timpson's backyard, just beyond his kitchen window, although Gill Lawson was the last, the very last person to admit to believing in vibes or ghosts or superstition, she had the most horrible feeling – a feeling so overwhelming she stepped back suddenly. And tripped, and went sprawling on the wet concrete. A bottle skittered, she swore. Too loudly.

Shit. She picked herself up in a hurry, wincing at the grazes on her palms. She'd landed on the bag, and her heart was hammering. Hobbling – her knee was grazed too, she got back to the gate, closed it carefully behind

357

her. One last look over her shoulder, but the windows stared back blankly, opaque now, not a twitching curtain.

Making her way painfully back up the hill Gill looked out for the couple, either one of them if they'd gone their separate ways, but saw no one. The light was almost gone. She focused on the student cafeteria, open to all in the money-saving initiatives the universities all seemed to be going in for, as if daytrippers might come out here to eat ham rolls under Rose Hill.

On a corner table by the window with a mug of tea, Gill set the backpack in front of her. All her stuff still in the purple bedroom: she hadn't even thought about which credit card she could use to pay the bill because no matter how pleased Steve was with the Queen's butcher he wasn't going to pay five nights in that place. And as for the mini-bar – well, maybe best not to think about that. Extortionate warm gin and tonic was better than no gin and tonic at all, or so it had seemed at one thirty in the morning and no sign of sleep.

Yatter, yatter, yatter: Gill couldn't seem to control the noise in her head sometimes, the excuses, the arguments. It felt like this was it: her and Carmichael. Like a toxic relationship that dragged you lower and lower but you couldn't seem to kill it. She needed to stop. She got out Bridget Webster's laptop and set it down. Check if she'd smashed it up – but it looked OK.

Gill had seen it there, on its shelf under the till, the girl had gone off into the stockroom for the white shirt Gill couldn't afford and there it had been, with its secrets. The girl had just told her, the CCTV gets downloaded and in that instant it hadn't been just investigative instinct that had put Gill's hand out to touch it, it had been something more. Her and her schoolfriends, nicking from Boots, laughing together, running hysterical for the bus. Did those girls he abused get to do that? Loss and anger and that old reckless streak. Back in trouble again.

It came on: twenty per cent charge. *User password*.

It was hopeless. Hopeless. A child's name, a husband's, their dates of birth? If she had all the time in the world, maybe. She searched the pregnant girl's friendly chatter for a clue, any clue, the chatter that had got progressively less friendly the harder Gill had pushed. That was Gill's life, wasn't it? It would be nice to just talk to someone, without pushing. Wouldn't it? Would she even know how to do that?

Outside it was almost dark now. From where she sat she could see the gatehouse, where Alan Timpson lived, down at the foot of the grassy hill that looked black in this light.

User password. How many lives did she have left? And then she remembered something, something she'd heard on the radio a while ago, an earnest computer guy just like Bridget's husband saying that some crazy percentage of computer users kept their password just as password, the one the thing came with. Even people who should know better, people whose husbands did tech. She typed, *password*.

Bingo.

Chapter Thirty

Matt was next to her as she called, his shoulder not touching but so close she could feel his warmth. She could feel him listening.

Carrie answered on the first ring: 'Sorry,' she said, 'Sorry Bridge, honest, I—'

'Are you there? Are you at Timpson's house?'

A sigh. 'The place was locked up, no answer at the door, I couldn't get in.'

'You *tried*?'

'Thought about smashing a window but then I got your message and I came back.' Bridget breathed out. Done something right for once. In time, for once. But Carrie was still talking. 'Your girl was there on the doorstep, on your doorstep, I mean. The pregnant one? I couldn't get in the house so I took her for a coffee, she told me about her husband. What a fucker, hey? She's well out of that. Are you back home?'

'Yes,' said Bridget. 'Is she still with you? Laura? Has she left him?'

Matt stood up and was pacing, anxious.

'We went back to her place,' Carrie said. 'I've just left her there.'

There was traffic noise behind her, and it sounded like she was walking: if Bridget knew Carrie she'd be off to find Magdalena, or the pub. She sounded pumped, breezy. 'She said she'd be OK. We called a locksmith, to change the locks on her house.'

'No, said Bridget immediately, and Matt stopped, a hand in his hair. He just wanted to get out, to do something practical, she could tell. 'Go back after her. It was Nick threw a brick through the window, he's angry, the police – he's violent. He might hurt her.'

A silence. Then Carrie said, 'Shit. Right, I'll go back round there.'

'Please,' said Bridget. 'Tell her to get out of there.'

'I'll go get and her and bring her back over, right now.'

'No, don't bring her—' but Carrie had gone.

Matt was sitting on the sofa beside her looking down at his hands, loose between his knees. 'There was a box,' he said quietly, not looking up. Bridget could still feel her breath out of control, and somewhere inside her a trembling.

'What was in the box?' Matt said, and then he did look up, at her. 'There are so many things, Bridge,' he said, and he sounded bone-weary, close to giving up. 'So many things you aren't telling me. The box you had in your bike basket, the one you had on your knees all the way home from his house last night. You ran upstairs with it the minute you got home. Do you think I don't see things?'

'No,' she said. 'I know you do see.'

'What was in that box?' Matt said, and there it was, impalpable, invisible, the barrier. They'd gone along together for years, decades, this way, not saying, not looking. Not asking. Respecting each other's right to privacy, is that how they'd have put it? She couldn't have lived otherwise.

'But I can't tell you,' said Bridget and she heard something, behind her head, insistent, and not sure if it was inside or out. 'I can't show you,' she said. And she looked into his face, frightened of seeing the end of it all there. But he was looking away, over her shoulder.

The sound hadn't been in her head: someone was at the kitchen door. Someone was tapping, tentative but insistent. Matt was on his feet.

'No' Bridget said, out of some understanding that she was going to have to manage without him. 'I'll go.' He followed her, all the same. She could see a shape through the opaque glass, narrow-shouldered, fair-haired. Matt was at her shoulder when she opened the door.

Isabel stood on the step, her bike leaning against the side of the house. Her hair was limp and damp, her blue eyes looked enormous and frightened.

'Isabel?' said Bridget and all she could think of was him. Carmichael, an image so vivid, walking towards her, that she almost stepped back. 'What's – what's happened?'

'I don't know what to do,' she said, her big eyes pleading. 'I think there's something really wrong, I think Finn might be going to do something stupid, I mean something dangerous. I told him you should never arrange to meet people you don't know and he just laughed. People you've met on the internet.'

362

'What?' Matt's voice was a register higher than usual, but Isabel wasn't looking at him, she was looking at Bridget.

'I lied to you,' she said miserably. 'I lied about knowing her. About knowing Phoebe. I've never met Phoebe.'

Critical battery.

A piece of luck, was what it was, though luck didn't feel like the right word to Gill, at this stage of the game. A kid walking into the bar and hauling the same laptop as Bridget Webster's – bottom end of the market, four years old at least – out of his bag. On the next table, no less. Pudding basin haircut and an uncertain smile and jeans certainly bought for him by his mum. Nice kid. *Lovely* kid.

She leaned towards him, over the screen hovering between life and death. Tapped the laptop and grimaced. 'You haven't got your charger cable on you, have you?'

Maybe she reminded him of his mum, or something because the kid brightened, wanting to be helpful. And hauled it out of his bag.

Was that luck? If it was, Gill's whole life was built on it, her career. And she'd been in the wrong place at the wrong time often enough, Christ knew. 'Lifesaver,' she murmured, smiling at him so broadly he had to smile back. There was even a plug, though she had to shift a bit to not attract attention from the woman behind the cakes, the university's electricity supply being almost certainly not intended for the likes of her.

Bridget Webster's screensaver was of two figures in rain-jackets standing on a hilltop in a damp green landscape, their backs to the camera. A tallish, spare man and a boy

363

of about eight, his thick dark hair escaping his hood. Holding hands. It took her ten minutes to locate the CCTV feed on the laptop: the kid whose cable she was using would have managed it in thirty seconds, no doubt. When the jerky images came up she wriggled a bit further round, because she didn't want the boy seeing any of it. Whatever it turned out to be.

She had to fast forward through about two weeks' worth of it, monitoring the date and time along the bottom of the screen, to get to the week before Carmichael disappeared. Stop start, stop, start. Pause, then fast forward.

She saw Bridget Webster. Saw her arriving early, saw her careful, hardworking, kind. She was always busy, on her feet, Gill saw her on hands and knees cleaning, saw her making tea for her pregnant assistant, the way she stood, the way she talked to customers. Bridget Webster was patient, she was considerate, she was thoughtful: was she relaxed? No. Almost never – but she had her strategies. She moved to and fro. Sometimes when she was alone she sat, she looked at her hands.

Gill sat back for a moment, both hands on the edge of the melamine table, holding herself distant from the screen because she had this feeling that if she wasn't careful it would pull her right out of this world and into that strange grey room with its rails of clothes, where Bridget Webster paced the floor.

How many victims of abuse had Gill spoken to, over the years? Many. Almost none of it had been written up: they didn't want people to know, there were injunctions, court cases, libel threats. They were bullied and intimidated. And they were ashamed. They fought to restore normality

364

to their lives and they didn't want that fucked up. Everything in the way Bridget Webster conducted herself in her small shop showed Gill that she was one of them: it was in the way she walked, the way she stood, the way she listened. The way she turned round too quickly sometimes.

Gill took her hands away from the table edge and with one finger touched the screen: *you've done it*, she wanted to say. *You've got away.*

And then on the screen the door of the shop opened and a man came in with a child. Not quite a child, somewhere between girl and woman, with light, flossy hair, a child on an adventure. The man was Anthony Carmichael.

He walked towards her and she backed away.

And then Gill found she couldn't look: on the next table the kid's head turned as she stood up and turned away. It was almost dark outside, that damp, saturated winter dark, the sun gone south too early, she left the computer open on the table and walked to the opposite corner of the student bar. The place had filled up while she was glued to the screen so now only the kid was watching her. She walked to where she could see down the hill to Alan Timpson's house.

A light was on in the tall gable window, not bright, and a figure standing there, dimly outlined, very still.

Chapter Thirty-One

Isabel had gabbled. Matt stepped between them almost instantly, taking her by the shoulders, but Bridget had put up a hand to him, gently.

'Let me,' she said. Isabel had turned to her gratefully.

'What's this about Finn, first?' she said, searching her face.

'I was just with him at the country park, I was there with my mum and dad and I saw him.'

'But you didn't see Phoebe.' Bridget spoke flatly, not daring to sound how she felt. Her terror might frighten the girl to speechlessness.

Isabel looked at her. Opened her mouth. Closed it again. She shook her head. 'He was just – wandering about,' she said. 'He'd had a message from – from Phoebe saying her parents had gone away for the weekend so he could come to her house.'

It was as though there was a hum in the room, at a low

level, as though some electrical appliance was malfunctioning, as though somewhere things were going wrong. Matt took a step towards the two of them, still standing in the doorway, Isabel still with her red anorak on, pale and tense. Neither had even sat down, a chair Bridget had pulled out sat forlorn and forgotten: Isabel hung her head, hanks of rain-darkened hair obscuring her face.

'Just because you haven't met her doesn't mean—' But Bridget broke off, hands at her face. Isabel raised her head reluctantly. She glanced quickly at Matt. The hum wouldn't go away, it crackled and fizzed. Bridget muttered into her hands, 'You said she was pretty.'

Isabel flushed. 'I—' she opened her mouth and Bridget looked from her to Matt and back again, pleading silently with them both, *Take this away. Take it away.*

'Isabel?'

Isabel had a hand to her mouth, shaking her head, no, no, and she was pale now, blue-pale as milk. She whispered, 'No, I just—' so quietly desperate that Bridget had to lean in, had to restrain the impulse to take hold of her and shake. 'I didn't want you to think I wanted to be his girlfriend, so I said, so I pretended—' Still whispering and despite herself Bridget nodded, understood, and at the same time it was as if a great mass had shifted, engulfing them.

'You've never met this girl,' she stated.

Isabel shook her head, mute. 'I was embarrassed, when you mentioned her—' The flush returned, briefly. 'I didn't even know he had a girlfriend then. Until you said.'

And had hated to hear of her existence, had felt despair, did Bridget remember that feeling? The tiniest echo of a

367

long-ago emotion, from the days before Carmichael, a boy, once upon a time, who hadn't known she existed, how could she have forgotten? That once she had been normal, a normal kid. A different world. And to cover up, Isabel had invented.

'He told you about her, though?' She *was* holding Isabel now, by the upper arms, as Matt paced behind them, barely containing himself. 'He went out with her last week, he got in late,' she said, panicking properly now. 'He did.' Seeking confirmation in the girl's face.

'When we went out yesterday he told me about her,' Isabel said, haltingly. Anguished. 'How much they loved each other, how she liked the same movies and computer games, she dresses up as some character, she sends him pictures. But when they were supposed to meet—' Staring into her face Bridget felt herself nodding, yes – but then Isabel broke off. And Matt was there between them, no longer able to contain himself.

She released Isabel and stepped back, and Matt took her place. Not touching. Careful not to. 'When they were supposed to meet,' he said. 'She didn't turn up.'

Bridget picked her phone from the table and dialled Finn's number. It went straight to answerphone. She raised her head, staring. She felt very cold: her fingers as she punched in a message, *call home now urgent* felt like they didn't belong to her. *Finn.*

'Hold on,' he said quietly. 'Isabel?' She nodded, mesmerised. 'Hold on. You haven't met this Phoebe, you haven't seen her or heard her voice.' Isabel shook her head, mute. Matt took a deep breath. 'Has *he*? Has he actually met her? It's not – is it just online?

368

Isabel was trembling now, holding on to her own elbows in an attempt to stop it. 'She couldn't come, when she was supposed to,' she said. 'Finn said – her dad is very strict. That's what he told me.' She looked around the room, desperate for escape.

'That's why she didn't come to eat with us,' said Bridget, numb. 'That was what he told us—' and she was already on the stairs, stumbling halfway up and turning, hanging on to the banister. Matt was on her heels, she heard something ragged in his breathing behind her that was almost a sob.

They both knew where they were going. Finn's room.

Posters on the walls, a heist movie poster, a car, a man standing arms folded with a gun, and one corner of the poster curling away from the wall. Socks on the floor, a heaped towel.

Bridget stood back in the doorway and let Matt go ahead: he was seated in front of the computer before she could catch her breath, he was bringing up a screen.

'How are you going to—' she began but he just raised a hand, intent.

Isabel called, halfway up the stairs and reluctantly Bridget went back. She was holding her phone in her hand, a talisman, waiting for it to come alive with his voice. Nothing.

Tears brimmed in the girl's big, light eyes, so pale you could see through her. 'I'm so – I'm so sorry—'

'Come here,' said Bridget, and put an arm round her, drew her down to the top step and sat beside her. She held on tight. 'It's not your fault,' she said, a lump in her throat like a stone. Inside her it pounded, hammered, the only thing that mattered. The only thing. 'Can you tell me anything else? How did they meet?' Behind them in Finn's room Matt clattered at the keyboard.

'They both played an online game,' Isabel said, desperate. 'I don't know too much – I don't play it. They have avatars. You know, like characters.' She rubbed her eyes, trying to think. Raised her head, her face clearing a little. 'Well, I mean,' and she hesitated, 'they're on Facebook, right? They have conversations on Facebook, I mean everyone does. You'd have to get to his page but—'

Bridget jumped up, but Matt had got there ahead of her, she heard a muttered exclamation and as she got to the door he was looking up at her, past the screen.

'He's logged out,' he said. 'I need to guess his password.'

'Facebook,' said Bridget. But he was already there, the screen was up, the Facebook homepage was asking for Finn's login details.

'First place I looked,' said Matt. 'I didn't think he'd even have a password, you know Finn, I mean, Christ, it's my job,' Matt never talked like this, never swore. 'I've talked to him about security but he's just a kid, this is his own home, I didn't – I thought—'

'They grow up,' Bridget whispered. 'They grow up.' She stood behind him, willing the page to open.

'I thought he'd have the password saved on the computer, I thought he wouldn't have listened to me about that, either.'

'He listens to you,' she said. 'It's not you.' So softly perhaps Matt didn't hear – and he was staring so hard at the screen, trying to will a word into the little box. 'Catfish,' he said.

'What?' He looked up at her. 'A catfish,' he repeated.

'Someone online pretending to be something they're not.'

Isabel was in the doorway. 'His avatar was called moonshine,' she said. They both stared.

Matt typed the words, Bridget saw him making himself go slowly. *Moonshine*. Pressed, return – and the page transformed, it bloomed photographs, messages, emojis, advertisements. Matt went unerringly to the chat icon, clicked. Private messages.

The first one was from Isabel. *Sorry*, it said.

Isabel spoke. 'But I know where—' wonderingly, something occurring to her.

But they were both focused on the screen, she was peripheral: the next chat was with Phoebe. *They aren't back till late*, it said. *Can't wait*.

Matt's finger moved across the touchpad, the cursor hovering over her name. Phoebe. Click on that and she'll show herself.

'I know where she lives,' said Isabel distinctly.

A profile had come up on the screen, and a photograph, but in that moment they weren't looking at the screen any more, although Isabel was. 'I knew she'd be pretty,' she said, disconsolate.

'What did you say?' said Bridget, stepping away from Matt towards her. 'You said you knew where she lived?'

'This girl's not Finn's age,' said Matt, frowning.

'This girl—' but Bridget was trying to stop herself taking hold of Isabel and shaking her. The face on the screen still a blur.

'Where does Phoebe live?' she said. 'Did he tell you?' Isabel flinched, trembling and Bridget made an effort. 'Please, Isabel,' she said. And the girl nodded, slowly.

'Somewhere in the university grounds,' she said, fumbling her words, frightened, desperate to do the right thing. 'It's why he was in the country park. Her dad works there. The strict dad. Finn told me not to – he didn't want you to know that. He wanted her to be just his thing. Private.'

'Her father works at the university?' Matt was bewildered now, twisting in the chair to look at her.

Bridget was cold, cold to her bones. Private. Just our thing, just between us. She stood up, reached for Matt. 'Stay here, now,' she said to Isabel, because it seemed the only safe thing to say. 'You stay right here.'

The girl on the screen was Magdalena.

It was as if Gill saw, but didn't see, what was happening down there. Her focus was somewhere else: a stage set was being prepared but the main event was going on somewhere off to the side.

Someone on a bicycle with lights made their slow way up the hill. A car left the car park. She saw the shape moving across the foot of the hill; she even moved closer to the glass to identify it in the dark. A boy with a shock of hair, carrying something big and awkward. Soon he would draw level with the house. Upstairs someone drew curtains.

The main event was being replayed in Gill's head, jerky, fuzzy figures in black and white advancing and receding on a screen. Could she un-see it, now? However much she wanted to.

Could Bridget Webster have pleaded self-defence? Bridget Webster, Bridget O'Neill as once was, when it mattered, when all this began. Could Bridget Webster, upstanding citizen, wife and mother, could she have gone to the police and spilled it all?

A plastic bag over the man's head. No.

It wasn't on screen, her doing that. But she had walked away from him sprawled half in, half out of the kitchen, she had walked jerky as a doll, across the floor of her small shop and through a door in the wall opposite the little kitchen. She had come back, with something balled up in her hand. Then she was on her knees: you could see the soles of her shoes as she knelt – and you could see a small spasmodic movement in one of his legs. Once, twice.

Anyone might have come in. Anyone might have paused, hand cupped either side of their head, and looked inside. Gill might have. And what would she have done, if she had?

I wonder what she did with him?

Someone's head turned, a girl with dreadlocks eyeing her sidelong, and Gill realised she'd said it out loud. She smiled, stiff, but the dreadlocked girl had already lost interest. Gill pondered her conscience. Did it make her a bad person, that she looked at a man dying and felt nothing?

The laptop sat there, humming softly, waiting for her. The kid on the next table would want his charger cable back, and she had to get back to the CCTV stream, to know what happened next. But she didn't move.

She hadn't quite felt *nothing*. She'd felt glad.

Below her the door to Timpson's house opened, a rectangle of light in the darkness.

Chapter Thirty-Two

They were in the van, the wipers flogging fast in heavy rain. The road ahead was a blur: all Bridget could see was the patchwork of letters and images that was Finn's computer screen.

She was doing the driving because he was going to call the police. They took a second to agree on that. Less than a second. She was being careful; she was so tense her hands on the wheel felt as though they'd seized up. Beside her Matt was on the phone to the police. She had to make herself breathe: in, out. She couldn't forget Isabel's face. They'd left her sitting at their kitchen table, pale with fear.

'No,' Matt repeated into the mobile, and under a veneer of patience his voice was hard as iron, and angry. *Be careful, Matt.* 'I work with him. I believe him to be a danger,' he repeated. 'Don't you understand?' *Be careful.* If he made them angry it would slow things down. 'My son has been groomed, and has gone missing.'

She'd started to say it as they closed the van doors, as she turned the key in the ignition.

Reversing carefully, she began to say, 'This is all my—' He'd stopped her mid-sentence.

They were at the junction now and indicating, because there was no time to stop the car to talk.

'If you blame yourself – if we start blaming ourselves, or each other—' Matt said, holding the mobile in his hand so tight his knuckles were white, and making her look at him. 'It won't end. It'll never end. So – don't. You are not to blame for anything.'

'I killed him,' she said. 'I should have been looking after Finn. You don't know what I've done.'

Matt's face turned towards her in the dark. 'Who?' he said, but she could hear from his voice he knew who.

'I killed him, the fucking bastard,' and she heard her voice rise, as though it belonged to someone else; it soared, it rejoiced.

'You killed him.' And Matt spoke so quietly she didn't know, in that suspended instant she had no idea what he was thinking, or what he would do next. *I killed him and Carrie and me – we –* And then it all crashed down, the high joyful song in her ears, all the rejoicing. 'I should have been looking after Finn,' she said, in horror.

This was where it came out, then. In the dark, cramped interior of her van in the smell of diesel, with the windscreen wipers going. This was the confessional, this was the police interview room.

'You *were* looking after Finn,' said Matt, and she could feel him looking at her, she glanced then quickly back. 'I know you were. Just drive.' And he began to dial the police.

Just like that, it was done.

Round the ring road, traffic hissing in the rain, the streetlights yellow in puddles, people going about their ordinary lives, waiting at pedestrian crossing and bus stops.

A truck pulled out in front of them, long and heavy and slow. It seemed to take whole minutes to engage its gears, as it slowed, accelerated, stopped. It was dirty: someone had scrawled *clean me* on the rear doors. Clean me? Bridget wanted to blow it up. *So fucking slow.*

Beside her Matt was grinding his teeth as the police were asking endless questions: she could hear the click of his jaw. He repeated Alan Timpson's name and address over and over, he told them they were on their way there. They put him on hold, and he hung up.

'They've got Nicholas Barnwell,' he said, the mobile clasped in both hands, like he wanted to smash it down somewhere. 'Found him drunk. He's admitted breaking the window.'

'Poor Laura,' she said automatically, then jerked back, to now. To the black terror they were driving through, the rain sideways against the windows and the truck slowing, again on the climb. Almost stationary. *Clean me.* 'Why didn't I look at what was happening, right there at home?'

'You know why,' said Matt. 'Neither of us looked and you had more excuse than me. But it doesn't matter. What matters is getting Finn back.'

She edged out, to look past the truck. The towers were up there, dead ahead, blinking red in the dark rainswept sky, something coming the other way but far enough off, far enough. Fuck it. She pulled out, the lights flaring, glittering in the rain, her foot down and the tyres screeching for a purchase. And suddenly they were past. The oncoming car blared its horn, a dazzle of lights, a brief glimpse of a pale angry face thrust towards them and after it had gone for a second the van held only stunned silence.

They turned across the base of the towers, bumping down the single-track road, and then Matt spoke.

'Rehearse it,' he said. Her head flicked to him, startled, then back to the road. 'Quick,' he said, 'go over what we'll say happened, because we haven't got long. The police will be there.'

She was driving as fast as she could on the narrow potholed road, and she didn't slow down. Matt talked at her in a low voice. 'We knew nothing until Isabel told us: we had our suspicions about Timpson and Carmichael when the journalist came looking for him but that was all. I – I recognised the picture as Carmichael's cleaner. I dropped something at his house one time. Keep you out of it. Out of his house.'

Her chest burned as if she'd been running. She could see light emerge as they crested the slope: a sliver of light, no more than that. A house, below the curve of the hill. Memorise it: we knew nothing until Isabel told us. Matt had his suspicions.

'I'll do the talking to start with,' said Matt.

'The journalist knows,' she said, dully, and she heard him take a breath, in. 'But it doesn't matter any more. I don't care.' And she didn't. 'As long as Finn's all right.'

Something slid below the chassis, one wheel on the grass, hitting the mud, two wheels, and the van lurched.

She would pray, but there was no one she believed in. *Take me instead.*

The wheels spun, they were at an angle and the engine revved uselessly: the van didn't move, they stalled. Bridget flung open the door and began to run, towards the dark house that sat half below the slope, muffled in a softer dark that was vegetation. She heard Matt behind her. Both knowing. Skidding on the cold, wet grass, she could hear her own breath: tried to keep the sliver of light in her sights but it tilted and jumped with every step.

The towers loomed above them as they ran, rectangles of light higher up. Once a woman threw herself from high up on Rose Hill. She must have had no son, was all Bridget could think, drenched in the rain, cold and terrified, her jeans slimed with mud and her legs heavy as lead but still running, running. *Go.*

A sign on the gate in university lettering, WARDEN: Bridget flung it aside, still in front, and then they were at his door, shoulder to shoulder and she was battering on it, pounding with both fists, then down to the letterbox and shouting, yelling through it with all the force of her lungs.

Finn. Finn.

Matt standing back and bellowing, up to the windows.

Finn. *Finn.*

On her knees in the wet Bridget shouted through the letterbox, she screamed. 'Let me in. Stay away from my son, stay away from him.' And suddenly she became aware that Matt wasn't behind her any more. There was the sound of smashing glass from somewhere round the back, and a shout. *I'm in.*

Inside there was a bellowing, it was Matt, bellowing like an animal, and then the door was wrenched open in front

378

of her, on to a dark hallway and Matt already running back into the house, down past a long stairway.

Let it not be too late. Don't touch him. Don't touch my son.

She heard a sound from upstairs, a whimper, frightened. She screamed, '*Finn!*' He was in there. He was crying for his mother: she could hear him, upstairs.

And then she was on the stairs, flying up in the dark, choking in the unfamiliar smell of a stranger's house, her every sense was assaulted by the place, the smell of bedclothes, curtains, damp, other people's food, she felt herself retch.

Finn, Finn, I'm coming, Mum's here, we're here. But she couldn't hear the words, her breath was gone, all used up on the stairs.

Flying, flying. Matt was behind her. And then she was on a landing, with three doors, all dark.

There was a scuffling then a small horrible sound, the worst sound, a sob but it told her: there. That door. In two steps she was across the landing and the door flew back ahead of her with such force it hit the wall behind it. The room was not quite dark, some light filtered through the closed curtain. It was warm, and there was a smell. A smell of chemical and animal together, and she saw movement in the dark.

She groped for a light switch, not knowing what she would see, but behind her Matt got there first, and light flooded the room, a shade swinging on a bedroom with one wall covered by mirrored wardrobe. The wrapped giant teddy bear discarded, face down in a corner.

The next thing she saw was Alan Timpson, fat in a

brown towelling bathrobe that revealed his thighs. *How did, how did he—?* he had one hand to his face and then she saw blood: there was blood on the front of the robe. But Matt had come round her, he was between them so she couldn't see, then she could. In the mirror she saw Finn's face, his torn shirt.

Matt's arms around his boy, their boy, she could see Finn's black unruly hair sticking up, his face buried in his father's neck. Alan Timpson was saying something, mumbling something. He was swaying, but not taking a step.

'Common assault,' he was saying.

In time.

Finn broke away and his arms were out to her. She saw his torn shirt but his trousers on, belt on and then she saw his knuckles were raw and she grabbed him, her arms around his back, broader than she knew. Looking over his shoulder she saw that the blood was coming from Timpson's nose. She saw Matt take a step towards him and then stop, three feet from him, blocking him. Just standing there.

'I didn't,' Finn was saying, into her cheek, gasping. 'I'm sorry, Mum. I didn't mean to—' Finn who'd never hit anyone in his life.

'Good boy,' she said. And said it again. And again. 'Good boy. Good boy.'

And then someone was calling, from downstairs.

The door was wide open when Gill got there: the hallway was dark, and then a light came on and she saw Bridget O'Neill at the top of the stairs. Bridget Webster now but she'd always be Bridget O'Neill to Gill. That girl in the school prize-giving picture taking a book from Anthony

Carmichael, so skinny you could snap her in half but not so fragile, it turned out.

Standing up there in mud-spattered jeans and a sweatshirt with a streak of mascara down one cheek she was still small but she looked like a prize-fighter to Gill. Her fists were clenched.

The laptop was under Gill's arm: she'd run with it down the hill, snatching it off the table and leaving the kid's cable dangling, his eyes on stalks. She saw Bridget look at it, then at her. She could hear a man talking, in a low voice, somewhere up there, another voice, raised, querulous, whining.

'It's you,' said Bridget O'Neill, clearly, looking at her.

In the next moment Gill heard the police sirens and with the sound she saw Bridget take a step back, shaking her head, as her husband emerged behind her on to the landing – and the boy. Their son: the three of them up there stood still a moment together, close: *holy*, was the word that came to Gill in that strange second, an uncharacteristic second, until she shook her head.

Then Matt Webster was coming down the stairs towards her: he was pale and there was blood on one cheek and on the hand she saw gripping the banister but he seemed very calm. His steps on the stairs were measured.

When he reached her he stopped and they both looked down at the laptop. Slowly she put it away in her backpack. Matt Webster stood in front of her still quite calm and waited for her to speak. A polite man.

Bridget and her son were coming down the stairs, awkward and slow because they seemed unwilling to let go, walking side by side. They came around Matt and Gill and walked out through the open front door. Then Gill spoke.

'I think it's best if I hang on to this, don't you?' she said. 'Until – well, let's say, until the police have done their bit with you?'

Matt looked at her a moment with his lips pursed, then he nodded. 'And then?' he said.

'Then – there are ways,' Gill said, carefully. 'Aren't there, well, you would know, ways of destroying a hard drive, aren't there? Beyond recovery.' He nodded, still not moving. 'And you'd show me, how to do that?' she said.

Wondering. If the engineer would still be in the purple lobby of the hotel in the far-off time when she would be able to crawl back there, and if he would ever get to look like this bloke.

And Matt Webster didn't smile but something came alive in his face. 'I'll show you,' he said.

It was almost eleven when they got back home: Matt had insisted the taxi take them from the police station back to the van, and a further twenty patient minutes spent getting it back on the road. Neither of them said they didn't want the police towing it, but both of them were thinking it. It was the two of them, now. When they pulled in Bridget saw the kitchen light was on.

The police station hadn't been what she'd expected. A Sunday night, not even late, and it had been clean and orderly, and they'd been treated with kindness. The female officer they'd come back with was brisk but solicitous, a male one was polite and warm. 'Let's get you home as soon as possible,' he said, a hand on Matt's shoulder.

Seven o'clock when they walked across the car park with the crackle of police walkie talkies flanking them.

Timpson had come in a separate car and they didn't have to see him again, the policewoman who walked them into the comfortable relatives' room said that straight away and Finn had nodded, saying nothing.

He was very pale: sometimes he looked at his sore knuckles wonderingly.

They'd talked to him with both her and Matt present. Then to her and Matt separately. Bridget remembered what to say, and she knew Matt would. No acting was necessary: she only had to live in the last three hours and all she felt was fear for Finn, and outrage.

Would it work? It might. It felt as though she was believed. Why shouldn't she be? They were Finn's parents. The police officers – three of them in the room – were only considerate. Only sympathetic. Perhaps – she hardly dared to think it – perhaps the system was on her side. Their side.

They mentioned Anthony Carmichael to her only once. The woman asked the question. Had Bridget known the girl, Magdalena Breska? They had brought her in, straight away; though Bridget hadn't seen her she'd heard a voice in the corridor, raised, indignant, that she knew was Magdalena's, though she kept her head down when she heard it.

'Her picture apparently had been used without her consent on the Facebook page for Phoebe James, using an email address traced to Dr Timpson's account,' said the policewoman wearily, with a trace of scepticism. 'It is the picture on her ID card, which her employer had for safekeeping.'

Had Bridget recognised her? She'd shaken her head in the quiet, dingy room. 'I don't think so. Matt said. Matt said she worked for – someone Alan Timpson knew.'

They would talk to Matt again, they said. About his suspicions, as computer officer.

'Anthony Carmichael,' the policewoman had said, without even looking up. 'Yes, we'd like to talk to Mr Carmichael.' And the moment had passed, they were standing up. 'You can take your son home, Mrs Webster,' she said.

Climbing out Bridget saw Laura's car on the drive, but only Carrie and Isabel were in the kitchen, sitting at the table, a pot of tea and three mugs.

'Where's Laura?'

Carrie was on her feet, jerked her head upstairs. 'She's got my bed,' she said. 'She was dead on her feet. I'll take the sofa.' Isabel had stood too, taller somehow already than Bridget remembered her but quiet and obedient still.

Bridget nodded, bone tired, smelling of the police car, ready in that moment just to disappear, to leave them all to it and evaporate but then half turning to check on Matt and Finn she caught something. Isabel's face turned towards Finn, and a look, an expression of joy and relief mixed that wiped everything out, even if just for those seconds. So simple, to be a child, Bridget thought, so simple, to be lit like that from inside like a window, and with the thought, something shifted.

They stood aside, the three adults, and Isabel went straight to Finn and hugged him. Bridget saw his shaggy head turn, over the slender girl's shoulder, she saw the overgrown boy marking off the signs, the kettle and the fridge magnets and the school timetable on the wall and the pencilled marks on the doorframe where he had grown taller. He was home. They were home.

Postscript

It seemed a hundred years since Gill Lawson had walked into this same station bar and half-recognised Carrie O'Neill, but it was only fifteen months. She bought a takeaway coffee and walked out into the early spring air. She turned on the spot, looking for those towers, but curiously considering they'd seemed to be everywhere last time she was here, she couldn't see them.

Gill had met up with Matt, on three occasions since that freezing wet November. Each time in London, each time on neutral ground. To make sure of certain things, and it had been reassuring to Gill that her priorities, which had felt like they were set in concrete (the story first, the story second, the story third fourth and fifth) had adjusted, without her even thinking about it. First, to make sure Finn was all right, that poor stunned kid she'd seen with his mother's arm around him, and it seemed he was: going out with Isabel for eight months now and heading off on holiday with her family this summer. Doing well at school.

Then that Bridget was OK.

Matt had nodded, thoughtful. 'We're thinking about moving abroad,' he said. 'Once Finn's at university.' They'd been sitting in a garden square near King's Cross, with pigeons pecking around their feet, Matt examining their movements. Then he'd raised his head. 'Her sister's there, you see?'

'Carrie.'

He'd nodded. 'Her and her girlfriend Ella, they got back together after all the – all the— Well. Ella's French, you see. Moved to the middle of nowhere, but—' He let it hang. 'And Finn's keen.'

'Good idea,' Bridget had said, carefully. 'No rush, but yes. Good idea.'

She was quite certain the police – even if the worst happened, even if Carmichael, wherever he was, was recovered and identified – would not pursue the circumstances of his death too far. Would not make the connection – because there was no connection, no record any more beyond that school photograph, that Bridget O'Neill had been abused by him.

Carmichael's car had been found at a dismal seaside resort, and the conclusion reached privately by the police – with the help of testimony from both Gill and Magdalena Breska that he had been about to be exposed, that he had been at the end of his tether and behaving irrationally – was that he had either fled the country, to disappear to Thailand or Brazil where, eventually he would resurface, or that he had committed suicide.

Gill had found Magdalena a job in London as a live-in housekeeper, and helped her with her residency application. She liked Magdalena, against all the odds. Did that make her safe? No such thing as a hundred per cent safe. You had to tolerate uncertainty.

There was Alan Timpson, of course – or there had been, keeping mulishly silent throughout his trial. Found guilty of grooming and a variety of child sex offences that would keep him on the sex offenders' register for the rest of his life, and sentenced to three years, of course it had still hung there, over them all, that he knew.

'Bridget says she admitted nothing to him,' Matt had said, beside her on a bench in Green Park last autumn, and Gill had seen the colour rise suddenly in his face, just saying her name Gill saw he was ready to fight for her. That was what mattered, she finally understood, it was why she'd pounded away at this for fifteen years. Standing next to another human being who needed protection and fighting for them: didn't have to be boyfriend, girlfriend, lover, son. Someone, was all.

She'd tried to get to Timpson after the trial, but he wouldn't talk to her. He was shtumm. It might mean he wouldn't talk to the police either – but it might not. He was a bastard, and as long as he was alive they would have to be afraid. How many nights had she prayed for him to hang himself, overdose, or for some violent cellmate to cut his throat? Not healthy, those thoughts.

None of those things had happened.

But she had news for Bridget. It was why she was coming. Alan Timpson was dead. Turned out he'd had cancer growing in his prostate for seven or eight years, undetected, undiagnosed, untreated: it had spread to his lungs and his brain, and it had killed him. She hoped it had been fucking painful.

Steve was authorising taxis these days. Gill climbed in and told the driver where she wanted to go.

Bridget stood at the window, her fingertips to the glass that was plastered with sale signs, watching.

That morning, alone in the house among packing cases, she had taken out the box of photographs and walked out into the back garden, where Matt had laid a fire in a steel drum, ready to go, before leaving for work. Cup of tea, bicycle helmet, last look up at her at the window. She dropped the photographs in, one by one, without looking at them. She had slowly stripped the box into pieces and burned that, too.

The signs on the shop window said, CLOSING DOWN SALE. EVERYTHING MUST GO.

You couldn't know, could you? You could never know for sure, what tomorrow would bring you. Even in another country, where a small stone house waited for them in the foothills of some mountains two valleys from where Ella had been born, and a job for Matt in the local college, and a small amount of money in the bank and Finn safe at university. You couldn't know. You could only hope.

The last of the stock was being packed up in boxes to be collected by a discount wholesaler. She'd sold the van for scrap and Laura and her baby had moved back up north to live with her mother, after coming for one last look around the shop, that small space where they'd moved warily around each other for those terrible weeks. The shop's lease had been taken over by a coffee shop chain: they were getting everything stripped out, steam cleaned and sandblasted. Standing in the doorway to the little kitchen Bridget had seen the trace of a smile on Laura's lips when she'd told her that. 'It did need a good clean,' she'd said. And Laura did look up then, the baby against her shoulder, up to the shelf where the box of Easter eggs and cherry blossom had filled a space, but only for a second and then, breezy, she was turning to leave.

Bridget had to go back, one last time; she had to make sure that there was no trace left, no stain, no clue, no odour. It might have looked as if she was just waiting, standing there in the middle of the shop, but she was looking, then she closed her eyes and she was listening, smelling, registering as she felt every molecule of the air on her skin. If there were ghosts, she would know; if she was going to be punished, then it would be here; if they were going to come for her, it would be now.

Then there was the wheeze and chug of an old diesel engine and Bridget opened her eyes to see an ancient black cab pulling up in the lane outside. When she saw the face at its window, with one part of her brain – the scrupulous part, the anxious part, the OCD part – she thought, *Matt must have told her I was here* but somewhere deeper, somewhere safer and more certain, Bridget thought, *she knew*. She took two steps to the door and opened it.

The cab pulled off, leaving its passenger in front of Bridget on the pavement. Hair untidy, white shirt that could do with a wash, the broad smile of an angel.

389

'I thought maybe you'd need me,' said Gill Lawson, pushing past her into the room where boxes stood and then turning back to set her hands square on Bridget's shoulders. 'But looks like there's nothing to see here.' Bridget felt a smile stretch her face, wider, then wider, and Gill's matched it. 'You're done?'

'All done,' Bridget said. 'We're all done.'